THE SHADOW-LINE
and Two Other Tales
TYPHOON
and
THE SECRET SHARER

Joseph Conrad was born Jozef Teodor Konrad Nalecz Korzeniowski in the Polish Ukraine, then under Russian rule, in 1857. His youth was spent in Poland, in Russia during his father's political exile there, in Cracow, and in southern France, where, between 1874 and 1878 he served his first apprenticeship at sea. In 1878 he shipped on a British freighter in the Mediterranean, and for sixteen years followed a seaman's career in many parts of the world. He became a British subject in 1886. During a period ashore in London in 1889 he began his first novel, *Almayer's Folly*, which was published in 1895. After his sea life ended in 1894 he devoted himself wholly to writing. Among his other novels are *The Nigger of the "Narcissus"* (1897), *Lord Jim* (1900), *Nostromo* (1904), *The Secret Agent* (1907), *Under Western Eyes* (1911), *Chance* (1914), *Victory* (1915), and *The Rescue* (1920). He also wrote seven books of shorter tales. His short novel *The Shadow-Line*, which is here combined with "Typhoon" and "The Secret Sharer," was published in 1917. Conrad died in England on August 3, 1924.

THE SHADOW-LINE

and Two Other Tales

TYPHOON

THE SECRET SHARER

by

JOSEPH CONRAD

"Worthy of my undying regard"

EDITED AND WITH AN INTRODUCTION
BY MORTON DAUWEN ZABEL

DOUBLEDAY ANCHOR BOOKS
DOUBLEDAY & COMPANY, INC., GARDEN CITY, NEW YORK

Library of Congress Catalog Card Number 59–9240

Contents

INTRODUCTION

I

If Conrad remains, after what is now more than half a century, the unchallenged master among English writers of sea tales, his claim to the title may be said to have been defined in the three stories collected in the present volume and in two others, "Youth" and *The Nigger of the "Narcissus."* The sea and its life of course figure in a large number of his other tales; it is a recurring presence from his first book to his last; and in some of them—*An Outcast of the Islands, Lord Jim, Nostromo, Chance, Victory, The Rescue, The Rover,* as in stories like "The End of the Tether," "Falk," "The Brute," "Freya of the Seven Isles," "The Black Mate"—its role is prominent. Yet however strongly or marginally these works count in this aspect of his achievement, the part the sea plays in them is either incidental to themes and action of another kind, or concerns characters and situations not strictly maritime, or is likely to be rendered in something less than Conrad's strongest art. A "tale of the sea" requires, if the term is to have accurate or specific value, a certain definition. It must involve a way of life and conduct, an ethic of dedication and purpose, an actuality of experience and vocation. One modern English writer, Marryat, and three Americans, Cooper, Dana, and Melville, had before Conrad given a classic quality and status to the sea tale in English. Poets and allegorists, epic scribes and chroniclers, several eminent novelists on occasion, one notable modern dramatist, minor and popular writers before and after Conrad almost without number, have shaped a long tradition of sea literature and made that tradition more conspicuous in English than in any other modern literature. The reasons are evident: "nowhere but in England," as Conrad said in the opening paragraph of "Youth," do "men and the sea [so] interpenetrate," the "sea entering into the life of most men, and the men knowing something or everything about the sea, in the way of amusement, of travel, or of bread-winning." Yet by one of the curious chances that play their part in the fortunes of literature, it was left to the Polish Conrad, soon after his first appearance as an English novelist in 1895, to raise that order of English narrative to a rank of serious and fully responsible art it had hardly achieved before his arrival and has scarcely shown with equal force since.

The event was soon apparent to those alert to such occasions, and Henry James was one of the first to recognize it. Eager as ever for signs of new energy, invention, or discovery in his art, particularly when these issued from an experience or sensibility unlike his own, he was able to respond to Conrad's work with an admiration and critical sympathy even more acute than the relish he had shown during the 'nineties for such other challenging talents of the hour as Kipling and Wells. "His successive books have been real literature, of a distinguished sort, the record of his experience, in navigating years, of Eastern seas, strange climes and far countries, all presented in a form more artistic than has been given to *any* 'Tales of the Sea' among English writers," James wrote in 1902. "*The Nigger of the 'Narcissus'* is in my opinion the very finest and strongest picture of the sea and sea-life that our language possesses—the masterpiece in a whole great class; and *Lord Jim* runs it very close."[1] Whether James had Melville in mind when he thus

[1] Letter of June 26, 1902, addressed to Edmund Gosse in support of a petition for a grant to Conrad from the Royal Literary Fund.

James had already expressed his conviction in a letter sent to Conrad in November 1900, on receiving *Lord Jim*, and he was to repeat it later, on one occasion in a letter of November 1, 1906, written after receiving *The Mirror of the Sea*: "I read you as I listen to rare music—with deepest depths of surrender,

committed himself—whether in fact he had ever read *Moby Dick*—does not appear, nor was he able at that point to speak for the work of this kind that still lay ahead in Conrad's future. But there is little English sea fiction in the half century since he spoke, and no single writer of it, to cause his estimate to be seriously contested, if qualified at all. It may be said with equal assurance today that Conrad is the English master of the sea story, and that his mastery is most fully realized, is given its most concentrated expression and authority, in *The Nigger*, "Youth," "Typhoon," "The Secret Sharer," and *The Shadow-Line*.[2]

The title was to give him serious doubts and some uneasy feeling in his later years, when he saw the fame of his "sea stuff" threatening to crowd out his other claims as a novelist in the minds of his readers and critics. He was fully aware of the romantic and superficial appeal of his *métier*,

---

and out of those depths I emerge slowly and reluctantly again to acknowledge that I return to life. To taste you as I do taste you is *really* thus to wander far away and to decently thank you is a postal transaction (quite another affair), for which I have to come *back*, and accept with a long sad sigh the community of our afflicted existence. . . . But the book itself is a wonder to me really—for its so bringing home the prodigy of your past experiences: bringing it home to me more personally and directly, I mean, the immense treasure and the inexhaustible adventures. No one has *known*—for intellectual use—the things you know, and you have, as the artist of the whole matter, an authority that no one has approached. I find you in it all, writing wonderfully, whatever you may say of your difficult medium and your *plume rebelle*. You knock about in the wide waters of expression like the raciest and boldest of privateers,—you have made the whole place your own: *en même temps que les droits les plus acquis vous y avez les plus rares bonheurs*. Nothing you have done has more in it. The root of the matter of saying [this is that] you stir me, in fine, to amazement and you touch me to tears, and I thank the powers who so mysteriously let you loose with such sensibilities, into such an undiscovered country—*for* sensibility."

James's view of other aspects of Conrad's work appears in his essay on "The New Novel" in *Notes on Novelists* (1914).

2 "Youth," "Heart of Darkness," and "The End of the Tether" are published in another volume in the Anchor Books series— *Youth: A Narrative, and Two Other Stories*, by Joseph Conrad— to which the present collection and its introduction serve as a companion volume.

and of the popular uses to which his material had been put by the facile entertainers of his day. It became his hope, when he finally arrived at the honors of a collected edition of his books, "to get freed from that infernal tail of ships and that obsession with my sea life" which even his best-intentioned publishers and critics had fixed on to promote his reputation. "After all, I may have been a seaman, but I am a writer of prose," he argued on one of these occasions. "Indeed, the nature of my writing runs the risk of being obscured by the nature of my material." "I admit it is natural," he allowed, but "such headings as 'Spinner of sea yarns—master mariner—seaman writer,'" came to rankle increasingly as he saw the celebrity for which he had waited during two anxious decades mount and the stricter ambition of his art become lost on many of his admirers. "You know how the public mind fastens on externals, on mere facts, such for instance as ships and voyages, without paying any attention to any deeper significance they may have," he pled to one of his interpreters, and to another: "a work of art is very seldom limited to one exclusive meaning and not necessarily tending to a definite conclusion. And this for the reason that the nearer it approaches art, the more it acquires a symbolic character." He was even carried to some curious special pleading in the matter: "Of course there are seamen in a good many of my books. That doesn't make them sea stories any more than the existence of de Barral in *Chance* . . . makes that novel a story of the financial world." And he was likely to end these arguments by wishing "that all those ships of mine were given a rest."[3]

So he spoke when age, success, the embarrassments of publicity, and perhaps a consciousness that his best work lay behind him spurred him to set his record in order and do what he could to guide the judgment of posterity. His discomfort may have had other causes—a feeling that he

[3] From letters to Richard Curle, July 14, 17, and 22, 1923, and to Barrett H. Clark, May 4, 1918, in *Joseph Conrad: Life and Letters*, by G. Jean-Aubry (1927). The question recurs in other letters of Conrad's later years and in some of the "Author's Notes" he wrote for his books between 1917 and 1920.

had worked his special vein of material unduly hard; a characteristic inclination to hold himself aloof from his imitators and well-wishers; possibly a suspicion that his maritime subject, like his exotic vein, had in his later books lent itself to the attenuations of romance and rhetoric and had so been overtaken by the evasive usage he could condemn in other practitioners of the genre. Both the subjects with which he began his career in literature—the East and the sea—were to involve Conrad in serious tests of his imaginative taste and judgment, and that he did not always meet those tests successfully was one of the problems that taxed his artist's conscience most severely, as it is a problem that taxes the critic of Conrad even today. It prompted some of the more painful scruples, self-questionings, and mortifications that run through his letters, and it elicited certain of the defensive passages in his "Author's Notes" for his books.

Yet there is no question that the sea was a supreme experience in his life; that it gave him a school of experience more important to him as a character and moral dramatist than any other he had known; that he viewed his relationship to it as something like a personal trust and calling; and that it gave him not only his richest single fund of material but the most powerful symbol of his art. Not even the inheritance of heroism, idealism, and tragedy that had come to him by his birth in Poland was to serve him so effectively in his practical and imaginative life. The sea first struck him as a lure to youthful fancy and day-dreaming when he read Hugo's *Travailleurs de la Mer* in his father's translation in the landlocked Ukraine. It had figured as an opportunity for romantic adventure during his four years in Marseilles. It became, in 1878, when his French escapades ended in fiasco and disgrace, a means of moral recovery and salvation. "I was pursuing a clear aim," he was to say of his refusal to return to Poland with the guardian-uncle who had come to rescue him from his difficulties in Marseilles and of his taking instead to the sea in earnest on the English freighter *Mavis*: "I was carrying out a deliberate plan of making out of myself, in the first place, a seaman worthy of the service, good enough to work by the side of the men with whom I was to live; and in the second place, I had to justify my existence to myself, to redeem a tacit moral pledge." His uncle's injunction had launched him on the most serious commitment of his early life: "You wanted to be a sailor, and you must be responsible for the consequences; you have forfeited my confidence. Work now to regain it; you will win it back if you apply yourself steadily and pull yourself together." It was in the sea and its ships that he found the sense of community, dedication, and responsibility that had failed him in Poland and France, and though his relations with it were eventually to show all the complexity of emotion and conflict of intelligence that could be expected in a man of Conrad's nature, his feeling of identification with its life and "passion" remained with him to the end. When in 1914 he called *The Nigger of the "Narcissus"* the "book by which, not as a novelist perhaps, but as an artist striving for the utmost sincerity of expression, I am willing to stand or fall," he spoke of that tale in terms that have a wider application to his work: "Its pages are the tribute of my unalterable and profound affection for the ships, the seamen, the winds and the great sea —the moulders of my youth, the companions of the best years of my life."

Nor did he, in his earlier days as a writer, hesitate to present himself as a disciple of its romantic historians, Marryat and Cooper. "There is an air of fable about it," he said of Marryat's work. "Its loss would be irreparable, like the curtailment of national story or the loss of a historical document. It is the beginning and the embodiment of an inspiring tradition." He saw Marryat as the laureate of "the Service":

His figures move about between water and sky, and the water and the sky are there only to frame the deeds of the Service. . . . His naïveties are perpetrated in a lurid light. . . . And yet they live; there is a truth in them, the truth of their time; a headlong, reckless audacity, an intimacy with violence, an unthinking fearlessness, and an exuberance of vitality which only years of war and victories can give. . . . He has created a priceless legend. . . . The tradition of the great past he has fixed in his pages will be cherished for ever as the guarantee of the future.

And of the sea in Cooper's novels he said that Cooper "could hear its voice, he could understand its silence, and he could interpret both for us in his prose with all that felicity and sureness of effect that belong to a poetical conception alone":

> In his sea tales the sea inter-penetrates with life; it is in a subtle way a factor in the problem of existence, and, for all its greatness, it is always in touch with the men who, bound on errands of war or gain, traverse its immense solitudes. His descriptions have the magistral ampleness of a gesture indicating the sweep of a vast horizon. They embrace the colours of sunset, the peace of starlight, the aspects of calm and storm, the great loneliness of the waters, the stillness of watchful coasts, and the alert readiness which marks men who live face to face with the promise and the menace of the sea. He knows the men and he knows the sea. His method may be often faulty, but his art is genuine. . . . In certain passages he reaches, very simply, the heights of inspired vision.

If these tributes have the appearance of an apologia for his own art, they also define an ancestry and indebtedness Conrad had no wish to conceal. "Perhaps no two authors of fiction influenced so many lives," he said, and acknowledging "the life of the writer of this appreciation" to be among them, he testified that their influence had "withstood the brutal shock of facts and the wear of laborious years," and that he had "never regretted his surrender" to their appeal.[4]

[4] "Tales of the Sea" in *Notes on Life and Letters* (1921), pp. 53–57. The essay was originally contributed to *The Outlook*, June 4, 1898.

II

When a writer undertakes to write about an element like the sea and makes it a major factor in his work—particularly when the writer is a novelist—he submits himself not only to great imaginative advantages but to certain radical tests and difficulties. The same thing can be said about Conrad's other early subject, the East. It can also be said of other areas that have appeared or reappeared in literature during the present century—primitive life, for one, with all it offers as a contrast to civilization and its discontents; the life and psychology of children; the new Unknown revealed by science and scientific theory; the conquest of the air which has seized the attention of poets and novelists in this first age of aviation and space exploration. All these have come into modern literature as countersubjects to the dominant claims of fact and realism that shaped the novel during its great ascendancy in the Nineteenth Century and that still define the basis of fiction and drama in the Twentieth. They make much the same appeal to the contemporary imagination that subjective fantasy or psychic allegory made to the Symbolists of eighty years ago when they resisted the strictures of Naturalism, or that Surrealism and other modes of irrational expression make in the present age of social and scientific authority. These subjects come to the artist as sanctions for personal and imaginative license: in one form or another they represent a reversion to primitive, intuitive, anti-authoritarian, or preconscious ways of truth. They imply a criticism of conscious reason, aggressive morality, the forms of corporate action and conduct. If they may be called implicitly anti-cultural, they seek their justification by becoming a means of resisting the tyranny or the inhumanity of intellect, mass thinking, and civilized convention.

Where once such subjects were explored under the inspiration of the Romantic vision they are now more likely to be investigated or dramatized under psychic or moral tenets. The fundamental incentive may be the same: the search for truth or reality through instinct; the recovery of an intimate relationship between man and the vital energy of nature. They embody a hope that by entering into relations with the strange, the fabulous, or the unknown a new revelation will be achieved, an unsuspected strength be imparted to the baffled or corrupted spirit of man.

> Nous nous embarquerons sur la mer des Ténèbres
> Avec le coeur joyeux d'un jeune passager. . . .
> Plonger au fond du gouffre, Enfer ou Ciel, qu'importe?
> Au fond de l'Inconnu pour trouver du *nouveau!*

The primitive has always been one means to this end, elemental or innocent nature another. Conrad had them both in his life, in his experience of the East and of the sea. It is likely he found himself responding with instinctive sympathy to Baudelaire's invocation of their force in "Le Voyage" —the Baudelaire whose *"stérilités des écrivains nerveux"* he admittedly shared and to whose sea-imagery he gave the salute of a fellow spirit in the epigraph of *The Shadow-Line.*[5]

He defined a basic antithesis of elements in his work when he described it as turning on contrasts of "civilization and jungle, land and sea, West and East." More than once he defended himself against the charge of liking "to write

[5] Conrad does not often quote or mention poets in his books and letters, though several are quoted in his epigraphs (Keats, Shakespeare, Milton, Chaucer, Symons). He seems to have taken Baudelaire particularly to heart. One of his confessions of sharing Baudelaire's *stérilités* appears in a letter to Edmund Gosse of March 23, 1905 ("Quincey too, I believe, has known that anguished suspension of all power of thought that comes to one often in the midst of a very revel of production, like the slave with his *memento mori* at a feast"). The lines at the head of *The Shadow-Line* are from "La Musique" (*Les Fleurs du Mal,* LXIX), whose symbolism is maritime: "La musique souvent me prend comme une mer!" and which closes:

> Je sens vibrer en moi toutes les passions
>   D'un vaisseau qui souffre;
> Le bon vent, la tempête et ses convulsions
>
>   Sur l'immense gouffre
> Me bercent. D'autres fois, calme plat, grand miroir
>   De mon désespoir!

of men who go to sea or live on lonely islands untrammelled by the pressure of worldly circumstances because such characters allowed freer play to [his] imagination," by arguing that the choice was inevitable to him. "I have not sought for special imaginative freedom or a larger play of fancy in my choice of characters and subjects. The nature of the knowledge, suggestions or hints used in my imaginative work has depended directly on the conditions of my active life." But the charge brought him to face the problem of the romantic or idealizing tendency in his art and of the degree to which it militated against the principles of fidelity, truth, and moral realism to which he had dedicated himself. It likewise brings Conrad's reader to deal with one of the radical criticisms that have in one form or another always been made of his work: that it rests on a "central obscurity" or irresolution; that his opinions on man and his fate, though "held under the semblance of eternity, girt with the sea, crowned with the stars," are "always promising to make some general philosophic statement about the universe" only to end "with a rough disclaimer"; and that his "central obscurity" results from the "constant discrepancies between his nearer and his further vision"—between, that is, his scrupulous respect for specific detail and the enigmatic, visionary, or cosmic quality he evokes beyond it.[6]

The point is inevitable to any intelligent reaction to Conrad's work, whether sympathetic or otherwise. It refers not only to the exotic, fabulous, and extravagant elements in his tales but to their tendency, especially in his later years, toward rhetorical emotion, their appeals to mystery and un-

[6] The criticism figures in a good many recent estimates of Conrad; it is given here in the words of E. M. Forster, one of its earliest formulators, in "Joseph Conrad: A Note" of 1921, in *Abinger Harvest* (1936). Forster continues: "If he lived only in his experiences, never lifting his eyes to what lies beyond them: or if, having seen what lies beyond, he would subordinate his experiences to it—then in either case he would be easier to read. But he is in neither case. He is too much of a seer to restrain his spirit; he is too much Joseph Conrad, too jealous of personal honour, to give any but the fullest value to deeds and dangers he has known."

reason. It bears particularly on his emphasis on the "inscrutable" in nature, woman, or history. What must be allowed is that Conrad himself seems to have been conscious of the problem; that it gave him his severest ordeal in the writing of his tales and in harmonizing their dramatic and moral concepts with the concrete realism of their action, characters, and words; and that he recognized the conflict as a challenge to his aims as an artist.[7]

His elaborate use of Eastern and primitive life gave him one form of the difficulty. He saw and felt the East in terms of a "vision" that answered some instinctive need of his nature, some necessity of identifying himself with the primitive condition of truth, undisguised by the deceptive appearances and subterfuges of civilized life. He saw in it "a stealthy Nemesis" that "lies in wait, pursues, overtakes so many of the conquering race, who are proud of their wisdom, of their knowledge, of their strength."[8] These are elusive forms of fate, and the truth Conrad ascribed to them obliged him to render their workings with all possible accuracy and probability—he was submitting himself to a serious imaginative and dramatic responsibility. Yet the strangeness, mystery, and fatality he felt obliged to show in his portrayal of the East and its people could also threaten his fidelity and throw him back on the devices of allegory and abstraction, sometimes on a damaging use of dramatic and atmospheric artifice.

[7] Conrad's dealings with the problem and what he felt it cost him in "the want of illuminating imagination" appear in several of his letters, a notable example being the one he wrote to Edward Garnett on November 12, 1900, after the publication of *Lord Jim: Joseph Conrad: Life and Letters* (1927), Vol. I, 298–99; also in Garnett's *Letters from Conrad 1895 to 1924* (London, n.d., but c. 1928), pp. 172–75. His larger credo was written early in his career, in the preface to *The Nigger of the "Narcissus"* (1897).

[8] The phrases here come from the closing pages of "Youth," but similar statements or implications appear in most of Conrad's tales of the East, Africa, or other remote settings. That Conrad's own fate as an exile and *déraciné* of a conquered and divided Poland may have incited his sympathy with the exploited East and his view of the nemesis it visits on its conquerors has been a subject for speculation among various interpreters.

His Eastern characters necessarily talk in a translated language—idealized, poetic, or remote. Their personalities and psychology recur to primitive, rudimentary, or simplified norms of behavior. Their landscape hovers in an air of mystery, darkness, impenetrability. Their conduct and motives lapse into unpredictable forms of irrationality, subtlety, or evasion. Whatever the logic of instinct Conrad ascribed to them, whatever the complexity he gave to his treatment of them or the values of primitive justice he traced in their life and history, they were bound to remain to a greater or lesser degree simplified types and thus an impediment to the kind of human and psychological fidelity he counted on for the more authentic substance of his art. "There is a bond between us and that humanity so far away," he said in defense of his exotic subject as early as 1895; and at times he could make the bond count for more than it has ever counted elsewhere in modern fiction. But it is a bond that inevitably remains tenuous and elusive in the work of a writer who accepts the principles of realism and dramatic fidelity. If it sometimes inspired Conrad to write some of the most powerful dramas of primitive life in modern fiction, it also encouraged him in the rhetorical abstraction that can seriously threaten both his drama and his prose.

The sea was similarly bound to appeal to him—as it has appealed to men of every age—in its aspects of primary or elemental force, its mindless oblivion and inhuman power: "too great, too mighty for common virtues," "faithful to no race after the manner of the kindly earth," with "no compassion, no faith, no law, no memory," no response to human need or vanity: an expression not only of the justice but of the indifference of nature. It is as such a presence that it figures in some of his most memorable passages—the voyage of the *Patna* in *Lord Jim;* the storm scenes of *The Nigger* and "Typhoon"; the great night scene of the silver-laden lighter on the Golfo Placido in *Nostromo;* the sinister calms that enclose the vessels in "The Secret Sharer" and *The Shadow-Line.* These are passages that deserve a place among the classic pictures of the sea in any age—*Odyssey, The Tempest, Moby Dick,* the poetic apostrophes of Coleridge, Hugo, Heine, Mallarmé, Baudelaire, Perse; and the physical scope and fidelity of Conrad's pictures, the brilliant detail of his renderings, certainly ensure him a high rank in that order of writing. To devise and sustain the long storm pictures of *The Nigger* and "Typhoon," and to bring their meteorological realism into such complex combination with the human drama pitched in their midst, requires much more than technical or professional knowledge. If the symbolic powers of Melville, Hardy, Hopkins, and Rimbaud are to be credited with having made original contributions to the treatment of elemental nature in modern literature, Conrad's share in that *mystique* must also be allowed. The "mysticism" is always more convincing in his tales when it avoids overt or hortatory expression and relies on sensory accuracy and implicit suggestion, but its urgency to Conrad is clear. It was to explain its role in his experience and imagination that he wrote *The Mirror of the Sea* and made of that book an essential document on his life and thought.

III

"This book is a very intimate revelation," he said of it thirteen years after its publication in 1906: "I have attempted here to lay bare with the unreserve of a last hour's confession the terms of my relation with the sea, which beginning mysteriously, like any great passion the inscrutable Gods send to mortals, went on unreasoning and invincible, surviving the test of disillusion, defying the disenchantment that lurks in every day of a strenuous life; went on full of love's delight and love's anguish, facing them in open-eyed exultation, without bitterness and without repining, from the first hour to the last." And to a critic who had complained that "in reading these chapters one is always hoping for the revelation; but the personality is never quite revealed," and that their "haphazard events" had the effect of "symbols of one knows not what sacred ritual taking place behind the veil," Conrad replied that in *The Mirror of the Sea*, "written in perfect sincerity," he had paid "the best tribute my piety can offer to the ultimate shapers of my character, convictions, and, in a sense, destiny—to the imperishable sea, to the ships that are no more, and to the simple men who have had their day."

It was the first of his two books of autobiography—*A Personal Record*, first called *Some Reminiscences*, came six years later, in 1912. Both books are remarkably Conradian. Both withhold as much as they reveal; in both Conrad takes the reader into what Forster calls "the severe little apartment that must, for want of a better word, be called his confidence" and at a certain definite moment "bows [him] out"; and both, by indulging the confidence in a manner at once frankly emotional and self-consciously reserved, go far in justifying the earlier critic's sense of a "sacred ritual taking place behind the veil." This is true even of *A Personal Record*, where the account deals chiefly with Conrad's youth in Poland, his years in France and in the East, and his beginnings and progress as a novelist. In *The Mirror of the Sea* the effect is central and essential, part of the book's conscious design, and thus valuable in what it does to illuminate the role of the sea in his tales generally.

That role, when it appears at its finest, is always strong in two values, in a twofold content and implication. The sense of ritual, rite, or "romance" is evident, but so is the sense of fact, reality, and physical fidelity that accompanies and substantiates it. When either of these works alone it is likely to show a lack of the best Conradian quality. The ritual or romance then resorts to the devices of rhetoric, invocation, self-conscious lyricism, an emotive style. And conversely, fact can deteriorate into data, technicalities, the conscious language of a code (the latter coming close to Kipling's usage, which Conrad seems to have wished to avoid). If his lines on Marryat and Cooper may be taken in evidence, Conrad was aware of the problem: it is a difficulty in most modern writing about the sea. When it met it successfully he did so, we become aware, because his twenty-year career on ships was long enough, exacting enough, to make him fully acquainted with the sea in its prosaic as much as in its poetic character: in its severest

reality as much as in its alluring romance. He wrote, in
other words, as a practiced and professional seaman. The
company he chose in Marryat and Cooper was his rightful
company; he consciously held aloof from that of Hugo,
Loti, Stevenson, and later romancers. "My life as a matter
of fact was far from being adventurous in itself": in after
years he is said to have confessed that the most vivid
memory the sea had left him was one of impatience, fatigue, and crushing boredom. Realism and disillusionment
checked and redressed whatever romanticism or bravado
had originally inspired him; the "Service" acted as a cor-
rective to Platonic self-conceit and vainglory. His strength
as an artist of sea life came from his skill in sustaining and
holding in balance both realities. It is their mutual claims
on him that makes the theme of *The Mirror of the Sea*.

The theme, implicit in all his finer stories of ships and
seamen, is stated in various passages in the tales, once most
effectively in *Lord Jim*:

> There is such magnificent vagueness in the expecta-
> tions that had driven each of us to sea, such a glorious
> indefiniteness, such a beautiful greed of adventures that
> are their own and only reward! What we get—well, we
> won't talk of that; but can one of us restrain a smile? In
> no other kind of life is the illusion more wide of reality—
> in no other is the beginning *all* illusion—the disenchant-
> ment more swift—the subjugation more complete. Hadn't
> we all commenced with the same desire, ended with the
> same knowledge, carried the memory of the same
> cherished glamour through the sordid days of impre-
> cation?

This points to a familiar antithesis or conflict in Conrad's
tales and temperament: the rival claims of appearance and
reality, illusion and disillusion, dream and recognition.
Their drama had begun in *Almayer's Folly* at the outset of
his literary career, and it was never to exhaust itself in his
speculations and obsessive inquisition. His trouble as a
dramatist came when he failed to find the concrete terms
or conditions for the drama: when dream or illusion remained too subjective or when reality remained too arbi-

trary, contrived, or artificial. It is this difficulty that shows itself both early and late in his career—in the first Malayan dramas, *Almayer's Folly* and *An Outcast of the Islands*, and in the final books, *The Arrow of Gold*, *The Rescue*, *The Rover*. The aura of "illusion" (the word is particularly insistent and over-urged at both ends of his production) then becomes as much a matter of contrivance or special-pleading as the violence or the melodrama of the action. The East on the one hand, romantic or apologetic self-projection on the other, end in dissipating dramatic and psychological fidelity. The political subjects to which Conrad applied himself in his middle period between 1903 and 1912 required a stricter discipline, a more objective and self-critical order of drama. They gave him a material that acted as a discipline of his self-indulgent and allegorizing bent, and it is this that accounts, in part at least, for the strength of *Nostromo*, *The Secret Agent*, and *Under Western Eyes*.

But the experience of ships and the sea provided that discipline in a more intimate form. While it can be said that this way of life invited both forms of the Conradian excess, it is necessary also to see that these existed, in his sea experience, in a continuously mutual and self-correcting combination. It is their co-existence and mutual necessity that he defines in *The Mirror*.

The "love that is given to ships" is there; so is the challenge and excitement of "initiation," the glamor of "the heroic age," the "strong magic" of calms and the "demonic character" of storms, the "cobwebs and gossamer" of sheets and sails, the "caprice of the winds"—"rulers of East and West," the heroic fantasy of "the nursery of the craft." But equally present is "the weight of the burden," the "severe technicality," the "character of the foe," above all the exactions of seacraft considered as "a fine art." In one significant sentence Conrad says that "*Odi et amo* may well be the confession of those who consciously or blindly have surrendered their existence to the fascination of the sea"; in another passage that "Impenetrable and heartless the sea has given nothing of itself to the suitors for its precarious favours. Unlike the earth, it cannot be subjugated at any cost of patience and toil. For all its fascination that has lured so many to a violent death, its immensity has never been loved as the mountains, the plains, the desert itself, have been loved."

Its lesson is finally endurance, responsibility, vigilance, in their strictest forms, and not their opposites. What results may at times seem to be a strongly disillusioned view of the element, but it never became a resentful or cynical one. In the sea Conrad found in inseparable union the forces of nature and action that best served his temper and imagination, a mode of experience in which fact and fantasy met on a common and necessary ground:

> I knew it capable of betraying the generous ardour of youth as implacably as, indifferent to evil and good, it would have betrayed the basest greed or the noblest heroism. My conception of its magnanimous greatness was gone. . . . Open to all and faithful to none, it exercises its fascination for the undoing of the best. To love it is not well. It knows no bond of plighted troth, no fidelity to misfortune, to long companionship, to long devotion. The promise it holds out perpetually is very great; but the only secret of its possession is strength, strength—the jealous, sleepless strength of a man guarding a coveted treasure within his gates.[9]

The eloquence of the phrasing, the personal pathos and metaphor, the emphasis on *anima*—none of these cancels the sense of something that was more important to the writer who put them to dramatic and allegoric use in his tales: his practiced knowledge of the sea as a test of mind and character. That knowledge remains basic to all of Con-

[9] Though *The Mirror of the Sea* mostly takes the form of reverie, definition, or meditation, it contains one notable passage of personal history, Conrad's first account of the *Tremolino* venture at Marseilles during his French years, 1874–78, and the episodes that later went into the writing of *The Arrow of Gold* (1919). This phase of his life, formerly described most fully by G. Jean-Aubry, has lately come under close and controversial scrutiny by recent biographers, notably by Jocelyn Baines in studies soon to contribute to a new biography and by Jerry Allen in *The Thunder and the Sunshine* (1958).

rad's more serious and convincing uses of the sea in his
books; and none of his protests against the popular fame
the sea brought him can deny its value to him as the central instrument of his moral imagination and the most
powerful single factor—reality or symbol—in his creative
achievement.

IV

"Typhoon," "The Secret Sharer," and *The Shadow-Line*,
brought together as they are in this volume, may be taken
as a trilogy on their common subject. They show in fact a
progression in their treatment of it. Each turns on a crisis of
shock, challenge, or initiation. Each centers in a trial of
"command." And the stories range from youth to age, the
two poles of the Conradian moral cycle, in their central
characters. They have the further value of marking three
notable points in Conrad's treatment of their material.
"Typhoon" was written in the midwinter of 1900–01, just
after the completion of *Lord Jim*, when he was rounding
off, with the seven tales of the *Youth* and *Typhoon* volumes, his first phase of authorship before embarking on
Nostromo and the books of his middle period. "The Secret
Sharer" came in 1909, almost exactly midway in his writing
career. *The Shadow-Line* was written between November
1914 and March 1915, at the beginning of his final phase
and as what most critics have taken to be his last work to
show his finer powers of style and imagination.[10]

[10] "Typhoon" was serialized in *The Pall Mall Magazine*, London, January–March, 1902, and in *The Critic*, New York, Feb-
ruary–May, 1902, and was first published in book form in New
York in 1902, in London in 1903. "The Secret Sharer" was serialized in *Harper's Magazine*, New York, August–September,
1910, and included in *'Twixt Land and Sea* in 1912. *The Shadow-
Line* was serialized in *The English Review*, London, September
1916–March 1917, and in the *Metropolitan Magazine*, New York,
October–November 1916, and was published as a book in 1917.
The dating of the writing of *The Shadow-Line* is given here as
Jean-Aubry gives it; Conrad himself says in his "Author's Note"
that it was "written in the last three months of the year 1916,"
but his dates are likely to be inaccurate.

A further factor of contrast and balance appears in the three tales. "If there is to be any classification by subjects," Conrad said of these stories, "I have done two Storm-pieces in *The Nigger of the 'Narcissus'* and in 'Typhoon'; and two Calm-pieces: 'The Secret Sharer' and *The Shadow-Line*." Storm at its wildest and deadliest plays its part in "Typhoon," calm in its most sinister and spectral malignity in *The Shadow-Line;* while another quiescence of sea and sky, a trance of stillness between foul weather and fair, acts its role in the drama of "The Secret Sharer."

The great storms of *The Nigger* and "Typhoon" engulf the ships in those tales with all the fury of conscious intention and hostility in the elements. In *The Nigger* the raging weather becomes a challenge of annihilation to the crew and thus accompanies and gives outward form to a cognate challenge in their midst—the fear, cowardice, and dread of death that are stirred to activity among them by the dying Negro. The threat of extinction becomes real not only outside the ship but within its hold. In "Typhoon" the storm is more positively external. Here Conrad did not exercise overtly his skill in dualistic drama or symbolism. Yet the power of the drama is hardly less impressive for being kept tacit, ironic, humorously rendered at the same time that it becomes physically all-engulfing.

In Captain MacWhirr, the stolid, incurious commander of the *Nan-Shan,* Conrad found a subject poles removed from the ordeals of dishonor, defeated egoism, or self-incriminating delusion, of enforced recognition and self-discovery, which he had already shown in his earlier stories and was to repeat in many later ones. But it was a subject that likewise demanded his assent and tribute. MacWhirr during all his years at sea has never yet met a danger that has disturbed his self-assurance. Honest with the "heavy obviousness of a lump of clay"; "ordinary, irresponsive, and unruffled"; exasperating in his "stupidity" to the uneasy mate Jukes; tolerable to the sea-wise engineer Solomon Rout chiefly because Rout prefers "the dullest ass of a skipper before a rogue"—this dullest and most prosaic of all Conrad's heroes appears in "Typhoon" as if to claim his rightful place among the men marked for merit or significance in the epic of the sea.

What marks him is stated in one of the key passages of Conrad's work, the paragraph at the end of Chapter I whose import echoes through the tales from first to last. "The sea . . . had never put itself out to startle the silent man." He has "seldom looked up"; "dirty weather he had known, of course . . . felt at the time and presently forgotten"; but he has "never been given a glimpse of immeasurable strength and of immoderate wrath, the wrath that passes exhausted but never appeased—the wrath and fury of the passionate sea":

> Captain MacWhirr had sailed over the surface of the oceans as some men go skimming over the years of existence to sink gently into a placid grave, ignorant of life to the last, without ever having been made to see all it may contain of perfidy, of violence, and of terror. There are on sea and land such men thus fortunate—or thus disdained by destiny or by the sea.

The words promise a judgment of contempt or dismissal on the impassive, dull-witted captain who has "just enough imagination to carry him through each successive day, and no more." Yet in the end it is neither the disdain of destiny nor Conrad's own disdain that is visited on him. When "dirty weather" strikes his ship (it is the only name he has for the wrath of the elements) he has his own way of "going through with it." The refinements of "storm strategy" had never counted in his seamanship: "A gale is a gale, Mr. Jukes, and a full-powered steamship has got to face it." It is he who keeps his head in the maelstrom; he who obstinately holds his post in a maddened universe; subdues the frenzied coolies and sees that the money from their broken sea chests is saved and redistributed; meets his almost unnerved self-conceit with sturdy courage; brings the boat through the cataclysm; and speaks his modest vow of dedication before the fallen barometer when he says of his ship: "I shouldn't like to lose her." "He was spared that annoyance," says Conrad; and the ironic comment echoes the eloquence he put into the four words he applied to old Singleton at the wheel during the fury that overwhelmed the *Narcissus*: "He steered with care."

"Typhoon" is a tribute to those who steer with care. Into MacWhirr's narrow and inflexible mind there enter none of the unnerving shocks and hauntings of men more signally marked for challenge, treachery, or self-discovery. He is as invulnerable to agony as he is incapable of conscious heroism. He represents in Conrad's hierarchy the lowest denominator of loyalty to the Service. He is miles removed from Jim, Marlow, Kurtz, Nostromo, Razumov, Heyst, Lingard: Conrad put his greater sympathy and insight into men of another cast. Into MacWhirr he put his secret envy and a humbler admiration—his knowledge of "the work to be done," his "sense of the fitness of things," his recognition of the courage in duty that merits the seaman's proudest reward: "Well done." MacWhirr too is "one of us."[11]

What gives the tale its strength is the fine control and accuracy of its rendering: the way in which the rising, fury, climax, and dropping of the typhoon reflect the conduct of the officers and coolies caught in its anger; the notation, at once laconic and humorous, of its effect on their natures; the comedy of decorum, punctilio, and stupefaction in their responses to the threat that almost destroys them; with, at the remote distance of the home ports across the world, the further comedy of the womenfolk who receive the news from their men. When Conrad wrote the tale he found a moment of poise in his descriptive and dramatic powers, between the riddled dramas of *Lord Jim* and *Nostromo*. Irony of some kind—humorous, sardonic, critical, pathetic, or tragic—was always a steadying factor in his work. He counted on it to hold his refractory materials and his personal involvement in them under control. It is a necessary

[11] "One admires what one lacks. That is why I admire perseverance and fidelity and constancy. And then I like to look on the good side of men, particularly if there is a suggestion of pathos in the situation." Conrad in a letter of August 26, 1891, to Madame Poradowska in Brussels (*Letters of Joseph Conrad to Marguerite Poradowska* [1940]).

Conrad's essay "Well Done" of 1918, one of his major statements on the seaman's code and ethic, is in *Notes on Life and Letters* (1921).

resource in his creation. In "Typhoon" the irony fuses the
elements of the tale into one of the strongest unities of
effect and content he ever arrived at and makes the story
of the *Nan-Shan* and her skipper, if not one of his subtlest
achievements, one of his surest.

"The Secret Sharer" shows the other and more salient
side of Conrad's mind and art. The story, written at a time
of acute preoccupation when he had both *Under Western
Eyes* and *Chance* on his hands, both defying completion,
is perhaps of all his tales the one most consciously written
as an emblem or epigram of his essential moral subject. Its
theme had worked in his tales from the beginning. It had
become overt in "Heart of Darkness," exhaustive in *Lord
Jim,* essential in *Nostromo;* and it was presently to arrive
at further extension in *Under Western Eyes*. The drama of
the other self, whether the Platonic ego, the unrecognized
unconscious, or the compulsive identity making its claim
on the precarious and untested conscience, had given focus
to the novels from the time of Almayer and Willems; it
had clearly laid an obsessive claim on Conrad's imagination as he progressed more deeply into his study of human
fate and character. "The Secret Sharer" not only gives a
name to the subject; it brings it to its most concise allegoric
expression, which means also to something resembling a
mythic condition. Division, duplicity, deception, the fated
duality of "self and soul," are radical throughout Conrad's
drama; and the experiences that are compelled by them—
recognition, sympathy, identification, self-knowledge—become their necessary cognates in all his major tales.

The story hinges on the precarious moment in the seaman's life when he takes his first command—when he passes
at a stroke from the shared life of a crew to the responsible
isolation of authority. Uneasy in his office; suddenly sensing
for the first time the peril of leaving the land for the solitary life of a ship; surrounded by the skeptical suspicion
of his crew; acutely aware of his untested authority, the
young captain enters on his command as if exposed to an
insecurity he has never before felt in his life. Alone on his
deck in the night watch which he has broken the rule of

the ship in keeping, he finds himself uneasily vulnerable to everything his exposure implies—self-doubt, stirrings of conscience, a sense of solitude and estrangement. And there it is, in the calm of night and out of the darkened water, that there comes to him the naked man who makes his appeal to his sympathy—Leggatt the murderer. Leggatt has killed a man; has done so for good reason yet against the law of men and ships; and has taken to the sea in flight from an impersonal justice: "a fugitive and a vagabond on the earth, with no brand of the curse on his sane forehead to stay a slaying hand." By an involuntary instinct that defies the law of his ship and office, the captain takes him aboard; condones his crime; conceals him in his cabin, gives him his own sleeping-suit to wear and his berth to lie in; finds himself sharing Leggatt's secret existence while denying it to the crew and the world. Another self has come to live in the masked rectitude of his life. "I was somewhat of a stranger to myself," the captain had felt when he took charge of his boat and its hostile crew; "I wondered how far I should turn out faithful to that ideal conception of one's own personality every man sets up for himself secretly." It is Leggatt, coming out of sea and darkness like a stealthy messenger from the unknown, who gives him his chance to find out.

The test Leggatt has met and acted on now becomes a test for the captain. He finds himself, for the first time, living a double life in which his authority must conceal the deception that defies and outlaws it. He carries through his deception of the crew; and when the time comes to give Leggatt his chance to return, naked once more, to the water, strike out for land, and "take his punishment" as "a free man, a proud swimmer striking out for a new destiny," he steers his ship so close to the rocky headland of Koh-ring that he risks as if by necessity its destruction. But not before he has snatched off his hat, his headpiece, and rammed it on Leggatt's head for protection against the sun that will beat mercilessly on him: only to find, as the keel nears the rocks, that the hat floats on the water and gives him a marker by which he can steer himself and his ship to safety.

The night, the silent sea, the naked swimmer, the concealment, the gift of the sleeping-suit, garb of the unconscious life, the lie enacted to the crew and the captain of the *Sephora*, the return of the fugitive to the sea, the hat that becomes a guide to steer by—the parts these play in the fable are evident. Conrad's intention in writing the tale becomes not only overt but explicit. The story risks offending against itself by making its secret too plain, its hero too aware of what is happening to him in his conspiracy with his other self. It is in the ordeals of Kurtz and Marlow, Lord Jim and Razumov, Decoud and Nostromo, that Conrad's drama of the alter ego takes on the richer force of psychic confusion and duplicity. He wrote "The Secret Sharer" as if to give an axiomatic statement of his central theme. Even so, the statement becomes something more than axiomatic. The spell of its atmosphere and imagery, the economy of action and event, the sustaining hint of meanings beyond the captain's conscious sense of collusion in guilt and secrecy, combine to make "The Secret Sharer" a fable that becomes focal not only in Conrad's own work but to an essential part of modern writing generally. It shows the conscious design and pregnant suggestiveness of archetypal fiction.

The Shadow-Line was written in a different mood and vein. Conrad was now approaching sixty. His work was beginning to take on an air of retrospect and epilogue. All his books after 1914 and his return from his last visit to Poland tend toward a retrospective pathos and conciliatory sentiment. The sustained tension of "Typhoon" and the greater novels, the concentrating conception of "The Secret Sharer," were hardly possible now. His last five novels turn on themes of surrender, acceptance, sacrifice, the truce with life and fate. These were not the subjects that inspired his greatest work. They give evidence of the fatigue and compromise that overtook his darker vision and more searching powers before the end. But whatever they cost him in a relaxation of those powers, in lassitude of imagination and awkwardness of writing, they take their place in his record as an aftermath of the severe exertions and vision that had sustained him during one of the greatest periods of energy to be found in the lives of modern authors. In *The Shadow-Line* he had one more tale to tell of what the sea had counted for in his life, one more of his essential subjects to bring to final statement.

The subject is stated in the opening lines. Once more it is the moment of life when a man finds that the "enchanted garden" of youth with its privilege of living "in advance of its days in all the beautiful continuity of hope which knows no pauses and no introspection" is closing behind him, and "perceives ahead a shadow-line warning one that the region of early youth, too, must be left behind." Jim, Marlow, Nostromo, Razumov, have all met that moment. Now it comes to another hero, again a young ship captain, who, arriving at his "first command," discovers that what promised to be the great heroic opportunity of his career has turned into a nightmare of menace, inadequacy, challenge in man and nature, a trap for the untested and the unwary.

In the prelude the young sailor in "the green sickness of late youth" throws up a good job for no good reason, is thought mad by his captain, and goes to the Officers' Home in an Eastern port to await his opportunity. There he is subjected to the shabby designs of the disgruntled steward and the demoralized Hamilton, both of them portents of what can become of a seaman's life and both conveying a presentiment of insecurity and "moral dissolution" that begins to infect the young man's soul. But the paternal Captain Giles comes to his rescue and speeds him on his new job—his first command, the situation and title Conrad first had in mind for the tale.

The mate, Mr. Burns, is resentful. He had expected promotion after the death of the old captain; soon turns sick and takes to his cabin with his hauntings by his old half-mad chief. The crew are suspicious. Gradually uneasiness and fear lay their hold on the ship. The winds die down. The vessel is trapped by doldrums in the Gulf of Siam, unable to gain the open sea. Ransome, the sanely rational cook, becomes the new captain's only ally, and he has a defective heart. An evil calm makes a dead sea of the waters. A slow delirium of impotence infects the ship.

Fever breaks out, striking down the crew. It is discovered that the dead captain had sold the ship's quinine and put a useless substitute in its place. The specter of the malevolent captain possesses the minds of Burns and the crew and touches the young captain himself. Sickness produces apathy, apathy hallucination. A dread of moral paralysis and impotence strikes the captain. His ship can neither move toward open water nor retreat to port. The "strange sense of insecurity" that had at the outset led him to suspect that he "might be no good" becomes all but overpowering. He finds himself "snared . . . as if in some poisonous trap." He feels the terror of what the faithful Ransome has had to learn to live with—a sickness of the heart.

It is that sickness that hovers like a warning over the tale. The fear that becomes a living presence on the ship is the lurking dread of spiritual apathy, impotence, discouragement, failure of heart, which most of Conrad's significant heroes are likely to experience and which this tale testifies to have been a fear in his own life and emotion. ("A strict piece of autobiography," he called *The Shadow-Line*: "another instance of the overwhelming greatness of our own emotion to ourselves.") At last the wind rises; rain falls; "the breeze [keeps] on freshening and [blows] true, true to a hair"; and because "the seaman's instinct alone survived in [his] moral dissolution," the captain finds himself able to summon his sickened crew to action and steer his ship to port. When Captain Giles meets him and asks him how he has come through his ordeal he protests that he is "not tired." "But I'll tell you, Captain Giles, how I feel. I feel old." "That will pass," says Giles. "The truth is that one must not make too much of anything in life, good or bad. . . . And there's another thing: a man should stand up to his bad luck, to his mistakes, to his conscience, and all that sort of thing. Why—what else would you have to fight against? . . . You will learn soon how not to be faint-hearted. A man has got to learn everything . . ."

When at the end the captain says good-bye to Ransome and shakes his hand for the last time, he recognizes one of the things he has learned. "I listened to him going up the companion stairs cautiously, step by step, in mortal fear of starting into sudden anger our common enemy it was his hard fate to carry consciously within his faithful breast." That enemy, the heart vulnerable to sickness and failure, will remain the captain's enemy too. He will carry its threat with him through life. Burns with his malcontent, Ransome with his courage, the ship with its evil spell—these he can now put behind him. They have yielded him their lessons. But they have left him with a knowledge that will remain and that will require all his "seaman's instinct" for safe passage through the years ahead.

"Both men and ships live in an unstable element," Conrad said in *The Mirror of the Sea*. That instability is the sphere and condition of his dramas, whether of life at sea or life in the world. The tests he met, the truths he learned, during his sailing years became the realities to which he addressed himself in his art. They are realities that assume many forms of peril, risk, and evil in his tales: now intimate or secret, now public, social, or historical, they rise as challenges to character and survival for men in every walk of life. It was in his tales of ships and seamen that Conrad brought them to some of the most effective and accurate expressions he ever arrived at, and it is their workings there that have made these stories classic of their kind—images in which "the sea interpenetrates with life" and becomes "a factor in the problem of existence."

Morton Dauwen Zabel

AUTHOR'S NOTES

TYPHOON[1]

The main characteristic of this volume consists in this, that all the stories composing it belong not only to the same period but have been written one after another in the order in which they appear in the book.

The period is that which follows on my connection with *Blackwood's Magazine*. I had just finished writing "The End of the Tether" and was casting about for some subject which could be developed in a shorter form than the tales in the volume of *Youth* when the instance of a steamship full of returning coolies from Singapore to some port in northern China occurred to my recollection. Years before I had heard it being talked about in the East as a recent occurrence. It was for us merely one subject of conversation amongst many others of the kind. Men earning their bread in any very specialized occupation will talk shop, not only because it is the most vital interest of their lives but also because they have not much knowledge of other subjects. They have never had the time to get acquainted with them. Life, for most of us, is not so much a hard as an exacting taskmaster.

I never met anybody personally concerned in this affair, the interest of which for us was, of course, not the bad weather but the extraordinary complication brought into the ship's life at a moment of exceptional stress by the

[1] From Conrad's "Author's Note," dated 1919, to the volume *Typhoon, and Other Stories* of 1903. The volume also contains the stories "Amy Foster," "Falk: A Reminiscence," and "Tomorrow." Only the part of Conrad's note relating to "Typhoon" is given here.

human element below her deck. Neither was the story itself ever enlarged upon in my hearing. In that company each of us could imagine easily what the whole thing was like. The financial difficulty of it, presenting also a human problem, was solved by a mind much too simple to be perplexed by anything in the world except men's idle talk for which it was not adapted.

From the first the mere anecdote, the mere statement I might say, that such a thing had happened on the high seas, appeared to me a sufficient subject for meditation. Yet it was but a bit of a sea yarn after all. I felt that to bring out its deeper significance which was quite apparent to me, something other, something more was required; a leading motive that would harmonize all these violent noises, and a point of view that would put all that elemental fury into its proper place.

What was needed of course was Captain MacWhirr. Directly I perceived him I could see that he was the man for the situation. I don't mean to say that I ever saw Captain MacWhirr in the flesh, or had ever come in contact with his literal mind and his dauntless temperament. MacWhirr is not an acquaintance of a few hours, or a few weeks, or a few months. He is the product of twenty years of life. My own life. Conscious invention had little to do with him. If it is true that Captain MacWhirr never walked and breathed on this earth (which I find for my part extremely difficult to believe) I can also assure my readers that he is perfectly authentic. I may venture to assert the same of every aspect of the story, while I confess that the particular typhoon of the tale was not a typhoon of my actual experience.

At its first appearance "Typhoon," the story, was classed by some critics as a deliberately intended storm-piece. Others picked out MacWhirr, in whom they perceived a definite symbolic intention. Neither was exclusively my intention. Both the typhoon and Captain MacWhirr presented themselves to me as the necessities of the deep conviction with which I approached the subject of the story. It was their opportunity. It was also my opportunity; and it would be vain to discourse about what I made of it in a handful of pages, since the pages themselves are here, between the covers of this volume, to speak for themselves.

This is a belated reflection. If it had occurred to me before it would have perhaps done away with the existence of this Author's Note; for, indeed, the same remark applies to every story in this volume. None of them are stories of experience in the absolute sense of the word. Experience in them is but the canvas of the attempted picture. Each of them has its more than one intention. With each the question is what the writer has done with his opportunity; and each answers the question for itself in words which, if I may say so without undue solemnity, were written with a conscientious regard for the truth of my own sensations. And each of those stories, to mean something, must justify itself in its own way to the conscience of each successive reader.

J. C.

1919

THE SECRET SHARER[2]

The only bond between these three stories is, so to speak, geographical, for their scene, be it land, be it sea, is situated in the same region which may be called the region of the Indian Ocean with its off-shoots and prolongations north of the equator even as far as the Gulf of Siam. In point of time they belong to the period immediately after the publication of that novel with the awkward title *Under Western Eyes* and, as far as the life of the writer is concerned, their appearance in a volume marks a definite change in the fortunes of his fiction. For there is no denying the fact that *Under Western Eyes* found no favour in the public eye, whereas the novel called *Chance* which followed *'Twixt*

[2] From Conrad's "Author's Note," dated 1920, to the volume *'Twixt Land and Sea* of 1912. The volume contains, besides "The Secret Sharer," two other tales: "A Smile of Fortune" and "Freya of the Seven Isles." Only the portion of Conrad's note that concerns "The Secret Sharer" is given here.

Land and Sea was received on its first appearance by many more readers than any other of my books.

This volume of three tales was also well received, publicly and privately and from a publisher's point of view. This little success was a most timely tonic for my enfeebled bodily frame. For this may indeed be called the book of a man's convalescence, at least as to three-fourths of it; because "The Secret Sharer," the middle story, was written much earlier than the other two.

For in truth the memories of *Under Western Eyes* are associated with the memory of a severe illness which seemed to wait like a tiger in the jungle on the turn of a path to jump on me the moment the last words of that novel were written. The memory of an illness is very much like the memory of a nightmare. On emerging from it in a much enfeebled state I was inspired to direct my tottering steps toward the Indian Ocean, a complete change of surroundings and atmosphere from the Lake of Geneva, as nobody would deny. Begun so languidly and with such a fumbling hand that the first twenty pages or more had to be thrown into the waste-paper basket, "A Smile of Fortune," the most purely Indian Ocean story of the three, has ended by becoming what the reader will see. I will only say for myself that I have been patted on the back for it by most unexpected people, personally unknown to me, the chief of them of course being the editor of a popular illustrated magazine who published it serially in one mighty instalment. Who will dare say after this that the change of air had not been an immense success?

The origins of the middle story, "The Secret Sharer," are quite other. It was written much earlier and was published first in *Harper's Magazine*, during the early part, I think, of 1911. Or perhaps the latter part? My memory on that point is hazy.[3] The basic fact of the tale I had in my possession for a good many years. It was in truth the common possession of the whole fleet of merchant ships trading to India, China, and Australia: a great company the last years of which coincided with my first years on the wider seas.

[3] "The Secret Sharer" was serialized in *Harper's Magazine* in August–September 1910.

The fact itself happened on board a very distinguished member of it, *Cutty Sark* by name and belonging to Mr. Willis, a notable ship-owner in his day, one of the kind (they are all underground now) who used personally to see his ships start on their voyages to those distant shores where they showed worthily the honoured house-flag of their owner. I am glad I was not too late to get at least one glimpse of Mr. Willis on a very wet and gloomy morning watching from the pier head of the New South Dock one of his clippers starting on a China voyage—an imposing figure of a man under the invariable white hat so well known in the Port of London, waiting till the head of his ship had swung down-stream before giving her a dignified wave of a big gloved hand. For all I know it may have been the *Cutty Sark* herself, though certainly not on that fatal voyage. I do not know the date of the occurrence on which the scheme of "The Secret Sharer" is founded; it came to light and even got into newspapers about the middle eighties, though I had heard of it before, as it were privately, among the officers of the great wool fleet in which my first years in deep water were served. It came to light under circumstances dramatic enough, I think, but which have nothing to do with my story. In the more specially maritime part of my writings this bit of presentation may take its place as one of my two Calm-pieces. For, if there is to be any classification by subjects, I have done two Storm-pieces in *The Nigger of the "Narcissus"* and in "Typhoon"; and two Calm-pieces: this one and *The Shadow-Line,* a book which belongs to a later period.

J. C.

1920

THE SHADOW-LINE [4]

This story, which I admit to be in its brevity a fairly complex piece of work, was not intended to touch on the

[4] Conrad's "Author's Note," dated 1920, to *The Shadow-Line* of 1917.

supernatural. Yet more than one critic has been inclined to take it in that way, seeing in it an attempt on my part to give the fullest scope to my imagination by taking it beyond the confines of the world of the living, suffering humanity. But as a matter of fact my imagination is not made of stuff so elastic as all that. I believe that if I attempted to put the strain of the supernatural on it it would fail deplorably and exhibit an unlovely gap. But I could never have attempted such a thing, because all my moral and intellectual being is penetrated by an invincible conviction that whatever falls under the dominion of our senses must be in nature and, however exceptional, cannot differ in its essence from all the other effects of the visible and tangible world of which we are a self-conscious part. The world of the living contains enough marvels and mysteries as it is; marvels and mysteries acting upon our emotions and intelligence in ways so inexplicable that it would almost justify the conception of life as an enchanted state. No, I am too firm in my consciousness of the marvellous to be ever fascinated by the mere supernatural, which (take it any way you like) is but a manufactured article, the fabrication of minds insensitive to the intimate delicacies of our relation to the dead and to the living, in their countless multitudes; a desecration of our tenderest memories; an outrage on our dignity.

Whatever my native modesty may be it will never condescend so low as to seek help for my imagination within those vain imaginings common to all ages and that in themselves are enough to fill all lovers of mankind with unutterable sadness. As to the effect of a mental or moral shock on a common mind, that is quite a legitimate subject for study and description. Mr. Burns's moral being receives a severe shock in his relations with his late captain, and this in his diseased state turns into a mere superstitious fancy compounded of fear and animosity. This fact is one of the elements of the story, but there is nothing supernatural in it, nothing so to speak from beyond the confines of this world, which in all conscience holds enough mystery and terror in itself.

Perhaps if I had published this tale, which I have had

for a long time in my mind, under the title of "First Command" no suggestion of the supernatural would have been found in it by any impartial reader, critical or otherwise. I will not consider here the origins of the feeling in which its actual title, *The Shadow-Line*, occurred to my mind. Primarily the aim of this piece of writing was the presentation of certain facts which certainly were associated with the change from youth, care-free and fervent, to the more self-conscious and more poignant period of maturer life. Nobody can doubt that before the supreme trial of a whole generation I had an acute consciousness of the minute and insignificant character of my own obscure experience. There could be no question here of any parallelism. That notion never entered my head. But there was a feeling of identity, though with an enormous difference of scale—as of one single drop measured against the bitter and stormy immensity of an ocean. And this was very natural too. For when we begin to meditate on the meaning of our own past it seems to fill all the world in its profundity and its magnitude. This book was written in the last three months of the year 1916. Of all the subjects of which a writer of tales is more or less conscious within himself this is the only one I found it possible to attempt at the time. The depth and the nature of the mood with which I approached it is best expressed perhaps in the dedication, which strikes me now as a most disproportionate thing—as another instance of the overwhelming greatness of our own emotion to ourselves.

This much having been said I may pass on now to a few remarks about the mere material of the story. As to locality it belongs to that part of the Eastern Seas from which I have carried away into my writing life the greatest number of suggestions. From my statement that I thought of this story for a long time under the title of "First Command" the reader may guess that it is concerned with my personal experience. As a matter of fact it *is* personal experience seen in perspective with the eye of the mind and coloured by that affection one can't help feeling for such events of one's life as one has no reason to be ashamed of. And that affection is as intense (I appeal here to universal experience) as the shame, and almost the anguish with which one remembers some unfortunate occurrences, down to mere mistakes in speech, that have been perpetrated by one in the past. The effect of perspective in memory is to make things loom large because the essentials stand out isolated from their surroundings of insignificant daily facts which have naturally faded out of one's mind. I remember that period of my sea-life with pleasure because, begun inauspiciously, it turned out in the end a success from a personal point of view, leaving a tangible proof in the terms of the letter the owners of the ship wrote to me two years afterwards when I resigned my command in order to come home. This resignation marked the beginning of another phase of my seaman's life, its terminal phase, if I may say so, which in its own way has coloured another portion of my writings. I didn't know then how near its end my sea-life was, and therefore I felt no sorrow except at parting with the ship. I was sorry also to break my connection with the firm which owned her and who were pleased to receive with friendly kindness and give their confidence to a man who had entered their service in an accidental manner and in very adverse circumstances. Without disparaging the earnestness of my purpose I suspect now that luck had no small part in the success of the trust reposed in me. And one cannot help remembering with pleasure the time when one's best efforts were seconded by a run of luck.

The words "Worthy of my undying regard" selected by me for the motto on the title-page are quoted from the text of the book itself; and, though one of my critics surmised that they applied to the ship, it is evident from the place where they stand that they refer to the men of that ship's company: complete strangers to their new captain and yet who stood by him so well during those twenty days that seemed to have been passed on the brink of a slow and agonizing destruction. And *that* is the greatest memory of all! For surely it is a great thing to have commanded a handful of men worthy of one's undying regard.

J. C.

TYPHOON

Far as the mariner on highest mast
Can see all round upon the calmed vast,
So wide was Neptune's hall . . .

KEATS

I

Captain MacWhirr, of the steamer *Nan-Shan*, had a physiognomy that, in the order of material appearances, was the exact counterpart of his mind: it presented no marked characteristics of firmness or stupidity; it had no pronounced characteristics whatever; it was simply ordinary, irresponsive, and unruffled.

The only thing his aspect might have been said to suggest, at times, was bashfulness; because he would sit, in business offices ashore, sunburnt and smiling faintly, with downcast eyes. When he raised them, they were perceived to be direct in their glance and of blue colour. His hair was fair and extremely fine, clasping from temple to temple the bald dome of his skull in a clamp as of fluffy silk. The hair of his face, on the contrary, carroty and flaming, resembled a growth of copper wire clipped short to the line of the lip; while, no matter how close he shaved, fiery metallic gleams passed, when he moved his head, over the surface of his cheeks. He was rather below the medium height, a bit round-shouldered, and so sturdy of limb that his clothes always looked a shade too tight for his arms and legs. As if unable to grasp what is due to the difference of latitudes, he wore a brown bowler hat, a complete suit of a brownish hue, and clumsy black boots. These harbour togs gave to his thick figure an air of stiff and uncouth smartness. A thin silver watch-chain looped his waistcoat, and he never left his ship for the shore without clutching in his powerful,

hairy fist an elegant umbrella of the very best quality, but
generally unrolled. Young Jukes, the chief mate, attending
his commander to the gangway, would sometimes venture
to say, with the greatest gentleness, "Allow me, sir"—and
possessing himself of the umbrella deferentially, would ele-
vate the ferrule, shake the folds, twirl a neat furl in a jiffy,
and hand it back; going through the performance with a
face of such portentous gravity, that Mr. Solomon Rout,
the chief engineer, smoking his morning cigar over the skylight, would turn away his head in order to hide a smile.
"Oh! aye! The blessed gamp. . . . Thank 'ee, Jukes, thank
'ee," would mutter Captain MacWhirr, heartily, without
looking up.

Having just enough imagination to carry him through
each successive day, and no more, he was tranquilly sure
of himself; and from the very same cause he was not in the
least conceited. It is your imaginative superior who is
touchy, overbearing, and difficult to please; but every ship
Captain MacWhirr commanded was the floating abode of
harmony and peace. It was, in truth, as impossible for him
to take a flight of fancy as it would be for a watchmaker to
put together a chronometer with nothing except a two-
pound hammer and a whip-saw in the way of tools. Yet the
uninteresting lives of men so entirely given to the actuality
of the bare existence have their mysterious side. It was impossible in Captain MacWhirr's case, for instance, to understand what under heaven could have induced that perfectly satisfactory son of a petty grocer in Belfast to run
away to sea. And yet he had done that very thing at the
age of fifteen. It was enough, when you thought it over,
to give you the idea of an immense, potent, and invisible
hand thrust into the ant-heap of the earth, laying hold of
shoulders, knocking heads together, and setting the unconscious faces of the multitude towards inconceivable goals
and in undreamt-of directions.

His father never really forgave him for this undutiful
stupidity. "We could have got on without him," he used to
say later on, "but there's the business. And he an only son,
too!" His mother wept very much after his disappearance.
As it had never occurred to him to leave word behind, he

was mourned over for dead till, after eight months, his first letter arrived from Talcahuano. It was short, and contained the statement: "We had very fine weather on our passage out." But evidently, in the writer's mind, the only important intelligence was to the effect that his captain had, on the very day of writing, entered him regularly on the ship's articles as Ordinary Seaman. "Because I can do the work," he explained. The mother again wept copiously, while the remark, "Tom's an ass," expressed the emotions of the father. He was a corpulent man, with a gift for sly chaffing, which to the end of his life he exercised in his intercourse with his son, a little pityingly, as if upon a half-witted person.

MacWhirr's visits to his home were necessarily rare, and in the course of years he despatched other letters to his parents, informing them of his successive promotions and of his movements upon the vast earth. In these missives could be found sentences like this: "The heat here is very great." Or: "On Christmas day at 4 P.M. we fell in with some icebergs." The old people ultimately became acquainted with a good many names of ships, and with the names of the skippers who commanded them—with the names of Scots and English shipowners—with the names of seas, oceans, straits, promontories—with outlandish names of lumber-ports, of rice-ports, of cotton-ports—with the names of islands—with the name of their son's young woman. She was called Lucy. It did not suggest itself to him to mention whether he thought the name pretty. And then they died.

The great day of MacWhirr's marriage came in due course, following shortly upon the great day when he got his first command.

All these events had taken place many years before the morning when, in the chart-room of the steamer *Nan-Shan,* he stood confronted by the fall of a barometer he had no reason to distrust. The fall—taking into account the excellence of the instrument, the time of the year, and the ship's position on the terrestrial globe—was of a nature ominously prophetic; but the red face of the man betrayed no sort of inward disturbance. Omens were as nothing to him, and he was unable to discover the message of a prophecy till the fulfilment had brought it home to his very door. "That's a fall, and no mistake," he thought. "There must be some uncommonly dirty weather knocking about."

The *Nan-Shan* was on her way from the southward to the treaty port of Fu-chau, with some cargo in her lower holds, and two hundred Chinese coolies returning to their village homes in the province of Fo-kien, after a few years of work in various tropical colonies. The morning was fine, the oily sea heaved without a sparkle, and there was a queer white misty patch in the sky like a halo of the sun. The fore-deck, packed with Chinamen, was full of sombre clothing, yellow faces, and pigtails, sprinkled over with a good many naked shoulders, for there was no wind, and the heat was close. The coolies lounged, talked, smoked, or stared over the rail; some, drawing water over the side, sluiced each other; a few slept on hatches, while several small parties of six sat on their heels surrounding iron trays with plates of rice and tiny teacups; and every single Celestial of them was carrying with him all he had in the world —a wooden chest with a ringing lock and brass on the corners, containing the savings of his labours: some clothes of ceremony, sticks of incense, a little opium maybe, bits of nameless rubbish of conventional value, and a small hoard of silver dollars, toiled for in coal lighters, won in gambling-houses or in petty trading, grubbed out of earth, sweated out in mines, on railway lines, in deadly jungle, under heavy burdens—amassed patiently, guarded with care, cherished fiercely.

A cross swell had set in from the direction of Formosa Channel about ten o'clock, without disturbing these passengers much, because the *Nan-Shan*, with her flat bottom, rolling chocks on bilges, and great breadth of beam, had the reputation of an exceptionally steady ship in a sea-way. Mr. Jukes, in moments of expansion on shore, would proclaim loudly that the "old girl was as good as she was pretty." It would never have occurred to Captain MacWhirr to express his favourable opinion so loud or in terms so fanciful.

She was a good ship, undoubtedly, and not old either. She had been built in Dumbarton less than three years before, to the order of a firm of merchants in Siam—Messrs. Sigg and Son. When she lay afloat, finished in every detail and ready to take up the work of her life, the builders contemplated her with pride.

"Sigg has asked us for a reliable skipper to take her out," remarked one of the partners; and the other, after reflecting for a while, said: "I think MacWhirr is ashore just at present." "Is he? Then wire him at once. He's the very man," declared the senior, without a moment's hesitation.

Next morning MacWhirr stood before them unperturbed, having travelled from London by the midnight express after a sudden but undemonstrative parting with his wife. She was the daughter of a superior couple who had seen better days.

"We had better be going together over the ship, Captain," said the senior partner; and the three men started to view the perfections of the *Nan-Shan* from stem to stern, and from her keelson to the trucks of her two stumpy polemasts.

Captain MacWhirr had begun by taking off his coat, which he hung on the end of a steam windlass embodying all the latest improvements.

"My uncle wrote of you favourably by yesterday's mail to our good friends—Messrs. Sigg, you know—and doubtless they'll continue you out there in command," said the junior partner. "You'll be able to boast of being in charge of the handiest boat of her size on the coast of China, Captain," he added.

"Have you? Thank 'ee," mumbled vaguely MacWhirr, to whom the view of a distant eventuality could appeal no more than the beauty of a wide landscape to a purblind tourist; and his eyes happening at the moment to be at rest upon the lock of the cabin door, he walked up to it, full of purpose, and began to rattle the handle vigorously, while he observed, in his low, earnest voice, "You can't trust the workmen nowadays. A brand-new lock, and it won't act at all. Stuck fast. See? See?"

As soon as they found themselves alone in their office across the yard: "You praised that fellow up to Sigg.

What is it you see in him?" asked the nephew, with faint contempt.

"I admit he has nothing of your fancy skipper about him, if that's what you mean," said the elder man, curtly. "Is the foreman of the joiners on the *Nan-Shan* outside? . . . Come in, Bates. How is it that you let Tait's people put us off with a defective lock on the cabin door? The Captain could see directly he set eye on it. Have it replaced at once. The little straws, Bates . . . the little straws. . . ."

The lock was replaced accordingly, and a few days afterwards the *Nan-Shan* steamed out to the East, without MacWhirr having offered any further remark as to her fittings, or having been heard to utter a single word hinting at pride in his ship, gratitude for his appointment, or satisfaction at his prospects.

With a temperament neither loquacious nor taciturn he found very little occasion to talk. There were matters of duty, of course—directions, orders, and so on; but the past being to his mind done with, and the future not there yet, the more general actualities of the day required no comment —because facts can speak for themselves with overwhelming precision.

Old Mr. Sigg liked a man of few words, and one that "you could be sure would not try to improve upon his instructions." MacWhirr satisfying these requirements, was continued in command of the *Nan-Shan*, and applied himself to the careful navigation of his ship in the China seas. She had come out on a British register, but after some time Messrs. Sigg judged it expedient to transfer her to the Siamese flag.

At the news of the contemplated transfer Jukes grew restless, as if under a sense of personal affront. He went about grumbling to himself, and uttering short scornful laughs. "Fancy having a ridiculous Noah's Ark elephant in the ensign of one's ship," he said once at the engine-room door. "Dash me if I can stand it; I'll throw up the billet. Don't it make *you* sick, Mr. Rout?" The chief engineer only cleared his throat with the air of a man who knows the value of a good billet.

The first morning the new flag floated over the stern of

the *Nan-Shan* Jukes stood looking at it bitterly from the bridge. He struggled with his feelings for a while, and then remarked, "Queer flag for a man to sail under, sir."

"What's the matter with the flag?" inquired Captain MacWhirr. "Seems all right to me." And he walked across to the end of the bridge to have a good look.

"Well, it looks queer to me," burst out Jukes, greatly exasperated, and flung off the bridge.

Captain MacWhirr was amazed at these manners. After a while he stepped quietly into the chart-room, and opened his International Signal Code-book at the plate where the flags of all the nations are correctly figured in gaudy rows. He ran his finger over them, and when he came to Siam he contemplated with great attention the red field and the white elephant. Nothing could be more simple; but to make sure he brought the book out on the bridge for the purpose of comparing the coloured drawing with the real thing at the flagstaff astern. When next Jukes, who was carrying on the duty that day with a sort of suppressed fierceness, happened on the bridge, his commander observed:

"There's nothing amiss with that flag."

"Isn't there?" mumbled Jukes, falling on his knees before a deck-locker and jerking therefrom viciously a spare lead-line.

"No. I looked up the book. Length twice the breadth and the elephant exactly in the middle. I thought the people ashore would know how to make the local flag. Stands to reason. You were wrong, Jukes. . . ."

"Well, sir," began Jukes, getting up excitedly, "all I can say——" He fumbled for the end of the coil of line with trembling hands.

"That's all right." Captain MacWhirr soothed him, sitting heavily on a little canvas folding-stool he greatly affected. "All you have to do is to take care they don't hoist the elephant upside-down before they get quite used to it."

Jukes flung the new lead-line over on the fore-deck with a loud "Here you are, bo'ss'en—don't forget to wet it thoroughly," and turned with immense resolution towards his commander; but Captain MacWhirr spread his elbows on the bridge-rail comfortably.

"Because it would be, I suppose, understood as a signal of distress," he went on. "What do you think? That elephant there, I take it, stands for something in the nature of the Union Jack in the flag. . . ."

"Does it!" yelled Jukes, so that every head on the *Nan-Shan's* decks looked towards the bridge. Then he sighed, and with sudden resignation: "It would certainly be a dam' distressful sight," he said, meekly.

Later in the day he accosted the chief engineer with a confidential, "Here, let me tell you the old man's latest."

Mr. Solomon Rout (frequently alluded to as Long Sol, Old Sol, or Father Rout), from finding himself almost invariably the tallest man on board every ship he joined, had acquired the habit of a stooping, leisurely condescension. His hair was scant and sandy, his flat cheeks were pale, his bony wrists and long scholarly hands were pale, too, as though he had lived all his life in the shade.

He smiled from on high at Jukes, and went on smoking and glancing about quietly, in the manner of a kind uncle lending an ear to the tale of an excited schoolboy. Then, greatly amused but impassive, he asked:

"And did you throw up the billet?"

"No," cried Jukes, raising a weary, discouraged voice above the harsh buzz of the *Nan-Shan's* friction winches. All of them were hard at work, snatching slings of cargo, high up, to the end of long derricks, only, as it seemed, to let them rip down recklessly by the run. The cargo chains groaned in the gins, clinked on coamings, rattled over the side; and the whole ship quivered, with her long gray flanks smoking in wreaths of steam. "No," cried Jukes, "I didn't. What's the good? I might just as well fling my resignation at this bulkhead. I don't believe you can make a man like that understand anything. He simply knocks me over."

At that moment Captain MacWhirr, back from the shore, crossed the deck, umbrella in hand, escorted by a mournful, self-possessed Chinaman, walking behind in paper-soled silk shoes, and who also carried an umbrella.

The master of the *Nan-Shan*, speaking just audibly and gazing at his boots as his manner was, remarked that it would be necessary to call at Fu-chau this trip, and desired Mr. Rout to have steam up to-morrow afternoon at one o'clock sharp. He pushed back his hat to wipe his forehead, observing at the same time that he hated going ashore anyhow; while overtopping him Mr. Rout, without deigning a word, smoked austerely, nursing his right elbow in the palm of his left hand. Then Jukes was directed in the same subdued voice to keep the forward 'tween-deck clear of cargo. Two hundred coolies were going to be put down there. The Bun Hin Company were sending that lot home. Twenty-five bags of rice would be coming off in a sampan directly, for stores. All seven-years'-men they were, said Captain MacWhirr, with a camphor-wood chest to every man. The carpenter should be set to work nailing three-inch battens along the deck below, fore and aft, to keep these boxes from shifting in a sea-way. Jukes had better look to it at once. "D'ye hear, Jukes?" This Chinaman here was coming with the ship as far as Fu-chau—a sort of interpreter he would be. Bun Hin's clerk he was, and wanted to have a look at the space. Jukes had better take him forward. "D'ye hear, Jukes?"

Jukes took care to punctuate these instructions in proper places with the obligatory "Yes, sir," ejaculated without enthusiasm. His brusque "Come along, John; make look see" set the Chinaman in motion at his heels.

"Wanchee look see, all same look see can do," said Jukes, who having no talent for foreign languages mangled the very pidgin-English cruelly. He pointed at the open hatch. "Catchee number one piecie place to sleep in. Eh?"

He was gruff, as became his racial superiority, but not unfriendly. The Chinaman, gazing sad and speechless into the darkness of the hatchway, seemed to stand at the head of a yawning grave.

"No catchee rain down there—savee?" pointed out Jukes. "Suppose all'ee same fine weather, one piecie coolie-man come top-side," he pursued, warming up imaginatively. "Make so— Phooooo!" He expanded his chest and blew out his cheeks. "Savee, John? Breathe—fresh air. Good. Eh?

Washee him piecie pants, chow-chow top-side—see, John?"

With his mouth and hands he made exuberant motions of eating rice and washing clothes; and the Chinaman, who concealed his distrust of this pantomime under a collected demeanour tinged by a gentle and refined melancholy, glanced out of his almond eyes from Jukes to the hatch and back again. "Velly good," he murmured, in a disconsolate undertone, and hastened smoothly along the decks, dodging obstacles in his course. He disappeared, ducking low under a sling of ten dirty gunny-bags full of some costly merchandise and exhaling a repulsive smell.

Captain MacWhirr meantime had gone on the bridge, and into the chart-room, where a letter, commenced two days before, awaited termination. These long letters began with the words, "My darling wife," and the steward, between the scrubbing of the floors and the dusting of chronometer-boxes, snatched at every opportunity to read them. They interested him much more than they possibly could the woman for whose eye they were intended; and this for the reason that they related in minute detail each successive trip of the *Nan-Shan*.

Her master, faithful to facts, which alone his consciousness reflected, would set them down with painstaking care upon many pages. The house in a northern suburb to which these pages were addressed had a bit of garden before the bow-windows, a deep porch of good appearance, coloured glass with imitation lead frame in the front door. He paid five-and-forty pounds a year for it, and did not think the rent too high, because Mrs. MacWhirr (a pretentious person with a scraggy neck and a disdainful manner) was admittedly ladylike, and in the neighbourhood considered as "quite superior." The only secret of her life was her abject terror of the time when her husband would come home to stay for good. Under the same roof there dwelt also a daughter called Lydia and a son, Tom. These two were but slightly acquainted with their father. Mainly, they knew him as a rare but privileged visitor, who of an evening smoked his pipe in the dining-room and slept in the house. The lanky girl, upon the whole, was rather ashamed of him; the boy was frankly and utterly indifferent in a straightforward, delightful, unaffected way manly boys have.

And Captain MacWhirr wrote home from the coast of China twelve times every year, desiring quaintly to be "remembered to the children," and subscribing himself "your loving husband," as calmly as if the words so long used by so many men were, apart from their shape, worn-out things, and of a faded meaning.

The China seas north and south are narrow seas. They are seas full of every-day, eloquent facts, such as islands, sand-banks, reefs, swift and changeable currents—tangled facts that nevertheless speak to a seaman in clear and definite language. Their speech appealed to Captain Mac-Whirr's sense of realities so forcibly that he had given up his state-room below and practically lived all his days on the bridge of his ship, often having his meals sent up, and sleeping at night in the chart-room. And he indited there his home letters. Each of them, without exception, contained the phrase, "The weather has been very fine this trip," or some other form of a statement to that effect. And this statement, too, in its wonderful persistence, was of the same perfect accuracy as all the others they contained.

Mr. Rout likewise wrote letters; only no one on board knew how chatty he could be pen in hand, because the chief engineer had enough imagination to keep his desk locked. His wife relished his style greatly. They were a childless couple, and Mrs. Rout, a big, high-bosomed, jolly woman of forty, shared with Mr. Rout's toothless and venerable mother a little cottage near Teddington. She would run over her correspondence, at breakfast, with lively eyes, and scream out interesting passages in a joyous voice at the deaf old lady, prefacing each extract by the warning shout, "Solomon says!" She had the trick of firing off Solomon's utterances also upon strangers, astonishing them easily by the unfamiliar text and the unexpectedly jocular vein of these quotations. On the day the new curate called for the first time at the cottage, she found occasion to remark, "As Solomon says: 'the engineers that go down to the sea in ships behold the wonders of sailor nature'"; when a change in the visitor's countenance made her stop and stare.

"Solomon. . . . Oh! . . . Mrs. Rout," stuttered the young man, very red in the face, "I must say . . . I don't. . . ."

"He's my husband," she announced in a great shout, throwing herself back in the chair. Perceiving the joke, she laughed immoderately with a handkerchief to her eyes, while he sat wearing a forced smile, and, from his inexperience of jolly women, fully persuaded that she must be deplorably insane. They were excellent friends afterwards; for, absolving her from irreverent intention, he came to think she was a very worthy person indeed; and he learned in time to receive without flinching other scraps of Solomon's wisdom.

"For my part," Solomon was reported by his wife to have said once, "give me the dullest ass for a skipper before a rogue. There is a way to take a fool; but a rogue is smart and slippery." This was an airy generalization drawn from the particular case of Captain MacWhirr's honesty, which, in itself, had the heavy obviousness of a lump of clay. On the other hand, Mr. Jukes, unable to generalize, unmarried, and unengaged, was in the habit of opening his heart after another fashion to an old chum and former shipmate, actually serving as second officer on board an Atlantic liner.

First of all he would insist upon the advantages of the Eastern trade, hinting at its superiority to the Western ocean service. He extolled the sky, the seas, the ships, and the easy life of the Far East. The *Nan-Shan*, he affirmed, was second to none as a sea-boat.

"We have no brass-bound uniforms, but then we are like brothers here," he wrote. "We all mess together and live like fighting-cocks. . . . All the chaps of the black-squad are as decent as they make that kind, and old Sol, the Chief, is a dry stick. We are good friends. As to our old man, you could not find a quieter skipper. Sometimes you would think he hadn't sense enough to see anything wrong. And yet it isn't that. Can't be. He has been in command for a good few years now. He doesn't do anything actually foolish, and gets his ship along all right without worrying anybody. I believe he hasn't brains enough to enjoy kicking up a row. I don't take advantage of him. I would scorn it.

Outside the routine of duty he doesn't seem to understand more than half of what you tell him. We get a laugh out of this at times; but it is dull, too, to be with a man like this—in the long-run. Old Sol says he hasn't much conversation. Conversation! O Lord! He never talks. The other day I had been yarning under the bridge with one of the engineers, and he must have heard us. When I came up to take my watch, he steps out of the chart-room and has a good look all round, peeps over at the sidelights, glances at the compass, squints upwards at the stars. That's his regular performance. By-and-by he says: 'Was that you talking just now in the port alleyway?' 'Yes, sir.' 'With the third engineer?' 'Yes, sir.' He walks off to starboard, and sits under the dodger on a little camp-stool of his, and for half an hour perhaps he makes no sound, except that I heard him sneeze once. Then after a while I hear him getting up over there, and he strolls across to port, where I was. 'I can't understand what you can find to talk about,' says he. 'Two solid hours. I am not blaming you. I see people ashore at it all day long, and then in the evening they sit down and keep at it over the drinks. Must be saying the same things over and over again. I can't understand.'

"Did you ever hear anything like that? And he was so patient about it. It made me quite sorry for him. But he is exasperating, too, sometimes. Of course one would not do anything to vex him even if it were worth while. But it isn't. He's so jolly innocent that if you were to put your thumb to your nose and wave your fingers at him he would only wonder gravely to himself what got into you. He told me once quite simply that he found it very difficult to make out what made people always act so queerly. He's too dense to trouble about, and that's the truth."

Thus wrote Mr. Jukes to his chum in the Western ocean trade, out of the fulness of his heart and the liveliness of his fancy.

He had expressed his honest opinion. It was not worth while trying to impress a man of that sort. If the world had been full of such men, life would have probably appeared to Jukes an unentertaining and unprofitable business. He was not alone in his opinion. The sea itself, as if sharing

Mr. Jukes' good-natured forbearance, had never put itself out to startle the silent man, who seldom looked up, and wandered innocently over the waters with the only visible purpose of getting food, raiment, and house-room for three people ashore. Dirty weather he had known, of course. He had been made wet, uncomfortable, tired in the usual way, felt at the time and presently forgotten. So that upon the whole he had been justified in reporting fine weather at home. But he had never been given a glimpse of immeasurable strength and of immoderate wrath, the wrath that passes exhausted but never appeased—the wrath and fury of the passionate sea. He knew it existed, as we know that crime and abominations exist; he had heard of it as a peaceable citizen in a town hears of battles, famines, and floods, and yet knows nothing of what these things mean—though, indeed, he may have been mixed up in a street row, have gone without his dinner once, or been soaked to the skin in a shower. Captain MacWhirr had sailed over the surface of the oceans as some men go skimming over the years of existence to sink gently into a placid grave, ignorant of life to the last, without ever having been made to see all it may contain of perfidy, of violence, and of terror. There are on sea and land such men thus fortunate—or thus disdained by destiny or by the sea.

II

Observing the steady fall of the barometer, Captain Mac-Whirr thought, "There's some dirty weather knocking about." This is precisely what he thought. He had had an experience of moderately dirty weather—the term dirty as applied to the weather implying only moderate discomfort to the seaman. Had he been informed by an indisputable authority that the end of the world was to be finally accomplished by a catastrophic disturbance of the atmosphere, he would have assimilated the information under the simple idea of dirty weather, and no other, because he had no experience of cataclysms, and belief does not necessarily imply comprehension. The wisdom of his county had pro-

nounced by means of an Act of Parliament that before he
could be considered as fit to take charge of a ship he should
be able to answer certain simple questions on the subject
of circular storms such as hurricanes, cyclones, typhoons;
and apparently he had answered them, since he was now
in command of the *Nan-Shan* in the China seas during the
season of typhoons. But if he had answered he remembered
nothing of it. He was, however, conscious of being made
uncomfortable by the clammy heat. He came out on the
bridge, and found no relief to this oppression. The air
seemed thick. He gasped like a fish, and began to believe
himself greatly out of sorts.

The *Nan-Shan* was ploughing a vanishing furrow upon
the circle of the sea that had the surface and the shimmer
of an undulating piece of gray silk. The sun, pale and without rays, poured down leaden heat in a strangely indecisive
light, and the Chinamen were lying prostrate about the
decks. Their bloodless, pinched, yellow faces were like the
faces of bilious invalids. Captain MacWhirr noticed two of
them especially, stretched out on their backs below the
bridge. As soon as they had closed their eyes they seemed
dead. Three others, however, were quarrelling barbarously
away forward; and one big fellow, half naked, with hercu-
lean shoulders, was hanging limply over a winch; another,
sitting on the deck, his knees up and his head drooping
sideways in a girlish attitude, was plaiting his pigtail with
infinite languor depicted in his whole person and in the
very movement of his fingers. The smoke struggled with
difficulty out of the funnel, and instead of streaming away
spread itself out like an infernal sort of cloud, smelling of
sulphur and raining soot all over the decks.

"What the devil are you doing there, Mr. Jukes?" asked
Captain MacWhirr.

This unusual form of address, though mumbled rather
than spoken, caused the body of Mr. Jukes to start as
though it had been prodded under the fifth rib. He had
had a low bench brought on the bridge, and sitting on it,
with a length of rope curled about his feet and a piece of
canvas stretched over his knees, was pushing a sail-needle

vigorously. He looked up, and his surprise gave to his eyes an expression of innocence and candour.

"I am only roping some of that new set of bags we made last trip for whipping up coals," he remonstrated, gently. "We shall want them for the next coaling, sir."

"What became of the others?"

"Why, worn out of course, sir."

Captain MacWhirr, after glaring down irresolutely at his chief mate, disclosed the gloomy and cynical conviction that more than half of them had been lost overboard, "if only the truth was known," and retired to the other end of the bridge. Jukes, exasperated by this unprovoked attack, broke the needle at the second stitch, and dropping his work got up and cursed the heat in a violent undertone.

The propeller thumped, the three Chinamen forward had given up squabbling very suddenly, and the one who had been plaiting his tail clasped his legs and stared dejectedly over his knees. The lurid sunshine cast faint and sickly shadows. The swell ran higher and swifter every moment, and the ship lurched heavily in the smooth, deep hollows of the sea.

"I wonder where that beastly swell comes from," said Jukes aloud, recovering himself after a stagger.

"North-east," grunted the literal MacWhirr, from his side of the bridge. "There's some dirty weather knocking about. Go and look at the glass."

When Jukes came out of the chart-room, the cast of his countenance had changed to thoughtfulness and concern. He caught hold of the bridge-rail and stared ahead.

The temperature in the engine-room had gone up to a hundred and seventeen degrees. Irritated voices were ascending through the skylight and through the fiddle of the stokehold in a harsh and resonant uproar, mingled with angry clangs and scrapes of metal, as if men with limbs of iron and throats of bronze had been quarrelling down there. The second engineer was falling foul of the stokers for letting the steam go down. He was a man with arms like a blacksmith, and generally feared; but that afternoon the stokers were answering him back recklessly, and slammed the furnace doors with the fury of despair. Then the noise ceased suddenly, and the second engineer appeared, emerging out of the stokehold streaked with grime and soaking wet like a chimney-sweep coming out of a well. As soon as his head was clear of the fiddle he began to scold Jukes for not trimming properly the stokehold ventilators; and in answer Jukes made with his hands deprecatory soothing signs meaning: "No wind—can't be helped—you can see for yourself." But the other wouldn't hear reason. His teeth flashed angrily in his dirty face. He didn't mind, he said, the trouble of punching their blanked heads down there, blank his soul, but did the condemned sailors think you could keep steam up in the God-forsaken boilers simply by knocking the blanked stokers about? No, by George! You had to get some draught, too—may he be everlastingly blanked for a swab-headed deck-hand if you didn't! And the chief, too, rampaging before the steam-gauge and carrying on like a lunatic up and down the engine-room ever since noon. What did Jukes think he was stuck up there for, if he couldn't get one of his decayed, good-for-nothing deck-cripples to turn the ventilators to the wind?

The relations of the "engine-room" and the "deck" of the *Nan-Shan* were, as is known, of a brotherly nature; therefore Jukes leaned over and begged the other in a restrained tone not to make a disgusting ass of himself; the skipper was on the other side of the bridge. But the second declared mutinously that he didn't care a rap who was on the other side of the bridge, and Jukes, passing in a flash from lofty disapproval into a state of exaltation, invited him in unflattering terms to come up and twist the beastly things to please himself, and catch such wind as a donkey of his sort could find. The second rushed up to the fray. He flung himself at the port ventilator as though he meant to tear it out bodily and toss it overboard. All he did was to move the cowl round a few inches, with an enormous expenditure of force, and seemed spent in the effort. He leaned against the back of the wheelhouse, and Jukes walked up to him.

"Oh, Heavens!" ejaculated the engineer in a feeble voice. He lifted his eyes to the sky, and then let his glassy stare descend to meet the horizon that, tilting up to an angle of forty degrees, seemed to hang on a slant for a while and settled down slowly. "Heavens! Phew! What's up, any-how?"

Jukes, straddling his long legs like a pair of compasses, put on an air of superiority. "We're going to catch it this time," he said. "The barometer is tumbling down like any-thing, Harry. And you trying to kick up that silly row. . . ."

The word "barometer" seemed to revive the second en-gineer's mad animosity. Collecting afresh all his energies, he directed Jukes in a low and brutal tone to shove the unmentionable instrument down his gory throat. Who cared for his crimson barometer? It was the steam—the steam—that was going down; and what between the firemen going faint and the chief going silly, it was worse than a dog's life for him; he didn't care a tinker's curse how soon the whole show was blown out of the water. He seemed on the point of having a cry, but after regaining his breath he mut-tered darkly, "I'll faint them," and dashed off. He stopped upon the fiddle long enough to shake his fist at the un-natural daylight, and dropped into the dark hole with a whoop.

When Jukes turned, his eyes fell upon the rounded back and the big red ears of Captain MacWhirr, who had come across. He did not look at his chief officer, but said at once, "That's a very violent man, that second engineer."

"Jolly good second, anyhow," grunted Jukes. "They can't keep up steam," he added, rapidly, and made a grab at the rail against the coming lurch.

Captain MacWhirr, unprepared, took a run and brought himself up with a jerk by an awning stanchion.

"A profane man," he said, obstinately. "If this goes on, I'll have to get rid of him the first chance."

"It's the heat," said Jukes. "The weather's awful. It would make a saint swear. Even up here I feel exactly as if I had my head tied up in a woollen blanket."

Captain MacWhirr looked up. "D'ye mean to say, Mr. Jukes, you ever had your head tied up in a blanket? What was that for?"

"It's a manner of speaking, sir," said Jukes, stolidly.

"Some of you fellows do go on! What's that about saints swearing? I wish you wouldn't talk so wild. What sort of saint would that be that would swear? No more saint than yourself, I expect. And what's a blanket got to do with it—or the weather either. . . . The heat does not make me swear —does it? It's filthy bad temper. That's what it is. And what's the good of your talking like this?"

Thus Captain MacWhirr expostulated against the use of images in speech, and at the end electrified Jukes by a contemptuous snort, followed by words of passion and resentment: "Damme! I'll fire him out of the ship if he don't look out."

And Jukes, incorrigible, thought: "Goodness me! Somebody's put a new inside to my old man. Here's temper, if you like. Of course it's the weather; what else? It would make an angel quarrelsome—let alone a saint."

All the Chinamen on deck appeared at their last gasp.

At its setting the sun had a diminished diameter and an expiring brown, rayless glow, as if millions of centuries elapsing since the morning had brought it near its end. A dense bank of cloud became visible to the northward; it had a sinister dark olive tint, and lay low and motionless upon the sea, resembling a solid obstacle in the path of the ship. She went floundering towards it like an exhausted creature driven to its death. The coppery twilight retired slowly, and the darkness brought out overhead a swarm of unsteady, big stars, that, as if blown upon, flickered exceedingly and seemed to hang very near the earth. At eight o'clock Jukes went into the chart-room to write up the ship's log.

He copied neatly out of the rough-book the number of miles, the course of the ship, and in the column for "wind" scrawled the word "calm" from top to bottom of the eight hours since noon. He was exasperated by the continuous, monotonous rolling of the ship. The heavy inkstand would slide away in a manner that suggested perverse intelligence in dodging the pen. Having written in the large space under the head of "Remarks" "Heat very oppressive," he stuck the end of the pen-holder in his teeth, pipe fashion, and mopped his face carefully.

"Ship rolling heavily in a high cross swell," he began again, and commented to himself, "Heavily is no word for it." Then he wrote: "Sunset threatening, with a low bank of clouds to N. and E. Sky clear overhead."

Sprawling over the table with arrested pen, he glanced out of the door, and in that frame of his vision he saw all the stars flying upwards between the teakwood jambs on a black sky. The whole lot took flight together and disappeared, leaving only a blackness flecked with white flashes, for the sea was as black as the sky and speckled with foam afar. The stars that had flown to the roll came back on the return swing of the ship, rushing downwards in their glittering multitude, not of fiery points, but enlarged to tiny discs brilliant with a clear wet sheen.

Jukes watched the flying big stars for a moment, and then wrote: "8 P.M. Swell increasing. Ship labouring and taking water on her decks. Battened down the coolies for the night. Barometer still falling." He paused, and thought to himself, "Perhaps nothing whatever'll come of it." And then he closed resolutely his entries: "Every appearance of a typhoon coming on."

On going out he had to stand aside, and Captain Mac-Whirr strode over the doorstep without saying a word or making a sign.

"Shut the door, Mr. Jukes, will you?" he cried from within.

Jukes turned back to do so, muttering ironically: "Afraid to catch cold, I suppose." It was his watch below, but he yearned for communion with his kind; and he remarked cheerily to the second mate: "Doesn't look so bad, after all—does it?"

The second mate was marching to and fro on the bridge, tripping down with small steps one moment, and the next climbing with difficulty the shifting slope of the deck. At the sound of Jukes' voice he stood still, facing forward, but made no reply.

"Hallo! That's a heavy one," said Jukes, swaying to meet the long roll till his lowered hand touched the planks. This time the second mate made in his throat a noise of an unfriendly nature.

He was an oldish, shabby little fellow, with bad teeth and no hair on his face. He had been shipped in a hurry in

Shanghai, that trip when the second officer brought from home had delayed the ship three hours in port by contriving (in some manner Captain MacWhirr could never understand) to fall overboard into an empty coal-lighter lying alongside, and had to be sent ashore to the hospital with concussion of the brain and a broken limb or two.

Jukes was not discouraged by the unsympathetic sound. "The Chinamen must be having a lovely time of it down there," he said. "It's lucky for them the old girl has the easiest roll of any ship I've ever been in. There now! This one wasn't so bad."

"You wait," snarled the second mate.

With his sharp nose, red at the tip, and his thin pinched lips, he always looked as though he were raging inwardly; and he was concise in his speech to the point of rudeness. All his time off duty he spent in his cabin with the door shut, keeping so still in there that he was supposed to fall asleep as soon as he had disappeared; but the man who came in to wake him for his watch on deck would invariably find him with his eyes wide open, flat on his back in the bunk, and glaring irritably from a soiled pillow. He never wrote any letters, did not seem to hope for news from anywhere; and though he had been heard once to mention West Hartlepool, it was with extreme bitterness, and only in connection with the extortionate charges of a boarding-house. He was one of those men who are picked up at need in the ports of the world. They are competent enough, appear hopelessly hard up, show no evidence of any sort of vice, and carry about them all the signs of manifest failure. They come aboard on an emergency, care for no ship afloat, live in their own atmosphere of casual connection amongst their shipmates who know nothing of them, and make up their minds to leave at inconvenient times. They clear out with no words of leave-taking in some God-forsaken port other men would fear to be stranded in, and go ashore in company of a shabby sea-chest, corded like a treasure-box, and with an air of shaking the ship's dust off their feet.

"You wait," he repeated, balanced in great swings with his back to Jukes, motionless and implacable.

"Do you mean to say we are going to catch it hot?" asked Jukes with boyish interest.

"Say? . . . I say nothing. You don't catch me," snapped the little second mate, with a mixture of pride, scorn, and cunning, as if Jukes' question had been a trap cleverly detected. "Oh, no! None of you here shall make a fool of me if I know it," he mumbled to himself.

Jukes reflected rapidly that this second mate was a mean little beast, and in his heart he wished poor Jack Allen had never smashed himself up in the coal-lighter. The far-off blackness ahead of the ship was like another night seen through the starry night of the earth—the starless night of the immensities beyond the created universe, revealed in its appalling stillness through a low fissure in the glittering sphere of which the earth is the kernel.

"Whatever there might be about," said Jukes, "we are steaming straight into it."

"*You've* said it," caught up the second mate, always with his back to Jukes. "You've said it, mind—not I."

"Oh, go to Jericho!" said Jukes, frankly; and the other emitted a triumphant little chuckle.

"You've said it," he repeated.

"And what of that?"

"I've known some real good men get into trouble with their skippers for saying a dam' sight less," answered the second mate feverishly. "Oh, no! You don't catch me."

"You seem deucedly anxious not to give yourself away," said Jukes, completely soured by such absurdity. "I wouldn't be afraid to say what I think."

"Aye, to me! That's no great trick. I am nobody, and well I know it."

The ship, after a pause of comparative steadiness, started upon a series of rolls, one worse than the other, and for a time Jukes, preserving his equilibrium, was too busy to open his mouth. As soon as the violent swinging had quieted down somewhat, he said: "This is a bit too much of a good thing. Whether anything is coming or not I think she ought to be put head on to that swell. The old man is just gone in to lie down. Hang me if I don't speak to him."

But when he opened the door of the chart-room he saw

his captain reading a book. Captain MacWhirr was not lying down: he was standing up with one hand grasping the edge of the bookshelf and the other holding open before his face a thick volume. The lamp wriggled in the gimbals, the loosened books toppled from side to side on the shelf, the long barometer swung in jerky circles, the table altered its slant every moment. In the midst of all this stir and movement Captain MacWhirr, holding on, showed his eyes above the upper edge, and asked, "What's the matter?"

"Swell getting worse, sir."

"Noticed that in here," muttered Captain MacWhirr. "Anything wrong?"

Jukes, inwardly disconcerted by the seriousness of the eyes looking at him over the top of the book, produced an embarrassed grin.

"Rolling like old boots," he said, sheepishly.

"Aye! Very heavy—very heavy. What do you want?"

At this Jukes lost his footing and began to flounder.

"I was thinking of our passengers," he said, in the manner of a man clutching at a straw.

"Passengers?" wondered the Captain, gravely. "What passengers?"

"Why, the Chinamen, sir," explained Jukes, very sick of this conversation.

"The Chinamen! Why don't you speak plainly? Couldn't tell what you meant. Never heard a lot of coolies spoken of as passengers before. Passengers, indeed! What's come to you?"

Captain MacWhirr, closing the book on his forefinger, lowered his arm and looked completely mystified. "Why are you thinking of the Chinamen, Mr. Jukes?" he inquired.

Jukes took a plunge, like a man driven to it. "She's rolling her decks full of water, sir. Thought you might put her head on perhaps—for a while. Till this goes down a bit—very soon, I dare say. Head to the eastward. I never knew a ship roll like this."

He held on in the doorway, and Captain MacWhirr, feeling his grip on the shelf inadequate, made up his mind to let go in a hurry, and fell heavily on the couch.

"Head to the eastward?" he said, struggling to sit up. "That's more than four points off her course."

"Yes, sir. Fifty degrees. . . . Would just bring her head far enough round to meet this. . . ."

Captain MacWhirr was now sitting up. He had not dropped the book, and he had not lost his place.

"To the eastward?" he repeated, with dawning astonishment. "To the . . . Where do you think we are bound to? You want me to haul a full-powered steamship four points off her course to make the Chinamen comfortable! Now, I've heard more than enough of mad things done in the world—but this. . . . If I didn't know you, Jukes, I would think you were in liquor. Steer four points off. . . . And what afterwards? Steer four points over the other way, I suppose, to make the course good. What put it into your head that I would start to tack a steamer as if she were a sailing-ship?"

"Jolly good thing she isn't," threw in Jukes, with bitter readiness. "She would have rolled every blessed stick out of her this afternoon."

"Aye! And you just would have had to stand and see them go," said Captain MacWhirr, showing a certain animation. "It's a dead calm, isn't it?"

"It is, sir. But there's something out of the common coming, for sure."

"Maybe. I suppose you have a notion I should be getting out of the way of that dirt," said Captain MacWhirr, speaking with the utmost simplicity of manner and tone, and fixing the oilcloth on the floor with a heavy stare. Thus he noticed neither Jukes' discomfiture nor the mixture of vexation and astonished respect on his face.

"Now, here's this book," he continued with deliberation, slapping his thigh with the closed volume. "I've been reading the chapter on the storms there."

This was true. He had been reading the chapter on the storms. When he had entered the chart-room, it was with no intention of taking the book down. Some influence in the air—the same influence, probably, that caused the steward to bring without orders the Captain's sea-boots and oilskin coat up to the chart-room—had as it were guided his hand to the shelf; and without taking the time to sit down he had waded with a conscious effort into the terminology of the subject. He lost himself amongst advancing semi-circles, left- and right-hand quadrants, the curves of the tracks, the probable bearing of the centre, the shifts of wind and the readings of barometer. He tried to bring all these things into a definite relation to himself, and ended by becoming contemptuously angry with such a lot of words and with so much advice, all head-work and supposition, without a glimmer of certitude.

"It's the damnedest thing, Jukes," he said. "If a fellow was to believe all that's in there, he would be running most of his time all over the sea trying to get behind the weather."

Again he slapped his leg with the book; and Jukes opened his mouth, but said nothing.

"Running to get behind the weather! Do you understand that, Mr. Jukes? It's the maddest thing!" ejaculated Captain MacWhirr, with pauses, gazing at the floor profoundly. "You would think an old woman had been writing this. It passes me. If that thing means anything useful, then it means that I should at once alter the course away, away to the devil somewhere, and come booming down on Fuchau from the northward at the tail of this dirty weather that's supposed to be knocking about in our way. From the north! Do you understand, Mr. Jukes? Three hundred extra miles to the distance, and a pretty coal bill to show. I couldn't bring myself to do that if every word in there was gospel truth, Mr. Jukes. Don't you expect me. . . ."

And Jukes, silent, marvelled at this display of feeling and loquacity.

"But the truth is that you don't know if the fellow is right, anyhow. How can you tell what a gale is made of till you get it? He isn't aboard here, is he? Very well. Here he says that the centre of them things bears eight points off the wind; but we haven't got any wind, for all the barometer falling. Where's his centre now?"

"We will get the wind presently," mumbled Jukes.

"Let it come, then," said Captain MacWhirr, with dignified indignation. "It's only to let you see, Mr. Jukes, that you don't find everything in books. All these rules for dodging breezes and circumventing the winds of heaven, Mr. Jukes, seem to me the maddest thing, when you come to look at it sensibly."

He raised his eyes, saw Jukes gazing at him dubiously, and tried to illustrate his meaning.

"About as queer as your extraordinary notion of dodging the ship head to sea, for I don't know how long, to make the Chinamen comfortable; whereas all we've got to do is to take them to Fu-chau, being timed to get there before noon on Friday. If the weather delays me—very well. There's your log-book to talk straight about the weather. But suppose I went swinging off my course and came in two days late, and they asked me: 'Where have you been all that time, Captain?' What could I say to that? 'Went around to dodge the bad weather,' I would say. 'It must've been dam' bad,' they would say. 'Don't know,' I would have to say; 'I've dodged clear of it.' See that, Jukes? I have been thinking it all out this afternoon."

He looked up again in his unseeing, unimaginative way. No one had ever heard him say so much at one time. Jukes, with his arms open in the doorway, was like a man invited to behold a miracle. Unbounded wonder was the intellectual meaning of his eye, while incredulity was seated in his whole countenance.

"A gale is a gale, Mr. Jukes," resumed the Captain, "and a full-powered steamship has got to face it. There's just so much dirty weather knocking about the world, and the proper thing is to go through it with none of what old Captain Wilson of the *Melita* calls 'storm strategy.' The other day ashore I heard him hold forth about it to a lot of shipmasters who came in and sat at a table next to mine. It seemed to me the greatest nonsense. He was telling them how he out-manœuvred, I think he said, a terrific gale, so that it never came nearer than fifty miles to him. A neat piece of headwork he called it. How he knew there was a terrific gale fifty miles off beats me altogether. It was like listening to a crazy man. I would have thought Captain Wilson was old enough to know better."

Captain MacWhirr ceased for a moment, then said, "It's your watch below, Mr. Jukes?"

Jukes came to himself with a start. "Yes, sir."

"Leave orders to call me at the slightest change," said the Captain. He reached up to put the book away, and tucked his legs upon the couch. "Shut the door so that it don't fly open, will you? I can't stand a door banging. They've put a lot of rubbishy locks into this ship, I must say."

Captain MacWhirr closed his eyes.

He did so to rest himself. He was tired, and he experienced that state of mental vacuity which comes at the end of an exhaustive discussion that has liberated some belief matured in the course of meditative years. He had indeed been making his confession of faith, had he only known it; and its effect was to make Jukes, on the other side of the door, stand scratching his head for a good while.

Captain MacWhirr opened his eyes.

He thought he must have been asleep. What was that loud noise? Wind? Why had he not been called? The lamp wriggled in its gimbals, the barometer swung in circles, the table altered its slant every moment; a pair of limp sea-boots with collapsed tops went sliding past the couch. He put out his hand instantly, and captured one.

Jukes' face appeared in a crack of the door: only his face, very red, with staring eyes. The flame of the lamp leaped, a piece of paper flew up, a rush of air enveloped Captain MacWhirr. Beginning to draw on the boot, he directed an expectant gaze at Jukes' swollen, excited features.

"Came on like this," shouted Jukes, "five minutes ago . . . all of a sudden."

The head disappeared with a bang, and a heavy splash and patter of drops swept past the closed door as if a pailful of melted lead had been flung against the house. A whistling could be heard now upon the deep vibrating noise outside. The stuffy chart-room seemed as full of draughts as a shed. Captain MacWhirr collared the other sea-boot on its violent passage along the floor. He was not flustered, but he could not find at once the opening for inserting his foot. The shoes he had flung off were scurrying from end to

end of the cabin, gambolling playfully over each other like
puppies. As soon as he stood up he kicked at them viciously,
but without effect.

He threw himself into the attitude of a lunging fencer,
to reach after his oilskin coat; and afterwards he staggered
all over the confined space while he jerked himself into it.
Very grave, straddling his legs far apart, and stretching
his neck, he started to tie deliberately the strings of his
sou'-wester under his chin, with thick fingers that trembled
slightly. He went through all the movements of a woman
putting on her bonnet before a glass, with a strained, listening attention, as though he had expected every moment to
hear the shout of his name in the confused clamour that
had suddenly beset his ship. Its increase filled his ears while
he was getting ready to go out and confront whatever it
might mean. It was tumultuous and very loud—made up
of the rush of the wind, the crashes of the sea, with that
prolonged deep vibration of the air, like the roll of an immense and remote drum beating the charge of the gale.

He stood for a moment in the light of the lamp, thick,
clumsy, shapeless in his panoply of combat, vigilant and
red-faced.

"There's a lot of weight in this," he muttered.

As soon as he attempted to open the door the wind
caught it. Clinging to the handle, he was dragged out over
the doorstep, and at once found himself engaged with the
wind in a sort of personal scuffle whose object was the
shutting of that door. At the last moment a tongue of air
scurried in and licked out the flame of the lamp.

Ahead of the ship he perceived a great darkness lying
upon a multitude of white flashes; on the starboard beam a
few amazing stars drooped, dim and fitful, above an immense waste of broken seas, as if seen through a mad drift
of smoke.

On the bridge a knot of men, indistinct and toiling, were
making great efforts in the light of the wheelhouse windows
that shone mistily on their heads and backs. Suddenly darkness closed upon one pane, then on another. The voices of
the lost group reached him after the manner of men's voices
in a gale, in shreds and fragments of forlorn shouting

snatched past the ear. All at once Jukes appeared at his side, yelling, with his head down.

"Watch — put in — wheelhouse shutters — glass — afraid — blow in."

Jukes heard his commander upbraiding.

"This—come—anything—warning—call me."

He tried to explain, with the uproar pressing on his lips.

"Light air—remained—bridge—sudden—north-east—could turn—thought—you—sure—hear."

They had gained the shelter of the weather-cloth, and could converse with raised voices, as people quarrel.

"I got the hands along to cover up all the ventilators. Good job I had remained on deck. I didn't think you would be asleep, and so . . . What did you say, sir? What?"

"Nothing," cried Captain MacWhirr. "I said—all right."

"By all the powers! We've got it this time," observed Jukes in a howl.

"You haven't altered her course?" inquired Captain Mac-Whirr, straining his voice.

"No, sir. Certainly not. Wind came out right ahead. And here comes the head sea."

A plunge of the ship ended in a shock as if she had landed her forefoot upon something solid. After a moment of stillness a lofty flight of sprays drove hard with the wind upon their faces.

"Keep her at it as long as we can," shouted Captain MacWhirr.

Before Jukes had squeezed the salt water out of his eyes all the stars had disappeared.

III

Jukes was as ready a man as any half-dozen young mates that may be caught casting a net upon the waters; and though he had been somewhat taken aback by the startling viciousness of the first squall, he had pulled himself together on the instant, had called out the hands and had rushed them along to secure such openings about the deck as had not been already battened down earlier in the evening. Shouting in his fresh, stentorian voice, "Jump, boys, and bear a hand!" he led in the work, telling himself the while that he had "just expected this."

But at the same time he was growing aware that this was rather more than he had expected. From the first stir of the air felt on his cheek the gale seemed to take upon itself the accumulated impetus of an avalanche. Heavy sprays enveloped the *Nan-Shan* from stem to stern, and instantly in the midst of her regular rolling she began to jerk and plunge as though she had gone mad with fright.

Jukes thought, "This is no joke." While he was exchanging explanatory yells with his captain, a sudden lowering of the darkness came upon the night, falling before their vision like something palpable. It was as if the masked lights of the world had been turned down. Jukes was uncritically glad to have his captain at hand. It relieved him as though that man had, by simply coming on deck, taken most of the gale's weight upon his shoulders. Such is the prestige, the privilege, and the burden of command.

Captain MacWhirr could expect no relief of that sort from any one on earth. Such is the loneliness of command. He was trying to see, with that watchful manner of a seaman who stares into the wind's eye as if into the eye of an adversary, to penetrate the hidden intention and guess the aim and force of the thrust. The strong wind swept at him out of a vast obscurity; he felt under his feet the uneasiness of his ship, and he could not even discern the shadow of her shape. He wished it were not so; and very still he waited, feeling stricken by a blind man's helplessness.

To be silent was natural to him, dark or shine. Jukes, at his elbow, made himself heard yelling cheerily in the gusts, "We must have got the worse of it at once, sir." A faint burst of lightning quivered all around, as if flashed into a cavern—into a black and secret chamber of the sea, with a floor of foaming crests.

It unveiled for a sinister, fluttering moment a ragged mass of clouds hanging low, the lurch of the long outlines of the ship, the black figures of men caught on the bridge, heads forward, as if petrified in the act of butting. The darkness palpitated down upon all this, and then the real thing came at last.

It was something formidable and swift, like the sudden smashing of a vial of wrath. It seemed to explode all round the ship with an overpowering concussion and a rush of great waters, as if an immense dam had been blown up to windward. In an instant the men lost touch of each other. This is the disintegrating power of a great wind: it isolates one from one's kind. An earthquake, a landslip, an avalanche, overtake a man incidentally, as it were—without passion. A furious gale attacks him like a personal enemy, tries to grasp his limbs, fastens upon his mind, seeks to rout his very spirit out of him.

Jukes was driven away from his commander. He fancied himself whirled a great distance through the air. Everything disappeared—even, for a moment, his power of thinking; but his hand had found one of the rail-stanchions. His distress was by no means alleviated by an inclination to disbelieve the reality of this experience. Though young, he had seen some bad weather, and had never doubted his ability to imagine the worst; but this was so much beyond his powers of fancy that it appeared incompatible with the existence of any ship whatever. He would have been incredulous about himself in the same way, perhaps, had he not been so harassed by the necessity of exerting a wrestling effort against a force trying to tear him away from his hold. Moreover, the conviction of not being utterly destroyed returned to him through the sensations of being half-drowned, bestially shaken, and partly choked.

It seemed to him he remained there precariously alone with the stanchion for a long, long time. The rain poured on him, flowed, drove in sheets. He breathed in gasps; and sometimes the water he swallowed was fresh and sometimes it was salt. For the most part he kept his eyes shut tight, as if suspecting his sight might be destroyed in the immense flurry of the elements. When he ventured to blink hastily, he derived some moral support from the green gleam of the starboard light shining feebly upon the flight of rain and sprays. He was actually looking at it when its ray fell upon the uprearing sea which put it out. He saw the head of the wave topple over, adding the mite of its crash to the tremendous uproar raging around him, and almost at the same instant the stanchion was wrenched away from his embracing arms. After a crushing thump on his back he found himself suddenly afloat and borne upwards. His first irresistible notion was that the whole China Sea had climbed on the bridge. Then, more sanely, he concluded himself gone overboard. All the time he was being tossed, flung, and rolled in great volumes of water, he kept on repeating mentally, with the utmost precipitation, the words: "My God! My God! My God! My God!"

All at once, in a revolt of misery and despair, he formed the crazy resolution to get out of that. And he began to thresh about with his arms and legs. But as soon as he commenced his wretched struggles he discovered that he had become somehow mixed up with a face, an oilskin coat, somebody's boots. He clawed ferociously all these things in turn, lost them, found them again, lost them once more, and finally was himself caught in the firm clasp of a pair of stout arms. He returned the embrace closely round a thick solid body. He had found his captain.

They tumbled over and over, tightening their hug. Suddenly the water let them down with a brutal bang; and, stranded against the side of the wheelhouse, out of breath and bruised, they were left to stagger up in the wind and hold on where they could.

Jukes came out of it rather horrified, as though he had escaped some unparalleled outrage directed at his feelings. It weakened his faith in himself. He started shouting aimlessly to the man he could feel near him in that fiendish blackness, "Is it you, sir? Is it you, sir?" till his temples seemed ready to burst. And he heard in answer a voice, as if crying far away, as if screaming to him fretfully from a very great distance, the one word "Yes!" Other seas swept again over the bridge. He received them defencelessly right over his bare head, with both his hands engaged in holding.

The motion of the ship was extravagant. Her lurches had an appalling helplessness: she pitched as if taking a header into a void, and seemed to find a wall to hit every time. When she rolled she fell on her side headlong, and she would be righted back by such a demolishing blow that Jukes felt her reeling as a clubbed man reels before he collapses. The gale howled and scuffled about gigantically in the darkness, as though the entire world were one black gully. At certain moments the air streamed against the ship as if sucked through a tunnel with a concentrated solid force of impact that seemed to lift her clean out of the water and keep her up for an instant with only a quiver running through her from end to end. And then she would begin her tumbling again as if dropped back into a boiling cauldron. Jukes tried hard to compose his mind and judge things coolly.

The sea, flattened down in the heavier gusts, would uprise and overwhelm both ends of the *Nan-Shan* in snowy rushes of foam, expanding wide, beyond both rails, into the night. And on this dazzling sheet, spread under the blackness of the clouds and emitting a bluish glow, Captain MacWhirr could catch a desolate glimpse of a few tiny specks black as ebony, the tops of the hatches, the battened companions, the heads of the covered winches, the foot of a mast. This was all he could see of his ship. Her middle structure, covered by the bridge which bore him, his mate, the closed wheelhouse where a man was steering shut up with the fear of being swept overboard together with the whole thing in one great crash—her middle structure was like a half-tide rock awash upon a coast. It was like an outlying rock with the water boiling up, streaming over, pouring off, beating round—like a rock in the surf to which shipwrecked people cling before they let go—only it rose, it sank, it rolled continuously, without respite and rest, like a rock that should have miraculously struck adrift from a coast and gone wallowing upon the sea.

The *Nan-Shan* was being looted by the storm with a senseless, destructive fury: trysails torn out of the extra gaskets, double-lashed awnings blown away, bridge swept clean, weather-cloths burst, rails twisted, light-screens smashed—and two of the boats had gone already. They had gone unheard and unseen, melting, as it were, in the shock and smother of the wave. It was only later, when upon the white flash of another high sea hurling itself amidships, Jukes had a vision of two pairs of davits leaping black and empty out of the solid blackness, with one over-hauled fall flying and an iron-bound block capering in the air, that he became aware of what had happened within about three yards of his back.

He poked his head forward, groping for the ear of his commander. His lips touched it—big, fleshy, very wet. He cried in an agitated tone, "Our boats are going now, sir."

And again he heard that voice, forced and ringing feebly, but with a penetrating effect of quietness in the enormous discord of noises, as if sent out from some remote spot of peace beyond the black wastes of the gale; again he heard a man's voice—the frail and indomitable sound that can be made to carry an infinity of thought, resolution and purpose, that shall be pronouncing confident words on the last day, when heavens fall, and justice is done—again he heard it, and it was crying to him, as if from very, very far—"All right."

He thought he had not managed to make himself under-stood. "Our boats—I say boats—the boats, sir! Two gone!"

The same voice, within a foot of him and yet so remote, yelled sensibly, "Can't be helped."

Captain MacWhirr had never turned his face, but Jukes caught some more words on the wind.

"What can—expect—when hammering through—such—— Bound to leave—something behind—stands to reason."

Watchfully Jukes listened for more. No more came. This was all Captain MacWhirr had to say; and Jukes could picture to himself rather than see the broad squat back before him. An impenetrable obscurity pressed down upon the ghostly glimmers of the sea. A dull conviction seized upon Jukes that there was nothing to be done.

If the steering-gear did not give way, if the immense volumes of water did not burst the deck in or smash one of the hatches, if the engines did not give up, if way could be kept on the ship against this terrific wind, and she did not bury herself in one of these awful seas, of whose white crests alone, topping high above her bows, he could now and then get a sickening glimpse—then there was a chance of her coming out of it. Something within him seemed to turn over, bringing uppermost the feeling that the *Nan-Shan* was lost.

"She's done for," he said to himself, with a surprising mental agitation, as though he had discovered an unexpected meaning in this thought. One of these things was bound to happen. Nothing could be prevented now, and nothing could be remedied. The men on board did not count, and the ship could not last. This weather was too impossible.

Jukes felt an arm thrown heavily over his shoulders; and to this overture he responded with great intelligence by catching hold of his captain round the waist.

They stood clasped thus in the blind night, bracing each other against the wind, cheek to cheek and lip to ear, in the manner of two hulks lashed stem to stern together.

And Jukes heard the voice of his commander hardly any louder than before, but nearer, as though, starting to march athwart the prodigious rush of the hurricane, it had approached him, bearing that strange effect of quietness like the serene glow of a halo.

"D'ye know where the hands got to?" it asked, vigorous and evanescent at the same time, overcoming the strength of the wind, and swept away from Jukes instantly.

Jukes didn't know. They were all on the bridge when the real force of the hurricane struck the ship. He had no idea where they had crawled to. Under the circumstances they were nowhere, for all the use that could be made of them. Somehow the Captain's wish to know distressed Jukes.

"Want the hands, sir?" he cried, apprehensively.

"Ought to know," asserted Captain MacWhirr. "Hold hard."

They held hard. An outburst of unchained fury, a vicious rush of the wind absolutely steadied the ship; she rocked only, quick and light like a child's cradle, for a terrific moment of suspense, while the whole atmosphere, as it seemed, streamed furiously past her, roaring away from the tenebrous earth.

It suffocated them, and with eyes shut they tightened their grasp. What from the magnitude of the shock might

have been a column of water running upright in the dark,
butted against the ship, broke short, and fell on her bridge,
crushingly, from on high, with a dead burying weight.

A flying fragment of that collapse, a mere splash, enveloped them in one swirl from their feet over their heads,
filling violently their ears, mouths and nostrils with salt
water. It knocked out their legs, wrenched in haste at their
arms, seethed away swiftly under their chins; and opening
their eyes, they saw the piled-up masses of foam dashing
to and fro amongst what looked like the fragments of a
ship. She had given way as if driven straight in. Their
panting hearts yielded, too, before the tremendous blow;
and all at once she sprang up again to her desperate plung-
ing, as if trying to scramble out from under the ruins.

The seas in the dark seemed to rush from all sides to
keep her back where she might perish. There was hate in
the way she was handled, and a ferocity in the blows that
fell. She was like a living creature thrown to the rage of a
mob: hustled terribly, struck at, borne up, flung down,
leaped upon. Captain MacWhirr and Jukes kept hold of
each other, deafened by the noise, gagged by the wind;
and the great physical tumult beating about their bodies,
brought, like an unbridled display of passion, a profound
trouble to their souls. One of those wild and appalling
shrieks that are heard at times passing mysteriously overhead in the steady roar of a hurricane, swooped, as if borne
on wings, upon the ship, and Jukes tried to outscream it.

"Will she live through this?"

The cry was wrenched out of his breast. It was as un-
intentional as the birth of a thought in the head, and he
heard nothing of it himself. It all became extinct at once—
thought, intention, effort—and of his cry the inaudible vibration added to the tempest waves of the air.

He expected nothing from it. Nothing at all. For indeed
what answer could be made? But after a while he heard
with amazement the frail and resisting voice in his ear,
the dwarf sound, unconquered in the giant tumult.

"She may!"

It was a dull yell, more difficult to seize than a whisper.
And presently the voice returned again, half submerged in

the vast crashes, like a ship battling against the waves of an ocean.

"Let's hope so!" it cried—small, lonely and unmoved, a stranger to the visions of hope or fear; and it flickered into disconnected words: "Ship. . . . This. . . . Never—Anyhow . . . for the best." Jukes gave it up.

Then, as if it had come suddenly upon the one thing fit to withstand the power of a storm, it seemed to gain force and firmness for the last broken shouts:

"Keep on hammering . . . builders . . . good men. . . . And chance it . . . engines. . . . Rout . . . good man."

Captain MacWhirr removed his arm from Jukes' shoulders, and thereby ceased to exist for his mate, so dark it was; Jukes, after a tense stiffening of every muscle, would let himself go limp all over. The gnawing of profound discomfort existed side by side with an incredible disposition to somnolence, as though he had been buffeted and worried into drowsiness. The wind would get hold of his head and try to shake it off his shoulders; his clothes, full of water, were as heavy as lead, cold and dripping like an armour of melting ice: he shivered—it lasted a long time; and with his hands closed hard on his hold, he was letting himself sink slowly into the depths of bodily misery. His mind became concentrated upon himself in an aimless, idle way, and when something pushed lightly at the back of his knees he nearly, as the saying is, jumped out of his skin.

In the start forward he bumped the back of Captain MacWhirr, who didn't move; and then a hand gripped his thigh. A lull had come, a menacing lull of the wind, the holding of a stormy breath—and he felt himself pawed all over. It was the boatswain. Jukes recognized these hands, so thick and enormous that they seemed to belong to some new species of man.

The boatswain had arrived on the bridge, crawling on all fours against the wind, and had found the chief mate's legs with the top of his head. Immediately he crouched and began to explore Jukes' person upwards with prudent, apologetic touches, as became an inferior.

He was an ill-favoured, undersized, gruff sailor of fifty, coarsely hairy, short-legged, long-armed, resembling an elderly ape. His strength was immense; and in his great lumpy paws, bulging like brown boxing-gloves on the end of furry forearms, the heaviest objects were handled like playthings. Apart from the grizzled pelt on his chest, the menacing demeanour and the hoarse voice, he had none of the classical attributes of his rating. His good nature almost amounted to imbecility: the men did what they liked with him, and he had not an ounce of initiative in his character, which was easy-going and talkative. For these reasons Jukes disliked him; but Captain MacWhirr, to Jukes' scornful disgust, seemed to regard him as a first-rate petty officer.

He pulled himself up by Jukes' coat, taking that liberty with the greatest moderation, and only so far as it was forced upon him by the hurricane.

"What is it, boss'n, what is it?" yelled Jukes, impatiently. What could that fraud of a boss'n want on the bridge? The typhoon had got on Jukes' nerves. The husky bellowings of the other, though unintelligible, seemed to suggest a state of lively satisfaction. There could be no mistake. The old fool was pleased with something.

The boatswain's other hand had found some other body, for in a changed tone he began to inquire: "Is it you, sir? Is it you, sir?" The wind strangled his howls.

"Yes!" cried Captain MacWhirr.

IV

All that the boatswain, out of a superabundance of yells, could make clear to Captain MacWhirr was the bizarre intelligence that "All them Chinamen in the fore 'tween-deck have fetched away, sir."

Jukes to leeward could hear these two shouting within six inches of his face, as you may hear on a still night half a mile away two men conversing across a field. He heard Captain MacWhirr's exasperated "What? What?" and the strained pitch of the other's hoarseness. "In a lump . . . seen them myself. . . . Awful sight, sir . . . thought . . . tell you."

Jukes remained indifferent, as if rendered irresponsible

by the force of the hurricane, which made the very thought of action utterly vain. Besides, being very young, he had found the occupation of keeping his heart completely steeled against the worst so engrossing that he had come to feel an overpowering dislike towards any other form of activity whatever. He was not scared; he knew this because, firmly believing he would never see another sunrise, he remained calm in that belief.

These are the moments of do-nothing heroics to which even good men surrender at times. Many officers of ships can no doubt recall a case in their experience when just such a trance of confounded stoicism would come all at once over a whole ship's company. Jukes, however, had no wide experience of men or storms. He conceived himself to be calm—inexorably calm; but as a matter of fact he was daunted, not abjectly, but only so far as a decent man may, without becoming loathsome to himself.

It was rather like a forced-on numbness of spirit. The long, long stress of a gale does it; the suspense of the interminably culminating catastrophe; and there is a bodily fatigue in the mere holding on to existence within the excessive tumult; a searching and insidious fatigue that penetrates deep into a man's breast to cast down and sadden his heart, which is incorrigible, and of all the gifts of the earth —even before life itself—aspires to peace.

Jukes was benumbed much more than he supposed. He held on—very wet, very cold, stiff in every limb; and in a momentary hallucination of swift visions (it is said that a drowning man thus reviews all his life) he beheld all sorts of memories altogether unconnected with his present situation. He remembered his father, for instance: a worthy business man, who at an unfortunate crisis in his affairs went quietly to bed and died forthwith in a state of resignation. Jukes did not recall these circumstances, of course, but remaining otherwise unconcerned he seemed to see distinctly the poor man's face; a certain game of nap played when quite a boy in Table Bay on board a ship, since lost with all hands; the thick eyebrows of his first skipper; and without any emotion, as he might years ago have walked listlessly into her room and found her sitting there with a book, he remembered his mother—dead, too, now—the resolute woman, left badly off, who had been very firm in his bringing up.

It could not have lasted more than a second, perhaps not so much. A heavy arm had fallen about his shoulders; Captain MacWhirr's voice was speaking his name into his ear.

"Jukes! Jukes!"

He detected the tone of deep concern. The wind had thrown its weight on the ship, trying to pin her down amongst the seas. They made a clean breach over her, as over a deep-swimming log; and the gathered weight of crashes menaced monstrously from afar. The breakers flung out of the night with a ghostly light on their crests—the light of sea-foam that in a ferocious, boiling-up pale flash showed upon the slender body of the ship the toppling rush, the downfall, and the seething mad scurry of each wave. Never for a moment could she shake herself clear of the water; Jukes, rigid, perceived in her motion the ominous sign of haphazard floundering. She was no longer struggling intelligently. It was the beginning of the end; and the note of busy concern in Captain MacWhirr's voice sickened him like an exhibition of blind and pernicious folly.

The spell of the storm had fallen upon Jukes. He was penetrated by it, absorbed by it; he was rooted in it with a rigour of dumb attention. Captain MacWhirr persisted in his cries, but the wind got between them like a solid wedge. He hung round Jukes' neck as heavy as a millstone, and suddenly the sides of their heads knocked together.

"Jukes! Mr. Jukes, I say!"

He had to answer that voice that would not be silenced. He answered in the customary manner: ". . . Yes, sir."

And directly, his heart, corrupted by the storm that breeds a craving for peace, rebelled against the tyranny of training and command.

Captain MacWhirr had his mate's head fixed firm in the crook of his elbow, and pressed it to his yelling lips mysteriously. Sometimes Jukes would break in, admonishing hastily: "Look out, sir!" or Captain MacWhirr would bawl an earnest exhortation to "Hold hard, there!" and the whole black universe seemed to reel together with the ship.

They paused. She floated yet. And Captain MacWhirr would resume his shouts. ". . . Says . . . whole lot . . . fetched away. . . . Ought to see . . . what's the matter."

Directly the full force of the hurricane had struck the ship, every part of her deck became untenable; and the sailors, dazed and dismayed, took shelter in the port alley-way under the bridge. It had a door aft, which they shut; it was very black, cold, and dismal. At each heavy fling of the ship they would groan all together in the dark, and tons of water could be heard scuttling about as if trying to get at them from above. The boatswain had been keeping up a gruff talk, but a more unreasonable lot of men, he said afterwards, he had never been with. They were snug enough there, out of harm's way, and not wanted to do anything, either; and yet they did nothing but grumble and complain peevishly like so many sick kids. Finally, one of them said that if there had been at least some light to see each other's noses by, it wouldn't be so bad. It was making him crazy, he declared, to lie there in the dark waiting for the blamed hooker to sink.

"Why don't you step outside, then, and be done with it at once?" the boatswain turned on him.

This called up a shout of execration. The boatswain found himself overwhelmed with reproaches of all sorts. They seemed to take it ill that a lamp was not instantly created for them out of nothing. They would whine after a light to get drowned by—anyhow! And though the unreason of their revilings was patent—since no one could hope to reach the lamp-room, which was forward—he became greatly distressed. He did not think it was decent of them to be nagging at him like this. He told them so, and was met by general contumely. He sought refuge, therefore, in an embittered silence. At the same time their grumbling and sighing and muttering worried him greatly, but by-and-by it occurred to him that there were six globe lamps hung in the 'tween-deck, and that there could be no harm in de-priving the coolies of one of them.

The Nan-Shan had an athwartship coal-bunker, which, being at times used as cargo space, communicated by an iron door with the fore 'tween-deck. It was empty then, and its manhole was the foremost one in the alleyway. The boatswain could get in, therefore, without coming out on deck at all; but to his great surprise he found he could induce no one to help him in taking off the manhole cover. He groped for it all the same, but one of the crew lying in his way refused to budge.

"Why, I only want to get you that blamed light you are crying for," he expostulated, almost pitifully.

Somebody told him to go and put his head in a bag. He regretted he could not recognize the voice, and that it was too dark to see, otherwise, as he said, he would have put a head on *that* son of a sea-cook, anyway, sink or swim. Nevertheless, he had made up his mind to show them he could get a light, if he were to die for it.

Through the violence of the ship's rolling, every movement was dangerous. To be lying down seemed labour enough. He nearly broke his neck dropping into the bunker. He fell on his back, and was sent shooting helplessly from side to side in the dangerous company of a heavy iron bar —a coal-trimmer's slice probably—left down there by somebody. This thing made him as nervous as though it had been a wild beast. He could not see it, the inside of the bunker coated with coal dust being perfectly and impenetrably black; but he heard it sliding and clattering, and striking here and there, always in the neighbourhood of his head. It seemed to make an extraordinary noise, too—to give heavy thumps as though it had been as big as a bridge girder. This was remarkable enough for him to notice while he was flung from port to starboard and back again, and clawing desperately the smooth sides of the bunker in the endeavour to stop himself. The door into the 'tween-deck not fitting quite true, he saw a thread of dim light at the bottom.

Being a sailor, and a still active man, he did not want much of a chance to regain his feet; and as luck would have it, in scrambling up he put his hand on the iron slice, picking it up as he rose. Otherwise he would have been afraid of the thing breaking his legs, or at least knocking him down again. At first he stood still. He felt unsafe in this darkness that seemed to make the ship's motion unfamiliar, unforeseen, and difficult to counteract. He felt so much shaken for a moment that he dared not move for fear of "taking charge again." He had no mind to get battered to pieces in that bunker.

He had struck his head twice; he was dazed a little. He seemed to hear yet so plainly the clatter and bangs of the iron slice flying about his ears that he tightened his grip to prove to himself he had it there safely in his hand. He was vaguely amazed at the plainness with which down there he could hear the gale raging. Its howls and shrieks seemed to take on, in the emptiness of the bunker, something of the human character, of human rage and pain—being not vast but infinitely poignant. And there were, with every roll, thumps, too—profound, ponderous thumps, as if a bulky object of five-ton weight or so had got play in the hold. But there was no such thing in the cargo. Something on deck? Impossible. Or alongside? Couldn't be.

He thought all this quickly, clearly, competently, like a seaman, and in the end remained puzzled. This noise, though, came deadened from outside, together with the washing and pouring of water on deck above his head. Was it the wind? Must be. It made down there a row like the shouting of a big lot of crazed men. And he discovered in himself a desire for a light, too—if only to get drowned by—and a nervous anxiety to get out of that bunker as quickly as possible.

He pulled back the bolt: the heavy iron plate turned on its hinges; and it was as though he had opened the door to the sounds of the tempest. A gust of hoarse yelling met him: the air was still; and the rushing of water overhead was covered by a tumult of strangled, throaty shrieks that produced an effect of desperate confusion. He straddled his legs the whole width of the doorway and stretched his neck. And at first he perceived only what he had come to seek: six small yellow flames swinging violently on the great body of the dusk.

It was stayed like the gallery of a mine, with a row of stanchions in the middle, and cross-beams overhead, penetrating into the gloom ahead—indefinitely. And to port there loomed, like the caving in of one of the sides, a bulky mass with a slanting outline. The whole place, with the shadows and the shapes, moved all the time. The boatswain glared: the ship lurched to starboard, and a great howl came from that mass that had the slant of fallen earth.

Pieces of wood whizzed past. Planks, he thought, inexpressibly startled, and flinging back his head. At his feet a man went sliding over, open-eyed, on his back, straining with uplifted arms for nothing: and another came bounding like a detached stone with his head between his legs and his hands clenched. His pigtail whipped in the air; he made a grab at the boatswain's legs, and from his opened hand a bright white disc rolled against the boatswain's foot. He recognized a silver dollar, and yelled at it with astonishment. With a precipitated sound of trampling and shuffling of bare feet, and with guttural cries, the mound of writhing bodies piled up to port detached itself from the ship's side and sliding, inert and struggling, shifted to starboard, with a dull, brutal thump. The cries ceased. The boatswain heard a long moan through the roar and whistling of the wind; he saw an inextricable confusion of heads and shoulders, naked soles kicking upwards, fists raised, tumbling backs, legs, pigtails, faces.

"Good Lord!" he cried, horrified, and banged-to the iron door upon this vision.

This was what he had come on the bridge to tell. He could not keep it to himself; and on board ship there is only one man to whom it is worth while to unburden yourself. On his passage back the hands in the alleyway swore at him for a fool. Why didn't he bring that lamp? What the devil did the coolies matter to anybody? And when he came out, the extremity of the ship made what went on inside of her appear of little moment.

At first he thought he had left the alleyway in the very moment of her sinking. The bridge ladders had been washed away, but an enormous sea filling the after deck floated him up. After that he had to lie on his stomach for some time, holding to a ring-bolt, getting his breath now and then, and swallowing salt water. He struggled farther on his hands and knees, too frightened and distracted to turn back. In this way he reached the after-part of the wheelhouse. In that comparatively sheltered spot he found the second mate. The boatswain was pleasantly surprised—his impression being that everybody on deck must have been washed away a long time ago. He asked eagerly where the Captain was.

The second mate was lying low, like a malignant little animal under a hedge.

"Captain? Gone overboard, after getting us into this mess." The mate, too, for all he knew or cared. Another fool. Didn't matter. Everybody was going by-and-by.

The boatswain crawled out again into the strength of the wind; not because he much expected to find anybody, he said, but just to get away from "that man." He crawled out as outcasts go to face an inclement world. Hence his great joy at finding Jukes and the Captain. But what was going on in the 'tween-deck was to him a minor matter by that time. Besides, it was difficult to make yourself heard. But he managed to convey the idea that the Chinamen had broken adrift together with their boxes, and that he had come up on purpose to report this. As to the hands, they were all right. Then, appeased, he subsided on the deck in a sitting posture, hugging with his arms and legs the stand of the engine-room telegraph—an iron casting as thick as a post. When that went, why, he expected he would go, too. He gave no more thought to the coolies.

Captain MacWhirr had made Jukes understand that he wanted him to go down below—to see.

"What am I to do then, sir?" And the trembling of his whole wet body caused Jukes' voice to sound like bleating.

"See first . . . Boss'n . . . says . . . adrift."

"That boss'n is a confounded fool," howled Jukes shakily.

The absurdity of the demand made upon him revolted Jukes. He was as unwilling to go as if the moment he had left the deck the ship were sure to sink.

"I must know . . . can't leave. . . ."

"They'll settle, sir."

"Fight . . . boss'n says they fight. . . . Why? Can't have . . . fighting . . . board ship. . . . Much rather keep you here . . . case . . . I should . . . washed overboard

myself. . . . Stop it . . . some way. You see and tell me
. . . through engine-room tube. Don't want you . . . come
up here . . . too often. Dangerous . . . moving about . . .
deck."

Jukes, held with his head in chancery, had to listen to
what seemed horrible suggestions.

"Don't want . . . you get lost . . . so long . . . ship isn't.
. . . Rout . . . Good man . . . Ship . . . may . . . through
this all right yet."

All at once Jukes understood he would have to go.

"Do you think she may?" he screamed.

But the wind devoured the reply, out of which Jukes
heard only the one word, pronounced with great energy
". . . . Always. . . ."

Captain MacWhirr released Jukes, and bending over the
boatswain, yelled, "Get back with the mate." Jukes only
knew that the arm was gone off his shoulders. He was dismissed with his orders—to do what? He was exasperated
into letting go his hold carelessly, and on the instant was
blown away. It seemed to him that nothing could stop him
from being blown right over the stern. He flung himself
down hastily, and the boatswain, who was following, fell on
him.

"Don't you get up yet, sir," cried the boatswain. "No
hurry!"

A sea swept over. Jukes understood the boatswain to
splutter that the bridge ladders were gone. "I'll lower you
down, sir, by your hands," he screamed. He shouted also
something about the smoke-stack being as likely to go overboard as not. Jukes thought it very possible, and imagined
the fires out, the ship helpless. . . . The boatswain by his
side kept on yelling. "What? What is it?" Jukes cried dis-
tressfully; and the other repeated, "What would my old
woman say if she saw me now?"

In the alleyway, where a lot of water had got in and
splashed in the dark, the men were still as death, till Jukes
stumbled against one of them and cursed him savagely for
being in the way. Two or three voices then asked, eager and
weak, "Any chance for us, sir?"

"What's the matter with you fools?" he said brutally. He

felt as though he could throw himself down amongst them and never move any more. But they seemed cheered; and in the midst of obsequious warnings, "Look out! Mind that manhole lid, sir," they lowered him into the bunker. The boatswain tumbled down after him, and as soon as he had picked himself up he remarked, "She would say, 'Serve you right, you old fool, for going to sea.'"

The boatswain had some means, and made a point of alluding to them frequently. His wife—a fat woman—and two grown-up daughters kept a greengrocer's shop in the East-end of London.

In the dark, Jukes, unsteady on his legs, listened to a faint thunderous patter. A deadened screaming went on steadily at his elbow, as it were; and from above the louder tumult of the storm descended upon these near sounds. His head swam. To him, too, in that bunker, the motion of the ship seemed novel and menacing, sapping his resolution as though he had never been afloat before.

He had half a mind to scramble out again; but the remembrance of Captain MacWhirr's voice made this impossible. His orders were to go and see. What was the good of it, he wanted to know. Enraged, he told himself he would see—of course. But the boatswain, staggering clumsily, warned him to be careful how he opened that door; there was a blamed fight going on. And Jukes, as if in great bodily pain, desired irritably to know what the devil they were fighting for.

"Dollars! Dollars, sir. All their rotten chests got burst open. Blamed money skipping all over the place, and they are tumbling after it head over heels—tearing and biting like anything. A regular little hell in there."

Jukes convulsively opened the door. The short boatswain peered under his arm.

One of the lamps had gone out, broken perhaps. Rancorous, guttural cries burst out loudly on their ears, and a strange panting sound, the working of all these straining breasts. A hard blow hit the side of the ship; water fell above with a stunning shock, and in the forefront of the gloom, where the air was reddish and thick, Jukes saw a head bang the deck violently, two thick calves waving on high, muscular arms twined round a naked body, a yellow-face, open-mouthed and with a set wild stare, look up and slide away. An empty chest clattered turning over; a man fell head first with a jump, as if lifted by a kick; and farther off, indistinct, others streamed like a mass of rolling stones down a bank, thumping the deck with their feet and flourishing their arms wildly. The hatchway ladder was loaded with coolies swarming on it like bees on a branch. They hung on the steps in a crawling, stirring cluster, beating madly with their fists the underside of the battened hatch, and the headlong rush of the water above was heard in the intervals of their yelling. The ship heeled over more, and they began to drop off: first one, then two, then all the rest went away together, falling straight off with a great cry.

Jukes was confounded. The boatswain, with gruff anxiety, begged him, "Don't you go in there, sir."

The whole place seemed to twist upon itself, jumping incessantly the while; and when the ship rose to a sea Jukes fancied that all these men would be shot upon him in a body. He backed out, swung the door to, and with trembling hands pushed at the bolt. . . .

As soon as his mate had gone Captain MacWhirr, left alone on the bridge, sidled and staggered as far as the wheelhouse. Its door being hinged forward, he had to fight the gale for admittance, and when at last he managed to enter, it was with an instantaneous clatter and a bang, as though he had been fired though the wood. He stood within, holding on to the handle.

The steering-gear leaked steam, and in the confined space the glass of the binnacle made a shiny oval of light in a thin white fog. The wind howled, hummed, whistled, with sudden booming gusts that rattled the doors and shutters in the vicious patter of sprays. Two coils of lead-line and a small canvas bag hung on a long lanyard, swung wide off, and came back clinging to the bulkheads. The gratings underfoot were nearly afloat; with every sweeping blow of a sea, water squirted violently through the cracks all round the door, and the man at the helm had flung down his cap, his coat, and stood propped against the gear-casing in a striped cotton shirt open on his breast. The little brass wheel in his hands had the appearance of a bright and fragile toy. The cords of his neck stood hard and lean, a dark patch lay in the hollow of his throat, and his face was still and sunken as in death.

Captain MacWhirr wiped his eyes. The sea that had nearly taken him overboard had, to his great annoyance, washed his sou'-wester hat off his bald head. The fluffy, fair hair, soaked and darkened, resembled a mean skein of cotton threads festooned round his bare skull. His face, glistening with sea-water, had been made crimson with the wind, with the sting of sprays. He looked as though he had come off sweating from before a furnace.

"You here?" he muttered, heavily.

The second mate had found his way into the wheelhouse some time before. He had fixed himself in a corner with his knees up, a fist pressed against each temple; and this attitude suggested rage, sorrow, resignation, surrender, with a sort of concentrated unforgiveness. He said mournfully and defiantly, "Well, it's my watch below now: ain't it?"

The steam gear clattered, stopped, clattered again, and the helmsman's eyeballs seemed to project out of a hungry face as if the compass card behind the binnacle glass had been meat. God knows how long he had been left there to steer, as if forgotten by all his shipmates. The bells had not been struck; there had been no reliefs; the ship's routine had gone down wind; but he was trying to keep her head north-north-east. The rudder might have been gone for all he knew, the fires out, the engines broken down, the ship ready to roll over like a corpse. He was anxious not to get muddled and lose control of her head, because the compass card swung far both ways, wriggling on the pivot, and sometimes seemed to whirl right round. He suffered from mental stress. He was horribly afraid, also, of the wheelhouse going. Mountains of water kept on tumbling against it. When the ship took one of her desperate dives the corners of his lips twitched.

Captain MacWhirr looked up at the wheelhouse clock. Screwed to the bulkhead, it had a white face on which the black hands appeared to stand quite still. It was half-past one in the morning.

"Another day," he muttered to himself.

The second mate heard him, and lifting his head as one grieving amongst ruins, "You won't see it break," he exclaimed. His wrists and his knees could be seen to shake violently. "No, by God! You won't. . . ."

He took his face again between his fists.

The body of the helmsman had moved slightly, but his head didn't budge on his neck—like a stone head fixed to look one way from a column. During a roll that all but took his booted legs from under him, and in the very stagger to save himself, Captain MacWhirr said austerely, "Don't you pay any attention to what that man says." And then, with an indefinable change of tone, very grave, he added, "He isn't on duty."

The sailor said nothing.

The hurricane boomed, shaking the little place, which seemed air-tight; and the light of the binnacle flickered all the time.

"You haven't been relieved," Captain MacWhirr went on, looking down. "I want you to stick to the helm, though, as long as you can. You've got the hang of her. Another man coming here might make a mess of it. Wouldn't do. No child's play. And the hands are probably busy with a job down below. . . . Think you can?"

The steering-gear leaped into an abrupt short clatter, stopped smouldering like an ember; and the still man, with a motionless gaze, burst out, as if all the passion in him had gone into his lips: "By Heavens, sir! I can steer for ever if nobody talks to me."

"Oh! aye! All right. . . ." The Captain lifted his eyes for the first time to the man, ". . . Hackett."

And he seemed to dismiss this matter from his mind. He stooped to the engine-room speaking-tube, blew in, and bent his head. Mr. Rout below answered, and at once Captain MacWhirr put his lips to the mouthpiece.

With the uproar of the gale around him he applied alternately his lips and his ear, and the engineer's voice mounted to him, harsh and as if out of the heat of an engagement. One of the stokers was disabled, the others had given in, the second engineer and the donkeyman were firing-up. The third engineer was standing by the steam-valve. The engines were being tended by hand. How was it above?

"Bad enough. It mostly rests with you," said Captain MacWhirr. Was the mate down there yet? No? Well, he would be presently. Would Mr. Rout let him talk through the speaking-tube?—through the deck speaking-tube, because he—the Captain—was going out again on the bridge directly. There was some trouble amongst the Chinamen. They were fighting, it seemed. Couldn't allow fighting anyhow. . . .

Mr. Rout had gone away, and Captain MacWhirr could feel against his ear the pulsation of the engines, like the beat of the ship's heart. Mr. Rout's voice down there shouted something distantly. The ship pitched headlong, the pulsation leaped with a hissing tumult, and stopped dead. Captain MacWhirr's face was impassive, and his eyes were fixed aimlessly on the crouching shape of the second mate. Again Mr. Rout's voice cried out in the depths, and the pulsating beats recommenced, with slow strokes—growing swifter.

Mr. Rout had returned to the tube. "It don't matter much what they do," he said, hastily; and then, with irritation, "She takes these dives as if she never meant to come up again."

"Awful sea," said the Captain's voice from above.

"Don't let me drive her under," barked Solomon Rout up the pipe.

"Dark and rain. Can't see what's coming," uttered the voice. "Must—keep—her—moving—enough to steer—and chance it," it went on to state distinctly.

"I am doing as much as I dare."

"We are—getting—smashed up—a good deal up here," proceeded the voice mildly. "Doing—fairly well—though. Of course, if the wheelhouse should go. . . ."

Mr. Rout, bending an attentive ear, muttered peevishly something under his breath.

But the deliberate voice up there became animated to

ask: "Jukes turned up yet?" Then, after a short wait, "I wish he would bear a hand. I want him to be done and come up here in case of anything. To look after the ship. I am all alone. The second mate's lost. . . ."

"What?" shouted Mr. Rout into the engine-room, taking his head away. Then up the tube he cried, "Gone overboard?" and clapped his ear to.

"Lost his nerve," the voice from above continued in a matter-of-fact tone. "Damned awkward circumstance."

Mr. Rout, listening with bowed neck, opened his eyes wide at this. However, he heard something like the sounds of a scuffle and broken exclamations coming down to him. He strained his hearing; and all the time Beale, the third engineer, with his arms uplifted, held between the palms of his hands the rim of a little black wheel projecting at the side of a big copper pipe. He seemed to be poising it above his head, as though it were a correct attitude in some sort of game.

To steady himself, he pressed his shoulder against the white bulkhead, one knee bent, and a sweat-rag tucked in his belt hanging on his hip. His smooth cheek was begrimed and flushed, and the coal dust on his eyelids, like the black pencilling of a make-up, enhanced the liquid brilliance of the whites, giving to his youthful face something of a feminine, exotic and fascinating aspect. When the ship pitched he would with hasty movements of his hands screw hard at the little wheel.

"Gone crazy," began the Captain's voice suddenly in the tube. "Rushed at me. . . . Just now. Had to knock him down. . . . This minute. You heard, Mr. Rout?"

"The devil!" muttered Mr. Rout. "Look out, Beale!"

His shout rang out like the blast of a warning trumpet, between the iron walls of the engine-room. Painted white, they rose high into the dusk of the skylight, sloping like a roof; and the whole lofty space resembled the interior of a monument, divided by floors of iron grating, with lights flickering at different levels, and a mass of gloom lingering in the middle, within the columnar stir of machinery under the motionless swelling of the cylinders. A loud and wild resonance, made up of all the noises of the hurricane, dwelt in the still warmth of the air. There was in it the smell of hot metal, of oil, and a slight mist of steam. The blows of the sea seemed to traverse it in an unringing, stunning shock, from side to side.

Gleams, like pale long flames, trembled upon the polish of metal; from the flooring below the enormous crank-heads emerged in their turns with a flash of brass and steel —going over; while the connecting-rods, big-jointed, like skeleton limbs, seemed to thrust them down and pull them up again with an irresistible precision. And deep in the half-light other rods dodged deliberately to and fro, crossheads nodded, discs of metal rubbed smoothly against each other, slow and gentle, in a commingling of shadows and gleams.

Sometimes all those powerful and unerring movements would slow down simultaneously, as if they had been the functions of a living organism, stricken suddenly by the blight of languor; and Mr. Rout's eyes would blaze darker in his long sallow face. He was fighting this fight in a pair of carpet slippers. A short shiny jacket barely covered his loins, and his white wrists protruded far out of the tight sleeves, as though the emergency had added to his stature, had lengthened his limbs, augmented his pallor, hollowed his eyes.

He moved, climbing high up, disappearing low down, with a restless, purposeful industry, and when he stood still, holding the guard-rail in front of the starting-gear, he would keep glancing to the right at the steam-gauge, at the water-gauge, fixed upon the white wall in the light of a swaying lamp. The mouths of two speaking-tubes gaped stupidly at his elbow, and the dial of the engine-room tele-graph resembled a clock of large diameter, bearing on its face curt words instead of figures. The grouped letters stood out heavily black, around the pivot-head of the indica-tor, emphatically symbolic of loud exclamations: AHEAD, ASTERN, SLOW, HALF, STAND BY; and the fat black hand pointed downwards to the word FULL, which, thus singled out, captured the eye as a sharp cry secures attention.

The wood-encased bulk of the low-pressure cylinder, frowning portly from above, emitted a faint wheeze at ev-ery thrust, and except for that low hiss the engines worked their steel limbs headlong or slow with a silent, determined smoothness. And all this, the white walls, the moving steel, the floor plates under Solomon Rout's feet, the floors of iron grating above his head, the dusk and the gleams, uprose and sank continuously, with one accord, upon the harsh wash of the waves against the ship's side. The whole loftiness of the place, booming hollow to the great voice of the wind, swayed at the top like a tree, would go over bodily, as if borne down this way and that by the tremendous blasts.

"You've got to hurry up," shouted Mr. Rout, as soon as he saw Jukes appear in the stokehold doorway.

Jukes' glance was wandering and tipsy; his red face was puffy, as though he had overslept himself. He had had an arduous road, and had travelled over it with immense vivacity, the agitation of his mind corresponding to the exertions of his body. He had rushed up out of the bunker, stumbling in the dark alleyway amongst a lot of bewildered men who, trod upon, asked "What's up, sir?" in awed mutters all round him—down the stokehold ladder, missing many iron rungs in his hurry, down into a place deep as a well, black as Tophet, tipping over back and forth like a see-saw. The water in the bilges thundered at each roll, and lumps of coal skipped to and fro, from end to end, rattling like an avalanche of pebbles on a slope of iron.

Somebody in there moaned with pain, and somebody else could be seen crouching over what seemed the prone body of a dead man; a lusty voice blasphemed; and the glow under each fire-door was like a pool of flaming blood radiating quietly in a velvety blackness.

A gust of wind struck upon the nape of Jukes' neck and next moment he felt it streaming about his wet ankles. The stokehold ventilators hummed; in front of the six fire-doors two wild figures, stripped to the waist, staggered and stooped, wrestling with two shovels.

"Hallo! Plenty of draught now," yelled the second engineer at once, as though he had been all the time looking out for Jukes. The donkeyman, a dapper little chap with a dazzling fair skin and a tiny, gingery moustache, worked in a sort of mute transport. They were keeping a full head of steam, and a profound rumbling, as of an empty furniture van trotting over a bridge, made a sustained bass to all the other noises of the place.

"Blowing off all the time," went on yelling the second. With a sound as of a hundred scoured saucepans, the orifice of a ventilator spat upon his shoulder a sudden gush of salt water, and he volleyed a stream of curses upon all things on earth including his own soul, ripping and raving, and all the time attending to his business. With a sharp clash of metal the ardent pale glare of the fire opened upon his bullet head, showing his spluttering lips, his insolent face, and with another clang closed like the white-hot wink of an iron eye.

"Where's the blooming ship? Can you tell me? blast my eyes! Under water—or what? It's coming down here in tons. Are the condemned cowls gone to Hades? Hey? Don't you know anything—you jolly sailor-man you . . . ?"

Jukes, after a bewildered moment, had been helped by a roll to dart through; and as soon as his eyes took in the comparative vastness, peace and brilliance of the engine-room, the ship, setting her stern heavily in the water, sent him charging head down upon Mr. Rout.

The chief's arm, long like a tentacle, and straightening as if worked by a spring, went out to meet him, and deflected his rush into a spin towards the speaking-tubes. At the same time Mr. Rout repeated earnestly:

"You've got to hurry up, whatever it is."

Jukes yelled "Are you there, sir?" and listened. Nothing. Suddenly the roar of the wind fell straight into his ear, but presently a small voice shoved aside the shouting hurricane quietly.

"You, Jukes?—Well?"

Jukes was ready to talk: it was only time that seemed to be wanting. It was easy enough to account for everything. He could perfectly imagine the coolies battened down in the reeking 'tween-deck, lying sick and scared between the rows of chests. Then one of these chests—or perhaps several at once—breaking loose in a roll, knocking out others, sides splitting, lids flying open, and all these clumsy Chinamen rising up in a body to save their property. Afterwards every fling of the ship would hurl that tramping, yelling mob here and there, from side to side, in a whirl of smashed wood, torn clothing, rolling dollars. A struggle once started, they would be unable to stop themselves. Nothing could stop them now except main force. It was a disaster. He had seen it, and that was all he could say. Some of them must be dead, he believed. The rest would go on fighting. . . .

He sent up his words, tripping over each other crowding the narrow tube. They mounted as if into a silence of an enlightened comprehension dwelling alone up there with a storm. And Jukes wanted to be dismissed from the face of that odious trouble intruding on the great need of the ship.

V

He waited. Before his eyes the engines turned with slow labour, that in the moment of going off into a mad fling would stop dead at Mr. Rout's shout, "Look out, Beale!" They paused in an intelligent immobility, stilled in mid-stroke, a heavy crank arrested on the cant, as if conscious of danger and the passage of time. Then, with a "Now, then!" from the chief, and the sound of a breath expelled through clenched teeth, they would accomplish the interrupted revolution and begin another.

There was the prudent sagacity of wisdom and the deliberation of enormous strength in their movements. This was their work—this patient coaxing of a distracted ship over the fury of the waves and into the very eye of the wind. At times Mr. Rout's chin would sink on his breast, and he watched them with knitted eyebrows as if lost in thought.

The voice that kept the hurricane out of Jukes' ear began: "Take the hands with you . . ." and left off unexpectedly.

"What could I do with them, sir?"

A harsh, abrupt, imperious clang exploded suddenly. The three pairs of eyes flew up to the telegraph dial to see the hand jump from FULL to STOP, as if snatched by a devil.

And then these three men in the engine-room had the intimate sensation of a check upon the ship, of a strange shrinking, as if she had gathered herself for a desperate leap.

"Stop her!" bellowed Mr. Rout.

Nobody—not even Captain MacWhirr, who alone on deck had caught sight of a white line of foam coming on at such a height that he couldn't believe his eyes—nobody was to know the steepness of that sea and the awful depth of the hollow the hurricane had scooped out behind the running wall of water.

It raced to meet the ship, and, with a pause, as of girding the loins, the *Nan-Shan* lifted her bows and leaped. The flames in all the lamps sank, darkening the engine-room. One went out. With a tearing crash and a swirling, raving tumult, tons of water fell upon the deck, as though the ship had darted under the foot of a cataract.

Down there they looked at each other, stunned.

"Swept from end to end, by God!" bawled Jukes.

She dipped into the hollow straight down, as if going over the edge of the world. The engine-room toppled forward menacingly, like the inside of a tower nodding in an earthquake. An awful racket, of iron things falling, came from the stokehold. She hung on this appalling slant long enough for Beale to drop on his hands and knees and begin to crawl as if he meant to fly on all fours out of the engine-room, and for Mr. Rout to turn his head slowly, rigid, cavernous, with the lower jaw dropping. Jukes had shut his eyes, and his face in a moment became hopelessly blank and gentle, like the face of a blind man.

At last she rose slowly, staggering, as if she had to lift a mountain with her bows.

Mr. Rout shut his mouth; Jukes blinked; and little Beale stood up hastily.

"Another one like this, and that's the last of her," cried the chief.

He and Jukes looked at each other, and the same thought came into their heads. The Captain! Everything must have been swept away. Steering-gear gone—ship like a log. All over directly.

"Rush!" ejaculated Mr. Rout thickly, glaring with enlarged, doubtful eyes at Jukes, who answered him by an irresolute glance.

The clang of the telegraph gong soothed them instantly. The black hand dropped in a flash from STOP to FULL.

"Now then, Beale!" cried Mr. Rout.

The steam hissed low. The piston-rods slid in and out. Jukes put his ear to the tube. The voice was ready for him. It said: "Pick up all the money. Bear a hand now. I'll want you up here." And that was all.

"Sir?" called up Jukes. There was no answer.

He staggered away like a defeated man from the field of battle. He had got, in some way or other, a cut above his left eyebrow—a cut to the bone. He was not aware of it in the least: quantities of the China Sea, large enough to break his neck for him, had gone over his head, had cleaned, washed, and salted that wound. It did not bleed, but only gaped red; and this gash over the eye, his dishevelled hair, the disorder of his clothes, gave him the aspect of a man worsted in a fight with fists.

"Got to pick up the dollars." He appealed to Mr. Rout, smiling pitifully at random.

"What's that?" asked Mr. Rout, wildly. "Pick up . . . ? I don't care. . . ." Then, quivering in every muscle, but with an exaggeration of paternal tone, "Go away now, for God's sake. You deck people'll drive me silly. There's that second mate been going for the old man. Don't you know? You fellows are going wrong for want of something to do. . . ."

At these words Jukes discovered in himself the beginnings of anger. Want of something to do—indeed. . . . Full of hot scorn against the chief, he turned to go the way he had come. In the stokehold the plump donkeyman toiled with his shovel mutely, as if his tongue had been cut out; but the second was carrying on like a noisy, undaunted maniac, who had preserved his skill in the art of stoking under a marine boiler.

"Hallo, you wandering officer! Hey! Can't you get some of your slush-slingers to wind up a few of them ashes? I am getting choked with them here. Curse it! Hallo! Hey!

Remember the articles: *Sailors and firemen to assist each other*. Hey! D'ye hear?"

Jukes was climbing out frantically, and the other, lifting up his face after him, howled, "Can't you speak? What are you poking about here for? What's your game, anyhow?"

A frenzy possessed Jukes. By the time he was back amongst the men in the darkness of the alleyway, he felt ready to wring all their necks at the slightest sign of hanging back. The very thought of it exasperated him. *He* couldn't hang back. They shouldn't.

The impetuosity with which he came amongst them carried them along. They had already been excited and startled at all his comings and goings—by the fierceness and rapidity of his movements; and more felt than seen in his rushes, he appeared formidable—busied with matters of life and death that brooked no delay. At his first word he heard them drop into the bunker one after another obediently, with heavy thumps.

They were not clear as to what would have to be done. "What is it? What is it?" they were asking each other. The boatswain tried to explain; the sounds of a great scuffle surprised them: and the mighty shocks, reverberating awfully in the black bunker, kept them in mind of their danger. When the boatswain threw open the door it seemed that an eddy of the hurricane, stealing through the iron sides of the ship, had set all these bodies whirling like dust: there came to them a confused uproar, a tempestuous tumult, a fierce mutter, gusts of screams dying away, and the tramping of feet mingling with the blows of the sea.

For a moment they glared amazed, blocking the doorway. Jukes pushed through them brutally. He said nothing, and simply darted in. Another lot of coolies on the ladder, struggling suicidally to break through the battened hatch to a swamped deck, fell off as before, and he disappeared under them like a man overtaken by a landslide.

The boatswain yelled excitedly: "Come along. Get the mate out. He'll be trampled to death. Come on."

They charged in, stamping on breasts, on fingers, on faces, catching their feet in heaps of clothing, kicking broken wood; but before they could get hold of him Jukes emerged waist deep in a multitude of clawing hands. In the instant he had been lost to view, all the buttons of his jacket had gone, its back had got split up to the collar, his waistcoat had been torn open. The central struggling mass of Chinamen went over to the roll, dark, indistinct, helpless, with a wild gleam of many eyes in the dim light of the lamps.

"Leave me alone—damn you. I am all right," screeched Jukes. "Drive them forward. Watch your chance when she pitches. Forward with 'em. Drive them against the bulkhead. Jam 'em up."

The rush of the sailors into the seething 'tween-deck was like a splash of cold water into a boiling cauldron. The commotion sank for a moment.

The bulk of Chinamen were locked in such a compact scrimmage that, linking their arms and aided by an appalling dive of the ship, the seamen sent it forward in one great shove, like a solid block. Behind their backs small clusters and loose bodies tumbled from side to side.

The boatswain performed prodigious feats of strength. With his long arms open, and each great paw clutching at a stanchion, he stopped the rush of seven entwined Chinamen rolling like a boulder. His joints cracked; he said, "Ha!" and they flew apart. But the carpenter showed the greater intelligence. Without saying a word to anybody he went back into the alleyway, to fetch several coils of cargo gear he had seen there—chain and rope. With these life-lines were rigged.

There was really no resistance. The struggle, however it began, had turned into a scramble of blind panic. If the coolies had started up after their scattered dollars they were by that time fighting only for their footing. They took each other by the throat merely to save themselves from being hurled about. Whoever got a hold anywhere would kick at the others who caught at his legs and hung on, till a roll sent them flying together across the deck.

The coming of the white devils was a terror. Had they come to kill? The individuals torn out of the ruck became very limp in the seamen's hands: some, dragged aside by the heels, were passive, like dead bodies, with open, fixed eyes. Here and there a coolie would fall on his knees as if begging for mercy; several, whom the excess of fear made unruly, were hit with hard fists between the eyes, and cowered; while those who were hurt submitted to rough handling, blinking rapidly without a plaint. Faces streamed with blood; there were raw places on the shaven heads, scratches, bruises, torn wounds, gashes. The broken porcelain out of the chests was mostly responsible for the latter. Here and there a Chinaman, wild-eyed, with his tail unplaited, nursed a bleeding sole.

They had been ranged closely, after having been shaken into submission, cuffed a little to allay excitement, addressed in gruff words of encouragement that sounded like promises of evil. They sat on the deck in ghastly, drooping rows, and at the end the carpenter, with two hands to help him, moved busily from place to place, setting taut and hitching the life-lines. The boatswain, with one leg and one arm embracing a stanchion, struggled with a lamp pressed to his breast, trying to get a light, and growling all the time like an industrious gorilla. The figures of seamen stooped repeatedly, with the movements of gleaners, and everything was being flung into the bunker: clothing, smashed wood, broken china, and the dollars, too, gathered up in men's jackets. Now and then a sailor would stagger towards the doorway with his arms full of rubbish; and dolorous, slanting eyes followed his movements.

With every roll of the ship the long rows of sitting Celestials would sway forward brokenly, and her headlong dives knocked together the line of shaven polls from end to end. When the wash of water rolling on the deck died away for a moment, it seemed to Jukes, yet quivering from his exertions, that in his mad struggle down there he had overcome the wind somehow: that a silence had fallen upon the ship, a silence in which the sea struck thunderously at her sides.

Everything had been cleared out of the 'tween-deck—all the wreckage, as the men said. They stood erect and tottering above the level of heads and drooping shoulders. Here and there a coolie sobbed for his breath. Where the high light fell, Jukes could see the salient ribs of one, the yellow, wistful face of another; bowed necks; or would meet a dull stare directed at his face. He was amazed that there had been no corpses; but the lot of them seemed at their last gasp, and they appeared to him more pitiful than if they had been all dead.

Suddenly one of the coolies began to speak. The light came and went on his lean, straining face; he threw his head up like a baying hound. From the bunker came the sounds of knocking and the tinkle of some dollars rolling loose; he stretched out his arm, his mouth yawned black, and the incomprehensible guttural hooting sounds, that did not seem to belong to a human language, penetrated Jukes with a strange emotion as if a brute had tried to be eloquent.

Two more started mouthing what seemed to Jukes fierce denunciations; the others stirred with grunts and growls. Jukes ordered the hands out of the 'tween-deck hurriedly. He left last himself, backing through the door, while the grunts rose to a loud murmur and hands were extended after him as after a malefactor. The boatswain shot the bolt, and remarked uneasily, "Seems as if the wind had dropped, sir."

The seamen were glad to get back into the alleyway. Secretly each of them thought that at the last moment he could rush out on deck—and that was a comfort. There is something horribly repugnant in the idea of being drowned under a deck. Now they had done with the Chinamen, they again became conscious of the ship's position.

Jukes on coming out of the alleyway found himself up to the neck in the noisy water. He gained the bridge, and discovered he could detect obscure shapes as if his sight had become preternaturally acute. He saw faint outlines. They recalled not the familiar aspect of the Nan-Shan, but something remembered—an old dismantled steamer he had seen years ago rotting on a mudbank. She recalled that wreck.

There was no wind, not a breath, except the faint currents created by the lurches of the ship. The smoke tossed out of the funnel was settling down upon her deck. He breathed it as he passed forward. He felt the deliberate throb of the engines, and heard small sounds that seemed to have survived the great uproar: the knocking of broken fittings, the rapid tumbling of some piece of wreckage on the bridge. He perceived dimly the squat shape of his captain holding on to a twisted bridge-rail, motionless and swaying as if rooted to the planks. The unexpected stillness of the air oppressed Jukes.

"We have done it, sir," he gasped.

"Thought you would," said Captain MacWhirr.

"Did you?" murmured Jukes to himself.

"Wind fell all at once," went on the Captain.

Jukes burst out: "If you think it was an easy job——"

But his captain, clinging to the rail, paid no attention. "According to the books the worst is not over yet."

"If most of them hadn't been half dead with seasickness and fright, not one of us would have come out of that 'tween-deck alive," said Jukes.

"Had to do what's fair by them," mumbled MacWhirr, stolidly. "You don't find everything in books."

"Why, I believe they would have risen on us if I hadn't ordered the hands out of that pretty quick," continued Jukes with warmth.

After the whisper of their shouts, their ordinary tones, so distinct, rang out very loud to their ears in the amazing stillness of the air. It seemed to them they were talking in a dark and echoing vault.

Through a jagged aperture in the dome of clouds the light of a few stars fell upon the black sea, rising and falling confusedly. Sometimes the head of a watery cone would topple on board and mingle with the rolling flurry of foam on the swamped deck; and the Nan-Shan wallowed heavily at the bottom of a circular cistern of clouds. This ring of dense vapours, gyrating madly round the calm of the centre, encompassed the ship like a motionless and unbroken wall of an aspect inconceivably sinister. Within, the sea, as if agitated by an internal commotion, leaped in peaked mounds that jostled each other, slapping heavily against her sides; and a low moaning sound, the infinite plaint of the storm's fury, came from beyond the limits of the menacing calm. Captain MacWhirr remained silent, and Jukes' ready ear caught suddenly the faint, long-drawn roar of some immense wave rushing unseen under that thick blackness, which made the appalling boundary of his vision.

"Of course," he started resentfully, "they thought we had caught at the chance to plunder them. Of course! You said —pick up the money. Easier said than done. They couldn't tell what was in our heads. We came in, smash—right into the middle of them. Had to do it by a rush."

"As long as it's done . . ." mumbled the Captain, without attempting to look at Jukes. "Had to do what's fair."

"We shall find yet there's the devil to pay when this is over," said Jukes, feeling very sore. "Let them only recover a bit, and you'll see. They will fly at our throats, sir. Don't forget, sir, she isn't a British ship now. These brutes know it well, too. The damned Siamese flag."

"We are on board, all the same," remarked Captain MacWhirr.

"The trouble's not over yet," insisted Jukes, prophetically, reeling and catching on. "She's a wreck," he added, faintly.

"The trouble's not over yet," assented Captain Mac-Whirr, half aloud. . . . "Look out for her a minute."

"Are you going off the deck, sir?" asked Jukes, hurriedly, as if the storm were sure to pounce upon him as soon as he had been left alone with the ship.

He watched her, battered and solitary, labouring heavily in a wild scene of mountainous black waters lit by the gleams of distant worlds. She moved slowly, breathing into the still core of the hurricane the excess of her strength in a white cloud of steam—and the deep-toned vibration of the escape was like the defiant trumpeting of a living creature of the sea impatient for the renewal of the contest. It ceased suddenly. The still air moaned. Above Jukes' head a few stars shone into a pit of black vapours. The inky edge of the cloud-disc frowned upon the ship under the patch of glittering sky. The stars, too, seemed to look at her intently, as if for the last time, and the cluster of their splendour sat like a diadem on a lowering brow.

Captain MacWhirr had gone into the chart-room. There was no light there; but he could feel the disorder of that place where he used to live tidily. His armchair was upset. The books had tumbled out on the floor; he scrunched a piece of glass under his boot. He groped for the matches, and found a box on a shelf with a deep ledge. He struck one, and puckering the corners of his eyes, held out the little flame towards the barometer whose glittering top of glass and metal nodded at him continuously.

It stood very low—incredibly low, so low that Captain MacWhirr grunted. The match went out, and hurriedly he extracted another, with thick, stiff fingers.

Again a little flame flared up before the nodding glass and metal of the top. His eyes looked at it, narrowed with attention, as if expecting an imperceptible sign. With his grave face he resembled a booted and misshapen pagan burning incense before the oracle of a Joss. There was no mistake. It was the lowest reading he had ever seen in his life.

Captain MacWhirr emitted a low whistle. He forgot himself till the flame diminished to a blue spark, burnt his fingers and vanished. Perhaps something had gone wrong with the thing!

There was an aneroid glass screwed above the couch. He turned that way, struck another match, and discovered the white face of the other instrument looking at him from the bulkhead, meaningly, not to be gainsaid, as though the wisdom of men were made unerring by the indifference of matter. There was no room for doubt now. Captain MacWhirr pshawed at it, and threw the match down.

The worst was to come, then—and if the books were right this worst would be very bad. The experience of the last six hours had enlarged his conception of what heavy weather could be like. "It'll be terrific," he pronounced, mentally. He had not consciously looked at anything by the light of the matches except at the barometer; and yet somehow he had seen that his water-bottle and the two tumblers had been flung out of their stand. It seemed to give him a more intimate knowledge of the tossing the ship had gone through. "I wouldn't have believed it," he thought. And his table had been cleared, too; his rulers, his pencils, the inkstand—all the things that had their safe appointed places—they were gone, as if a mischievous hand had plucked them out one by one and flung them on the wet floor. The hurricane had broken in upon the orderly arrangements of his privacy. This had never happened before, and the feeling of dismay reached the very seat of his composure. And the worst was to come yet! He was glad the trouble in the 'tween-deck had been discovered in time. If the ship had to go after all, then, at least, she wouldn't be going to the bottom with a lot of people in her fighting teeth and claw. That would have been odious. And in that feeling there was a humane intention and a vague sense of the fitness of things.

These instantaneous thoughts were yet in their essence heavy and slow, partaking of the nature of the man. He extended his hand to put back the matchbox in its corner of the shelf. There were always matches there—by his order. The steward had his instructions impressed upon him long before. "A box . . . just there, see? Not so very full . . . where I can put my hand on it, steward. Might want a light in a hurry. Can't tell on board ship *what* you might want in a hurry. Mind, now."

And of course on his side he would be careful to put it back in its place scrupulously. He did so now, but before he removed his hand it occurred to him that perhaps he would never have occasion to use that box any more. The vividness of the thought checked him and for an infinitesimal fraction of a second his fingers closed again on the small object as though it had been the symbol of all these little habits that chain us to the weary round of life. He released it at last, and letting himself fall on the settee, listened for the first sounds of returning wind.

Not yet. He heard only the wash of water, the heavy splashes, the dull shocks of the confused seas boarding his ship from all sides. She would never have a chance to clear her decks.

But the quietude of the air was startlingly tense and unsafe, like a slender hair holding a sword suspended over his head. By this awful pause the storm penetrated the defences of the man and unsealed his lips. He spoke out in the solitude and the pitch darkness of the cabin, as if addressing another being awakened within his breast.

"I shouldn't like to lose her," he said half aloud.

He sat unseen, apart from the sea, from his ship, isolated, as if withdrawn from the very current of his own existence, where such freaks as talking to himself surely had no place. His palms reposed on his knees, he bowed his short neck and puffed heavily, surrendering to a strange sensation of weariness he was not enlightened enough to recognize for the fatigue of mental stress.

From where he sat he could reach the door of a wash-stand locker. There should have been a towel there. There was. Good. . . . He took it out, wiped his face, and afterwards went on rubbing his wet head. He towelled himself with energy in the dark, and then remained motionless with the towel on his knees. A moment passed, of a stillness so profound that no one could have guessed there was a man sitting in that cabin. Then a murmur arose.

"She may come out of it yet."

When Captain MacWhirr came out on deck, which he did brusquely, as though he had suddenly become conscious of having stayed away too long, the calm had lasted already more than fifteen minutes—long enough to make itself intolerable even to his imagination. Jukes, motionless on the fore-part of the bridge, began to speak at once. His voice, blank and forced as though he were talking through hard-set teeth, seemed to flow away on all sides into the darkness, deepening again upon the sea.

"I had the wheel relieved. Hackett began to sing out that he was done. He's lying in there alongside the steering-gear with a face like death. At first I couldn't get anybody to crawl out and relieve the poor devil. That boss'en's worse than no good, I always said. Thought I would have had to go myself and haul out one of them by the neck."

"Ah, well," muttered the Captain. He stood watchful by Jukes' side.

"The second mate's in there, too, holding his head. Is he hurt, sir?"

"No—crazy," said Captain MacWhirr, curtly.

"Looks as if he had a tumble, though."

"I had to give him a push," explained the Captain.

Jukes gave an impatient sigh.

"It will come very sudden," said Captain MacWhirr, "and from over there, I fancy. God only knows though. These books are only good to muddle your head and make you jumpy. It will be bad, and there's an end. If we only can steam her round in time to meet it. . . ."

A minute passed. Some of the stars winked rapidly and vanished.

"You left them pretty safe?" began the Captain abruptly, as though the silence were unbearable.

"Are you thinking of the coolies, sir? I rigged life-lines all ways across that 'tween-deck."

"Did you? Good idea, Mr. Jukes."

"I didn't . . . think you cared to . . . know," said Jukes —the lurching of the ship cut his speech as though somebody had been jerking him around while he talked—"how I got on with . . . that infernal job. We did it. And it may not matter in the end."

"Had to do what's fair, for all—they are only Chinamen. Give them the same chance with ourselves—hang it all. She isn't lost yet. Bad enough to be shut up below in a gale——"

"That's what I thought when you gave me the job, sir," interjected Jukes, moodily.

"——without being battered to pieces," pursued Captain MacWhirr with rising vehemence. "Couldn't let that go on in my ship, if I knew she hadn't five minutes to live. Couldn't bear it, Mr. Jukes."

A hollow echoing noise, like that of a shout rolling in a rocky chasm, approached the ship and went away again. The last star, blurred, enlarged, as if returning to the fiery mist of its beginning, struggled with the colossal depth of blackness hanging over the ship—and went out.

"Now for it!" muttered Captain MacWhirr. "Mr. Jukes."

"Here, sir."

The two men were growing indistinct to each other.

"We must trust her to go through it and come out on the other side. That's plain and straight. There's no room for Captain Wilson's storm-strategy here."

"No, sir."

"She will be smothered and swept again for hours," mumbled the Captain. "There's not much left by this time above deck for the sea to take away—unless you or me."

"Both, sir," whispered Jukes, breathlessly.

"You are always meeting trouble half way, Jukes," Captain MacWhirr remonstrated quaintly. "Though it's a fact that the second mate is no good. D'ye hear, Mr. Jukes? You would be left alone if. . . ."

Captain MacWhirr interrupted himself, and Jukes, glancing on all sides, remained silent.

"Don't you be put out by anything," the Captain continued, mumbling rather fast. "Keep her facing it. They may say what they like, but the heaviest seas run with the wind. Facing it—always facing it—that's the way to get through. You are a young sailor. Face it. That's enough for any man. Keep a cool head."

"Yes, sir," said Jukes, with a flutter of the heart.

In the next few seconds the Captain spoke to the engine-room and got an answer.

For some reason Jukes experienced an access of confidence, a sensation that came from outside like a warm breath, and made him feel equal to every demand. The distant muttering of the darkness stole into his ears. He noted it unmoved, out of that sudden belief in himself, as a man safe in a shirt of mail would watch a point.

The ship laboured without intermission amongst the black hills of water, paying with this hard tumbling the price of her life. She rumbled in her depths, shaking a white plummet of steam into the night, and Jukes' thought skimmed like a bird through the engine-room, where Mr. Rout—good man—was ready. When the rumbling ceased it seemed to him that there was a pause of every sound, a dead pause in which Captain MacWhirr's voice rang out startlingly.

"What's that? A puff of wind?"—it spoke much louder than Jukes had ever heard it before—"On the bow. That's right. She may come out of it yet."

The mutter of the winds drew near apace. In the forefront could be distinguished a drowsy waking plaint passing on, and far off the growth of a multiple clamour, marching and expanding. There was the throb as of many drums in it, a vicious rushing note, and like the chant of a tramping multitude.

Jukes could no longer see his captain distinctly. The darkness was absolutely piling itself upon the ship. At most he made out movements, a hint of elbows spread out, of a head thrown up.

Captain MacWhirr was trying to do up the top button of his oilskin coat with unwonted haste. The hurricane, with its power to madden the seas, to sink ships, to uproot trees, to overturn strong walls and dash the very birds of the air to the ground, had found this taciturn man in its path, and, doing its utmost, had managed to wring out a few words. Before the renewed wrath of winds swooped on his ship, Captain MacWhirr was moved to declare, in a tone of vexation, as it were: "I wouldn't like to lose her."

He was spared that annoyance.

VI

On a bright sunshiny day, with the breeze chasing her smoke far ahead, the *Nan-Shan* came into Fu-chau. Her arrival was at once noticed on shore, and the seamen in harbour said: "Look! Look at that steamer. What's that? Siamese—isn't she? Just look at her!"

She seemed, indeed, to have been used as a running target for the secondary batteries of a cruiser. A hail of minor shells could not have given her upper works a more broken, torn, and devastated aspect: and she had about her the worn, weary air of ships coming from the far ends of the world—and indeed with truth, for in her short passage she had been very far; sighting, verily, even the coast of the Great Beyond, whence no ship ever returns to give up her crew to the dust of the earth. She was incrusted and gray with salt to the trucks of her masts and to the top of her funnel; as though (as some facetious seaman said) "the crowd on board had fished her out somewhere from the bottom of the sea and brought her in here for salvage." And further, excited by the felicity of his own wit, he offered to give five pounds for her—"as she stands."

Before she had been quite an hour at rest, a meagre little man, with a red-tipped nose and a face cast in an angry mould, landed from a sampan on the quay of the

Foreign Concession, and incontinently turned to shake his fist at her.

A tall individual, with legs much too thin for a rotund stomach, and with watery eyes, strolled up and remarked, "Just left her—eh? Quick work."

He wore a soiled suit of blue flannel with a pair of dirty cricketing shoes; a dingy gray moustache drooped from his lip, and daylight could be seen in two places between the rim and the crown of his hat.

"Hallo! what are you doing here?" asked the ex-second mate of the *Nan-Shan*, shaking hands hurriedly.

"Standing by for a job—chance worth taking—got a quiet hint," explained the man with the broken hat, in jerky, apathetic wheezes.

The second shook his fist again at the *Nan-Shan*. "There's a fellow there that ain't fit to have the command of a scow," he declared, quivering with passion, while the other looked about listlessly.

"Is there?"

But he caught sight on the quay of a heavy seaman's chest, painted brown under a fringed sailcloth cover, and lashed with new manila line. He eyed it with awakened interest.

"I would talk and raise trouble if it wasn't for that damned Siamese flag. Nobody to go to—or I would make it hot for him. The fraud! Told his chief engineer—that's another fraud for you—I had lost my nerve. The greatest lot of ignorant fools that ever sailed the seas. No! You can't think . . ."

"Got your money all right?" inquired his seedy acquaintance suddenly.

"Yes. Paid me off on board," raged the second mate. "'Get your breakfast on shore,' says he."

"Mean skunk!" commented the tall man, vaguely, and passed his tongue on his lips. "What about having a drink of some sort?"

"He struck me," hissed the second mate.

"No! Struck! You don't say?" The man in blue began to bustle about sympathetically. "Can't possibly talk here. I want to know all about it. Struck—eh? Let's get a fellow to carry your chest. I know a quiet place where they have some bottled beer. . . ."

Mr. Jukes, who had been scanning the shore through a pair of glasses, informed the chief engineer afterwards that "our late second mate hasn't been long in finding a friend. A chap looking uncommonly like a bummer. I saw them walk away together from the quay."

The hammering and banging of the needful repairs did not disturb Captain MacWhirr. The steward found in the letter he wrote, in a tidy chart-room, passages of such absorbing interest that twice he was nearly caught in the act. But Mrs. MacWhirr, in the drawing-room of the forty-pound house, stifled a yawn—perhaps out of self-respect—for she was alone.

She reclined in a plush-bottomed and gilt hammock-chair near a tiled fireplace, with Japanese fans on the mantel and a glow of coals in the grate. Lifting her hands, she glanced wearily here and there into the many pages. It was not her fault they were so prosy, so completely uninteresting—from "My darling wife" at the beginning, to "Your loving husband" at the end. She couldn't be really expected to understand all these ship affairs. She was glad, of course, to hear from him, but she had never asked herself why, precisely.

". . . They are called typhoons . . . The mate did not seem to like it . . . Not in books . . . Couldn't think of letting it go on. . . ."

The paper rustled sharply. ". . . . A calm that lasted more than twenty minutes," she read perfunctorily; and the next words her thoughtless eyes caught, on the top of another page, were: "see you and the children again. . . ." She had a movement of impatience. He was always thinking of coming home. He had never had such a good salary before. What was the matter now?

It did not occur to her to turn back overleaf to look. She would have found it recorded there that between 4 and 6 A.M. on December 25th, Captain MacWhirr did actually think that his ship could not possibly live another hour in such a sea, and that he would never see his wife and children again. Nobody was to know this (his letters got mislaid so quickly)—nobody whatever but the steward, who had been greatly impressed by that disclosure. So much so, that he tried to give the cook some idea of the "narrow squeak we all had" by saying solemnly, "The old man himself had a dam' poor opinion of our chance."

"How do you know?" asked, contemptuously, the cook, an old soldier. "He hasn't told you, maybe?"

"Well, he did give me a hint to that effect," the steward brazened it out.

"Get along with you! He will be coming to tell *me* next," jeered the old cook, over his shoulder.

Mrs. MacWhirr glanced farther, on the alert. ". . . Do what's fair. . . . Miserable objects. . . . Only three, with a broken leg each, and one . . . Thought had better keep the matter quiet . . . hope to have done the fair thing. . . ."

She let fall her hands. No: there was nothing more about coming home. Must have been merely expressing a pious wish. Mrs. MacWhirr's mind was set at ease, and a black marble clock, priced by the local jeweller at £3 18s. 6d., had a discreet stealthy tick.

The door flew open, and a girl in the long-legged, short-frocked period of existence, flung into the room. A lot of colourless, rather lanky hair was scattered over her shoulders. Seeing her mother, she stood still, and directed her pale prying eyes upon the letter.

"From father," murmured Mrs. MacWhirr. "What have you done with your ribbon?"

The girl put her hands up to her head and pouted.

"He's well," continued Mrs. MacWhirr, languidly. "At least I think so. He never says." She had a little laugh. The girl's face expressed a wandering indifference, and Mrs. MacWhirr surveyed her with fond pride.

"Go and get your hat," she said after a while. "I am going out to do some shopping. There is a sale at Linom's."

"Oh, how jolly!" uttered the child, impressively, in unexpectedly grave vibrating tones, and bounded out of the room.

It was a fine afternoon, with a gray sky and dry sidewalks. Outside the draper's Mrs. MacWhirr smiled upon a

woman in a black mantle of generous proportions armoured
in jet and crowned with flowers blooming falsely above a
bilious matronly countenance. They broke into a swift little
babble of greetings and exclamations both together, very
hurried, as if the street were ready to yawn open and swallow all that pleasure before it could be expressed.

Behind them the high glass doors were kept on the swing.
People couldn't pass, men stood aside waiting patiently,
and Lydia was absorbed in poking the end of her parasol
between the stone flags. Mrs. MacWhirr talked rapidly.

"Thank you very much. He's not coming home yet. Of
course it's very sad to have him away, but it's such a comfort to know he keeps so well." Mrs. MacWhirr drew
breath. "The climate there agrees with him," she added,
beamingly, as if poor MacWhirr had been away touring
in China for the sake of his health.

Neither was the chief engineer coming home yet. Mr.
Rout knew too well the value of a good billet.

"Solomon says wonders will never cease," cried Mrs.
Rout joyously at the old lady in her armchair by the fire.
Mr. Rout's mother moved slightly, her withered hands lying
in black half-mittens on her lap.

The eyes of the engineer's wife fairly danced on the paper. "That captain of the ship he is in—a rather simple man,
you remember, mother?—has done something rather clever,
Solomon says."

"Yes, my dear," said the old woman meekly, sitting with
bowed silvery head, and that air of inward stillness characteristic of very old people who seem lost in watching the
last flickers of life. "I think I remember."

Solomon Rout, Old Sol, Father Sol, the Chief, "Rout,
good man"—Mr. Rout, the condescending and paternal
friend of youth, had been the baby of her many children—
all dead by this time. And she remembered him best as a
boy of ten—long before he went away to serve his apprenticeship in some great engineering works in the North. She
had seen so little of him since, she had gone through so
many years, that she had now to retrace her steps very far
back to recognize him plainly in the mist of time. Some-

times it seemed that her daughter-in-law was talking of some strange man.

Mrs. Rout junior was disappointed. "H'm. H'm." She turned the page. "How provoking! He doesn't say what it is. Says I couldn't understand how much there was in it. Fancy! What could it be so very clever? What a wretched man not to tell us!"

She read on without further remark soberly, and at last sat looking into the fire. The chief wrote just a word or two of the typhoon; but something had moved him to express an increased longing for the companionship of the jolly woman. "If it hadn't been that mother must be looked after, I would send you your passage-money to-day. You could set up a small house out here. I would have a chance to see you sometimes then. We are not growing younger. . . ."

"He's well, mother," sighed Mrs. Rout, rousing herself.

"He always was a strong healthy boy," said the old woman placidly.

But Mr. Jukes' account was really animated and very full. His friend in the Western ocean trade imparted it freely to the other officers of his liner. "A chap I know writes to me about an extraordinary affair that happened on board his ship in that typhoon—you know—that we read of in the papers two months ago. It's the funniest thing! Just see for yourself what he says. I'll show you his letter."

There were phrases in it calculated to give the impression of light-hearted, indomitable resolution. Jukes had written them in good faith, for he felt thus when he wrote. He described with lurid effect the scenes in the 'tween-deck. ". . . It struck me in a flash that those confounded Chinamen couldn't tell we weren't a desperate kind of robbers. 'Tisn't good to part the Chinaman from his money if he is the stronger party. We need have been desperate indeed to go thieving in such weather, but what could these beggars know of us? So, without thinking of it twice, I got the hands away in a jiffy. Our work was done—that the old man had set his heart on. We cleared out without staying to inquire how they felt. I am convinced that if they had not been so unmercifully shaken, and afraid—each individual one of them—to stand up, we would have been torn to pieces. Oh! It was pretty complete, I can tell you; and you may run to and fro across the Pond to the end of time before you find yourself with such a job on your hands."

After this he alluded professionally to the damage done to the ship, and went on thus:

"It was when the weather quieted down that the situation became confoundedly delicate. It wasn't made any better by us having been lately transferred to the Siamese flag; though the skipper can't see that it makes any difference —'as long as *we* are on board'—he says. There are feelings that this man simply hasn't got—and there's an end of it. You might just as well try to make a bedpost understand. But apart from this it is an infernally lonely state for a ship to be going about the China seas with no proper consuls, not even a gunboat of her own anywhere, nor a body to go to in case of some trouble.

"My notion was to keep these Johnnies under hatches for another fifteen hours or so; as we weren't much farther than that from Fu-chau. We would find there, most likely, some sort of a man-of-war, and once under her guns we were safe enough; for surely any skipper of a man-of-war—English, French or Dutch—would see white men through as far as row on board goes. We could get rid of them and their money afterwards by delivering them to their Mandarin or Taotai, or whatever they call these chaps in goggles you see being carried about in sedan-chairs through their stinking streets.

"The old man wouldn't see it somehow. He wanted to keep the matter quiet. He got that notion into his head, and a steam windlass couldn't drag it out of him. He wanted as little fuss made as possible, for the sake of the ship's name and for the sake of the owners—'for the sake of all concerned,' says he, looking at me very hard. It made me angry hot. Of course you couldn't keep a thing like that quiet; but the chests had been secured in the usual manner and were safe enough for any earthly gale, while this had been an altogether fiendish business I couldn't give you even an idea of.

"Meantime, I could hardly keep on my feet. None of us had a spell of any sort for nearly thirty hours, and there the old man sat rubbing his chin, rubbing the top of his head, and so bothered he didn't even think of pulling his long boots off.

"'I hope, sir,' says I, 'you won't be letting them out on deck before we make ready for them in some shape or other.' Not, mind you, that I felt very sanguine about controlling these beggars if they meant to take charge. A trouble with a cargo of Chinamen is no child's play. I was dam' tired, too. 'I wish,' said I, 'you would let us throw the whole lot of these dollars down to them and leave them to fight it out amongst themselves, while we get a rest.'

"'Now you talk wild, Jukes,' says he, looking up in his slow way that makes you ache all over, somehow. 'We must plan out something that would be fair to all parties.'

"I had no end of work on hand, as you may imagine, so I set the hands going, and then I thought I would turn in a bit. I hadn't been asleep in my bunk ten minutes when in rushes the steward and begins to pull at my leg.

"'For God's sake, Mr. Jukes, come out! Come on deck quick, sir. Oh, do come out!'

"The fellow scared all the sense out of me. I didn't know what had happened: another hurricane—or what. Could hear no wind.

"'The Captain's letting them out. Oh, he is letting them out! Jump on deck, sir, and save us. The chief engineer has just run below for his revolver.'

"That's what I understood the fool to say. However, Father Rout swears he went in there only to get a clean pocket-handkerchief. Anyhow, I made one jump into my trousers and flew on deck aft. There was certainly a good deal of noise going on forward of the bridge. Four of the hands with the boss'en were at work abaft. I passed up to them some of the rifles all the ships on the China coast carry in the cabin, and led them on the bridge. On the way I ran against Old Sol, looking startled and sucking at an unlighted cigar.

"'Come along,' I shouted to him.

"We charged, the seven of us, up to the chart-room. All was over. There stood the old man with his sea-boots still drawn up to the hips and in shirt-sleeves—got warm thinking it out, I suppose. Bun Hin's dandy clerk at his elbow, as dirty as a sweep, was still green in the face. I could see directly I was in for something.

"'What the devil are these monkey tricks, Mr. Jukes?' asks the old man, as angry as ever he could be. I tell you frankly it made me lose my tongue. 'For God's sake, Mr. Jukes,' says he, 'do take away these rifles from the men. Somebody's sure to get hurt before long if you don't. Damme, if this ship isn't worse than Bedlam! Look sharp now. I want you up here to help me and Bun Hin's China-man to count that money. You wouldn't mind lending a hand, too, Mr. Rout, now you are here. The more of us the better.'

"He had settled it all in his mind while I was having a snooze. Had we been an English ship, or only going to land our cargo of coolies in an English port, like Hong-Kong, for instance, there would have been no end of inquiries and bother, claims for damages and so on. But these Chinamen know their officials better than we do.

"The hatches had been taken off already, and they were all on deck after a night and a day down below. It made you feel queer to see so many gaunt, wild faces together. The beggars stared about at the sky, at the sea, at the ship, as though they had expected the whole thing to have been blown to pieces. And no wonder! They had had a doing that would have shaken the soul out of a white man. But then they say a Chinaman has no soul. He has, though, something about him that is deuced tough. There was a fellow (amongst others of the badly hurt) who had had his eye all but knocked out. It stood out of his head the size of half a hen's egg. This would have laid out a white man on his back for a month: and yet there was that chap elbowing here and there in the crowd and talking to the others as if nothing had been the matter. They made a great hubbub amongst themselves, and whenever the old man showed his bald head on the foreside of the bridge, they would all leave off jawing and look at him from below.

"It seems that after he had done his thinking he made that Bun Hin's fellow go down and explain to them the only way they could get their money back. He told me after-

wards that, all the coolies having worked in the same place
and for the same length of time, he reckoned he would be
doing the fair thing by them as near as possible if he shared
all the cash we had picked up equally among the lot. You
couldn't tell one man's dollars from another's, he said, and
if you asked each man how much money he brought on
board he was afraid they would lie, and he would find himself a long way short. I think he was right there. As to giving up the money to any Chinese official he could scare up
in Fu-chau, he said he might just as well put the lot in his
own pocket at once for all the good it would be to them.
I suppose they thought so, too.

"We finished the distribution before dark. It was rather
a sight: the sea running high, the ship a wreck to look at,
these Chinamen staggering up on the bridge one by one
for their share, and the old man still booted, and in his shirt-
sleeves, busy paying out at the chart-room door, perspiring
like anything, and now and then coming down sharp on
myself or Father Rout about one thing or another not quite
to his mind. He took the share of those who were disabled
himself to them on the No. 2 hatch. There were three dollars left over, and these went to the three most damaged
coolies, one to each. We turned-to afterwards, and shovelled
out on deck heaps of wet rags, all sorts of fragments of
things without shape, and that you couldn't give a name
to, and let them settle the ownership themselves.

"This certainly is coming as near as can be to keeping
the thing quiet for the benefit of all concerned. What's your
opinion, you pampered mail-boat swell? The old chief says
that this was plainly the only thing that could be done. The
skipper remarked to me the other day, 'There are things you
find nothing about in books.' I think that he got out of it
very well for such a stupid man."

THE SECRET SHARER

On my right hand there were lines of fishing stakes resembling a mysterious system of half-submerged bamboo fences, incomprehensible in its division of the domain of tropical fishes, and crazy of aspect as if abandoned forever by some nomad tribe of fishermen now gone to the other end of the ocean; for there was no sign of human habitation as far as the eye could reach. To the left a group of barren islets, suggesting ruins of stone walls, towers, and blockhouses, had its foundations set in a blue sea that itself looked solid, so still and stable did it lie below my feet; even the track of light from the westering sun shone smoothly, without that animated glitter which tells of an imperceptible ripple. And when I turned my head to take a parting glance at the tug which had just left us anchored outside the bar, I saw the straight line of the flat shore joined to the stable sea, edge to edge, with a perfect and unmarked closeness, in one leveled floor half brown, half blue under the enormous dome of the sky. Corresponding in their insignificance to the islets of the sea, two small clumps of trees, one on each side of the only fault in the impeccable joint, marked the mouth of the river Meinam we had just left on the first preparatory stage of our homeward journey; and, far back on the inland level, a larger and loftier mass, the grove surrounding the great Paknam pagoda, was the only thing on which the eye could rest from the vain task of exploring the monotonous sweep of the horizon. Here and there gleams as of a few scattered pieces of silver marked the windings of the great river; and on the nearest of them, just within the bar, the tug steaming right into the land became lost to my sight, hull and funnel and masts, as though the impassive earth had swallowed her up without an effort, without a tremor. My eye followed the light cloud of her smoke, now here, now there, above the plain, according to the devious curves of the stream, but always fainter and farther away, till I lost it at last behind the miter-shaped hill of the great pagoda. And then I was left alone with my ship, anchored at the head of the Gulf of Siam.

She floated at the starting point of a long journey, very still in an immense stillness, the shadows of her spars flung far to the eastward by the setting sun. At that moment I was alone on her decks. There was not a sound in her— and around us nothing moved, nothing lived, not a canoe on the water, not a bird in the air, not a cloud in the sky. In this breathless pause at the threshold of a long passage we seemed to be measuring our fitness for a long and arduous enterprise, the appointed task of both our existences to be carried out, far from all human eyes, with only sky and sea for spectators and for judges.

There must have been some glare in the air to interfere with one's sight, because it was only just before the sun left us that my roaming eyes made out beyond the highest ridges of the principal islet of the group something which did away with the solemnity of perfect solitude. The tide of darkness flowed on swiftly; and with tropical suddenness a swarm of stars came out above the shadowy earth, while I lingered yet, my hand resting lightly on my ship's rail as if on the shoulder of a trusted friend. But, with all that multitude of celestial bodies staring down at one, the comfort of quiet communion with her was gone for good. And there were also disturbing sounds by this time—voices, footsteps forward; the steward flitted along the main-deck, a busily ministering spirit; a hand bell tinkled urgently under the poop deck. . . .

I found my two officers waiting for me near the supper

table, in the lighted cuddy. We sat down at once, and as I helped the chief mate, I said:

"Are you aware that there is a ship anchored inside the islands? I saw her mastheads above the ridge as the sun went down."

He raised sharply his simple face, overcharged by a terrible growth of whisker, and emitted his usual ejaculations: "Bless my soul, sir! You don't say so!"

My second mate was a round-cheeked, silent young man, grave beyond his years, I thought; but as our eyes happened to meet I detected a slight quiver on his lips. I looked down at once. It was not my part to encourage sneering on board my ship. It must be said, too, that I knew very little of my officers. In consequence of certain events of no particular significance, except to myself, I had been appointed to the command only a fortnight before. Neither did I know much of the hands forward. All these people had been together for eighteen months or so, and my position was that of the only stranger on board. I mention this because it has some bearing on what is to follow. But what I felt most was my being a stranger to the ship; and if all the truth must be told, I was somewhat of a stranger to myself. The youngest man on board (barring the second mate), and untried as yet by a position of the fullest responsibility, I was willing to take the adequacy of the others for granted. They had simply to be equal to their tasks; but I wondered how far I should turn out faithful to that ideal conception of one's own personality every man sets up for himself secretly.

Meantime the chief mate, with an almost visible effect of collaboration on the part of his round eyes and frightful whiskers, was trying to evolve a theory of the anchored ship. His dominant trait was to take all things into earnest consideration. He was of a painstaking turn of mind. As he used to say, he "liked to account to himself" for practically everything that came in his way, down to a miserable scorpion he had found in his cabin a week before. The why and the wherefore of that scorpion—how it got on board and came to select his room rather than the pantry (which was a dark place and more what a scorpion would be partial to), and how on earth it managed to drown itself in the inkwell of his writing desk—had exercised him infinitely. The ship within the islands was much more easily accounted for; and just as we were about to rise from table he made his pronouncement. She was, he doubted not, a ship from home lately arrived. Probably she drew too much water to cross the bar except at the top of spring tides. Therefore she went into that natural harbor to wait for a few days in preference to remaining in an open roadstead.

"That's so," confirmed the second mate, suddenly, in his slightly hoarse voice. "She draws over twenty feet. She's the Liverpool ship *Sephora* with a cargo of coal. Hundred and twenty-three days from Cardiff."

We looked at him in surprise.

"The tugboat skipper told me when he came on board for your letters, sir," explained the young man. "He expects to take her up the river the day after tomorrow."

After thus overwhelming us with the extent of his information he slipped out of the cabin. The mate observed regretfully that he "could not account for that young fellow's whims." What prevented him telling us all about it at once, he wanted to know.

I detained him as he was making a move. For the last two days the crew had had plenty of hard work, and the night before they had very little sleep. I felt painfully that I—a stranger—was doing something unusual when I directed him to let all hands turn in without setting an anchor watch. I proposed to keep on deck myself till one o'clock or thereabouts. I would get the second mate to relieve me at that hour.

"He will turn out the cook and the steward at four," I concluded, "and then give you a call. Of course at the slightest sign of any sort of wind we'll have the hands up and make a start at once."

He concealed his astonishment. "Very well, sir." Outside the cuddy he put his head in the second mate's door to inform him of my unheard-of caprice to take a five hours' anchor watch on myself. I heard the other raise his voice incredulously—"What? The Captain himself?" Then a few more murmurs, a door closed, then another. A few moments later I went on deck.

My strangeness, which had made me sleepless, had prompted that unconventional arrangement, as if I had expected in those solitary hours of the night to get on terms with the ship of which I knew nothing, manned by men of whom I knew very little more. Fast alongside a wharf, littered like any ship in port with a tangle of unrelated things, invaded by unrelated shore people, I had hardly seen her yet properly. Now, as she lay cleared for sea, the stretch of her main-deck seemed to me very fine under the stars. Very fine, very roomy for her size, and very inviting. I descended the poop and paced the waist, my mind picturing to myself the coming passage through the Malay Archipelago, down the Indian Ocean, and up the Atlantic. All its phases were familiar enough to me, every characteristic, all the alternatives which were likely to face me on the high seas —everything! . . . except the novel responsibility of command. But I took heart from the reasonable thought that the ship was like other ships, the men like other men, and that the sea was not likely to keep any special surprises expressly for my discomfiture.

Arrived at that comforting conclusion, I bethought myself of a cigar and went below to get it. All was still down there. Everybody at the after end of the ship was sleeping profoundly. I came out again on the quarter-deck, agreeably at ease in my sleeping suit on that warm breathless night, barefooted, a glowing cigar in my teeth, and, going forward, I was met by the profound silence of the fore end of the ship. Only as I passed the door of the forecastle I heard a deep, quiet, trustful sigh of some sleeper inside. And suddenly I rejoiced in the great security of the sea as compared with the unrest of the land, in my choice of that untempted life presenting no disquieting problems, invested with an elementary moral beauty by the absolute straightforwardness of its appeal and by the singleness of its purpose.

The riding light in the forerigging burned with a clear, untroubled, as if symbolic, flame, confident and bright in the mysterious shades of the night. Passing on my way aft

along the other side of the ship, I observed that the rope
side ladder, put over, no doubt, for the master of the tug
when he came to fetch away our letters, had not been
hauled in as it should have been. I became annoyed at this,
for exactitude in some small matters is the very soul of
discipline. Then I reflected that I had myself peremptorily
dismissed my officers from duty, and by my own act had
prevented the anchor watch being formally set and things
properly attended to. I asked myself whether it was wise
ever to interfere with the established routine of duties even
from the kindest of motives. My action might have made
me appear eccentric. Goodness only knew how that ab-
surdly whiskered mate would "account" for my conduct,
and what the whole ship thought of that informality of their
new captain. I was vexed with myself.

Not from compunction certainly, but, as it were mechani-
cally, I proceeded to get the ladder in myself. Now a side
ladder of that sort is a light affair and comes in easily, yet
my vigorous tug, which should have brought it flying on
board, merely recoiled upon my body in a totally unexpected jerk. What the devil! . . . I was so astounded by
the immovableness of that ladder that I remained stock-
still, trying to account for it to myself like that imbecile
mate of mine. In the end, of course, I put my head over
the rail.

The side of the ship made an opaque belt of shadow on
the darkling glassy shimmer of the sea. But I saw at once
something elongated and pale floating very close to the
ladder. Before I could form a guess a faint flash of phosphorescent light, which seemed to issue suddenly from the
naked body of a man, flickered in the sleeping water with
the elusive, silent play of summer lightning in a night sky.
With a gasp I saw revealed to my stare a pair of feet, the
long legs, a broad livid back immersed right up to the neck
in a greenish cadaverous glow. One hand, awash, clutched
the bottom rung of the ladder. He was complete but for
the head. A headless corpse! The cigar dropped out of my
gaping mouth with a tiny plop and a short hiss quite audible in the absolute stillness of all things under heaven. At
that I suppose he raised up his face, a dimly pale oval in

the shadow of the ship's side. But even then I could only barely make out down there the shape of his black-haired head. However, it was enough for the horrid, frost-bound sensation which had gripped me about the chest to pass off. The moment of vain exclamations was past, too. I only climbed on the spare spar and leaned over the rail as far as I could, to bring my eyes nearer to that mystery floating alongside.

As he hung by the ladder, like a resting swimmer, the sea lightning played about his limbs at every stir; and he appeared in it ghastly, silvery, fishlike. He remained as mute as a fish, too. He made no motion to get out of the water, either. It was inconceivable that he should not attempt to come on board, and strangely troubling to suspect that perhaps he did not want to. And my first words were prompted by just that troubled incertitude.

"What's the matter?" I asked in my ordinary tone, speaking down to the face upturned exactly under mine.

"Cramp," it answered, no louder. Then slightly anxious, "I say, no need to call anyone."

"I was not going to," I said.

"Are you alone on deck?"

"Yes."

I had somehow the impression that he was on the point of letting go the ladder to swim away beyond my ken—mysterious as he came. But, for the moment, this being appearing as if he had risen from the bottom of the sea (it was certainly the nearest land to the ship) wanted only to know the time. I told him. And he, down there, tentatively:

"I suppose your captain's turned in?"

"I am sure he isn't," I said.

He seemed to struggle with himself, for I heard something like the low, bitter murmur of doubt. "What's the good?" His next words came out with a hesitating effort.

"Look here, my man. Could you call him out quietly?"

I thought the time had come to declare myself.

"*I* am the captain."

I heard a "By Jove!" whispered at the level of the water. The phosphorescence flashed in the swirl of the water all about his limbs, his other hand seized the ladder.

"My name's Leggatt."

The voice was calm and resolute. A good voice. The self-possession of that man had somehow induced a corresponding state in myself. It was very quietly that I remarked:

"You must be a good swimmer."

"Yes. I've been in the water practically since nine o'clock. The question for me now is whether I am to let go this ladder and go on swimming till I sink from exhaustion, or—to come on board here."

I felt this was no mere formula of desperate speech, but a real alternative in the view of a strong soul. I should have gathered from this that he was young; indeed, it is only the young who are ever confronted by such clear issues. But at the time it was pure intuition on my part. A mysterious communication was established already between us two—in the face of that silent, darkened tropical sea. I was young, too; young enough to make no comment. The man in the water began suddenly to climb up the ladder, and I hastened away from the rail to fetch some clothes.

Before entering the cabin I stood still, listening in the lobby at the foot of the stairs. A faint snore came through the closed door of the chief mate's room. The second mate's door was on the hook, but the darkness in there was absolutely soundless. He, too, was young and could sleep like a stone. Remained the steward, but he was not likely to wake up before he was called. I got a sleeping suit out of my room and, coming back on deck, saw the naked man from the sea sitting on the main hatch, glimmering white in the darkness, his elbows on his knees and his head in his hands. In a moment he had concealed his damp body in a sleeping suit of the same gray-stripe pattern as the one I was wearing and followed me like my double on the poop. Together we moved right aft, barefooted, silent.

"What is it?" I asked in a deadened voice, taking the lighted lamp out of the binnacle, and raising it to his face.

"An ugly business."

He had rather regular features; a good mouth; light eyes under somewhat heavy, dark eyebrows; a smooth, square forehead; no growth on his cheeks; a small, brown mustache, and a well-shaped, round chin. His expression was concentrated, meditative, under the inspecting light of the lamp I held up to his face; such as a man thinking hard in solitude might wear. My sleeping suit was just right for his size. A well-knit young fellow of twenty-five at most. He caught his lower lip with the edge of white, even teeth.

"Yes," I said, replacing the lamp in the binnacle. The warm, heavy tropical night closed upon his head again.

"There's a ship over there," he murmured.

"Yes, I know. The *Sephora*. Did you know of us?"

"Hadn't the slightest idea. I am the mate of her——" He paused and corrected himself. "I should say I *was*."

"Aha! Something wrong?"

"Yes. Very wrong indeed. I've killed a man."

"What do you mean? Just now?"

"No, on the passage. Weeks ago. Thirty-nine south. When I say a man——"

"Fit of temper," I suggested, confidently.

The shadowy, dark head, like mine, seemed to nod imperceptibly above the ghostly gray of my sleeping suit. It was, in the night, as though I had been faced by my own reflection in the depths of a somber and immense mirror.

"A pretty thing to have to own up to for a Conway boy," murmured my double, distinctly.

"You're a Conway boy?"

"I am," he said, as if startled. Then, slowly . . . "Perhaps you too——"

It was so; but being a couple of years older I had left before he joined. After a quick interchange of dates a silence fell; and I thought suddenly of my absurd mate with his terrific whiskers and the "Bless my soul—you don't say so" type of intellect. My double gave me an inkling of his thoughts by saying: "My father's a parson in Norfolk. Do you see me before a judge and jury on that charge? For myself I can't see the necessity. There are fellows that an angel from heaven—— And I am not that. He was one of those creatures that are just simmering all the time with a silly sort of wickedness. Miserable devils that have no business to live at all. He wouldn't do his duty and wouldn't let anybody else do theirs. But what's the good of talking!

You know well enough the sort of ill-conditioned snarling cur——"

He appealed to me as if our experiences had been as identical as our clothes. And I knew well enough the pestiferous danger of such a character where there are no means of legal repression. And I knew well enough also that my double there was no homicidal ruffian. I did not think of asking him for details, and he told me the story roughly in brusque, disconnected sentences. I needed no more. I saw it all going on as though I were myself inside that other sleeping suit.

"It happened while we were setting a reefed foresail, at dusk. Reefed foresail! You understand the sort of weather. The only sail we had left to keep the ship running; so you may guess what it had been like for days. Anxious sort of job, that. He gave me some of his cursed insolence at the sheet. I tell you I was overdone with this terrific weather that seemed to have no end to it. Terrific, I tell you—and a deep ship. I believe the fellow himself was half crazed with funk. It was no time for gentlemanly reproof, so I turned round and felled him like an ox. He up and at me. We closed just as an awful sea made for the ship. All hands saw it coming and took to the rigging, but I had him by the throat, and went on shaking him like a rat, the men above us yelling, 'Look out! look out!' Then a crash as if the sky had fallen on my head. They say that for over ten minutes hardly anything was to be seen of the ship—just the three masts and a bit of the forecastle head and of the poop all awash driving along in a smother of foam. It was a miracle that they found us, jammed together behind the forebitts. It's clear that I meant business, because I was holding him by the throat still when they picked us up. He was black in the face. It was too much for them. It seems they rushed us aft together, gripped as we were, screaming 'Murder!' like a lot of lunatics, and broke into the cuddy. And the ship running for her life, touch and go all the time, any minute her last in a sea fit to turn your hair gray only a-looking at it. I understand that the skipper, too, started raving like the rest of them. The man had been deprived of sleep for more than a week, and to have this sprung on him at the height of a furious gale nearly drove him out of his mind. I wonder they didn't fling me overboard after getting the carcass of their precious shipmate out of my fingers. They had rather a job to separate us, I've been told. A sufficiently fierce story to make an old judge and a respectable jury sit up a bit. The first thing I heard when I came to myself was the maddening howling of that endless gale, and on that the voice of the old man. He was hanging on to my bunk, staring into my face out of his sou'wester.

"'Mr. Leggatt, you have killed a man. You can act no longer as chief mate of this ship.'"

His care to subdue his voice made it sound monotonous. He rested a hand on the end of the skylight to steady himself with, and all that time did not stir a limb, so far as I could see. "Nice little tale for a quiet tea party," he concluded in the same tone.

One of my hands, too, rested on the end of the skylight; neither did I stir a limb, so far as I knew. We stood less than a foot from each other. It occurred to me that if old "Bless my soul—you don't say so" were to put his head up the companion and catch sight of us, he would think he was seeing double, or imagine himself come upon a scene of weird witchcraft; the strange captain having a quiet confabulation by the wheel with his own gray ghost. I became very much concerned to prevent anything of the sort. I heard the other's soothing undertone.

"My father's a parson in Norfolk," it said. Evidently he had forgotten he had told me this important fact before. Truly a nice little tale.

"You had better slip down into my stateroom now," I said, moving off stealthily. My double followed my movements; our bare feet made no sound; I let him in, closed the door with care, and, after giving a call to the second mate, returned on deck for my relief.

"Not much sign of any wind yet," I remarked when he approached.

"No, sir. Not much," he assented, sleepily, in his hoarse voice, with just enough deference, no more, and barely suppressing a yawn.

"Well, that's all you have to look out for. You have got your orders."

"Yes, sir."

I paced a turn or two on the poop and saw him take up his position face forward with his elbow in the ratlines of the mizzen rigging before I went below. The mate's faint snoring was still going on peacefully. The cuddy lamp was burning over the table on which stood a vase with flowers, a polite attention from the ship's provision merchant—the last flowers we should see for the next three months at the very least. Two bunches of bananas hung from the beam symmetrically, one on each side of the rudder casing. Everything was as before in the ship—except that two of her captain's sleeping suits were simultaneously in use, one motionless in the cuddy, the other keeping very still in the captain's stateroom.

It must be explained here that my cabin had the form of the capital letter L, the door being within the angle and opening into the short part of the letter. A couch was to the left, the bed place to the right; my writing desk and the chronometers' table faced the door. But anyone opening it, unless he stepped right inside, had no view of what I call the long (or vertical) part of the letter. It contained some lockers surmounted by a bookcase; and a few clothes, a thick jacket or two, caps, oilskin coat, and such like, hung on hooks. There was at the bottom of that part a door opening into my bathroom, which could be entered also directly from the saloon. But that way was never used.

The mysterious arrival had discovered the advantage of this particular shape. Entering my room, lighted strongly by a big bulkhead lamp swung on gimbals above my writing desk, I did not see him anywhere till he stepped out quietly from behind the coats hung in the recessed part.

"I heard somebody moving about, and went in there at once," he whispered.

I, too, spoke under my breath.

"Nobody is likely to come in here without knocking and getting permission."

He nodded. His face was thin and the sunburn faded, as though he had been ill. And no wonder. He had been,

I heard presently, kept under arrest in his cabin for nearly seven weeks. But there was nothing sickly in his eyes or in his expression. He was not a bit like me, really; yet, as we stood leaning over my bed place, whispering side by side, with our dark heads together and our backs to the door, anybody bold enough to open it stealthily would have been treated to the uncanny sight of a double captain busy talking in whispers with his other self.

"But all this doesn't tell me how you came to hang on to our side ladder," I inquired, in the hardly audible murmurs we used, after he had told me something more of the proceedings on board the *Sephora* once the bad weather was over.

"When we sighted Java Head I had had time to think all those matters out several times over. I had six weeks of doing nothing else, and with only an hour or so every evening for a tramp on the quarter-deck."

He whispered, his arms folded on the side of my bed place, staring through the open port. And I could imagine perfectly the manner of this thinking out—a stubborn if not a steadfast operation; something of which I should have been perfectly incapable.

"I reckoned it would be dark before we closed with the land," he continued, so low that I had to strain my hearing near as we were to each other, shoulder touching shoulder almost. "So I asked to speak to the old man. He always seemed very sick when he came to see me—as if he could not look me in the face. You know, that foresail saved the ship. She was too deep to have run long under bare poles. And it was I that managed to set it for him. Anyway, he came. When I had him in my cabin—he stood by the door looking at me as if I had the halter round my neck already—I asked him right away to leave my cabin door unlocked at night while the ship was going through Sunda Straits. There would be the Java coast within two or three miles, off Angier Point. I wanted nothing more. I've had a prize for swimming my second year in the Conway."

"I can believe it," I breathed out.

"God only knows why they locked me in every night. To see some of their faces you'd have thought they were afraid

I'd go about at night strangling people. Am I a murdering brute? Do I look it? By Jove! if I had been he wouldn't have trusted himself like that into my room. You'll say I might have chucked him aside and bolted out, there and then—it was dark already. Well, no. And for the same reason I wouldn't think of trying to smash the door. There would have been a rush to stop me at the noise, and I did not mean to get into a confounded scrimmage. Somebody else might have got killed—for I would not have broken out only to get chucked back, and I did not want any more of that work. He refused, looking more sick than ever. He was afraid of the men, and also of that old second mate of his who had been sailing with him for years—a gray-headed old humbug; and his steward, too, had been with him devil knows how long—seventeen years or more—a dogmatic sort of loafer who hated me like poison, just because I was the chief mate. No chief mate ever made more than one voyage in the *Sephora*, you know. Those two old chaps ran the ship. Devil only knows what the skipper wasn't afraid of (all his nerve went to pieces altogether in that hellish spell of bad weather we had)—of what the law would do to him —of his wife, perhaps. Oh, yes! she's on board. Though I don't think she would have meddled. She would have been only too glad to have me out of the ship in any way. The 'brand of Cain' business, don't you see. That's all right. I was ready enough to go off wandering on the face of the earth—and that was price enough to pay for an Abel of that sort. Anyhow, he wouldn't listen to me. 'This thing must take its course. I represent the law here.' He was shaking like a leaf. 'So you won't?' 'No!' 'Then I hope you will be able to sleep on that,' I said, and turned my back on him. 'I wonder that *you* can,' cries he, and locks the door.

"Well after that, I couldn't. Not very well. That was three weeks ago. We have had a slow passage through the Java Sea; drifted about Carimata for ten days. When we anchored here they thought, I suppose, it was all right. The nearest land (and that's five miles) is the ship's destination; the consul would soon set about catching me; and there would have been no object in bolting to these islets there. I don't suppose there's a drop of water on them. I don't know how it was, but tonight that steward, after bringing me my supper, went out to let me eat it, and left the door unlocked. And I ate it—all there was, too. After I had finished I strolled out on the quarter-deck. I don't know that I meant to do anything. A breath of fresh air was all I wanted, I believe. Then a sudden temptation came over me. I kicked off my slippers and was in the water before I had made up my mind fairly. Somebody heard the splash and they raised an awful hullabaloo. 'He's gone! Lower the boats! He's committed suicide! No, he's swimming.' Certainly I was swimming. It's not so easy for a swimmer like me to commit suicide by drowning. I landed on the nearest islet before the boat left the ship's side. I heard them pulling about in the dark, hailing, and so on, but after a bit they gave up. Everything quieted down and the anchorage became as still as death. I sat down on a stone and began to think. I felt certain they would start searching for me at daylight. There was no place to hide on those stony things —and if there had been, what would have been the good? But now I was clear of that ship, I was not going back. So after a while I took off all my clothes, tied them up in a bundle with a stone inside, and dropped them in the deep water on the outer side of that islet. That was suicide enough for me. Let them think what they liked, but I didn't mean to drown myself. I meant to swim till I sank—but that's not the same thing. I struck out for another of these little islands, and it was from that one that I first saw your riding light. Something to swim for. I went on easily, and on the way I came upon a flat rock a foot or two above water. In the daytime, I dare say, you might make it out with a glass from your poop. I scrambled up on it and rested myself for a bit. Then I made another start. That last spell must have been over a mile."

His whisper was getting fainter and fainter, and all the time he stared straight out through the porthole, in which there was not even a star to be seen. I had not interrupted him. There was something that made comment impossible in his narrative, or perhaps in himself; a sort of feeling, a quality, which I can't find a name for. And when he ceased, all I found was a futile whisper: "So you swam for our light?"

"Yes—straight for it. It was something to swim for. I couldn't see any stars low down because the coast was in the way, and I couldn't see the land, either. The water was like glass. One might have been swimming in a confounded thousand-feet deep cistern with no place for scrambling out anywhere; but what I didn't like was the notion of swimming round and round like a crazed bullock before I gave out; and as I didn't mean to go back . . . No. Do you see me being hauled back, stark naked, off one of these little islands by the scruff of the neck and fighting like a wild beast? Somebody would have got killed for certain, and I did not want any of that. So I went on. Then your ladder——"

"Why didn't you hail the ship?" I asked, a little louder.

He touched my shoulder lightly. Lazy footsteps came right over our heads and stopped. The second mate had crossed from the other side of the poop and might have been hanging over the rail for all we knew.

"He couldn't hear us talking—could he?" My double breathed into my very ear, anxiously.

His anxiety was in answer, a sufficient answer, to the question I had put to him. An answer containing all the difficulty of that situation. I closed the porthole quietly, to make sure. A louder word might have been overheard.

"Who's that?" he whispered then.

"My second mate. But I don't know much more of the fellow than you do."

And I told him a little about myself. I had been appointed to take charge while I least expected anything of the sort, not quite a fortnight ago. I didn't know either the ship or the people. Hadn't had the time in port to look about me or size anybody up. And as to the crew, all they knew was that I was appointed to take the ship home. For the rest, I was almost as much of a stranger on board as himself, I said. And at the moment I felt it most acutely. I felt that it would take very little to make me a suspect person in the eyes of the ship's company.

He had turned about meantime; and we, the two

strangers in the ship, faced each other in identical attitudes.

"Your ladder——" he murmured, after a silence. "Who'd have thought of finding a ladder hanging over at night in a ship anchored out here! I felt just then a very unpleasant faintness. After the life I've been leading for nine weeks, anybody would have got out of condition. I wasn't capable of swimming round as far as your rudder chains. And, lo and behold! there was a ladder to get hold of. After I gripped it I said to myself, 'What's the good?' When I saw a man's head looking over I thought I would swim away presently and leave him shouting—in whatever language it was. I didn't mind being looked at. I—I liked it. And then you speaking to me so quietly—as if you had expected me —made me hold on a little longer. It had been a confounded lonely time—I don't mean while swimming. I was glad to talk a little to somebody that didn't belong to the *Sephora*. As to asking for the captain, that was a mere impulse. It could have been no use, with all the ship knowing about me and the other people pretty certain to be round here in the morning. I don't know—I wanted to be seen, to talk with somebody, before I went on. I don't know what I would have said. . . . 'Fine night, isn't it?' or something of the sort."

"Do you think they will be round here presently?" I asked with some incredulity.

"Quite likely," he said, faintly.

He looked extremely haggard all of a sudden. His head rolled on his shoulders.

"H'm. We shall see then. Meantime get into that bed," I whispered. "Want help? There."

It was a rather high bed place with a set of drawers underneath. This amazing swimmer really needed the lift I gave him by seizing his leg. He tumbled in, rolled over on his back, and flung one arm across his eyes. And then, with his face nearly hidden, he must have looked exactly as I used to look in that bed. I gazed upon my other self for a while before drawing across carefully the two green serge curtains which ran on a brass rod. I thought for a moment of pinning them together for greater safety, but I sat down on the couch, and once there I felt unwilling to rise and hunt for a pin. I would do it in a moment. I was extremely tired, in a peculiarly intimate way, by the strain of stealthiness, by the effort of whispering and the general secrecy of this excitement. It was three o'clock by now and I had been on my feet since nine, but I was not sleepy; I could not have gone to sleep. I sat there, fagged out, looking at the curtains, trying to clear my mind of the confused sensation of being in two places at once, and greatly bothered by an exasperating knocking in my head. It was a relief to discover suddenly that it was not in my head at all, but on the outside of the door. Before I could collect myself the words "Come in" were out of my mouth, and the steward entered with a tray, bringing in my morning coffee. I had slept, after all, and I was so frightened that I shouted, "This way! I am here, steward," as though he had been miles away. He put down the tray on the table next the couch and only then said, very quietly, "I can see you are here, sir." I felt him give me a keen look, but I dared not meet his eyes just then. He must have wondered why I had drawn the curtains of my bed before going to sleep on the couch. He went out, hooking the door open as usual.

I heard the crew washing decks above me. I knew I would have been told at once if there had been any wind. Calm, I thought, and I was doubly vexed. Indeed, I felt dual more than ever. The steward reappeared suddenly in the doorway. I jumped up from the couch so quickly that he gave a start.

"What do your want here?"

"Close your port, sir—they are washing decks."

"It is closed," I said, reddening.

"Very well, sir." But he did not move from the doorway and returned my stare in an extraordinary, equivocal manner for a time. Then his eyes wavered, all his expression changed, and in a voice unusually gentle, almost coaxingly:

"May I come in to take the empty cup away, sir?"

"Of course!" I turned my back on him while he popped in and out. Then I unhooked and closed the door and even pushed the bolt. This sort of thing could not go on very long. The cabin was as hot as an oven, too. I took a peep at my double, and discovered that he had not moved, his arm was still over his eyes; but his chest heaved; his hair was wet; his chin glistened with perspiration. I reached over him and opened the port.

"I must show myself on deck," I reflected.

Of course, theoretically, I could do what I liked, with no one to say nay to me within the whole circle of the horizon; but to lock my cabin door and take the key away I did not dare. Directly I put my head out of the companion I saw the group of my two officers, the second mate barefooted, the chief mate in long India-rubber boots, near the break of the poop, and the steward halfway down the poop ladder talking to them eagerly. He happened to catch sight of me and dived, the second ran down on the main-deck shouting some order or other, and the chief mate came to meet me, touching his cap.

There was a sort of curiosity in his eye that I did not like. I don't know whether the steward had told them that I was "queer" only, or downright drunk, but I know the man meant to have a good look at me. I watched him coming with a smile which, as he got into point-blank range, took effect and froze his very whiskers. I did not give him time to open his lips.

"Square the yards by lifts and braces before the hands go to breakfast."

It was the first particular order I had given on board that ship; and I stayed on deck to see it executed, too. I had felt the need of asserting myself without loss of time. That sneering young cub got taken down a peg or two on that occasion, and I also seized the opportunity of having a good look at the face of every foremast man as they filed past me to go to the after braces. At breakfast time, eating nothing myself, I presided with such frigid dignity that the two mates were only too glad to escape from the cabin as soon as decency permitted; and all the time the dual working of my mind distracted me almost to the point of insanity. I was constantly watching myself, my secret self, as dependent on my actions as my own personality, sleeping in that bed, behind that door which faced me as I sat at the head of the table. It was very much like being mad, only it was worse because one was aware of it.

I had to shake him for a solid minute, but when at last he opened his eyes it was in the full possession of his senses, with an inquiring look.

"All's well so far," I whispered. "Now you must vanish into the bathroom."

He did so, as noiseless as a ghost, and then I rang for the steward, and facing him boldly, directed him to tidy up my stateroom while I was having my bath—"and be quick about it." As my tone admitted of no excuses, he said, "Yes, sir," and ran off to fetch his dustpan and brushes. I took a bath and did most of my dressing, splashing, and whistling softly for the steward's edification, while the secret sharer of my life stood drawn up bolt upright in that little space, his face looking very sunken in daylight, his eyelids lowered under the stern, dark line of his eyebrows drawn together by a slight frown.

When I left him there to go back to my room the steward was finishing dusting. I sent for the mate and engaged him in some insignificant conversation. It was, as it were, trifling with the terrific character of his whiskers; but my object was to give him an opportunity for a good look at my cabin. And then I could at last shut, with a clear conscience, the door of my stateroom and get my double back into the recessed part. There was nothing else for it. He had to sit still on a small folding stool, half smothered by the heavy coats hanging there. We listened to the steward going into the bathroom out of the saloon, filling the water bottles there, scrubbing the bath, setting things to rights, whisk, bang, clatter—out again into the saloon—turn the key—click. Such was my scheme for keeping my second self invisible. Nothing better could be contrived under the circumstances. And there we sat; I at my writing desk ready to appear busy with some papers, he behind me out of sight of the door. It would not have been prudent to talk in daytime; and I could not have stood the excitement of that queer sense of whispering to myself. Now and then, glancing over my shoulder, I saw him far back there, sitting rigidly on the low stool, his bare feet close together, his arms folded, his head hanging on his breast—and perfectly still. Anybody would have taken him for me.

I was fascinated by it myself. Every moment I had to glance over my shoulder. I was looking at him when a voice outside the door said:

"Beg pardon, sir."

"Well!" . . . I kept my eyes on him, and so when the voice outside the door announced, "There's a ship's boat coming our way, sir," I saw him give a start—the first movement he had made for hours. But he did not raise his bowed head.

"All right. Get the ladder over."

I hesitated. Should I whisper something to him? But what? His immobility seemed to have been never disturbed. What could I tell him he did not know already? . . . Finally I went on deck.

II

The skipper of the *Sephora* had a thin red whisker all round his face, and the sort of complexion that goes with hair of that color; also the particular, rather smeary shade of blue in the eyes. He was not exactly a showy figure; his shoulders were high, his stature but middling—one leg slightly more bandy than the other. He shook hands, looking vaguely around. A spiritless tenacity was his main characteristic, I judged. I behaved with a politeness which seemed to disconcert him. Perhaps he was shy. He mumbled to me as if he were ashamed of what he was saying; gave his name (it was something like Archbold—but at this distance of years I hardly am sure), his ship's name, and a few other particulars of that sort, in the manner of a criminal making a reluctant and doleful confession. He had had terrible weather on the passage out—terrible—terrible—wife aboard, too.

By this time we were seated in the cabin and the steward brought in a tray with a bottle and glasses. "Thanks! No." Never took liquor. Would have some water, though. He drank two tumblerfuls. Terrible thirsty work. Ever since daylight had been exploring the islands round his ship.

"What was that for—fun?" I asked, with an appearance of polite interest.

"No!" He sighed. "Painful duty."

As he persisted in his mumbling and I wanted my double to hear every word, I hit upon the notion of informing him that I regretted to say I was hard of hearing.

"Such a young man, too!" he nodded, keeping his smeary blue, unintelligent eyes fastened upon me. "What was the cause of it—some disease?" he inquired, without the least sympathy and as if he thought that, if so, I'd got no more than I deserved.

"Yes; disease," I admitted in a cheerful tone which seemed to shock him. But my point was gained, because he had to raise his voice to give me his tale. It is not worth while to record that version. It was just over two months since all this had happened, and he had thought so much about it that he seemed completely muddled as to its bearings, but still immensely impressed.

"What would you think of such a thing happening on board your own ship? I've had the *Sephora* for these fifteen years. I am a well-known shipmaster."

He was densely distressed—and perhaps I should have sympathized with him if I had been able to detach my mental vision from the unsuspected sharer of my cabin as though he were my second self. There he was on the other side of the bulkhead, four or five feet from us, no more, as we sat in the saloon. I looked politely at Captain Archbold (if that was his name), but it was the other I saw, in a gray sleeping suit, seated on a low stool, his bare feet close together, his arms folded, and every word said between us falling into the ears of his dark head bowed on his chest.

"I have been at sea now, man and boy, for seven-and-thirty years, and I've never heard of such a thing happening in an English ship. And that it should be my ship. Wife on board, too."

I was hardly listening to him.

"Don't you think," I said, "that the heavy sea which, you told me, came aboard just then might have killed the man?

I have seen the sheer weight of a sea kill a man very neatly, by simply breaking his neck."

"Good God!" he uttered, impressively, fixing his smeary blue eyes on me. "The sea! No man killed by the sea ever looked like that." He seemed positively scandalized at my suggestion. And as I gazed at him certainly not prepared for anything original on his part, he advanced his head close to mine and thrust his tongue out at me so suddenly that I couldn't help starting back.

After scoring over my calmness in this graphic way he nodded wisely. If I had seen the sight, he assured me, I would never forget it as long as I lived. The weather was too bad to give the corpse a proper sea burial. So next day at dawn they took it up on the poop, covering its face with a bit of bunting; he read a short prayer, and then, just as it was, in its oilskins and long boots, they launched it amongst those mountainous seas that seemed ready every moment to swallow up the ship herself and the terrified lives on board of her.

"That reefed foresail saved you," I threw in.

"Under God—it did," he exclaimed fervently. "It was by a special mercy, I firmly believe, that it stood some of those hurricane squalls."

"It was the setting of that sail which——" I began.

"God's own hand in it," he interrupted me. "Nothing less could have done it. I don't mind telling you that I hardly dared give the order. It seemed impossible that we could touch anything without losing it, and then our last hope would have been gone."

The terror of that gale was on him yet. I let him go on for a bit, then said, casually—as if returning to a minor subject:

"You were very anxious to give up your mate to the shore people, I believe?"

He was. To the law. His obscure tenacity on that point had in it something incomprehensible and a little awful; something, as it were, mystical, quite apart from his anxiety that he should not be suspected of "countenancing any doings of that sort." Seven-and-thirty virtuous years at sea, of which over twenty of immaculate command, and the last fifteen in the *Sephora*, seemed to have laid him under some pitiless obligation.

"And you know," he went on, groping shame-facedly amongst his feelings, "I did not engage that young fellow. His people had some interest with my owners. I was in a way forced to take him on. He looked very smart, very gentlemanly, and all that. But do you know—I never liked him, somehow. I am a plain man. You see, he wasn't exactly the sort for the chief mate of a ship like the *Sephora*."

I had become so connected in thoughts and impressions with the secret sharer of my cabin that I felt as if I, personally, were being given to understand that I, too, was not the sort that would have done for the chief mate of a ship like the *Sephora*. I had no doubt of it in my mind.

"Not at all the style of man. You understand," he insisted, superfluously, looking hard at me.

I smiled urbanely. He seemed at a loss for a while.

"I suppose I must report a suicide."

"Beg pardon?"

"Sui-cide! That's what I'll have to write to my owners directly I get in."

"Unless you manage to recover him before tomorrow," I assented, dispassionately. . . . "I mean, alive."

He mumbled something which I really did not catch, and I turned my ear to him in a puzzled manner. He fairly bawled:

"The land—I say, the mainland is at least seven miles off my anchorage."

"About that."

My lack of excitement, of curiosity, of surprise, of any sort of pronounced interest, began to arouse his distrust. But except for the felicitous pretense of deafness I had not tried to pretend anything. I had felt utterly incapable of playing the part of ignorance properly, and therefore was afraid to try. It is also certain that he had brought some ready-made suspicions with him, and that he viewed my politeness as a strange and unnatural phenomenon. And yet how else could I have received him? Not heartily! That was impossible for psychological reasons, which I need not state here. My only object was to keep off his inquiries.

Surlily? Yes, but surliness might have provoked a point-blank question. From its novelty to him and from its nature, punctilious courtesy was the manner best calculated to restrain the man. But there was the danger of his breaking through my defense bluntly. I could not, I think, have met him by a direct lie, also for psychological (not moral) reasons. If he had only known how afraid I was of his putting my feeling of identity with the other to the test! But, strangely enough—(I thought of it only afterwards)—I believe that he was not a little disconcerted by the reverse side of that weird situation, by something in me that reminded him of the man he was seeking—suggested a mysterious similitude to the young fellow he had distrusted and disliked from the first.

However that might have been, the silence was not very prolonged. He took another oblique step.

"I reckon I had no more than a two-mile pull to your ship. Not a bit more."

"And quite enough, too, in this awful heat," I said.

Another pause full of mistrust followed. Necessity, they say, is mother of invention, but fear, too, is not barren of ingenious suggestions. And I was afraid he would ask me point-blank for news of my other self.

"Nice little saloon, isn't it?" I remarked, as if noticing for the first time the way his eyes roamed from one closed door to the other. "And very well fitted out, too. Here, for instance," I continued, reaching over the back of my seat negligently and flinging the door open, "is my bathroom."

He made an eager movement, but hardly gave it a glance. I got up, shut the door of the bathroom, and invited him to have a look round, as if I were very proud of my accommodation. He had to rise and be shown round, but he went through the business without any raptures whatever.

"And now we'll have a look at my stateroom," I declared, in a voice as loud as I dared to make it, crossing the cabin to the starboard side with purposely heavy steps.

He followed me in and gazed around. My intelligent double had vanished. I played my part.

"Very convenient—isn't it?"

"Very nice. Very comf . . ." He didn't finish and went

out brusquely as if to escape from some unrighteous wiles of mine. But it was not to be. I had been too frightened not to feel vengeful; I felt I had him on the run, and I meant to keep him on the run. My polite insistence must have had something menacing in it, because he gave in suddenly. And I did not let him off a single item; mate's room, pantry, storerooms, the very sail locker which was also under the poop—he had to look into them all. When at last I showed him out on the quarter-deck he drew a long, spiritless sigh, and mumbled dismally that he must really be going back to his ship now. I desired my mate, who had joined us, to see to the captain's boat.

The man of whiskers gave a blast on the whistle which he used to wear hanging round his neck, and yelled, "*Sephora's* away!" My double down there in my cabin must have heard, and certainly could not feel more relieved than I. Four fellows came running out from somewhere forward and went over the side, while my own men, appearing on deck too, lined the rail. I escorted my visitor to the gangway ceremoniously, and nearly overdid it. He was a tenacious beast. On the very ladder he lingered, and in that unique, guiltily conscientious manner of sticking to the point:

"I say . . . you . . . you don't think that——"

I covered his voice loudly:

"Certainly not. . . . I am delighted. Good-by."

I had an idea of what he meant to say, and just saved myself by the privilege of defective hearing. He was too shaken generally to insist, but my mate, close witness of that parting, looked mystified and his face took on a thoughtful cast. As I did not want to appear as if I wished to avoid all communication with my officers, he had the opportunity to address me.

"Seems a very nice man. His boat's crew told our chaps a very extraordinary story, if what I am told by the steward is true. I suppose you had it from the captain, sir?"

"Yes. I had a story from the captain."

"A very horrible affair—isn't it, sir?"

"It is."

"Beats all these tales we hear about murders in Yankee ships."

"I don't think it beats them. I don't think it resembles them in the least."

"Bless my soul—you don't say so! But of course I've no acquaintance whatever with American ships, not I, so I couldn't go against your knowledge. It's horrible enough for me. . . . But the queerest part is that those fellows seemed to have some idea the man was hidden aboard here. They had really. Did you ever hear of such a thing?"

"Preposterous—isn't it?"

We were walking to and fro athwart the quarter-deck. No one of the crew forward could be seen (the day was Sunday), and the mate pursued:

"There was some little dispute about it. Our chaps took offense. 'As if we would harbor a thing like that,' they said. 'Wouldn't you like to look for him in our coalhole?' Quite a tiff. But they made it up in the end. I suppose he did drown himself. Don't you, sir?"

"I don't suppose anything."

"You have no doubt in the matter, sir?"

"None whatever."

I left him suddenly. I felt I was producing a bad impression, but with my double down there it was most trying to be on deck. And it was almost as trying to be below. Altogether a nerve-trying situation. But on the whole I felt less torn in two when I was with him. There was no one in the whole ship whom I dared take into my confidence. Since the hands had got to know his story, it would have been impossible to pass him off for anyone else, and an accidental discovery was to be dreaded now more than ever. . . .

The steward being engaged in laying the table for dinner, we could talk only with our eyes when I first went down. Later in the afternoon we had a cautious try at whispering. The Sunday quietness of the ship was against us; the stillness of air and water around her was against us; the elements, the men were against us—everything was against us in our secret partnership; time itself—for this could not go on forever. The very trust in Providence was,

I suppose, denied to his guilt. Shall I confess that this thought cast me down very much? And as to the chapter of accidents which counts for so much in the book of success, I could only hope that it was closed. For what favorable accident could be expected?

"Did you hear everything?" were my first words as soon as we took up our position side by side, leaning over my bed place.

He had. And the proof of it was his earnest whisper, "The man told you he hardly dared to give the order."

I understood the reference to be to that saving foresail.

"Yes. He was afraid of it being lost in the setting."

"I assure you he never gave the order. He may think he did, but he never gave it. He stood there with me on the break of the poop after the main topsail blew away, and whimpered about our last hope—positively whimpered about it and nothing else—and the night coming on! To hear one's skipper go on like that in such weather was enough to drive any fellow out of his mind. It worked me up into a sort of desperation. I just took it into my own hands and went away from him, boiling, and—— But what's the use telling you? *You* know! . . . Do you think that if I had not been pretty fierce with them I should have got the men to do anything? Not It! The bo's'n perhaps? Perhaps! It wasn't a heavy sea—it was a sea gone mad! I suppose the end of the world will be something like that; and a man may have the heart to see it coming once and be done with it—but to have to face it day after day—— I don't blame anybody. I was precious little better than the rest. Only—I was an officer of that old coal wagon, anyhow——"

"I quite understand," I conveyed that sincere assurance into his ear. He was out of breath with whispering; I could hear him pant slightly. It was all very simple. The same strung-up force which had given twenty-four men a chance, at least, for their lives, had, in a sort of recoil, crushed an unworthy mutinous existence.

But I had no leisure to weigh the merits of the matter—footsteps in the saloon, a heavy knock. "There's enough wind to get under way with, sir." Here was the call of a new claim upon my thoughts and even upon my feelings.

"Turn the hands up," I cried through the door. "I'll be on deck directly."

I was going out to make the acquaintance of my ship. Before I left the cabin our eyes met—the eyes of the only two strangers on board. I pointed to the recessed part where the little campstool awaited him and laid my finger on my lips. He made a gesture—somewhat vague—a little mysterious, accompanied by a faint smile, as if of regret.

This is not the place to enlarge upon the sensations of a man who feels for the first time a ship move under his feet to his own independent word. In my case they were not unalloyed. I was not wholly alone with my command; for there was that stranger in my cabin. Or rather, I was not completely and wholly with her. Part of me was absent. That mental feeling of being in two places at once affected me physically as if the mood of secrecy had penetrated my very soul. Before an hour had elapsed since the ship had begun to move, having occasion to ask the mate (he stood by my side) to take a compass bearing of the pagoda, I caught myself reaching up to his ear in whispers. I say I caught myself, but enough had escaped to startle the man. I can't describe it otherwise than by saying that he shied. A grave, preoccupied manner, as though he were in possession of some perplexing intelligence, did not leave him henceforth. A little later I moved away from the rail to look at the compass with such a stealthy gait that the helmsman noticed it—and I could not help noticing the unusual roundness of his eyes. These are trifling instances, though it's to no commander's advantage to be suspected of ludicrous eccentricities. But I was also more seriously affected. There are to a seaman certain words, gestures, that should in given conditions come as naturally, as instinctively as the winking of a menaced eye. A certain order should spring on to his lips without thinking; a certain sign should get itself made, so to speak, without reflection. But all unconscious alertness had abandoned me. I had to make an effort of will to recall myself back (from the cabin) to the conditions of the moment. I felt that I was appearing an irresolute commander to those people who were watching me more or less critically.

And, besides, there were the scares. On the second day out, for instance, coming off the deck in the afternoon (I had straw slippers on my bare feet) I stopped at the open pantry door and spoke to the steward. He was doing something there with his back to me. At the sound of my voice he nearly jumped out of his skin, as the saying is, and incidentally broke a cup.

"What on earth's the matter with you?" I asked, astonished.

He was extremely confused. "Beg your pardon, sir. I made sure you were in your cabin."

"You see I wasn't."

"No, sir. I could have sworn I had heard you moving in there not a moment ago. It's most extraordinary . . . very sorry, sir."

I passed on with an inward shudder. I was so identified with my secret double that I did not even mention the fact in those scanty, fearful whispers we exchanged. I suppose he had made some slight noise of some kind or other. It would have been miraculous if he hadn't at one time or another. And yet, haggard as he appeared, he looked always perfectly self-controlled, more than calm—almost invulnerable. On my suggestion he remained almost entirely in the bathroom, which, upon the whole, was the safest place. There could be really no shadow of an excuse for anyone ever wanting to go in there, once the steward had done with it. It was a very tiny place. Sometimes he reclined on the floor, his legs bent, his head sustained on one elbow. At others I would find him on the campstool, sitting in his gray sleeping suit and with his cropped dark hair like a patient, unmoved convict. At night I would smuggle him into my bed place, and we would whisper together, with the regular footfalls of the officer of the watch passing and repassing over our heads. It was an infinitely miserable time. It was lucky that some tins of fine preserves were stowed in a locker in my stateroom; hard bread I could always get hold of; and so he lived on stewed chicken, *pâté de foie gras*, asparagus, cooked oysters, sardines—on all sorts of abominable sham delicacies out of tins. My early-morning coffee he always drank; and it was all I dared do for him in that respect.

Every day there was the horrible maneuvering to go through so that my room and then the bathroom should be done in the usual way. I came to hate the sight of the steward, to abhor the voice of that harmless man. I felt that it was he who would bring on the disaster of discovery. It hung like a sword over our heads.

The fourth day out, I think (we were then working down the east side of the Gulf of Siam, tack for tack, in light winds and smooth water)—the fourth day, I say, of this miserable juggling with the unavoidable, as we sat at our evening meal, that man, whose slightest movement I dreaded, after putting down the dishes ran up on deck busily. This could not be dangerous. Presently he came down again; and then it appeared that he had remembered a coat of mine which I had thrown over a rail to dry after having been wetted in a shower which had passed over the ship in the afternoon. Sitting stolidly at the head of the table I became terrified at the sight of the garment on his arm. Of course he made for my door. There was no time to lose.

"Steward," I thundered. My nerves were so shaken that I could not govern my voice and conceal my agitation. This was the sort of thing that made my terrifically whiskered mate tap his forehead with his forefinger. I had detected him using that gesture while talking on deck with a confidential air to the carpenter. It was too far to hear a word, but I had no doubt that this pantomime could only refer to the strange new captain.

"Yes, sir," the pale-faced steward turned resignedly to me. It was this maddening course of being shouted at, checked without rhyme or reason, arbitrarily chased out of my cabin, suddenly called into it, sent flying out of his pantry on incomprehensible errands, that accounted for the growing wretchedness of his expression.

"Where are you going with that coat?"

"To your room, sir."

"Is there another shower coming?"

"I'm sure I don't know, sir. Shall I go up again and see, sir?"

"No! never mind."

My object was attained, as of course my other self in there would have heard everything that passed. During this interlude my two officers never raised their eyes off their respective plates; but the lip of that confounded cub, the second mate, quivered visibly.

I expected the steward to hook my coat on and come out at once. He was very slow about it; but I dominated my nervousness sufficiently not to shout after him. Suddenly I became aware (it could be heard plainly enough) that the fellow for some reason or other was opening the door of the bathroom. It was the end. The place was literally not big enough to swing a cat in. My voice died in my throat and I went stony all over. I expected to hear a yell of surprise and terror, and made a movement, but had not the strength to get on my legs. Everything remained still. Had my second self taken the poor wretch by the throat? I don't know what I could have done next moment if I had not seen the steward come out of my room, close the door, and then stand quietly by the sideboard.

"Saved," I thought. "But, no! Lost! Gone! He was gone!"

I laid my knife and fork down and leaned back in my chair. My head swam. After a while, when sufficiently recovered to speak in a steady voice, I instructed my mate to put the ship round at eight o'clock himself.

"I won't come on deck," I went on. "I think I'll turn in, and unless the wind shifts I don't want to be disturbed before midnight. I feel a bit seedy."

"You did look middling bad a little while ago," the chief mate remarked without showing any great concern.

They both went out, and I stared at the steward clearing the table. There was nothing to be read on that wretched man's face. But why did he avoid my eyes, I asked myself. Then I thought I should like to hear the sound of his voice.

"Steward!"

"Sir!" Startled as usual.

"Where did you hang up that coat?"

"In the bathroom, sir." The usual anxious tone. "It's not quite dry yet, sir."

For some time longer I sat in the cuddy. Had my double vanished as he had come? But of his coming there was an explanation, whereas his disappearance would be inexplicable. . . . I went slowly into my dark room, shut the door, lighted the lamp, and for a time dared not turn round. When at last I did I saw him standing bolt-upright in the narrow recessed part. It would not be true to say I had a shock, but an irresistible doubt of his bodily existence flitted through my mind. Can it be, I asked myself, that he is not visible to other eyes than mine? It was like being haunted. Motionless, with a grave face, he raised his hands slightly at me in a gesture which meant clearly, "Heavens! what a narrow escape!" Narrow indeed. I think I had come creeping quietly as near insanity as any man who has not actually gone over the border. That gesture restrained me, so to speak.

The mate with the terrific whiskers was now putting the ship on the other tack. In the moment of profound silence which follows upon the hands going to their stations I heard on the poop his raised voice: "Hard alee!" and the distant shout of the order repeated on the main-deck. The sails, in that light breeze, made but a faint fluttering noise. It ceased. The ship was coming round slowly; I held my breath in the renewed stillness of expectation; one wouldn't have thought that there was a single living soul on her decks. A sudden brisk shout, "Mainsail haul!" broke the spell, and in the noisy cries and rush overhead of the men running away with the main brace we two, down in my cabin, came together in our usual position by the bed place.

He did not wait for my question. "I heard him fumbling here and just managed to squat myself down in the bath," he whispered to me. "The fellow only opened the door and put his arm in to hang the coat up. All the same——"

"I never thought of that," I whispered back, even more appalled than before at the closeness of the shave, and marveling at that something unyielding in his character which was carrying him through so finely. There was no agitation in his whisper. Whoever was being driven distracted, it was not he. He was sane. And the proof of his sanity was continued when he took up the whispering again.

"It would never do for me to come to life again."

It was something that a ghost might have said. But what he was alluding to was his old captain's reluctant admission of the theory of suicide. It would obviously serve his turn —if I had understood at all the view which seemed to govern the unalterable purpose of his action.

"You must maroon me as soon as ever you can get amongst these islands off the Cambodge shore," he went on.

"Maroon you! We are not living in a boy's adventure tale," I protested. His scornful whispering took me up.

"We aren't indeed! There's nothing of a boy's tale in this. But there's nothing else for it. I want no more. You don't suppose I am afraid of what can be done to me? Prison or gallows or whatever they may please. But you don't see me coming back to explain such things to an old fellow in a wig and twelve respectable tradesmen, do you? What can they know whether I am guilty or not—or of *what* I am guilty, either? That's my affair. What does the Bible say? 'Driven off the face of the earth.' Very well, I am off the face of the earth now. As I came at night so I shall go."

"Impossible!" I murmured. "You can't."

"Can't? . . . Not naked like a soul on the Day of Judgment. I shall freeze on to this sleeping suit. The Last Day is not yet—and . . . you have understood thoroughly. Didn't you?"

I felt suddenly ashamed of myself. I may say truly that I understood—and my hesitation in letting that man swim away from my ship's side had been a mere sham sentiment, a sort of cowardice.

"It can't be done now till next night," I breathed out. "The ship is on the off-shore tack and the wind may fail us."

"As long as I know that you understand," he whispered. "But of course you do. It's a great satisfaction to have got somebody to understand. You seem to have been there on purpose." And in the same whisper, as if we two whenever we talked had to say things to each other which were not fit for the world to hear, he added, "It's very wonderful."

We remained side by side talking in our secret way—but sometimes silent or just exchanging a whispered word or two at long intervals. And as usual he stared through the port. A breath of wind came now and again into our faces. The ship might have been moored in dock, so gently and on an even keel she slipped through the water, that did not murmur even at our passage, shadowy and silent like a phantom sea.

At midnight I went on deck, and to my mate's great surprise put the ship round on the other tack. His terrible whiskers flitted round me in silent criticism. I certainly should not have done it if it had been only a question of getting out of that sleepy gulf as quickly as possible. I believe he told the second mate, who relieved him, that it was a great want of judgment. The other only yawned. That intolerable cub shuffled about so sleepily and lolled against the rails in such a slack, improper fashion that I came down on him sharply.

"Aren't you properly awake yet?"

"Yes, sir! I am awake."

"Well, then, be good enough to hold yourself as if you were. And keep a lookout. If there's any current we'll be closing with some islands before daylight."

The east side of the gulf is fringed with islands, some solitary, others in groups. On the blue background of the high coast they seem to float on silvery patches of calm water, arid and gray, or dark green and rounded like clumps of evergreen bushes, with the larger ones, a mile or two long, showing the outlines of ridges, ribs of gray rock under the dank mantle of matted leafage. Unknown to trade, to travel, almost to geography, the manner of life they harbor is an unsolved secret. There must be villages—settlements of fishermen at least—on the largest of them, and some communication with the world is probably kept up by native craft. But all that forenoon, as we headed for them, fanned along by the faintest of breezes, I saw no sign of man or canoe in the field of the telescope I kept on pointing at the scattered group.

At noon I gave no orders for a change of course, and the

mate's whiskers became much concerned and seemed to be offering themselves unduly to my notice. At last I said:

"I am going to stand right in. Quite in—as far as I can take her."

The stare of extreme surprise imparted an air of ferocity also to his eyes, and he looked truly terrific for a moment.

"We're not doing well in the middle of the gulf," I continued, casually. "I am going to look for the land breezes tonight."

"Bless my soul! Do you mean, sir, in the dark amongst the lot of all them islands and reefs and shoals?"

"Well—if there are any regular land breezes at all on this coast one must get close inshore to find them, mustn't one?"

"Bless my soul!" he exclaimed again under his breath. All that afternoon he wore a dreamy, contemplative appearance which in him was a mark of perplexity. After dinner I went into my stateroom as if I meant to take some rest. There we two bent our dark heads over a half-unrolled chart lying on my bed.

"There," I said. "It's got to be Koh-ring. I've been looking at it ever since sunrise. It has got two hills and a low point. It must be inhabited. And on the coast opposite there is what looks like the mouth of a biggish river—with some towns, no doubt, not far up. It's the best chance for you that I can see."

"Anything. Koh-ring let it be."

He looked thoughtfully at the chart as if surveying chances and distances from a lofty height—and following with his eyes his own figure wandering on the blank land of Cochin-China, and then passing off that piece of paper clean out of sight into uncharted regions. And it was as if the ship had two captains to plan her course for her. I had been so worried and restless running up and down that I had not had the patience to dress that day. I had remained in my sleeping suit, with straw slippers and a soft floppy hat. The closeness of the heat in the gulf had been most oppressive, and the crew were used to seeing me wandering in that airy attire.

"She will clear the south point as she heads now," I whispered into his ear. "Goodness only knows when, though, but certainly after dark. I'll edge her in to half a mile, as far as I may be able to judge in the dark——"

"Be careful," he murmured, warningly—and I realized suddenly that all my future, the only future for which I was fit, would perhaps go irretrievably to pieces in any mishap to my first command.

I could not stop a moment longer in the room. I motioned him to get out of sight and made my way on the poop. That unplayful cub had the watch. I walked up and down for a while thinking things out, then beckoned him over.

"Send a couple of hands to open the two quarter-deck ports," I said, mildly.

He actually had the impudence, or else so forgot himself in his wonder at such an incomprehensible order, as to repeat:

"Open the quarter-deck ports! What for, sir?"

"The only reason you need concern yourself about is because I tell you to do so. Have them open wide and fastened properly."

He reddened and went off, but I believe made some jeering remark to the carpenter as to the sensible practice of ventilating a ship's quarter-deck. I know he popped into the mate's cabin to impart the fact to him because the whiskers came on deck, as it were by chance, and stole glances at me from below—for signs of lunacy or drunkenness, I suppose.

A little before supper, feeling more restless than ever, I rejoined, for a moment, my second self. And to find him sitting so quietly was surprising, like something against nature, inhuman.

I developed my plan in a hurried whisper.

"I shall stand in as close as I dare and then put her round. I will presently find means to smuggle you out of here into the sail locker, which communicates with the lobby. But there is an opening, a sort of square for hauling the sails out, which gives straight on the quarter-deck and which is never closed in fine weather, so as to give air to the sails. When the ship's way is deadened in stays and all the hands are aft at the main braces you will have a clear road to slip out and get overboard through the open quarter-deck port. I've had them both fastened up. Use a rope's end to lower yourself into the water so as to avoid a splash—you know. It could be heard and cause some beastly complication."

He kept silent for a while, then whispered, "I understand."

"I won't be there to see you go," I began with an effort. "The rest . . . I only hope I have understood, too."

"You have. From first to last"—and for the first time there seemed to be a faltering, something strained in his whisper. He caught hold of my arm, but the ringing of the supper bell made me start. He didn't though; he only released his grip.

After supper I didn't come below again till well past eight o'clock. The faint, steady breeze was loaded with dew; and the wet, darkened sails held all there was of propelling power in it. The night, clear and starry, sparkled darkly, and the opaque, lightless patches shifting slowly against the low stars were the drifting islets. On the port bow there was a big one more distant and shadowily imposing by the great space of sky it eclipsed.

On opening the door I had a back view of my very own self looking at a chart. He had come out of the recess and was standing near the table.

"Quite dark enough," I whispered.

He stepped back and leaned against my bed with a level, quiet glance. I sat on the couch. We had nothing to say to each other. Over our heads the officer of the watch moved here and there. Then I heard him move quickly. I knew what that meant. He was making for the companion; and presently his voice was outside my door.

"We are drawing in pretty fast, sir. Land looks rather close."

"Very well," I answered. "I am coming on deck directly."

I waited till he was gone out of the cuddy, then rose. My double moved too. The time had come to exchange our last whispers, for neither of us was ever to hear each other's natural voice.

"Look here!" I opened a drawer and took out three sovereigns. "Take this anyhow. I've got six and I'd give you the lot, only I must keep a little money to buy some fruit and vegetables for the crew from native boats as we go through Sunda Straits."

He shook his head.

"Take it," I urged him, whispering desperately. "No one can tell what——"

He smiled and slapped meaningly the only pocket of the sleeping jacket. It was not safe, certainly. But I produced a large old silk handkerchief of mine, and tying the three pieces of gold in a corner, pressed it on him. He was touched, I suppose, because he took it at last and tied it quickly round his waist under the jacket, on his bare skin.

Our eyes met; several seconds elapsed, till, our glances still mingled, I extended my hand and turned the lamp out. Then I passed through the cuddy, leaving the door of my room wide open. . . . "Steward!"

He was still lingering in the pantry in the greatness of his zeal, giving a rub-up to a plated cruet stand the last thing before going to bed. Being careful not to wake up the mate, whose room was opposite, I spoke in an undertone.

He looked round anxiously. "Sir!"

"Can you get me a little hot water from the galley?"

"I am afraid, sir, the galley fire's been out for some time now."

"Go and see."

He flew up the stairs.

"Now," I whispered, loudly, into the saloon—too loudly, perhaps, but I was afraid I couldn't make a sound. He was by my side in an instant—the double captain slipped past the stairs—through a tiny dark passage . . . a sliding door. We were in the sail locker, scrambling on our knees over the sails. A sudden thought struck me. I saw myself wandering barefooted, bareheaded, the sun beating on my dark poll. I snatched off my floppy hat and tried hurriedly in the dark to ram it on my other self. He dodged and fended off silently. I wonder what he thought had come to me before he understood and suddenly desisted. Our hands met gropingly, lingered united in a steady, motionless clasp for a second. . . . No word was breathed by either of us when they separated.

I was standing quietly by the pantry door when the steward returned.

"Sorry, sir. Kettle barely warm. Shall I light the spirit lamp?"

"Never mind."

I came out on deck slowly. It was now a matter of conscience to shave the land as close as possible—for now he must go overboard whenever the ship was put in stays. Must! There could be no going back for him. After a moment I walked over to leeward and my heart flew into my mouth at the nearness of the land on the bow. Under any other circumstances I would not have held on a minute longer. The second mate had followed me anxiously.

I looked on till I felt I could command my voice.

"She will weather," I said then in a quiet tone.

"Are you going to try that, sir?" he stammered out incredulously.

I took no notice of him and raised my tone just enough to be heard by the helmsman.

"Keep her good full."

"Good full, sir."

The wind fanned my cheek, the sails slept, the world was silent. The strain of watching the dark loom of the land grow bigger and denser was too much for me. I had shut my eyes—because the ship must go closer. She must! The stillness was intolerable. Were we standing still?

When I opened my eyes the second view started my heart with a thump. The black southern hill of Koh-ring seemed to hang right over the ship like a towering fragment of the ever-lasting night. On that enormous mass of blackness there was not a gleam to be seen, not a sound to be heard. It was gliding irresistibly towards us and yet seemed already within reach of the hand. I saw the vague figures of the watch grouped in the waist, gazing in awed silence.

"Are you going on, sir?" inquired an unsteady voice at my elbow.

I ignored it. I had to go on.

"Keep her full. Don't check her way. That won't do now," I said, warningly.

"I can't see the sails very well," the helmsman answered me, in strange, quavering tones.

Was she close enough? Already she was, I won't say in the shadow of the land, but in the very blackness of it, already swallowed up as it were, gone too close to be recalled, gone from me altogether.

"Give the mate a call," I said to the young man who stood at my elbow as still as death. "And turn all hands up."

My tone had a borrowed loudness reverberated from the height of the land. Several voices cried out together: "We are all on deck, sir."

Then stillness again, with the great shadow gliding closer, towering higher, without a light, without a sound. Such a hush had fallen on the ship that she might have been a bark of the dead floating in slowly under the very gate of Erebus.

"My God! Where are we?"

It was the mate moaning at my elbow. He was thunderstruck, and as it were deprived of the moral support of his whiskers. He clapped his hands and absolutely cried out, "Lost!"

"Be quiet," I said, sternly.

He lowered his tone, but I saw the shadowy gesture of his despair. "What are we doing here?"

"Looking for the land wind."

He made as if to tear his hair, and addressed me recklessly.

"She will never get out. You have done it, sir. I knew it'd end in something like this. She will never weather, and you are too close now to stay. She'll drift ashore before she's round. O my God!"

I caught his arm as he was raising it to batter his poor devoted head, and shook it violently.

"She's ashore already," he wailed, trying to tear himself away.

"Is she? . . . Keep good full there!"

"Good full, sir," cried the helmsman in a frightened, thin, childlike voice.

I hadn't let go the mate's arm and went on shaking it. "Ready about, do you hear? You go forward"—shake—"and stop there"—shake—"and hold your noise"—shake—"and see these head-sheets properly overhauled"—shake, shake—shake.

And all the time I dared not look towards the land lest my heart should fail me. I released my grip at last and he ran forward as if fleeing for dear life.

I wondered what my double there in the sail locker thought of this commotion. He was able to hear everything —and perhaps he was able to understand why, on my conscience, it had to be thus close—no less. My first order "Hard alee!" re-echoed ominously under the towering shadow of Koh-ring as if I had shouted in a mountain gorge. And then I watched the land intently. In that smooth water and light wind it was impossible to feel the ship coming-to. No! I could not feel her. And my second self was making now ready to ship out and lower himself overboard. Perhaps he was gone already . . . ?

The great black mass brooding over our very mastheads began to pivot away from the ship's side silently. And now I forgot the secret stranger ready to depart, and remembered only that I was a total stranger to the ship. I did not know her. Would she do it? How was she to be handled?

I swung the mainyard and waited helplessly. She was perhaps stopped, and her very fate hung in the balance, with the black mass of Koh-ring like the gate of the everlasting night towering over her taffrail. What would she do now? Had she way on her yet? I stepped to the side swiftly, and on the shadowy water I could see nothing except a faint phosphorescent flash revealing the glassy smoothness of the sleeping surface. It was impossible to tell —and I had not learned yet the feel of my ship. Was she moving? What I needed was something easily seen, a piece of paper, which I could throw overboard and watch. I had nothing on me. To run down for it I didn't dare. There was no time. All at once my strained, yearning stare distinguished a white object floating within a yard of the ship's side. White on the black water. A phosphorescent flash passed under it. What was that thing? . . . I recognized my own floppy hat. It must have fallen off his head . . . and he didn't bother. Now I had what I wanted—the saving mark for my eyes. But I hardly thought of my other self, now gone from the ship, to be hidden forever from all friendly faces, to be a fugitive and a vagabond on the earth, with no brand of the curse on his sane forehead to stay a slaying hand . . . too proud to explain.

And I watched the hat—the expression of my sudden pity for his mere flesh. It had been meant to save his homeless head from the dangers of the sun. And now—behold—it was saving the ship, by serving me for a mark to help out the ignorance of my strangeness. Ha! It was drifting forward, warning me just in time that the ship had gathered sternway.

"Shift the helm," I said in a low voice to the seaman standing still like a statue.

The man's eyes glistened wildly in the binnacle light as he jumped round to the other side and spun round the wheel.

I walked to the break of the poop. On the overshadowed deck all hands stood by the forebraces waiting for my order. The stars ahead seemed to be gliding from right to left. And all was so still in the world that I heard the quiet remark, "She's round," passed in a tone of intense relief between two seamen.

"Let go and haul."

The foreyards ran round with a great noise, amidst cheery cries. And now the frightful whiskers made themselves heard giving various orders. Already the ship was drawing ahead. And I was alone with her. Nothing! no one in the world should stand now between us, throwing a shadow on the way of silent knowledge and mute affection, the perfect communion of a seaman with his first command.

Walking to the taffrail, I was in time to make out, on the very edge of a darkness thrown by a towering black mass like the very gateway of Erebus—yes, I was in time to catch an evanescent glimpse of my white hat left behind to mark the spot where the secret sharer of my cabin and of my thoughts, as though he were my second self, had lowered himself into the water to take his punishment: a free man, a proud swimmer striking out for a new destiny.

THE SHADOW-LINE

A Confession

"Worthy of my undying regard"

> . . . D'autres fois, calme plat, grand miroir
> De mon désespoir.
>
> BAUDELAIRE

I

Only the young have such moments. I don't mean the very young. No. The very young have, properly speaking, no moments. It is the privilege of early youth to live in advance of its days in all the beautiful continuity of hope which knows no pauses and no introspection.

One closes behind one the little gate of mere boyishness —and enters an enchanted garden. Its very shades glow with promise. Every turn of the path has its seduction. And it isn't because it is an undiscovered country. One knows well enough that all mankind had streamed that way. It is the charm of universal experience from which one expects an uncommon or personal sensation—a bit of one's own.

One goes on recognising the landmarks of the predecessors, excited, amused, taking the hard luck and the good luck together—the kicks and the halfpence, as the saying is —the picturesque common lot that holds so many possibilities for the deserving or perhaps for the lucky. Yes. One goes on. And the time, too, goes on—till one perceives ahead a shadow-line warning one that the region of early youth, too, must be left behind.

This is the period of life in which such moments of which I have spoken are likely to come. What moments? Why, the moments of boredom, of weariness, of dissatisfaction. Rash moments. I mean moments when the still young are inclined to commit rash actions, such as getting married suddenly or else throwing up a job for no reason.

This is not a marriage story. It wasn't so bad as that with me. My action, rash as it was, had more the character of divorce—almost of desertion. For no reason on which a sensible person could put a finger I threw up my job—chucked my berth—left the ship of which the worst that could be said was that she was a steamship and therefore, perhaps, not entitled to that blind loyalty which. . . . However, it's no use trying to put a gloss on what even at the time I myself half suspected to be a caprice.

It was in an Eastern port. She was an Eastern ship, inasmuch as then she belonged to that port. She traded among dark islands on a blue reef-scarred sea, with the Red Ensign over the taffrail and at her masthead a houseflag, also red, but with a green border and with a white crescent in it. For an Arab owned her, and a Syed at that. Hence the green border on the flag. He was the head of a great House of Straits Arabs, but as loyal a subject of the complex British Empire as you could find east of the Suez Canal. World politics did not trouble him at all, but he had a great occult power amongst his own people.

It was all one to us who owned the ship. He had to employ white men in the shipping part of his business, and many of those he so employed had never set eyes on him from the first to the last day. I myself saw him but once, quite accidentally on a wharf—an old, dark little man blind in one eye, in a snowy robe and yellow slippers. He was having his hand severely kissed by a crowd of Malay pilgrims to whom he had done some favour, in the way of food and money. His almsgiving, I have heard, was most extensive, covering almost the whole Archipelago. For isn't it said that "The charitable man is the friend of Allah"?

Excellent (and picturesque) Arab owner, about whom one needed not to trouble one's head, a most excellent Scottish ship—for she was that from the keel up—excellent sea-boat, easy to keep clean, most handy in every way, and if it had not been for her internal propulsion, worthy of any man's love, I cherish to this day a profound respect for her memory. As to the kind of trade she was engaged in and the character of my shipmates, I could not have been happier if I had had the life and the men made to my order by a benevolent Enchanter.

And suddenly I left all this. I left it in that, to us, inconsequential manner in which a bird flies away from a comfortable branch. It was as though all unknowing I had heard a whisper or seen something. Well—perhaps! One day I was perfectly right and the next everything was gone—glamour, flavour, interest, contentment—everything. It was one of those moments, you know. The green sickness of late youth descended on me and carried me off. Carried me off that ship, I mean.

We were only four white men on board, with a large crew of Kalashes and two Malay petty officers. The Captain stared hard as if wondering what ailed me. But he was a sailor, and he, too, had been young at one time. Presently a smile came to lurk under his thick iron-grey moustache, and he observed that, of course, if I felt I must go he couldn't keep me by main force. And it was arranged that I should be paid off the next morning. As I was going out of the chart-room he added suddenly, in a peculiar, wistful tone, that he hoped I would find what I was so anxious to go and look for. A soft, cryptic utterance which seemed to reach deeper than any diamond-hard tool could have done. I do believe he understood my case.

But the second engineer attacked me differently. He was a sturdy young Scot, with a smooth face and light eyes. His honest red countenance emerged out of the engine-room companion and then the whole robust man, with shirt sleeves turned up, wiping slowly the massive fore-arms with a lump of cotton-waste. And his light eyes expressed bitter distaste, as though our friendship had turned to ashes. He said weightily: "Oh! Aye! I've been thinking it was about time for you to run away home and get married to some silly girl."

It was tacitly understood in the port that John Nieven

was a fierce misogynist; and the absurd character of the
sally convinced me that he meant to be nasty—very nasty
—had meant to say the most crushing thing he could think
of. My laugh sounded deprecatory. Nobody but a friend
could be so angry as that. I became a little crestfallen. Our
chief engineer also took a characteristic view of my action,
but in a kindlier spirit.

He was young, too, but very thin, and with a mist of
fluffy brown beard all round his haggard face. All day long,
at sea or in harbour, he could be seen walking hastily up
and down the after-deck, wearing an intense, spiritually
rapt expression, which was caused by a perpetual consciousness of unpleasant physical sensations in his internal
economy. For he was a confirmed dyspeptic. His view of
my case was very simple. He said it was nothing but de-
ranged liver. Of course! He suggested I should stay for another trip and meantime dose myself with a certain patent
medicine in which his own belief was absolute. "I'll tell you
what I'll do. I'll buy you two bottles, out of my own pocket.
There. I can't say fairer than that, can I?"

I believe he would have perpetrated the atrocity (or gen-
erosity) at the merest sign of weakening on my part. By
that time, however, I was more discontented, disgusted,
and dogged than ever. The past eighteen months, so full
of new and varied experience, appeared a dreary, prosaic
waste of days. I felt—how shall I express it?—that there was
no truth to be got out of them.

What truth? I should have been hard put to it to explain.
Probably, if pressed, I would have burst into tears simply.
I was young enough for that.

Next day the Captain and I transacted our business in
the Harbour Office. It was a lofty, big, cool, white room,
where the screened light of day glowed serenely. Everybody in it—the officials, the public—was in white. Only the
heavy polished desks gleamed darkly in a central avenue,
and some papers lying on them were blue. Enormous
punkahs sent from on high a gentle draught through that
immaculate interior and upon our perspiring heads.

The official behind the desk we approached grinned
amiably and kept it up till, in answer to his perfunctory

question, "Sign off and on again?" my Captain answered, "No! Signing off for good." And then his grin vanished in sudden solemnity. He did not look at me again till he handed me my papers with a sorrowful expression, as if they had been my passports for Hades.

While I was putting them away he murmured some question to the Captain, and I heard the latter answer good-humouredly:

"No. He leaves us to go home."

"Oh!" the other exclaimed, nodding mournfully over my sad condition.

I didn't know him outside the official building, but he leaned forward over the desk to shake hands with me, compassionately, as one would with some poor devil going out to be hanged; and I am afraid I performed my part ungraciously, in the hardened manner of an impenitent criminal.

No homeward-bound mail-boat was due for three or four days. Being now a man without a ship, and having for a time broken my connection with the sea—become, in fact, a mere potential passenger—it would have been more appropriate perhaps if I had gone to stay at an hotel. There it was, too, within a stone's throw of the Harbour Office, low, but somehow palatial, displaying its white, pillared pavilions surrounded by trim grass plots. I would have felt a passenger indeed in there! I gave it a hostile glance and directed my steps towards the Officers' Sailors' Home.

I walked in the sunshine, disregarding it, and in the shade of the big trees on the Esplanade without enjoying it. The heat of the tropical East descended through the leafy boughs, enveloping my thinly clad body, clinging to my rebellious discontent, as if to rob it of its freedom.

The Officers' Home was a large bungalow with a wide verandah and a curiously suburban-looking little garden of bushes and a few trees between it and the street. That institution partook somewhat of the character of a residental club, but with a slightly Governmental flavour about it, because it was administered by the Harbour Office. Its manager was officially styled Chief Steward. He was an unhappy, wizened little man, who if put into a jockey's rig would have looked the part to perfection. But it was obvious that at some time or other in his life, in some capacity or other, he had been connected with the sea. Possibly in the comprehensive capacity of a failure.

I should have thought his employment a very easy one, but he used to affirm for some reason or other that his job would be the death of him some day. It was rather mysterious. Perhaps everything naturally was too much trouble for him. He certainly seemed to hate having people in the house.

On entering it I thought he must be feeling pleased. It was as still as a tomb. I could see no one in the living rooms; and the verandah, too, was empty, except for a man at the far end dozing prone in a long chair. At the noise of my footsteps he opened one horribly fish-like eye. He was a stranger to me. I retreated from there, and, crossing the dining-room—a very bare apartment with a motionless punkah hanging over the centre table—I knocked at a door labelled in black letters: "Chief Steward."

The answer to my knock being a vexed and doleful plaint: "Oh, dear! Oh, dear! What is it now?" I went in at once.

It was a strange room to find in the tropics. Twilight and stuffiness reigned in there. The fellow had hung enormously ample, dusty, cheap lace curtains over his windows, which were shut. Piles of cardboard boxes, such as milliners and dressmakers use in Europe, cumbered the corners; and by some means he had procured for himself the sort of furniture that might have come out of a respectable parlour in the East End of London—a horsehair sofa, armchairs of the same. I glimpsed grimy antimacassars scattered over that horrid upholstery, which was awe-inspiring, insomuch that one could not guess what mysterious accident, need, or fancy had collected it there. Its owner had taken off his tunic, and in white trousers and a thin short-sleeved singlet prowled behind the chair-backs nursing his meagre elbows.

An exclamation of dismay escaped him when he heard that I had come for a stay; but he could not deny that there were plenty of vacant rooms.

"Very well. Can you give me the one I had before?"

He emitted a faint moan from behind a pile of cardboard boxes on the table, which might have contained gloves or handkerchiefs or neckties. I wonder what the fellow did keep in them? There was a smell of decaying coral, or Oriental dust, of zoological specimens in that den of his. I could only see the top of his head and his unhappy eyes levelled at me over the barrier.

"It's only for a couple of days," I said, intending to cheer him up.

"Perhaps you would like to pay in advance?" he suggested eagerly.

"Certainly not!" I burst out directly I could speak. "Never heard of such a thing! This is the most infernal cheek. . . ."

He had seized his head in both hands—a gesture of despair which checked my indignation.

"Oh, dear! Oh, dear! Don't fly out like this. I am asking everybody."

"I don't believe it," I said bluntly.

"Well, I am going to. And if you gentlemen all agreed to pay in advance I could make Hamilton pay up too. He's always turning up ashore dead broke, and even when he has some money he won't settle his bills. I don't know what to do with him. He swears at me and tells me I can't chuck a white man out into the street here. So if you only would. . . ."

I was amazed. Incredulous too. I suspected the fellow of gratuitous impertinence. I told him with marked emphasis that I would see him and Hamilton hanged first, and requested him to conduct me to my room with no more of his nonsense. He produced then a key from somewhere and led the way out of his lair, giving me a vicious sidelong look in passing.

"Any one I know staying here?" I asked him before he left my room.

He had recovered his usual pained impatient tone, and said that Captain Giles was there, back from a Solo Sea trip. Two other guests were staying also. He paused. And, of course, Hamilton, he added.

"Oh, yes! Hamilton," I said, and the miserable creature took himself off with a final groan.

His impudence still rankled when I came into the dining-room at tiffin time. He was there on duty overlooking the Chinamen servants. The tiffin was laid on one end only of the long table, and the punkah was stirring the hot air lazily—mostly above a barren waste of polished wood.

We were four around the cloth. The dozing stranger from the chair was one. Both his eyes were partly opened now, but they did not seem to see anything. He was supine. The dignified person next him, with short side whiskers and a carefully scraped chin, was, of course, Hamilton. I have never seen any one so full of dignity for the station in life Providence had been pleased to place him in. I had been told that he regarded me as a rank outsider. He raised not only his eyes, but his eyebrows as well, at the sound I made pulling back my chair.

Captain Giles was at the head of the table. I exchanged a few words of greeting with him and sat down on his left. Stout and pale, with a great shiny dome of a bald forehead and prominent brown eyes, he might have been anything but a seaman. You would not have been surprised to learn that he was an architect. To me (I know how absurd it is) he looked like a church-warden. He had the appearance of a man from whom you would expect sound advice, moral sentiments, with perhaps a platitude or two thrown in on occasion, not from a desire to dazzle, but from honest conviction.

Though very well known and appreciated in the shipping world, he had no regular employment. He did not want it. He had his own peculiar position. He was an expert. An expert in—how shall I say it?—in intricate navigation. He was supposed to know more about remote and imperfectly charted parts of the Archipelago than any man living. His brain must have been a perfect warehouse of reefs, positions, bearings, images of headlands, shapes of obscure coasts, aspects of innumerable islands, desert and otherwise. Any ship, for instance, bound on a trip to Palawan or somewhere that way would have Captain Giles on board, either in temporary command or "to assist the master." It was said that he had a retaining fee from a wealthy firm of Chinese steamship owners, in view of such services. Besides, he was always ready to relieve any man who wished to take a spell ashore for a time. No owner was ever known to object to an arrangement of that sort. For it seemed to be the established opinion at the port that Captain Giles was as good as the best, if not a little better. But in Hamilton's view he was an "outsider." I believe that for Hamilton the generalisation "outsider" covered the whole lot of us; though I suppose that he made some distinctions in his mind.

I didn't try to make conversation with Captain Giles, whom I had not seen more than twice in my life. But, of course, he knew who I was. After a while, inclining his big shiny head my way, he addressed me first in his friendly fashion. He presumed from seeing me there, he said, that I had come ashore for a couple of days' leave.

He was a low-voiced man. I spoke a little louder, saying that: No—I had left the ship for good.

"A free man for a bit," was his comment.

"I suppose I may call myself that—since eleven o'clock," I said.

Hamilton had stopped eating at the sound of our voices. He laid down his knife and fork gently, got up, and muttering something about "this infernal heat cutting one's appetite," went out of the room. Almost immediately we heard him leave the house down the verandah steps.

On this Captain Giles remarked easily that the fellow had no doubt gone off to look after my old job. The Chief Steward, who had been leaning against the wall, brought his face of an unhappy goat nearer to the table and addressed us dolefully. His object was to unburden himself of his eternal grievance against Hamilton. The man kept him in hot water with the Harbour Office as to the state of his accounts. He wished to goodness he would get my job, though in truth what would it be? Temporary relief at best.

I said: "You needn't worry. He won't get my job. My successor is on board already."

He was surprised, and I believe his face fell a little at the news. Captain Giles gave a soft laugh. We got up and went out on the verandah, leaving the supine stranger to be dealt with by the Chinamen. The last thing I saw they had put a plate with a slice of pineapple on it before him and stood back to watch what would happen. But the experiment seemed a failure. He sat insensible.

It was imparted to me in a low voice by Captain Giles that this was an officer of some Rajah's yacht which had come into our port to be dry-docked. Must have been "seeing life" last night, he added, wrinkling his nose in an intimate, confidential way which pleased me vastly. For Captain Giles had prestige. He was credited with wonderful adventures and with some mysterious tragedy in his life. And no man had a word to say against him. He continued:

"I remember him first coming ashore here some years ago. Seems only the other day. He was a nice boy. Oh! these nice boys!"

I could not help laughing aloud. He looked startled, then joined in the laugh. "No! No! I didn't mean that," he cried. "What I meant is that some of them do go soft mighty quick out here."

Jocularly I suggested the beastly heat as the first cause. But Captain Giles disclosed himself possessed of a deeper philosophy. Things out East were made easy for white men. That was all right. The difficulty was to go on keeping white, and some of these nice boys did not know how. He gave me a searching look, and in a benevolent, heavy-uncle manner asked point blank:

"Why did you throw up your berth?"

I became angry all of a sudden; for you can understand how exasperating such a question was to a man who didn't know. I said to myself that I ought to shut up that moralist; and to him aloud I said with challenging politeness:

"Why . . . ? Do you disapprove?"

He was too disconcerted to do more than mutter confusedly: "I! . . . In a general way . . ." and then gave me up. But he retired in good order, under the cover of a heavily humorous remark that he, too, was getting soft, and that this was his time for taking his little siesta—when he was on shore. "Very bad habit. Very bad habit."

The simplicity of the man would have disarmed a touchiness even more youthful than mine. So when next day at tiffin he bent his head towards me and said that he had met my late Captain last evening, adding in an undertone: "He's very sorry you left. He had never had a mate that suited him so well," I answered him earnestly, without any affectation, that I certainly hadn't been so comfortable in any ship or with any commander in all my sea-going days.

"Well—then," he murmured.

"Haven't you heard, Captain Giles, that I intend to go home?"

"Yes," he said benevolently. "I have heard that sort of thing so often before."

"What of that?" I cried. I thought he was the most dull, unimaginative man I had ever met. I don't know what more I would have said, but the much-belated Hamilton came in just then and took his usual seat. So I dropped into a mumble.

"Anyhow, you shall see it done this time."

Hamilton, beautifully shaved, gave Captain Giles a curt nod, but didn't even condescend to raise his eyebrows at me; and when he spoke it was only to tell the Chief Steward that the food on his plate wasn't fit to be set before a gentleman. The individual addressed seemed much too unhappy to groan. He only cast his eyes up to the punkah and that was all.

Captain Giles and I got up from the table, and the stranger next to Hamilton followed our example, manœuvring himself to his feet with difficulty. He, poor fellow, not because he was hungry but I verily believe only to recover his self-respect, had tried to put some of that unworthy food into his mouth. But after dropping his fork twice and generally making a failure of it, he had sat still with an air of intense mortification combined with a ghastly glazed stare. Both Giles and I had avoided looking his way at table.

On the verandah he stopped short on purpose to address to us anxiously a long remark which I failed to understand completely. It sounded like some horrible unknown language. But when Captain Giles, after only an instant for reflection, answered him with homely friendliness, "Aye, to be sure. You are right there," he appeared very much gratified indeed, and went away (pretty straight too) to seek a distant long chair.

"What was he trying to say?" I asked with disgust.

"I don't know. Mustn't be down too much on a fellow. He's feeling pretty wretched, you may be sure; and to-morrow he'll feel worse yet."

Judging by the man's appearance it seemed impossible. I wondered what sort of complicated debauch had reduced him to that unspeakable condition. Captain Giles' benevolence was spoiled by a curious air of complacency which I disliked. I said with a little laugh:

"Well, he will have you to look after him."

He made a deprecatory gesture, sat down, and took up a paper. I did the same. The papers were old and uninteresting, filled up mostly with dreary stereotyped descriptions of Queen Victoria's first jubilee celebrations. Probably we should have quickly fallen into a tropical afternoon doze if it had not been for Hamilton's voice raised in the dining-room. He was finishing his tiffin there. The big double doors stood wide open permanently, and he could not have had any idea how near to the doorway our chairs were placed. He was heard in a loud, supercilious tone answering some statement ventured by the Chief Steward.

"I am not going to be rushed into anything. They will be glad enough to get a gentleman I imagine. There is no hurry."

A loud whispering from the steward succeeded and then again Hamilton was heard with even intenser scorn.

"What? That young ass who fancies himself for having been chief mate with Kent so long? . . . Preposterous."

Giles and I looked at each other. Kent being the name of my late commander, Captain Giles' whisper, "He's talking of you," seemed to me sheer waste of breath. The Chief Steward must have stuck to his point whatever it was, because Hamilton was heard again more supercilious, if possible, and also very emphatic:

"Rubbish, my good man! One doesn't *compete* with a rank outsider like that. There's plenty of time."

Then there was pushing of chairs, footsteps in the next room, and plaintive expostulations from the Steward, who was pursuing Hamilton, even out of doors through the main entrance.

"That's a very insulting sort of man," remarked Captain Giles—superfluously, I thought. "Very insulting. You haven't offended him in some way, have you?"

"Never spoke to him in my life," I said grumpily. "Can't imagine what he means by competing. He has been trying for my job after I left—and didn't get it. But that isn't exactly competition."

Captain Giles balanced his big benevolent head thoughtfully. "He didn't get it," he repeated very slowly. "No, not likely either, with Kent. Kent is no end sorry you left him. He gives you the name of a good seaman too."

I flung away the paper I was still holding. I sat up, I slapped the table with my open palm. I wanted to know why he would keep harping on that, my absolutely private affair. It was exasperating, really.

Captain Giles silenced me by the perfect equanimity of his gaze. "Nothing to be annoyed about," he murmured reasonably, with an evident desire to soothe the childish irritation he had aroused. And he was really a man of an appearance so inoffensive that I tried to explain myself as much as I could. I told him that I did not want to hear any more about what was past and gone. It had been very nice while it lasted, but now it was done with I preferred not to talk about it or even think about it. I had made up my mind to go home.

He listened to the whole tirade in a particular, lending-the-ear attitude, as if trying to detect a false note in it somewhere; then straightened himself up and appeared to ponder sagaciously over the matter.

"Yes. You told me you meant to go home. Anything in view there?"

Instead of telling him that it was none of his business I said sullenly:

"Nothing that I know of."

I had indeed considered that rather blank side of the situation I had created for myself by leaving suddenly my very satisfactory employment. And I was not very pleased with it. I had it on the tip of my tongue to say that common sense had nothing to do with my action, and that therefore it didn't deserve the interest Captain Giles seemed to be taking in it. But he was puffing at a short wooden pipe now, and looked so guileless, dense, and commonplace, that it seemed hardly worth while to puzzle him either with truth or sarcasm.

He blew a cloud of smoke, then surprised me by a very abrupt: "Paid your passage money yet?"

Overcome by the shameless pertinacity of a man to whom it was rather difficult to be rude, I replied with exaggerated meekness that I had not done so yet. I thought there would be plenty of time to do that to-morrow.

And I was about to turn away, withdrawing my privacy from his fatuous, objectless attempts to test what sort of stuff it was made of, when he laid down his pipe in an extremely significant manner, you know, as if a critical moment had come, and leaned sideways over the table between us.

"Oh! You haven't yet!" He dropped his voice mysteriously. "Well, then I think you ought to know that there's something going on here."

I had never in my life felt more detached from all earthly goings on. Freed from the sea for a time, I preserved the sailor's consciousness of complete independence from all land affairs. How could they concern me? I gazed at Captain Giles' animation with scorn rather than with curiosity.

To his obviously preparatory question whether our Steward had spoken to me that day I said he hadn't. And what's more he would have had precious little encouragement if he had tried to. I didn't want the fellow to speak to me at all.

Unrebuked by my petulance, Captain Giles, with an air of immense sagacity, began to tell me a minute tale about a Harbour Office peon. It was absolutely pointless. A peon was seen walking that morning on the verandah with a letter in his hand. It was in an official envelope. As the habit of these fellows is, he had shown it to the first white man he came across. That man was our friend in the arm-chair.

He, as I knew, was not in a state to interest himself in any sublunary matters. He could only wave the peon away. The peon then wandered on along the verandah and came upon Captain Giles, who was there by an extraordinary chance. . . .

At this point he stopped with a profound look. The letter, he continued, was addressed to the Chief Steward. Now what could Captain Ellis, the Master Attendant, want to write to the Steward for? The fellow went every morning, anyhow, to the Harbour Office with his report, for orders or what not. He hadn't been back more than an hour before there was an office peon chasing him with a note. Now what was that for?

And he began to speculate. It was not for this—and it could not be for that. As to that other thing it was unthinkable.

The fatuousness of all this made me stare. If the man had not been somehow a sympathetic personality I would have resented it like an insult. As it was, I felt only sorry for him. Something remarkably earnest in his gaze prevented me from laughing in his face. Neither did I yawn at him. I just stared.

His tone became a shade more mysterious. Directly the fellow (meaning the Steward) got that note he rushed for his hat and bolted out of the house. But it wasn't because the note called him to the Harbour Office. He didn't go there. He was not absent long enough for that. He came darting back in no time, flung his hat away, and raced about the dining-room moaning and slapping his forehead. All these exciting facts and manifestations had been observed by Captain Giles. He had, it seems, been meditating upon them ever since.

I began to pity him profoundly. And in a tone which I tried to make as little sarcastic as possible I said that I was glad he had found something to occupy his morning hours.

With his disarming simplicity he made me observe, as if it were a matter of some consequence, how strange it was that he should have spent the morning indoors at all.

He generally was out before tiffin, visiting various offices, seeing his friends in the harbour, and so on. He had felt out of sorts somewhat on rising. Nothing much. Just enough to make him feel lazy.

All this with a sustained, holding stare which, in conjunction with the general inanity of the discourse, conveyed the impression of mild, dreary lunacy. And when he hitched his chair a little and dropped his voice to the low note of mystery, it flashed upon me that high professional reputation was not necessarily a guarantee of sound mind.

It never occurred to me then that I didn't know in what soundness of mind exactly consisted and what a delicate and, upon the whole, unimportant matter it was. With some idea of not hurting his feelings I blinked at him in an interested manner. But when he proceeded to ask me mysteriously whether I remembered what had passed just now between that Steward of ours and "that man Hamilton," I only grunted sour assent and turned away my head.

"Aye. But do you remember every word?" he insisted tactfully.

"I don't know. It's none of my business," I snapped out, consigning, moreover, the Steward and Hamilton aloud to eternal perdition.

I meant to be very energetic and final, but Captain Giles continued to gaze at me thoughtfully. Nothing could stop him. He went on to point out that my personality was involved in that conversation. When I tried to preserve the semblance of unconcern he became positively cruel. I heard what the man had said? Yes? What did I think of it then? —he wanted to know.

Captain Giles' appearance excluding the suspicion of mere sly malice, I came to the conclusion that he was simply the most tactless idiot on earth. I almost despised myself for the weakness of attempting to enlighten his common understanding. I started to explain that I did not think anything whatever. Hamilton was not worth a thought. What such an offensive loafer . . .— "Aye! that he is," interjected Captain Giles— . . . thought or said was below any decent man's contempt, and I did not propose to take the slightest notice of it.

This attitude seemed to me so simple and obvious that I was really astonished at Giles giving no sign of assent. Such perfect stupidity was almost interesting.

"What would you like me to do?" I asked laughing. "I can't start a row with him because of the opinion he has formed of me. Of course, I've heard of the contemptuous way he alludes to me. But he doesn't intrude his contempt on my notice. He has never expressed it in my hearing. For even just now he didn't know we could hear him. I should only make myself ridiculous."

That hopeless Giles went on puffing at his pipe moodily. All at once his face cleared, and he spoke.

"You missed my point."

"Have I? I am very glad to hear it," I said.

With increasing animation he stated again that I had missed his point. Entirely. And in a tone of growing self-conscious complacency he told me that few things escaped his attention, and he was rather used to thinking them out, and generally from his experience of life and men arrived at the right conclusion.

This bit of self-praise, of course, fitted excellently the laborious inanity of the whole conversation. The whole thing strengthened in me that obscure feeling of life being but a waste of days, which, half-unconsciously, had driven me out of a comfortable berth, away from men I liked, to flee from the menace of emptiness . . . and to find inanity at the first turn. Here was a man of recognised character and achievement disclosed as an absurd and dreary chatterer. And it was probably like this everywhere—from east to west, from the bottom to the top of the social scale.

A great discouragement fell on me. A spiritual drowsiness. Giles' voice was going on complacently; the very voice of the universal hollow conceit. And I was no longer angry with it. There was nothing original, nothing new, startling, informing to expect from the world: no opportunities to find out something about oneself, no wisdom to acquire, no fun to enjoy. Everything was stupid and overrated, even as Captain Giles was. So be it.

The name of Hamilton suddenly caught my ear and roused me up.

"I thought we had done with him," I said, with the greatest possible distaste.

"Yes. But considering what we happened to hear just now I think you ought to do it."

"Ought to do it?" I sat up bewildered. "Do what?"

Captain Giles confronted me very much surprised.

"Why! Do what I have been advising you to try. You go and ask the Steward what was there in that letter from the Harbour Office. Ask him straight out."

I remained speechless for a time. Here was something unexpected and original enough to be altogether incomprehensible. I murmured, astounded:

"But I thought it was Hamilton that you . . ."

"Exactly. Don't you let him. You do what I tell you. You tackle that Steward. You'll make him jump, I bet," insisted Captain Giles, waving his smouldering pipe impressively at me. Then he took three rapid puffs at it.

His aspect of triumphant acuteness was indescribable. Yet the man remained a strangely sympathetic creature. Benevolence radiated from him ridiculously, mildly, impressively. It was irritating, too. But I pointed out coldly, as one who deals with the incomprehensible, that I didn't see any reason to expose myself to a snub from the fellow. He was a very unsatisfactory steward and a miserable wretch besides, but I would just as soon think of tweaking his nose.

"Tweaking his nose," said Captain Giles in a scandalised tone. "Much use it would be to you."

That remark was so irrelevant that one could make no answer to it. But the sense of the absurdity was beginning at last to exercise its well-known fascination. I felt I must not let the man talk to me any more. I got up, observing curtly that he was too much for me—that I couldn't make him out.

Before I had time to move away he spoke again in a changed tone of obstinacy and puffing nervously at his pipe.

"Well—he's a—no account cuss—anyhow. You just—ask him. That's all."

That new manner impressed me—or rather made me pause. But sanity asserting its sway, at once I left the verandah after giving him a mirthless smile. In a few strides I found myself in the dining-room, now cleared and empty. But during that short time various thoughts occurred to me, such as: that Giles had been making fun of me, expecting some amusement at my expense; that I probably looked silly and gullible; that I knew very little of life. . . .

The door facing me across the dining-room flew open to my extreme surprise. It was the door inscribed with the word "Steward" and the man himself ran out of his stuffy Philistinish lair in his absurd hunted animal manner, making for the garden door.

To this day I don't know what made me call after him: "I say! Wait a minute." Perhaps it was the sidelong glance he gave me; or possibly I was yet under the influence of Captain Giles' mysterious earnestness. Well, it was an impulse of some sort; an effect of that force somewhere within our lives which shapes them this way or that. For if these words had not escaped from my lips (my will had nothing to do with that) my existence would, to be sure, have been still a seaman's existence, but directed on now to me utterly inconceivable lines.

No. My will had nothing to do with it. Indeed, no sooner had I made that fateful noise than I became extremely sorry for it. Had the man stopped and faced me I would have had to retire in disorder. For I had no notion to carry out Captain Giles' idiotic joke, either at my own expense or at the expense of the Steward.

But here the old human instinct of the chase came into play. He pretended to be deaf, and I, without thinking a second about it, dashed along my own side of the dining table and cut him off at the very door.

"Why can't you answer when you are spoken to?" I asked roughly.

He leaned against the side of the door. He looked extremely wretched. Human nature is, I fear, not very nice right through. There are ugly spots in it. I found myself growing angry, and that, I believe, only because my quarry looked so woe-begone. Miserable beggar!

I went for him without more ado. "I understand there

was an official communication to the Home from the Harbour Office this morning. Is that so?"

Instead of telling me to mind my own business, as he might have done, he began to whine with an undertone of impudence. He couldn't see me anywhere this morning. He couldn't be expected to run all over the town after me.

"Who wants you to?" I cried. And then my eyes became opened to the inwardness of things and speeches the triviality of which had been so baffling and tiresome.

I told him I wanted to know what was in that letter. My sternness of tone and behaviour was only half assumed. Curiosity can be a very fierce sentiment—at times.

He took refuge in a silly, muttering sulkiness. It was nothing to me, he mumbled. I had told him I was going home. And since I was going home he didn't see why he should. . . .

That was the line of his argument, and it was irrelevant enough to be almost insulting. Insulting to one's intelligence, I mean.

In that twilight region between youth and maturity, in which I had my being then, one is peculiarly sensitive to that kind of insult. I am afraid my behaviour to the Steward became very rough indeed. But it wasn't in him to face out anything or anybody. Drug habit or solitary tippling, perhaps. And when I forgot myself so far as to swear at him he broke down and began to shriek.

I don't mean to say that he made a great outcry. It was a cynical shrieking confession, only faint—piteously faint. It wasn't very coherent either, but sufficiently so to strike me dumb at first. I turned my eyes from him in righteous indignation, and perceived Captain Giles in the verandah doorway surveying quietly the scene, his own handiwork, if I may express it in that way. His smouldering black pipe was very noticeable in his big, paternal fist. So, too, was the glitter of his heavy gold watch-chain across the breast of his white tunic. He exhaled an atmosphere of virtuous sagacity thick enough for any innocent soul to fly to confidently. I flew to him.

"You would never believe it," I cried. "It was a notification that a master is wanted for some ship. There's a command apparently going about and this fellow puts the thing in his pocket."

The Steward screamed out in accents of loud despair, "You will be the death of me!"

The mighty slap he gave his wretched forehead was very loud, too. But when I turned to look at him he was no longer there. He had rushed away somewhere out of sight. This sudden disappearance made me laugh.

This was the end of the incident—for me. Captain Giles, however, staring at the place where the Steward had been, began to haul at his gorgeous gold chain till at last the watch came up from the deep pocket like solid truth from a well. Solemnly he lowered it down again and only then said:

"Just three o'clock. You will be in time—if you don't lose any, that is."

"In time for what?" I asked.

"Good Lord! For the Harbour Office. This must be looked into."

Strictly speaking, he was right. But I've never had much taste for investigation, for showing people up and all that, no doubt, ethically meritorious kind of work. And my view of the episode was purely ethical. If any one had to be the death of the Steward I didn't see why it shouldn't be Captain Giles himself, a man of age and standing, and a permanent resident. Whereas I, in comparison, felt myself a mere bird of passage in that port. In fact, it might have been said that I had already broken off my connection. I muttered that I didn't think—it was nothing to me. . . .

"Nothing!" repeated Captain Giles, giving some signs of quiet, deliberate indignation. "Kent warned me you were a peculiar young fellow. You will tell me next that a command is nothing to you—and after all the trouble I've taken, too!"

"The trouble!" I murmured, uncomprehending. What trouble? All I could remember was being mystified and bored by his conversation for a solid hour after tiffin. And he called that taking a lot of trouble.

He was looking at me with a self-complacency which would have been odious in any other man. All at once, as if a page of a book had been turned over disclosing a word which made plain all that had gone before, I perceived that this matter had also another than an ethical aspect.

And still I did not move. Captain Giles lost his patience a little. With an angry puff at his pipe he turned his back on my hesitation.

But it was not hesitation on my part. I had been, if I may express myself so, put out of gear mentally. But as soon as I had convinced myself that this stale, unprofitable world of my discontent contained such a thing as a command to be seized, I recovered my powers of locomotion.

It's a good step from the Officers' Home to the Harbour Office; but with the magic word "Command" in my head I found myself suddenly on the quay as if transported there in the twinkling of an eye, before a portal of dressed white stone above a flight of shallow white steps.

All this seemed to glide towards me swiftly. The whole great roadstead to the right was just a mere flicker of blue, and the dim cool hall swallowed me up out of the heat and glare of which I had not been aware till the very moment I passed in from it.

The broad inner staircase insinuated itself under my feet somehow. Command is a strong magic. The first human beings I perceived distinctly since I had parted with the indignant back of Captain Giles was the crew of the harbour steam-launch lounging on the spacious landing about the curtained archway of the shipping office.

It was there that my buoyancy abandoned me. The atmosphere of officialdom would kill anything that breathes the air of human endeavour, would extinguish hope and fear alike in the supremacy of paper and ink. I passed heavily under the curtain which the Malay coxswain of the harbour launch raised for me. There was nobody in the office except the clerks, writing in two industrious rows. But the head shipping-master hopped down from his elevation and hurried along on the thick mats to meet me in the broad central passage.

He had a Scottish name, but his complexion was of a rich olive hue, his short beard was jet black, and his eyes, also black, had a languishing expression. He asked confidentially:

"You want to see Him?"

All lightness of spirit and body having departed from me at the touch of officialdom, I looked at the scribe without animation and asked in my turn wearily:

"What do you think? Is it any use?"

"My goodness! He has asked for you twice to-day."

This emphatic He was the supreme authority, the Marine Superintendent, the Harbour-Master—a very great person in the eyes of every single quill-driver in the room. But that was nothing to the opinion he had of his own greatness.

Captain Ellis looked upon himself as a sort of divine (pagan) emanation, the deputy-Neptune for the circumambient seas. If he did not actually rule the waves, he pretended to rule the fate of the mortals whose lives were cast upon the waters.

This uplifting illusion made him inquisitorial and peremptory. And as his temperament was choleric there were fellows who were actually afraid of him. He was redoubtable, not in virtue of his office, but because of his unwarrantable assumptions. I had never had anything to do with him before.

I said: "Oh! He has asked for me twice. Then perhaps I had better go in."

"You must! You must!"

The shipping-master led the way with a mincing gait round the whole system of desks to a tall and important-looking door, which he opened with a deferential action of the arm.

He stepped right in (but without letting go of the handle) and, after gazing reverently down the room for a while, beckoned me in by a silent jerk of the head. Then he slipped out at once and shut the door after me most delicately.

Three lofty windows gave on the harbour. There was nothing in them but the dark-blue sparkling sea and the paler luminous blue of the sky. My eye caught in the depths and distances of these blue tones the white speck of some big ship just arrived and about to anchor in the outer roadstead. A ship from home—after perhaps ninety days at sea. There is something touching about a ship coming in from sea and folding her white wings for a rest.

The next thing I saw was the top-knot of silver hair surmounting Captain Ellis' smooth red face, which would have been apoplectic if it hadn't had such a fresh appearance.

Our deputy-Neptune had no beard on his chin, and there was no trident to be seen standing in a corner anywhere, like an umbrella. But his hand was holding a pen— the official pen, far mightier than the sword in making or marring the fortune of simple toiling men. He was looking over his shoulder at my advance.

When I had come well within range he saluted me by a nerve-shattering: "Where have you been all this time?"

As it was no concern of his I did not take the slightest notice of the shot. I said simply that I had heard there was a master needed for some vessel, and being a sailing-ship man I thought I would apply. . . .

He interrupted me. "Why! Hang it! *You* are the right man for that job—if there had been twenty others after it. But no fear of that. They are all afraid to catch hold. That's what's the matter."

He was very irritated. I said innocently: "Are they, sir? I wonder why?"

"Why!" he fumed. "Afraid of the sails. Afraid of a white crew. Too much trouble. Too much work. Too long out here. Easy life and deck-chairs more their mark. Here I sit with the Consul-General's cable before me, and the only man fit for the job not to be found anywhere. I began to think you were funking it too. . . ."

"I haven't been long getting to the office," I remarked calmly.

"You have a good name out here, though," he growled savagely without looking at me.

"I am very glad to hear it from you, sir," I said.

"Yes. But you are not on the spot when you are wanted. You know you weren't. That steward of yours wouldn't dare to neglect a message from this office. Where the devil did you hide yourself for the best part of the day?"

I only smiled kindly down on him, and he seemed to recollect himself, and asked me to take a seat. He explained that the master of a British ship having died in Bankok the Consul-General had cabled to him a request for a competent man to be sent out to take command.

Apparently, in his mind, I was the man from the first, though for the looks of the thing the notification addressed to the Sailors' Home was general. An agreement had already been prepared. He gave it to me to read, and when I handed it back to him with the remark that I accepted its terms, the deputy-Neptune signed it, stamped it with his own exalted hand, folded it in four (it was a sheet of blue foolscap), and presented it to me—a gift of extraordinary potency, for, as I put it in my pocket, my head swam a little.

"This is your appointment to the command," he said with a certain gravity. "An official appointment binding the owners to conditions which you have accepted. Now—when will you be ready to go?"

I said I would be ready that very day if necessary. He caught me at my word with great readiness. The steamer *Melita* was leaving for Bankok that evening about seven. He would request her captain officially to give me a passage and wait for me till ten o'clock.

Then he rose from his office chair, and I got up too. My head swam, there was no doubt about it, and I felt a heaviness of limbs as if they had grown bigger since I had sat down on that chair. I made my bow.

A subtle change in Captain Ellis' manner became perceptible as though he had laid aside the trident of deputy-Neptune. In reality, it was only his official pen that he had dropped on getting up.

II

He shook hands with me: "Well, there you are, on your own, appointed officially under my responsibility."

He was actually walking with me to the door. What a distance off it seemed! I moved like a man in bonds. But we reached it at last. I opened it with the sensation of dealing with mere dream-stuff, and then at the last moment the fellowship of seamen asserted itself, stronger than the difference of age and station. It asserted itself in Captain Ellis' voice.

"Good-bye—and good luck to you," he said so heartily that I could only give him a grateful glance. Then I turned and went out, never to see him again in my life. I had not made three steps into the outer office when I heard behind my back a gruff, loud, authoritative voice, the voice of our deputy-Neptune.

It was addressing the head shipping-master, who, having let me in, had, apparently, remained hovering in the middle distance ever since.

"Mr. R., let the harbour launch have steam up to take the captain here on board the *Melita* at half-past nine to-night."

I was amazed at the startled assent of R.'s "Yes, sir." He ran before me out on the landing. My new dignity sat yet so lightly on me that I was not aware that it was I, the Captain, the object of this last graciousness. It seemed as if all of a sudden a pair of wings had grown on my shoulders. I merely skimmed along the polished floor.

But R. was impressed.

"I say!" he exclaimed on the landing, while the Malay crew of the steam-launch standing by looked stonily at the man for whom they were going to be kept on duty so late, away from their gambling, from their girls, or their pure domestic joys. "I say! His own launch. What have you done to him?"

His stare was full of respectful curiosity. I was quite confounded.

"Was it for me? I hadn't the slightest notion," I stammered out.

He nodded many times. "Yes. And the last person who had it before you was a Duke. So, there!"

I think he expected me to faint on the spot. But I was in too much of a hurry for emotional displays. My feelings were already in such a whirl that this staggering information did not seem to make the slightest difference. It fell into the seething cauldron of my brain, and I carried it off with me after a short but effusive passage of leave-taking with R.

The favour of the great throws an aureole round the fortunate object of its selection. That excellent man inquired whether he could do anything for me. He had known me only by sight, and he was well aware he would never see me again; I was, in common with the other seamen of the port, merely a subject for official writing, filling up of forms with all the artificial superiority of a man of pen and ink to the men who grapple with realities outside the consecrated walls of official buildings. What ghosts we must have been to him! Mere symbols to juggle with in books and heavy registers, without brains and muscles and perplexities; something hardly useful and decidedly inferior.

And he—the office hours being over—wanted to know if he could be of any use to me!

I ought, properly speaking—I ought to have been moved to tears. But I did not even think of it. It was only another miraculous manifestation of that day of miracles. I parted from him as if he had been a mere symbol. I floated down the staircase. I floated out of the official and imposing portal. I went on floating along.

I use that word rather than the word "flew," because I have a distinct impression that, though uplifted by my aroused youth, my movements were deliberate enough. To that mixed white, brown, and yellow portion of mankind, out abroad on their own affairs, I presented the appearance of a man walking rather sedately. And nothing in the way of abstraction could have equalled my deep detachment from the forms and colours of this world. It was, as it were, absolute.

And yet, suddenly, I recognised Hamilton. I recognised him without effort, without a shock, without a start. There he was, strolling towards the Harbour Office with his stiff, arrogant dignity. His red face made him noticeable at a distance. It flamed, over there, on the shady side of the street.

He had perceived me too. Something (unconscious exuberance of spirits perhaps) moved me to wave my hand to him elaborately. This lapse from good taste happened before I was aware that I was capable of it.

The impact of my impudence stopped him short, much as a bullet might have done. I verily believe he staggered, though as far as I could see he didn't actually fall. I had gone past in a moment and did not turn my head. I had forgotten his existence.

The next ten minutes might have been ten seconds or ten centuries for all my consciousness had to do with it. People might have been falling dead around me, houses crumbling, guns firing, I wouldn't have known. I was thinking: "By Jove! I have got it." It being the command. It had come about in a way utterly unforeseen in my modest day-dreams.

I perceived that my imagination had been running in conventional channels and that my hopes had always been drab stuff. I had envisaged a command as a result of a slow course of promotion in the employ of some highly respectable firm. The reward of faithful service. Well, faithful service was all right. One would naturally give that for one's own sake, for the sake of the ship, for the love of the life of one's choice; not for the sake of the reward.

There is something distasteful in the notion of a reward.

And now here I had my command, absolutely in my pocket, in a way undeniable indeed, but most unexpected; beyond my imaginings, outside all reasonable expectations, and even notwithstanding the existence of some sort of obscure intrigue to keep it away from me. It is true that the intrigue was feeble, but it helped the feeling of wonder—as if I had been specially destined for that ship I did not know, by some power higher than the prosaic agencies of the commercial world.

A strange sense of exultation began to creep into me. If I had worked for that command ten years or more there would have been nothing of the kind. I was a little frightened.

"Let us be calm," I said to myself.

Outside the door of the Officers' Home the wretched Steward seemed to be waiting for me. There was a broad flight of a few steps, and he ran to and fro on the top of it as if chained there. A distressed cur. He looked as though his throat were too dry for him to bark.

I regret to say I stopped before going in. There had been a revolution in my moral nature. He waited open-mouthed, breathless, while I looked at him for half a minute.

"And you thought you could keep me out of it," I said scathingly.

"You said you were going home," he squeaked miserably. "You said so. You said so."

"I wonder what Captain Ellis will have to say to that excuse," I uttered slowly with a sinister meaning.

His lower jaw had been trembling all the time and his voice was like the bleating of a sick goat. "You have given me away? You have done for me?"

Neither his distress nor yet the sheer absurdity of it was able to disarm me. It was the first instance of harm being attempted to be done to me—at any rate, the first I had ever found out. And I was still young enough, still too much on this side of the shadow-line, not to be surprised and indignant at such things.

I gazed at him inflexibly. Let the beggar suffer. He slapped his forehead and I passed in, pursued, into the dining-room, by his screech: "I always said you'd be the death of me."

This clamour not only overtook me, but went ahead, as it were, on to the verandah and brought out Captain Giles.

He stood before me in the doorway in all the commonplace solidity of his wisdom. The gold chain glittered on his breast. He clutched a smouldering pipe.

I extended my hand to him warmly and he seemed surprised, but did respond heartily enough in the end, with a faint smile of superior knowledge which cut my thanks short as if with a knife. I don't think that more than one word came out. And even for that one, judging by the temperature of my face, I had blushed as if for a bad action. Assuming a detached tone, I wondered how on earth he had managed to spot the little underhand game that had been going on.

He murmured complacently that there were but few things done in the town that he could not see the inside of.

And as to this house, he had been using it off and on for nearly ten years. Nothing that went on in it could escape his great experience. It had been no trouble to him. No trouble at all.

Then in his quiet thick tone he wanted to know if I had complained formally of the Steward's action.

I said that I hadn't—though, indeed, it was not for want of opportunity. Captain Ellis had gone for me bald-headed in a most ridiculous fashion for being out of the way when wanted.

"Funny old gentleman," interjected Captain Giles. "What did you say to that?"

"I said simply that I came along the very moment I heard of his message. Nothing more. I didn't want to hurt the Steward. I would scorn to harm such an object. No. I made no complaint, but I believe he thinks I've done so. Let him think. He's got a fright that he won't forget in a hurry, for Captain Ellis would kick him out into the middle of Asia. . . ."

"Wait a moment," said Captain Giles, leaving me suddenly. I sat down feeling very tired, mostly in my head. Before I could start a train of thought he stood again before me, murmuring the excuse that he had to go and put the fellow's mind at ease.

I looked up with surprise. But in reality I was indifferent. He explained that he had found the Steward lying face downwards on the horsehair sofa. He was all right now.

"He would not have died of fright," I said contemptuously.

"No. But he might have taken an overdose out of one of those little bottles he keeps in his room," Captain Giles argued seriously. "The confounded fool has tried to poison himself once—a couple of years ago."

"Really," I said without emotion. "He doesn't seem very fit to live, anyhow."

"As to that, it may be said of a good many."

"Don't exaggerate like this!" I protested, laughing irritably. "But I wonder what this part of the world would do if you were to leave off looking after it, Captain Giles? Here you have got me a command and saved the Steward's life in one afternoon. Though why you should have taken all that interest in either of us is more than I can understand."

Captain Giles remained silent for a minute.

Then gravely:

"He's not a bad steward really. He can find a good cook, at any rate. And, what's more, he can keep him when found. I remember the cooks we had here before his time. . . ."

I must have made a movement of impatience, because he interrupted himself with an apology for keeping me yarning there, while no doubt I needed all my time to get ready.

What I really needed was to be alone for a bit. I seized this opening hastily. My bedroom was a quiet refuge in an apparently uninhabited wing of the building. Having absolutely nothing to do (for I had not unpacked my things), I sat down on the bed and abandoned myself to the influences of the hour. To the unexpected influences. . . .

And first I wondered at my state of mind. Why was I not more surprised? Why? Here I was, invested with a command in the twinkling of an eye, not in the common course of human affairs, but more as if by enchantment. I ought to have been lost in astonishment. But I wasn't. I was very much like people in fairy tales. Nothing ever astonishes them. When a fully appointed gala coach is produced out of a pumpkin to take her to a ball Cinderella does not exclaim. She gets in quietly and drives away to her high fortune.

Captain Ellis (a fierce sort of fairy) had produced a command out of a drawer almost as unexpectedly as in a fairy tale. But a command is an abstract idea, and it seemed a sort of "lesser marvel" till it flashed upon me that it involved the concrete existence of a ship.

A ship! My ship! She was mine, more absolutely mine for possession and care than anything in the world; an object of responsibility and devotion. She was there waiting for me, spellbound, unable to move, to live, to get out into the world (till I came), like an enchanted princess. Her call had come to me as if from the clouds. I had never suspected her existence. I didn't know how she looked, I had barely heard her name, and yet we were indissolubly united for a certain portion of our future, to sink or swim together!

A sudden passion of anxious impatience rushed through my veins and gave me such a sense of the intensity of existence as I have never felt before or since. I discovered how much of a seaman I was, in heart, in mind, and, as it were, physically—a man exclusively of sea and ships; the sea the only world that counted, and the ships the test of manliness, of temperament, of courage and fidelity—and of love.

I had an exquisite moment. It was unique also. Jumping up from my seat, I paced up and down my room for a long time. But when I came into the dining-room I behaved with sufficient composure. Only I couldn't eat anything at dinner.

Having declared my intention not to drive but to walk down to the quay, I must render the wretched Steward justice that he bestirred himself to find me some coolies for the luggage. They departed, carrying all my worldly possessions (except a little money I had in my pocket) slung from a long pole. Captain Giles volunteered to walk down with me.

We followed the sombre, shaded alley across the Esplanade. It was moderately cool there under the trees. Captain Giles remarked, with a sudden laugh: "I know who's jolly thankful at having seen the last of you."

I guessed that he meant the Steward. The fellow had borne himself to me in a sulkily frightened manner at the last. I expressed my wonder that he should have tried to do me a bad turn for no reason at all.

"Don't you see that what he wanted was to get rid of our friend Hamilton by dodging him in front of you for that job? That would have removed him for good, see?"

"Heavens!" I exclaimed, feeling humiliated somehow. "Can it be possible? What a fool he must be! That overbearing, impudent loafer! Why! He couldn't . . . And yet he's nearly done it, I believe; for the Harbour Office was bound to send somebody."

"Aye. A fool like our Steward can be dangerous sometimes," declared Captain Giles sententiously. "Just because he is a fool," he added, imparting further instruction in his complacent low tones. "For," he continued in the manner of a set demonstration, "no sensible person would risk being kicked out of the only berth between himself and starvation just to get rid of a simple annoyance—a small worry. Would he now?"

"Well, no," I conceded, restraining a desire to laugh at that something mysteriously earnest in delivering the conclusions of his wisdom as though they were the product of prohibited operations. "But that fellow looks as if he were rather crazy. He must be."

"As to that, I believe everybody in the world is a little mad," he announced quietly.

"You make no exceptions?" I inquired, just to hear his answer.

He kept silent for a little while, then got home in an effective manner.

"Why! Kent says that even of you."

"Does he?" I retorted, extremely embittered all at once against my former captain. "There's nothing of that in the written character from him which I've got in my pocket. Has he given you any instances of my lunacy?"

Captain Giles explained in a conciliating tone that it had been only a friendly remark in reference to my abrupt leaving the ship for no apparent reason.

I muttered grumpily: "Oh! leaving his ship," and mended my pace. He kept up by my side in the deep gloom of the avenue as if it were his conscientious duty to see me out of the colony as an undesirable character. He panted a little, which was rather pathetic in a way. But I was not moved. On the contrary. His discomfort gave me a sort of malicious pleasure.

Presently I relented, slowed down, and said:

"What I really wanted was to get a fresh grip. I felt it was time. Is that so very mad?"

He made no answer. We were issuing from the avenue. On the bridge over the canal a dark, irresolute figure seemed to be awaiting something or somebody.

It was a Malay policeman, barefooted, in his blue uni-

form. The silver band on his little round cap shone dimly
in the light of the street lamp. He peered in our direction
timidly.

Before we could come up to him he turned about and
walked in front of us in the direction of the jetty. The
distance was some hundred yards; and then I found my
coolies squatting on their heels. They had kept the pole
on their shoulders, and all my worldly goods, still tied to
the pole, were resting on the ground between them. As far
as the eye could reach along the quay there was not another
soul abroad except the police peon, who saluted us.

It seems he had detained the coolies as suspicious characters, and had forbidden them the jetty. But at a sign from
me he took off the embargo with alacrity. The two patient
fellows, rising together with a faint grunt, trotted off along
the planks, and I prepared to take my leave of Captain
Giles, who stood there with an air as though his mission
were drawing to a close. It could not be denied that he had
done it all. And while I hesitated about an appropriate
sentence he made himself heard:

"I expect you'll have your hands pretty full of tangled
up business."

I asked him what made him think so; and he answered
that it was his general experience of the world. Ship a long
time away from her port, owners inaccessible by cable, and
the only man who could explain matters dead and buried.

"And you yourself new to the business in a way," he
concluded in a sort of unanswerable tone.

"Don't insist," I said. "I know it only too well. I only wish
you could impart to me some small portion of your experience before I go. As it can't be done in ten minutes I
had better not begin to ask you. There's that harbour
launch waiting for me too. But I won't feel really at peace
till I have that ship of mine out in the Indian Ocean."

He remarked casually that from Bankok to the Indian
Ocean was a pretty long step. And this murmur, like a dim
flash from a dark lantern, showed me for a moment the
broad belt of islands and reefs between that unknown ship,
which was mine, and the freedom of the great waters of
the globe.

But I felt no apprehension. I was familiar enough with the Archipelago by that time. Extreme patience and extreme care would see me through the region of broken land, of faint airs and of dead water to where I would feel at last my command swing on the great swell and list over to the great breath of regular winds, that would give her the feeling of a large, more intense life. The road would be long. All roads are long that lead towards one's heart's desire. But this road my mind's eye could see on a chart, professionally, with all its complications and difficulties, yet simple enough in a way. One is a seaman or one is not. And I had no doubt of being one.

The only part I was a stranger to was the Gulf of Siam. And I mentioned this to Captain Giles. Not that I was concerned very much. It belonged to the same region the nature of which I knew, into whose very soul I seemed to have looked during the last months of that existence with which I had broken now, suddenly, as one parts with some enchanting company.

"The Gulf . . . Ay! A funny piece of water—that," said Captain Giles.

Funny, in this connection, was a vague word. The whole thing sounded like an opinion uttered by a cautious person mindful of actions for slander.

I didn't inquire as to the nature of that funniness. There was really no time. But at the very last he volunteered a warning.

"Whatever you do, keep to the east side of it. The west side is dangerous at this time of the year. Don't let anything tempt you over. You'll find nothing but trouble there."

Though I could hardly imagine what could tempt me to involve my ship amongst the currents and reefs of the Malay shore, I thanked him for the advice.

He gripped my extended arm warmly, and the end of our acquaintance came suddenly in the words: "Good-night."

That was all he said: "Good-night." Nothing more. I don't know what I intended to say, but surprise made me swallow it, whatever it was. I choked slightly, and then exclaimed with a sort of nervous haste: "Oh! Good-night, Captain Giles, good-night."

His movements were always deliberate, but his back had receded some distance along the deserted quay before I collected myself enough to follow his example and made a half turn in the direction of the jetty.

Only my movements were not deliberate. I hurried down to the steps and leaped into the launch. Before I had fairly landed in her stern-sheets the slim little craft darted away from the jetty with a sudden swirl of her propeller and the hard, rapid puffing of the exhaust in her vaguely gleaming brass funnel amidships.

The misty churning at her stern was the only sound in the world. The shore lay plunged in the silence of the deepest slumber. I watched the town recede still and soundless in the hot night, till the abrupt hail, "Steam-launch, ahoy!" made me spin round face forward. We were close to a white, ghostly steamer. Lights shone on her decks, in her port-holes. And the same voice shouted from her: "Is that our passenger?"

"It is," I yelled.

Her crew had been obviously on the jump. I could hear them running about. The modern spirit of haste was loudly vocal in the orders to "Heave away on the cable"—to "Lower the side-ladder," and in urgent requests to me to "Come along, sir! We have been delayed three hours for you. . . . Our time is seven o'clock, you know!"

I stepped on the deck. I said, "No! I don't know." The spirit of modern hurry was embodied in a thin, long-armed, long-legged man, with a closely clipped grey beard. His meagre hand was hot and dry. He declared feverishly:

"I am hanged if I would have waited another five minutes—harbour-master or no harbour-master."

"That's your own business," I said. "I didn't ask you to wait for me."

"I hope you don't expect any supper," he burst out. "This isn't a boarding-house afloat. You are the first passenger I ever had in my life and I hope to goodness you will be the last."

I made no answer to this hospitable communication; and, indeed, he didn't wait for any, bolting away on to his bridge to get his ship under way.

For the four days he had me on board he did not depart from that half-hostile attitude. His ship having been delayed three hours on my account, he couldn't forgive me for not being a more distinguished person. He was not exactly outspoken about it, but that feeling of annoyed wonder was peeping out perpetually in his talk.

He was absurd.

He was also a man of much experience, which he liked to trot out; but no greater contrast with Captain Giles could have been imagined. He would have amused me if I had wanted to be amused. But I did not want to be amused. I was like a lover looking forward to a meeting. Human hostility was nothing to me. I thought of my unknown ship. It was amusement enough, torment enough, occupation enough.

He perceived my state, for his wits were sufficiently sharp for that, and he poked sly fun at my preoccupation in the manner some nasty, cynical old men assume towards the dreams and illusions of youth. I, on my side, refrained from questioning him as to the appearance of my ship, though I knew that being in Bankok every month or so he must have known her by sight. I was not going to expose the ship, my ship! to some slighting reference.

He was the first really unsympathetic man I had ever come in contact with. My education was far from being finished, though I didn't know it. No! I didn't know it.

All I knew was that he disliked me and had some contempt for my person. Why? Apparently because his ship had been delayed three hours on my account. Who was I to have such a thing done for me? Such a thing had never been done for him. It was a sort of jealous indignation.

My expectation, mingled with fear, was wrought to its highest pitch. How slow had been the days of the passage and how soon they were over. One morning early, we crossed the bar, and while the sun was rising splendidly over the flat spaces of the land we steamed up the innumerable bends, passed under the shadow of the great gilt pagoda, and reached the outskirts of the town.

There it was, spread largely on both banks, the Oriental capital which had as yet suffered no white conqueror; an

expanse of brown houses of bamboo, of mats, of leaves, of
a vegetable-matter style of architecture, sprung out of the
brown soil on the banks of the muddy river. It was amazing
to think that in those miles of human habitations there was
not probably half a dozen pounds of nails. Some of those
houses of sticks and grass, like the nests of an aquatic race,
clung to the low shores. Others seemed to grow out of the
water; others again floated in long anchored rows in the
very middle of the stream. Here and there in the distance,
above the crowded mob of low, brown roof ridges, towered
great piles of masonry, King's Palace, temples, gorgeous
and dilapidated, crumbling under the vertical sunlight, tremendous, overpowering, almost palpable, which seemed to
enter one's breast with the breath of one's nostrils and soak
into one's limbs through every pore of one's skin.

The ridiculous victim of jealousy had for some reason or
other to stop his engines just then. The steamer drifted
slowly up with the tide. Oblivious of my new surroundings
I walked the deck, in anxious, deadened abstraction, a commingling of romantic reverie with a very practical survey
of my qualifications. For the time was approaching for me
to behold my command and to prove my worth in the
ultimate test of my profession.

Suddenly I heard myself called by that imbecile. He was
beckoning me to come up on his bridge.

I didn't care very much for that, but as it seemed that
he had something particular to say I went up the ladder.

He laid his hand on my shoulder and gave me a slight
turn, pointing with his other arm at the same time.

"There! That's your ship, Captain," he said. I felt a
thump in my breast—only one, as if my heart had then
ceased to beat. There were ten or more ships moored along
the bank, and the one he meant was partly hidden from
my sight by her next astern. He said: "We'll drift abreast
her in a moment."

What was his tone? Mocking? Threatening? Or only indifferent? I could not tell. I suspected some malice in this
unexpected manifestation of interest.

He left me, and I leaned over the rail of the bridge looking over the side. I dared not raise my eyes. Yet it had to

be done—and, indeed, I could not have helped myself. I believe I trembled.

But directly my eyes had rested on my ship all my fear vanished. It went off swiftly, like a bad dream. Only that a dream leaves no shame behind it, and that I felt a momentary shame at my unworthy suspicions.

Yes, there she was. Her hull, her rigging filled my eye with a great content. That feeling of life-emptiness which had made me so restless for the last few months lost its bitter plausibility, its evil influence, dissolved in a flow of joyous emotion.

At the first glance I saw that she was a high-class vessel, a harmonious creature in the lines of her fine body, in the proportioned tallness of her spars. Whatever her age and her history, she had preserved the stamp of her origin. She was one of those craft that in virtue of their design and complete finish will never look old. Amongst her companions moored to the bank, and all bigger than herself, she looked like a creature of high breed—an Arab steed in a string of cart-horses.

A voice behind me said in a nasty equivocal tone: "I hope you are satisfied with her, Captain." I did not even turn my head. It was the master of the steamer, and whatever he meant, whatever he thought of her, I knew that, like some rare women, she was one of those creatures whose mere existence is enough to awaken an unselfish delight. One feels that it is good to be in the world in which she has her being.

That illusion of life and character which charms one in men's finest handiwork radiated from her. An enormous baulk of teak-wood timber swung over her hatchway; lifeless matter, looking heavier and bigger than anything aboard of her. When they started lowering it the surge of the tackle sent a quiver through her from water-line to the trucks up the fine nerves of her rigging, as though she had shuddered at the weight. It seemed cruel to load her so. . . .

Half-an-hour later, putting my foot on her deck for the first time, I received the feeling of deep physical satisfaction. Nothing could equal the fullness of that moment, the

ideal completeness of that emotional experience which had
come to me without the preliminary toil and disenchant-
ments of an obscure career.

My rapid glance ran over her, enveloped, appropriated
the form concreting the abstract sentiment of my command. A lot of details perceptible to a seaman struck my
eye vividly in that instant. For the rest, I saw her disen-
gaged from the material conditions of her being. The shore
to which she was moored was as if it did not exist. What
were to me all the countries of the globe? In all the parts
of the world washed by navigable waters our relation to
each other would be the same—and more intimate than
there are words to express in the language. Apart from that,
every scene and episode would be a mere passing show.
The very gang of yellow coolies busy about the main hatch
was less substantial than the stuff dreams are made of. For
who on earth would dream of Chinamen? . . .

I went aft, ascended the poop, where, under the awning,
gleamed the brasses of the yacht-like fittings, the polished
surfaces of the rails, the glass of the skylights. Right aft two
seamen, busy cleaning the steering-gear, with the reflected
ripples of light running playfully up their bent backs, went
on with their work, unaware of me and of the almost af-
fectionate glance I threw at them in passing towards the
companion-way of the cabin.

The doors stood wide open, the slide was pushed right
back. The half-turn of the staircase cut off the view of the
lobby. A low humming ascended from below, but it stopped
abruptly at the sound of my descending footsteps.

III

The first thing I saw down there was the upper part of a
man's body projecting backwards, as it were, from one of
the doors at the foot of the stairs. His eyes looked at me
very wide and still. In one hand he held a dinner plate, in
the other a cloth.

"I am your new captain," I said quietly.

In a moment, in the twinkling of an eye, he had got rid

of the plate and the cloth and jumped to open the cabin door. As soon as I passed into the saloon he vanished, but only to reappear instantly, buttoning up a jacket he had put on with the swiftness of a "quick-change" artist.

"Where's the chief mate?" I asked.

"In the hold, I think, sir. I saw him go down the after-hatch ten minutes ago."

"Tell him I am on board."

The mahogany table under the skylight shone in the twilight like a dark pool of water. The sideboard, surmounted by a wide looking-glass in an ormolu frame, had a marble top. It bore a pair of silver-plated lamps and some other pieces—obviously a harbour display. The saloon itself was panelled in two kinds of wood in the excellent, simple taste prevailing when the ship was built.

I sat down in the arm-chair at the head of the table—the captain's chair, with a small tell-tale compass swung above it—a mute reminder of unremitting vigilance.

A succession of men had sat in that chair. I became aware of that thought suddenly, vividly, as though each had left a little of himself between the four walls of these ornate bulkheads; as if a sort of composite soul, the soul of command, had whispered suddenly to mine of long days at sea and of anxious moments.

"You, too!" it seemed to say, "you, too, shall taste of that peace and that unrest in a searching intimacy with your own self—obscure as we were and as supreme in the face of all the winds and all the seas, in an immensity that receives no impress, preserves no memories, and keeps no reckoning of lives."

Deep within the tarnished ormolu frame, in the hot half-light sifted through the awning, I saw my own face propped between my hands. And I stared back at myself with the perfect detachment of distance, rather with curiosity than with any other feeling, except of some sympathy for this latest representative of what for all intents and purposes was a dynasty; continuous not in blood, indeed, but in its experience, in its training, in its conception of duty, and in the blessed simplicity of its traditional point of view on life.

It struck me that this quietly staring man whom I was watching, both as if he were myself and somebody else, was not exactly a lonely figure. He had his place in a line of men whom he did not know, of whom he had never heard; but who were fashioned by the same influences, whose souls in relation to their humble life's work had no secrets for him.

Suddenly I perceived that there was another man in the saloon, standing a little on one side and looking intently at me. The chief mate. His long, red moustache determined the character of his physiognomy, which struck me as pugnacious in (strange to say) a ghastly sort of way.

How long had he been there looking at me, appraising me in my unguarded day-dreaming state? I would have been more disconcerted if, having the clock set in the top of the mirror-frame right in front of me, I had not noticed that its long hand had hardly moved at all.

I could not have been in that cabin more than two minutes altogether. Say three. . . . So he could not have been watching me more than a mere fraction of a minute, luckily. Still, I regretted the occurrence.

But I showed nothing of it as I rose leisurely (it had to be leisurely) and greeted him with perfect friendliness.

There was something reluctant and at the same time attentive in his bearing. His name was Burns. We left the cabin and went round the ship together. His face in the full light of day appeared very worn, meagre, even haggard. Somehow I had a delicacy as to looking too often at him; his eyes, on the contrary, remained fairly glued on my face. They were greenish and had an expectant expression.

He answered all my questions readily enough, but my ear seemed to catch a tone of unwillingness. The second officer, with three or four hands, was busy forward. The mate mentioned his name and I nodded to him in passing. He was very young. He struck me as rather a cub.

When we returned below I sat down on one end of a deep, semi-circular, or, rather, semi-oval settee, upholstered in red plush. It extended right across the whole after-end of the cabin. Mr. Burns, motioned to sit down, dropped into one of the swivel-chairs round the table, and kept his eyes on me as persistently as ever, and with that strange air as if all this were make-believe and he expected me to get up, burst into a laugh, slap him on the back, and vanish from the cabin.

There was an odd stress in the situation which began to make me uncomfortable. I tried to react against this vague feeling.

"It's only my inexperience," I thought.

In the face of that man, several years, I judged, older than myself, I became aware of what I had left already behind me—my youth. And that was indeed poor comfort. Youth is a fine thing, a mighty power—as long as one does not think of it. I felt I was becoming self-conscious. Almost against my will I assumed a moody gravity. I said: "I see you have kept her in very good order, Mr. Burns."

Directly I had uttered these words I asked myself angrily why the deuce did I want to say that? Mr. Burns in answer had only blinked at me. What on earth did he mean?

I fell back on a question which had been in my thoughts for a long time—the most natural question on the lips of any seaman whatever joining a ship. I voiced it (confound this self-consciousness) in a *dégagé* cheerful tone: "I suppose she can travel—what?"

Now a question like this might have been answered normally, either in accents of apologetic sorrow or with a visibly suppressed pride, in a "I don't want to boast, but you shall see" sort of tone. There are sailors, too, who would have been roughly outspoken: "Lazy brute," or openly delighted: "She's a flyer." Two ways, if four manners.

But Mr. Burns found another way, a way of his own which had, at all events, the merit of saving his breath, if no other.

Again he did not say anything. He only frowned. And it was an angry frown. I waited. Nothing more came.

"What's the matter? . . . Can't you tell after being nearly two years in the ship?" I addressed him sharply.

He looked as startled for a moment as though he had discovered my presence only that very moment. But this passed off almost at once. He put on an air of indifference. But I suppose he thought it better to say something. He said that a ship needed, just like a man, the chance to show the best she could do, and that this ship had never had a chance since he had been on board of her. Not that he could remember. The last captain . . . He paused.

"Has he been so very unlucky?" I asked with frank incredulity. Mr. Burns turned his eyes away from me. No, the late captain was not an unlucky man. One couldn't say that. But he had not seemed to want to make use of his luck.

Mr. Burns—man of enigmatic moods—made this statement with an inanimate face and staring wilfully at the rudder-casing. The statement itself was obscurely suggestive. I asked quietly:

"Where did he die?"

"In this saloon. Just where you are sitting now," answered Mr. Burns.

I repressed a silly impulse to jump up; but upon the whole I was relieved to hear that he had not died in the bed which was now to be mine. I pointed out to the chief mate that what I really wanted to know was where he had buried his late captain.

Mr. Burns said that it was at the entrance to the Gulf. A roomy grave; a sufficient answer. But the mate, overcoming visibly something within him—something like a curious reluctance to believe in my advent (as an irrevocable fact, at any rate), did not stop at that—though, indeed, he may have wished to do so.

As a compromise with his feelings, I believe, he addressed himself persistently to the rudder-casing, so that to me he had the appearance of a man talking in solitude, a little unconsciously, however.

His tale was that at seven bells in the forenoon watch he had all hands mustered on the quarter-deck and told them that they had better go down to say good-bye to the captain.

Those words, as if grudged to an intruding personage, were enough for me to evoke vividly that strange ceremony: The bare-footed, bare-headed seamen crowding shyly into that cabin, a small mob pressed against that sideboard, uncomfortable rather than moved, shirts open on sunburnt chests, weather-beaten faces, and all staring at the dying man with the same grave and expectant expression.

"Was he conscious?" I asked.

"He didn't speak, but he moved his eyes to look at them," said the mate.

After waiting a moment Mr. Burns motioned the crew to leave the cabin, but he detained the two eldest men to stay with the captain while he went on deck with his sextant to "take the sun." It was getting towards noon and he was anxious to obtain a good observation for latitude. When he returned below to put his sextant away he found that the two men had retreated out into the lobby. Through the open door he had a view of the captain lying easy against the pillows. He had "passed away" while Mr. Burns was taking his observation. As near noon as possible. He had hardly changed his position.

Mr. Burns sighed, glanced at me inquisitively, as much as to say, "Aren't you going yet?" and then turned his thoughts from his new captain back to the old, who, being dead, had no authority, was not in anybody's way, and was much easier to deal with.

Mr. Burns dealt with him at some length. He was a peculiar man—of about sixty-five—iron grey, hard-faced, obstinate, and uncommunicative. He used to keep the ship loafing at sea for inscrutable reasons. Would come on deck at night sometimes, take some sail off her, God only knows why or wherefore, then go below, shut himself up in his cabin, and play on the violin for hours—till daybreak perhaps. In fact, he spent most of his time day or night playing the violin. That was when the fit took him. Very loud, too.

It came to this, that Mr. Burns mustered his courage one day and remonstrated earnestly with the captain. Neither he nor the second mate could get a wink of sleep in their watches below for the noise. . . . And how could they be expected to keep awake while on duty? he pleaded. The answer of that stern man was that if he and the second mate didn't like the noise, they were welcome to pack up their traps and walk over the side. When this alternative was offered the ship happened to be 600 miles from the nearest land.

Mr. Burns at this point looked at me with an air of curiosity. I began to think that my predecessor was a remarkably peculiar old man.

But I had to hear stranger things yet. It came out that this stern, grim, wind-tanned, rough, sea-salted, tactiturn sailor of sixty-five was not only an artist, but a lover as well. In Haiphong, when they got there after a course of most unprofitable peregrinations (during which the ship was nearly lost twice), he got himself, in Mr. Burns' own words, "mixed up" with some woman. Mr. Burns had had no personal knowledge of that affair, but positive evidence of it existed in the shape of a photograph taken in Haiphong. Mr. Burns found it in one of the drawers in the captain's room.

In due course I, too, saw that amazing human document (I even threw it overboard later). There he sat with his hands reposing on his knees, bald, squat, grey, bristly, recalling a wild boar somehow; and by his side towered an awful, mature, white female with rapacious nostrils and a cheaply ill-omened stare in her enormous eyes. She was disguised in some semi-oriental, vulgar, fancy costume. She resembled a low-class medium or one of those women who tell fortunes by cards for half-a-crown. And yet she was striking. A professional sorceress from the slums. It was incomprehensible. There was something awful in the thought that she was the last reflection of the world of passion for the fierce soul which seemed to look at one out of the sardonically savage face of that old seaman. However, I noticed that she was holding some musical instrument— guitar or mandolin—in her hand. Perhaps that was the secret of her sortilege.

For Mr. Burns that photograph explained why the unloaded ship was kept sweltering at anchor for three weeks in a pestilential hot harbour without air. They lay there and gasped. The captain, appearing now and then on short visits, mumbled to Mr. Burns unlikely tales about some letters he was waiting for.

Suddenly, after vanishing for a week, he came on board

in the middle of the night and took the ship out to sea with the first break of dawn. Daylight showed him looking wild and ill. The mere getting clear of the land took two days, and somehow or other they bumped slightly on a reef. However, no leak developed, and the captain, growling "no matter," informed Mr. Burns that he had made up his mind to take the ship to Hong-Kong and dry-dock her there.

At this Mr. Burns was plunged into despair. For indeed, to beat up to Hong-Kong against a fierce monsoon, with a ship not sufficiently ballasted and with her supply of water not completed, was an insane project.

But the captain growled peremptorily, "Stick her at it," and Mr. Burns, dismayed and enraged, stuck her at it, and kept her at it, blowing away sails, straining the spars, exhausting the crew—nearly maddened by the absolute conviction that the attempt was impossible and was bound to end in some catastrophe.

Meantime the captain, shut up in his cabin and wedged in a corner of his settee against the crazy bounding of the ship, played the violin—or, at any rate, made continuous noise on it.

When he appeared on deck he would not speak and not always answer when spoken to. It was obvious that he was ill in some mysterious manner, and beginning to break up.

As the days went by the sounds of the violin became less and less loud, till at last only a feeble scratching would meet Mr. Burns' ear as he stood in the saloon listening outside the door of the captain's state-room.

One afternoon in perfect desperation he burst into that room and made such a scene, tearing his hair and shouting such horrid imprecations that he cowed the contemptuous spirit of the sick man. The water-tanks were low, they had not gained 50 miles in a fortnight. She would never reach Hong-Kong.

It was like fighting desperately towards destruction for the ship and the men. This was evident without argument. Mr. Burns, losing all restraint, put his face close to his captain's and fairly yelled: "You, sir, are going out of the world. But I can't wait till you are dead before I put the helm up. You must do it yourself. You must do it now!"

The man on the couch snarled in contempt: "So I am going out of the world—am I?"

"Yes, sir—you haven't many days left in it," said Mr. Burns calming down. "One can see it by your face."

"My face, eh? . . . Well, put the helm up and be damned to you."

Burns flew on deck, got the ship before the wind, then came down again, composed but resolute.

"I've shaped a course for Pulo Condor, sir," he said. "When we make it, if you are still with us, you'll tell me into what port you wish me to take the ship and I'll do it."

The old man gave him a look of savage spite, and said these atrocious words in deadly, slow tones:

"If I had my wish, neither the ship nor any of you would ever reach a port. And I hope you won't."

Mr. Burns was profoundly shocked. I believe he was positively frightened at the time. It seems, however, that he managed to produce such an effective laugh that it was the old man's turn to be frightened. He shrank within himself and turned his back on him.

"And his head was not gone then," Mr. Burns assured me excitedly. "He meant every word of it."

Such was practically the late captain's last speech. No connected sentence passed his lips afterwards. That night he used the last of his strength to throw his fiddle over the side. No one had actually seen him in the act, but after his death Mr. Burns couldn't find the thing anywhere. The empty case was very much in evidence, but the fiddle was clearly not in the ship. And where else could it have gone to but overboard?

"Threw his violin overboard!" I exclaimed.

"He did," cried Mr. Burns excitedly. "And it's my belief he would have tried to take the ship down with him if it had been in human power. He never meant her to see home again. He wouldn't write to his owners, he never wrote to his old wife either—he wasn't going to. He had made up his mind to cut adrift from everything. That's what it was. He didn't care for business, or freights, or for making a passage—or anything. He meant to have gone wandering about the world till he lost her with all hands."

Mr. Burns looked like a man who had escaped great danger. For a little he would have exclaimed: "If it hadn't been for me!" And the transparent innocence of his indignant eyes was underlined quaintly by the arrogant pair of moustaches which he proceeded to twist, and as if extend, horizontally.

I might have smiled if I had not been busy with my own sensations, which were not those of Mr. Burns. I was already the man in command. My sensations could not be like those of any other man on board. In that community I stood, like a king in his country, in a class all by myself. I mean an hereditary king, not a mere elected head of a state. I was brought there to rule by an agency as remote from the people and as inscrutable almost to them as the Grace of God.

And like a member of a dynasty, feeling a semi-mystical bond with the dead, I was profoundly shocked by my immediate predecessor.

That man had been in all essentials but his age just such another man as myself. Yet the end of his life was a complete act of treason, the betrayal of a tradition which seemed to me as imperative as any guide on earth could be. It appeared that even at sea a man could become the victim of evil spirits. I felt on my face the breath of unknown powers that shape our destinies.

Not to let the silence last too long I asked Mr. Burns if he had written to his captain's wife. He shook his head. He had written to nobody.

In a moment he became sombre. He never thought of writing. It took him all his time to watch incessantly the loading of the ship by a rascally Chinese stevedore. In this Mr. Burns gave me the first glimpse of the real chief mate's soul which dwelt uneasily in his body.

He mused, then hastened on with gloomy force.

"Yes! The captain died as near noon as possible. I looked through his papers in the afternoon. I read the service over him at sunset and then I stuck the ship's head north and brought her in here. I—brought—her—in."

He struck the table with his fist.

"She would hardly have come in by herself," I observed. "But why didn't you make for Singapore instead?"

His eyes wavered. "The nearest port," he muttered sullenly.

I had framed the question in perfect innocence, but this answer (the difference in distance was insignificant) and his manner offered me a clue to the simple truth. He took the ship to a port where he expected to be confirmed in his temporary command from lack of a qualified master to put over his head. Whereas Singapore, he surmised justly, would be full of qualified men.

But his naïve reasoning forgot to take into account the telegraph cable reposing on the bottom of the very Gulf up which he had turned that ship which he imagined himself to have saved from destruction. Hence the bitter flavour of our interview. I tasted it more and more distinctly—and it was less and less to my taste.

"Look here, Mr. Burns," I began, very firmly. "You may as well understand that I did not run after this command. It was pushed in my way. I've accepted it. I am here to take the ship home first of all, and you may be sure that I shall see to it that every one of you on board here does his duty to that end. This is all I have to say—for the present."

He was on his feet by this time, but instead of taking his dismissal he remained with trembling, indignant lips, and looking at me hard as though, really, after this, there was nothing for me to do in common decency but to vanish from his outraged sight. Like all very simple emotional states this was moving. I felt sorry for him—almost sympathetic, till (seeing that I did not vanish) he spoke in a tone of forced restraint.

"If I hadn't a wife and a child at home you may be sure, sir, I would have asked you to let me go the very minute you came on board."

I answered him with a matter-of-course calmness as though some remote third person were in question.

"And I, Mr. Burns, would not have let you go. You have signed the ship's articles as chief officer, and till they are terminated at the final port of discharge I shall expect you to attend to your duty and give me the benefit of your experience to the best of your ability."

Stony incredulity lingered in his eyes; but it broke down before my friendly attitude. With a slight upward toss of his arms (I got to know that gesture well afterwards) he bolted out of the cabin.

We might have saved ourselves that little passage of harmless sparring. Before many days had elapsed it was Mr. Burns who was pleading with me anxiously not to leave him behind; while I could only return him but doubtful answers. The whole thing took on a somewhat tragic complexion.

And this horrible problem was only an extraneous episode, a mere complication in the general problem of how to get that ship—which was mine with her appurtenances and her men, with her body and her spirit now slumbering in that pestilential river—how to get her out to sea.

Mr. Burns, while still acting captain, had hastened to sign a charter-party which in an ideal world without guile would have been an excellent document. Directly I ran my eye over it I foresaw trouble ahead unless the people of the other part were quite exceptionally fair-minded and open to argument.

Mr. Burns, to whom I imparted my fears, chose to take great umbrage at them. He looked at me with that usual incredulous stare, and said bitterly:

"I suppose, sir, you want to make out I've acted like a fool?"

I told him, with my systematic kindliness which always seemed to augment his surprise, that I did not want to make out anything. I would leave that to the future.

And, sure enough, the future brought in a lot of trouble. There were days when I used to remember Captain Giles with nothing short of abhorrence. His confounded acuteness had let me in for this job; while his prophecy that I "would have my hands full" coming true, made it appear as if done on purpose to play an evil joke on my young innocence.

Yes. I had my hands full of complications which were most valuable as "experience." People have a great opinion of the advantages of experience. But in that connection experience means always something disagreeable as opposed to the charm and innocence of illusions.

I must say I was losing mine rapidly. But on these instructive complications I must not enlarge more than to say that they could all be résuméd in the one word: Delay.

A mankind which has invented the proverb, "Time is money," will understand my vexation. The word "Delay" entered the secret chamber of my brain, resounded there like a tolling bell which maddens the ear, affected all my senses, took on a black colouring, a bitter taste, a deadly meaning.

"I am really sorry to see you worried like this. Indeed, I am . . ."

It was the only humane speech I used to hear at that time. And it came from a doctor, appropriately enough.

A doctor is humane by definition. But that man was so in reality. His speech was not professional. I was not ill. But other people were, and that was the reason of his visiting the ship.

He was the doctor of our Legation and, of course, of the Consulate too. He looked after the ship's health, which generally was poor, and trembling, as it were, on the verge of a break-up. Yes. The men ailed. And thus time was not only money, but life as well.

I had never seen such a steady ship's company. As the doctor remarked to me: "You seem to have a most respectable lot of seamen." Not only were they consistently sober, but they did not even want to go ashore. Care was taken to expose them as little as possible to the sun. They were employed on light work under the awnings. And the humane doctor commended me.

"Your arrangements appear to me to be very judicious, my dear Captain."

It is difficult to express how much that pronouncement comforted me. The doctor's round full face framed in a light-coloured whisker was the perfection of a dignified amenity. He was the only human being in the world who seemed to take the slightest interest in me. He would generally sit in the cabin for half-an-hour or so at every visit.

I said to him one day:

"I suppose the only thing now is to take care of them as you are doing, till I can get the ship to sea?"

He inclined his head, shutting his eyes under the large spectacles, and murmured:

"The sea . . . undoubtedly."

The first member of the crew fairly knocked over was the steward—the first man to whom I had spoken on board. He was taken ashore (with choleraic symptoms) and died there at the end of a week. Then, while I was still under the startling impression of this first home-thrust of the climate, Mr. Burns gave up and went to bed in a raging fever without saying a word to anybody.

I believe he had partly fretted himself into that illness; the climate did the rest with the swiftness of an invisible monster ambushed in the air, in the water, in the mud of the river bank. Mr. Burns was a predestined victim.

I discovered him lying on his back, glaring sullenly and radiating heat on one like a small furnace. He would hardly answer my questions, and only grumbled: Couldn't a man take an afternoon off duty with a bad headache—for once?

That evening, as I sat in the saloon after dinner, I could hear him muttering continuously in his room. Ransome, who was clearing the table, said to me:

"I am afraid, sir, I won't be able to give the mate all the attention he's likely to need. I will have to be forward in the galley a great part of my time."

Ransome was the cook. The mate had pointed him out to me the first day, standing on the deck, his arms crossed on his broad chest, gazing on the river.

Even at a distance his well-proportioned figure, something thoroughly sailor-like in his poise, made him noticeable. On nearer view the intelligent, quiet eyes, a well-bred face, the disciplined independence of his manner made up an attractive personality. When, in addition, Mr. Burns told me that he was the best seaman in the ship, I expressed my surprise that in his earliest prime and of such appearance he should sign on as cook on board a ship.

"It's his heart," Mr. Burns had said. "There's something

wrong with it. He mustn't exert himself too much or he may drop dead suddenly."

And he was the only one the climate had not touched—perhaps because, carrying a deadly enemy in his breast, he had schooled himself into a systematic control of feelings and movements. When one was in the secret this was apparent in his manner. After the poor steward died, and as he could not be replaced by a white man in this Oriental port, Ransome had volunteered to do the double work.

"I can do it all right, sir, as long as I go about it quietly," he had assured me.

But obviously he couldn't be expected to take up sick-nursing in addition. Moreover, the doctor peremptorily ordered Mr. Burns ashore.

With a seaman on each side holding him up under the arms, the mate went over the gangway more sullen than ever. We built him up with pillows in the gharry, and he made an effort to say brokenly:

"Now—you've got—what you wanted—got me out of—the ship."

"You were never more mistaken in your life, Mr. Burns," I said quietly, duly smiling at him; and the trap drove off to a sort of sanatorium, a pavilion of bricks which the doctor had in the grounds of his residence.

I visited Mr. Burns regularly. After the first few days, when he didn't know anybody, he received me as if I had come either to gloat over a crushed enemy or else to curry favour with a deeply-wronged person. It was either one or the other, just as it happened according to his fantastic sick-room moods. Whichever it was, he managed to convey it to me even during the period when he appeared almost too weak to talk. I treated him to my invariable kindliness.

Then one day, suddenly, a surge of downright panic burst through all this craziness.

If I left him behind in this deadly place he would die. He felt it, he was certain of it. But I wouldn't have the heart to leave him ashore. He had a wife and child in Sydney.

He produced his wasted fore-arms from under the sheet

which covered him and clasped his fleshless claws. He would die! He would die here. . . .

He absolutely managed to sit up, but only for a moment, and when he fell back I really thought that he would die there and then. I called to the Bengali dispenser, and hastened away from the room.

Next day he upset me thoroughly by renewing his entreaties. I returned an evasive answer, and left him the picture of ghastly despair. The day after I went in with reluctance, and he attacked me at once in a much stronger voice and with an abundance of argument which was quite startling. He presented his case with a sort of crazy vigour, and asked me finally how would I like to have a man's death on my conscience? He wanted me to promise that I would not sail without him.

I said that I really must consult the doctor first. He cried out at that. The doctor! Never! That would be a death sentence.

The effort had exhausted him. He closed his eyes, but went on rambling in a low voice. I had hated him from the start. The late captain had hated him too. Had wished him dead. Had wished all hands dead. . . .

"What do you want to stand in with that wicked corpse for, sir? He'll have you too," he ended, blinking his glazed eyes vacantly.

"Mr. Burns," I cried, very much discomposed, "what on earth are you talking about?"

He seemed to come to himself, though he was too weak to start.

"I don't know," he said languidly. "But don't ask that doctor, sir. You and I are sailors. Don't ask him, sir. Some day perhaps you will have a wife and child yourself."

And again he pleaded for the promise that I would not leave him behind. I had the firmness of mind not to give it to him. Afterwards this sternness seemed criminal; for my mind was made up. That prostrated man, with hardly strength enough to breathe and ravaged by a passion of fear, was irresistible. And, besides, he had happened to hit on the right words. He and I were sailors. That was a claim, for I had no other family. As to the wife-and-child (some day) argument it had no force. It sounded merely bizarre.

I could imagine no claim that would be stronger and more absorbing than the claim of that ship, of these men snared in the river by silly commercial complications, as if in some poisonous trap.

However, I had nearly fought my way out. Out to sea. The sea—which was pure, safe, and friendly. Three days more.

That thought sustained and carried me on my way back to the ship. In the saloon the doctor's voice greeted me, and his large form followed his voice, issuing out of the starboard spare cabin where the ship's medicine chest was kept securely lashed in the bed-place.

Finding that I was not on board he had gone in there, he said, to inspect the supply of drugs, bandages, and so on. Everything was completed and in order.

I thanked him; I had just been thinking of asking him to do that very thing, as in a couple of days, as he knew, we were going to sea, where all our troubles of every sort would be over at last.

He listened gravely and made no answer. But when I opened to him my mind as to Mr. Burns he sat down by my side, and, laying his hand on my knee amicably, begged me to think what it was I was exposing myself to.

The man was just strong enough to bear being moved and no more. But he couldn't stand a return of the fever. I had before me a passage of sixty days perhaps, beginning with intricate navigation and ending probably with a lot of bad weather. Could I run the risk of having to go through it single-handed, with no chief officer and with a second quite a youth? . . .

He might have added that it was my first command too. He did probably think of that fact, for he checked himself. It was very present to my mind.

He advised me earnestly to cable to Singapore for a chief officer, even if I had to delay my sailing for a week.

"Not a day," I said. The very thought gave me the shivers. The hands seemed fairly fit, all of them, and this was the time to get them away. Once at sea I was not afraid of facing anything. The sea was now the only remedy for all my troubles.

The doctor's glasses were directed at me like two lamps searching the genuineness of my resolution. He opened his lips as if to argue further, but shut them again without saying anything. I had a vision of poor Burns so vivid in his exhaustion, helplessness, and anguish, that it moved me more than the reality I had come away from only an hour before. It was purged from the drawbacks of his personality, and I could not resist it.

"Look here," I said. "Unless you tell me officially that the man must not be moved I'll make arrangements to have him brought on board to-morrow, and shall take the ship out of the river next morning, even if I have to anchor outside the bar for a couple of days to get her ready for sea."

"Oh! I'll make all the arrangements myself," said the doctor at once. "I spoke as I did only as a friend—as a well-wisher, and that sort of thing."

He rose in his dignified simplicity and gave me a warm handshake, rather solemnly, I thought. But he was as good as his word. When Mr. Burns appeared at the gangway carried on a stretcher, the doctor himself walked by its side. The programme had been altered in so far that this transportation had been left to the last moment, on the very morning of our departure.

It was barely an hour after sunrise. The doctor waved his big arm to me from the shore and walked back at once to his trap, which had followed him empty to the riverside. Mr. Burns, carried across the quarter-deck, had the appearance of being absolutely lifeless. Ransome went down to settle him in his cabin. I had to remain on deck to look after the ship, for the tug had got hold of our towrope already.

The splash of our shore-fasts falling in the water produced a complete change of feeling in me. It was like the imperfect relief of awakening from a nightmare. But when the ship's head swung down the river away from that town, Oriental and squalid, I missed the expected elation of that striven-for moment. What there was, undoubtedly, was a relaxation of tension which translated itself into a sense of weariness after an inglorious fight.

About mid-day we anchored a mile outside the bar. The afternoon was busy for all hands. Watching the work from the poop, where I remained all the time, I detected in it some of the languor of the six weeks spent in the steaming heat of the river. The first breeze would blow that away. Now the calm was complete. I judged that the second officer—a callow youth with an unpromising face—was not, to put it mildly, of that invaluable stuff from which a commander's right hand is made. But I was glad to catch along the main deck a few smiles on those seamen's faces at which I had hardly had time to have a good look as yet. Having thrown off the mortal coil of shore affairs, I felt myself familiar with them and yet a little strange, like a long-lost wanderer among his kin.

Ransome flitted continually to and fro between the galley and the cabin. It was a pleasure to look at him. The man positively had grace. He alone of all the crew had not had a day's illness in port. But with the knowledge of that uneasy heart within his breast I could detect the restraint he put on the natural sailor-like agility of his movements. It was as though he had something very fragile or very explosive to carry about his person and was all the time aware of it.

I had occasion to address him once or twice. He answered me in his pleasant quiet voice and with a faint, slightly wistful smile. Mr. Burns appeared to be resting. He seemed fairly comfortable.

After sunset I came out on deck again to meet only a still void. The thin, featureless crust of the coast could not be distinguished. The darkness had risen around the ship like a mysterious emanation from the dumb and lonely waters. I leaned on the rail and turned my ear to the shadows of the night. Not a sound. My command might have been a planet flying vertiginously on its appointed path in a space of infinite silence. I clung to the rail as if my sense of balance were leaving me for good. How absurd. I hailed nervously.

"On deck there!"

The immediate answer, "Yes, sir," broke the spell. The anchor-watch man ran up the poop ladder smartly. I told him to report at once the slightest sign of a breeze coming.

Going below I looked in on Mr. Burns. In fact, I could not avoid seeing him, for his door stood open. The man was so wasted that, in that white cabin, under a white sheet, and with his diminished head sunk in the white pillow, his red moustaches captured one's eyes exclusively, like something artificial—a pair of moustaches from a shop exhibited there in the harsh light of the bulkhead-lamp without a shade.

While I stared with a sort of wonder he asserted himself by opening his eyes and even moving them in my direction. A minute stir.

"Dead calm, Mr. Burns," I said resignedly.

In an unexpectedly distinct voice Mr. Burns began a rambling speech. Its tone was very strange, not as if affected by his illness, but as if of a different nature. It sounded unearthly. As to the matter, I seemed to make out that it was the fault of the "old man"—the late captain—ambushed down there under the sea with some evil intention. It was a weird story.

I listened to the end; then stepping into the cabin I laid my hand on the mate's forehead. It was cool. He was light-headed only from extreme weakness. Suddenly he seemed to become aware of me, and in his own voice—of course, very feeble—he asked regretfully:

"Is there no chance at all to get under way, sir?"

"What's the good of letting go our hold of the ground only to drift, Mr. Burns?" I answered.

He sighed, and I left him to his immobility. His hold on life was as slender as his hold on sanity. I was oppressed by my lonely responsibilities. I went into my cabin to seek relief in a few hours' sleep, but almost before I closed my eyes the man on deck came down reporting a light breeze. Enough to get under way with, he said.

And it was no more than just enough. I ordered the windlass manned, the sails loosed, and the topsails set. But by the time I had cast the ship I could hardly feel any breath of wind. Nevertheless, I trimmed the yards and put everything on her. I was not going to give up the attempt.

IV

With her anchor at the bow and clothed in canvas to her very trucks, my command seemed to stand as motionless as a model ship set on the gleams and shadows of polished marble. It was impossible to distinguish land from water in the enigmatical tranquillity of the immense forces of the world. A sudden impatience possessed me.

"Won't she answer the helm at all?" I said irritably to the man whose strong brown hands grasping the spokes of the wheel stood out lighted on the darkness, like a symbol of mankind's claim to the direction of its own fate.

He answered me:

"Yes, sir. She's coming-to slowly."

"Let her head come up to south."

"Aye, aye, sir."

I paced the poop. There was not a sound but that of my footsteps, till the man spoke again.

"She is at south now, sir."

I felt a slight tightness of the chest before I gave out the first course of my first command to the silent night, heavy with dew and sparkling with stars. There was a finality in the act committing me to the endless vigilance of my lonely task.

"Steady her head at that," I said at last. "The course is south."

"South, sir," echoed the man.

I sent below the second mate and his watch and remained in charge, walking the deck through the chill, somnolent hours that precede the dawn.

Slight puffs came and went, and whenever they were strong enough to wake up the black water the murmur alongside ran through my very heart in a delicate crescendo of delight and died away swiftly. I was bitterly tired. The very stars seemed weary of waiting for daybreak. It came at last with a mother-of-pearl sheen at the zenith, such as

I had never seen before in the tropics, unglowing, almost grey, with a strange reminder of high latitudes.

The voice of the look-out man hailed from forward:

"Land on the port bow, sir."

"All right."

Leaning on the rail I never even raised my eyes. The motion of the ship was imperceptible. Presently Ransome brought me the cup of morning coffee. After I had drunk it I looked ahead, and in the still streak of very bright pale orange light I saw the land profiled flatly as if cut out of black paper and seeming to float on the water as light as cork. But the rising sun turned it into mere dark vapour, a doubtful, massive shadow trembling in the hot glare.

The watch finished washing decks. I went below and stopped at Mr. Burns' door (he could not bear to have it shut), but hesitated to speak to him till he moved his eyes. I gave him the news.

"Sighted Cape Liant at daylight. About fifteen miles."

He moved his lips then, but I heard no sound till I put my ear down, and caught the peevish comment: "This is crawling. . . . No luck."

"Better luck than standing still, anyhow," I pointed out resignedly, and left him to whatever thoughts or fancies haunted his hopeless prostration.

Later that morning, when relieved by my second officer, I threw myself on my couch and for some three hours or so I really found oblivion. It was so perfect that on waking up I wondered where I was. Then came the immense relief of the thought: on board my ship! At sea! At sea!

Through the port-holes I beheld an unruffled, sun-smitten horizon. The horizon of a windless day. But its spaciousness alone was enough to give me a sense of a fortunate escape, a momentary exultation of freedom.

I stepped out into the saloon with my heart lighter than it had been for days. Ransome was at the sideboard preparing to lay the table for the first sea dinner of the passage. He turned his head, and something in his eyes checked my modest elation.

Instinctively I asked: "What is it now?" not expecting in the least the answer I got. It was given with that sort of contained serenity which was characteristic of the man.

"I am afraid we haven't left all sickness behind us, sir."

"We haven't! What's the matter?"

He told me then that two of our men had been taken bad with fever in the night. One of them was burning and the other was shivering, but he thought that it was pretty much the same thing. I thought so too. I felt shocked by the news. "One burning, the other shivering, you say? No. We haven't left the sickness behind. Do they look very ill?"

"Middling bad, sir." Ransome's eyes gazed steadily into mine. We exchanged smiles. Ransome's a little wistful, as usual, mine no doubt grim enough, to correspond with my secret exasperation.

I asked:

"Was there any wind at all this morning?"

"Can hardly say that, sir. We've moved all the time though. The land ahead seems a little nearer."

That was it. A little nearer. Whereas if we had only had a little more wind, only a very little more, we might, we should, have been abreast of Liant by this time and increasing our distance from that contaminated shore. And it was not only the distance. It seemed to me that a stronger breeze would have blown away the infection which clung to the ship. It obviously did cling to the ship. Two men. One burning, one shivering. I felt a distinct reluctance to go and look at them. What was the good? Poison is poison. Tropical fever is tropical fever. But that it should have stretched its claw after us over the sea seemed to me an extraordinary and unfair licence. I could hardly believe that it could be anything worse than the last desperate pluck of the evil from which we were escaping into the clean breath of the sea. If only that breath had been a little stronger. However, there was the quinine against the fever. I went into the spare cabin where the medicine chest was kept to prepare two doses. I opened it full of faith as a man opens a miraculous shrine. The upper part was inhabited by a collection of bottles, all square-shouldered and as like each other as peas. Under that orderly array there were two drawers, stuffed as full of things as one could imagine—paper packages, bandages, cardboard boxes officially labelled. The lower of the two, in one of its compartments, contained our provision of quinine.

There were five bottles, all round and all of a size. One was about a third full. The other four remained still wrapped up in paper and sealed. But I did not expect to see an envelope lying on top of them. A square envelope, belonging, in fact, to the ship's stationery.

It lay so that I could see it was not closed down, and on picking it up and turning it over I perceived that it was addressed to myself. It contained a half-sheet of notepaper, which I unfolded with a queer sense of dealing with the uncanny, but without any excitement as people meet and do extraordinary things in a dream.

"My dear Captain," it began, but I ran to the signature. The writer was the doctor. The date was that of the day on which, returning from my visit to Mr. Burns in the hospital, I had found the excellent doctor waiting for me in the cabin; and when he told me that he had been putting in time inspecting the medicine chest for me. How bizarre! While expecting me to come in at any moment he had been amusing himself by writing me a letter, and then as I came in had hastened to stuff it into the medicine chest drawer. A rather incredible proceeding. I turned to the text in wonder.

In a large, hurried, but legible hand the good, sympathetic man for some reason, either of kindness or more likely impelled by the irresistible desire to express his opinion, with which he didn't want to damp my hopes before, was warning me not to put my trust in the beneficial effects of a change from land to sea. "I didn't want to add to your worries by discouraging your hopes," he wrote. "I am afraid that, medically speaking, the end of your troubles is not yet." In short, he expected me to have to fight a probable return of tropical illness. Fortunately I had a good provision of quinine. I should put my trust in that, and administer it steadily, when the ship's health would certainly improve.

I crumpled up the letter and rammed it into my pocket. Ransome carried off two big doses to the men forward. As to myself, I did not go on deck as yet. I went instead to the door of Mr. Burns' room, and gave him that news too.

It was impossible to say the effect it had on him. At first I thought that he was speechless. His head lay sunk in the pillow. He moved his lips enough, however, to assure me that he was getting much stronger; a statement shockingly untrue on the face of it.

That afternoon I took my watch as a matter of course. A great over-heated stillness enveloped the ship and seemed to hold her motionless in a flaming ambience composed in two shades of blue. Faint, hot puffs eddied nervelessly from her sails. And yet she moved. She must have. For, as the sun was setting, we had drawn abreast of Cape Liant and dropped it behind us: an ominous retreating shadow in the last gleams of twilight.

In the evening, under the crude glare of his lamp, Mr. Burns seemed to have come more to the surface of his bedding. It was as if a depressing hand had been lifted off him. He answered my few words by a comparatively long, connected speech. He asserted himself strongly. If he escaped being smothered by this stagnant heat, he said, he was confident that in a very few days he would be able to come up on deck and help me.

While he was speaking I trembled lest this effort of energy should leave him lifeless before my eyes. But I cannot deny that there was something comforting in his willingness. I made a suitable reply, but pointed out to him that the only thing that could really help us was wind—a fair wind.

He rolled his head impatiently on the pillow. And it was not comforting in the least to hear him begin to mutter crazily about the late captain, that old man buried in latitude 8° 20', right in our way—ambushed at the entrance of the Gulf.

"Are you still thinking of your late captain, Mr. Burns?" I said. "I imagine the dead feel no animosity against the living. They care nothing for them."

"You don't know that one," he breathed out feebly.

"No. I didn't know him, and he didn't know me. And so he can't have any grievance against me, anyway."

"Yes. But there's all the rest of us on board," he insisted.

I felt the inexpugnable strength of common sense being insidiously menaced by this gruesome, by this insane delusion. And I said:

"You mustn't talk so much. You will tire yourself."

"And there is the ship herself," he persisted in a whisper.

"Now, not a word more," I said, stepping in and laying my hand on his cool forehead. It proved to me that this atrocious absurdity was rooted in the man himself and not in the disease, which, apparently, had emptied him of every power, mental and physical, except that one fixed idea.

I avoided giving Mr. Burns any opening for conversation for the next few days. I merely used to throw him a hasty, cheery word when passing his door. I believe that if he had had the strength he would have called out after me more than once. But he hadn't the strength. Ransome, however, observed to me one afternoon that the mate "seemed to be picking up wonderfully."

"Did he talk any nonsense to you of late?" I asked casually.

"No, sir." Ransome was startled by the direct question; but, after a pause, he added equably: "He told me this morning, sir, that he was sorry he had to bury our late captain right in the ship's way, as one may say, out of the Gulf."

"Isn't this nonsense enough for you?" I asked, looking confidently at the intelligent, quiet face on which the secret uneasiness in the man's breast had thrown a transparent veil of care.

Ransome didn't know. He had not given a thought to the matter. And with a faint smile he flitted away from me on his never-ending duties, with his usual guarded activity.

Two more days passed. We had advanced a little way —a very little way—into the larger space of the Gulf of Siam. Seizing eagerly upon the elation of the first command thrown into my lap, by the agency of Captain Giles, I had yet an uneasy feeling that such luck as this has got perhaps to be paid for in some way. I had held, professionally, a review of my chances. I was competent enough for that. At least, I thought so. I had a general sense of my preparedness which only a man pursuing a calling he loves can know. That feeling seemed to me the most natural thing in the world. As natural as breathing. I imagined I could not have lived without it.

I don't know what I expected. Perhaps nothing else than that special intensity of existence which is the quintessence of youthful aspirations. Whatever I expected I did not expect to be beset by hurricanes. I knew better than that. In the Gulf of Siam there are no hurricanes. But neither did I expect to find myself bound hand and foot to the hopeless extent which was revealed to me as the days went on.

Not that the evil spell held us always motionless. Mysterious currents drifted us here and there, with a stealthy power made manifest by the changing vistas of the islands fringing the east shore of the Gulf. And there were winds too, fitful and deceitful. They raised hopes only to dash them into the bitterest disappointment, promises of advance ending in lost ground, expiring in sighs, dying into dumb stillness in which the currents had it all their own way—their own inimical way.

The Island of Koh-ring, a great, black, upheaved ridge amongst a lot of tiny islets, lying upon the glassy water like a triton amongst minnows, seemed to be the centre of the fatal circle. It seemed impossible to get away from it. Day after day it remained in sight. More than once, in a favourable breeze, I would take its bearing in the fast ebbing twilight, thinking that it was for the last time. Vain hope. A night of fitful airs would undo the gains of temporary favour, and the rising sun would throw out the black relief of Koh-ring, looking more barren, inhospitable, and grim than ever.

"It's like being bewitched, upon my word," I said once to Mr. Burns, from my usual position in the doorway.

He was sitting up in his bed-place. He was progressing towards the world of living men, if he could hardly have been said to have rejoined it yet. He nodded to me his frail and bony head in a wisely mysterious assent.

"Oh, yes, I know what you mean," I said. "But you cannot expect me to believe that a dead man has the power to put out of joint the meteorology of this part of the world. Though indeed it seems to have gone utterly wrong. The land and sea breezes have got broken up into small pieces. We cannot depend upon them for five minutes together."

"It won't be very long now before I can come up on deck," muttered Mr. Burns, "and then we shall see."

Whether he meant this for a promise to grapple with supernatural evil I couldn't tell. At any rate, it wasn't the kind of assistance I needed. On the other hand, I had been living on deck practically night and day so as to take advantage of every chance to get my ship a little more to the southward. The mate, I could see, was extremely weak yet, and not quite rid of his delusion, which to me appeared but a symptom of his disease. At all events, the hopefulness of an invalid was not to be discouraged. I said:

"You will be most welcome there, I am sure, Mr. Burns. If you go on improving at this rate you'll be presently one of the healthiest men in the ship."

This pleased him, but his extreme emaciation converted his self-satisfied smile into a ghastly exhibition of long teeth under the red moustache.

"Aren't the fellows improving, sir?" he asked soberly, with an extremely sensible expression of anxiety on his face.

I answered him only with a vague gesture and went away from the door. The fact was that disease played with us capriciously very much as the winds did. It would go from one man to another with a lighter or heavier touch, which always left its mark behind, staggering some, knocking others over for a time, leaving this one, returning to another, so that all of them had now an invalidish aspect and a hunted, apprehensive look in their eyes; while Ransome and I, the only two completely untouched, went amongst them assiduously distributing quinine. It was a double fight. The adverse weather held us in front and the disease pressed on our rear. I must say that the men were very good. The constant toil of trimming the yards they faced willingly. But all spring was out of their limbs, and as I looked at them from the poop I could not keep from my mind the dreadful impression that they were moving in poisoned air.

Down below, in his cabin, Mr. Burns had advanced so far as not only to be able to sit up, but even to draw up his legs. Clasping them with bony arms, like an animated skeleton, he emitted deep, impatient sighs.

"The great thing to do, sir," he would tell me on every occasion, when I gave him the chance, "the great thing is to get the ship past 8° 20' of latitude. Once she's past that we're all right."

At first I used only to smile at him, though, God knows, I had not much heart left for smiles. But at last I lost my patience.

"Oh, yes. The latitude 8° 20'. That's where you buried your late captain, isn't it?" Then with severity: "Don't you think, Mr. Burns, it's about time you dropped all that nonsense?"

He rolled at me his deep-sunken eyes in a glance of invincible obstinacy. But for the rest, he only muttered, just loud enough for me to hear, something about "Not surprised . . . find . . . play us some beastly trick yet . . ."

Such passages as this were not exactly wholesome for my resolution. The stress of adversity was beginning to tell on me. At the same time I felt a contempt for that obscure weakness of my soul. I said to myself disdainfully that it should take much more than that to affect in the smallest degree my fortitude.

I didn't know then how soon and from what unexpected direction it would be attacked.

It was the very next day. The sun had risen clear of the southern shoulder of Koh-ring, which still hung, like an evil attendant, on our port quarter. It was intensely hateful to my sight. During the night we had been heading all round the compass, trimming the yards again and again, to what I fear must have been for the most part imaginary puffs of air. Then just about sunrise we got for an hour an inexplicable, steady breeze, right in our teeth. There was no sense in it. It fitted neither with the season of the year, nor with the secular experience of seamen as recorded in books, nor with the aspect of the sky. Only purposeful malevolence could account for it. It sent us travelling at a great pace away from our proper course; and if we had been out on pleasure sailing bent it would have been a delightful breeze, with the awakened sparkle of the sea, with the sense of motion and a feeling of unwonted freshness. Then all at once, as if disdaining to carry farther the sorry jest, it dropped and died out completely in less than five minutes. The ship's head swung where it listed; the stilled sea took on the polish of a steel plate in the calm.

I went below, not because I meant to take some rest, but simply because I couldn't bear to look at it just then. The indefatigable Ransome was busy in the saloon. It had become a regular practice with him to give me an informal health report in the morning. He turned away from the sideboard with his usual pleasant, quiet gaze. No shadow rested on his intelligent forehead.

"There are a good many of them middling bad this morning, sir," he said in a calm tone.

"What? All knocked out?"

"Only two actually in their bunks, sir, but . . ."

"It's the last night that has done for them. We have had to pull and haul all the blessed time."

"I heard, sir. I had a mind to come out and help only, you know. . . ."

"Certainly not. You mustn't. . . . The fellows lie at night about the decks, too. It isn't good for them."

Ransome assented. But men couldn't be looked after like children. Moreover, one could hardly blame them for trying for such coolness and such air as there were to be found on deck. He himself, of course, knew better.

He was, indeed, a reasonable man. Yet it would have been hard to say that the others were not. The last few days had been for us like the ordeal of the fiery furnace. One really couldn't quarrel with their common, imprudent humanity making the best of the moments of relief, when the night brought in the illusion of coolness and the starlight twinkled through the heavy, dew-laden air. Moreover, most of them were so weakened that hardly anything could be done without everybody that could totter mustering on the braces. No, it was no use remonstrating with them. But I fully believed that quinine was of very great use indeed.

I believed in it. I pinned my faith to it. It would save the men, the ship, break the spell by its medicinal virtue, make time of no account, the weather but a passing worry, and, like a magic powder working against mysterious malefices, secure the first passage of my first command against the evil powers of calms and pestilence. I looked upon it as more precious than gold, and unlike gold, of which there ever hardly seems to be enough anywhere, the ship had a sufficient store of it. I went in to get it with the purpose of weighing out doses. I stretched my hand with the feeling of a man reaching for an unfailing panacea, took up a fresh bottle and unrolled the wrapper, noticing as I did so that the ends, both top and bottom, had come unsealed. . . .

But why record all the swift steps of the appalling discovery. You have guessed the truth already. There was the wrapper, the bottle, and the white powder inside, some sort of powder! But it wasn't quinine. One look at it was quite enough. I remember that at the very moment of picking up the bottle, before I even dealt with the wrapper, the weight of the object I had in my hand gave me an instant of premonition. Quinine is as light as feathers; and my nerves must have been exasperated into an extraordinary sensibility. I let the bottle smash itself on the floor. The stuff, whatever it was, felt gritty under the sole of my shoe. I snatched up the next bottle and then the next. The weight alone told the tale. One after another they fell, breaking at my feet, not because I threw them down in my dismay, but slipping through my fingers as if this disclosure were too much for my strength.

It is a fact that the very greatness of a mental shock helps one to bear up against it, by producing a sort of temporary insensibility. I came out of the state-room stunned, as if something heavy had dropped on my head. From the other side of the saloon, across the table, Ransome, with a duster in his hand, stared open-mouthed. I don't think that I looked wild. It is quite possible that I appeared to be in a hurry because I was instinctively hastening up on deck. An example of this training become instinct. The difficulties, the dangers, the problems of a ship at sea must be met on deck.

To this fact, as it were of nature, I responded instinctively; which may be taken as a proof that for a moment I must have been robbed of my reason.

I was certainly off my balance, a prey to impulse, for at the bottom of the stairs I turned and flung myself at the doorway of Mr. Burns' cabin. The wildness of his aspect checked my mental disorder. He was sitting up in his bunk, his body looking immensely long, his head drooping a little sideways, with affected complacency. He flourished, in his trembling hand, on the end of a fore-arm no thicker than a stout walking-stick, a shining pair of scissors which he tried before my very eyes to jab at his throat.

I was to a certain extent horrified; but it was rather a secondary sort of effect, not really strong enough to make me yell at him in some such manner as: "Stop!" . . . "Heavens!" . . . "What are you doing?"

In reality he was simply overtaxing his returning strength in a shaky attempt to clip off the thick growth of his red beard. A large towel was spread over his lap, and a shower of stiff hairs, like bits of copper wire, was descending on it at every snip of the scissors.

He turned to me his face grotesque beyond the fantasies of mad dreams, one cheek all bushy as if with a swollen flame, the other denuded and sunken, with the untouched long moustache on that side asserting itself, lonely and fierce. And while he stared thunderstruck, with the gaping scissors on his fingers, I shouted my discovery at him fiendishly, in six words, without comment.

V

I heard the clatter of the scissors escaping from his hand, noted the perilous heave of his whole person over the edge of the bunk after them, and then, returning to my first purpose, pursued my course on to the deck. The sparkle of the sea filled my eyes. It was gorgeous and barren, monotonous and without hope under the empty curve of the sky. The sails hung motionless and slack, the very folds of their sagging surfaces moved no more than carved granite. The impetuosity of my advent made the man at the helm start slightly. A block aloft squeaked incomprehensibly, for what on earth could have made it do so? It was a whistling note like a bird's. For a long, long time I faced an empty world, steeped in an infinity of silence, through which the sunshine poured and flowed for some mysterious purpose. Then I heard Ransome's voice at my elbow.

"I have put Mr. Burns back to bed, sir."

"You have?"

"Well, sir, he got out, all of a sudden, but when he let go of the edge of his bunk he fell down. He isn't lightheaded, though, it seems to me."

"No," I said dully, without looking at Ransome. He waited for a moment, then, cautiously as if not to give offence: "I don't think we need lose much of that stuff, sir," he said, "I can sweep it up, every bit of it almost, and then we could sift the glass out. I will go about it at once. It will not make the breakfast late, not ten minutes."

"Oh, yes," I said bitterly. "Let the breakfast wait, sweep up every bit of it, and then throw the damned lot overboard!"

The profound silence returned, and when I looked over my shoulder Ransome—the intelligent, serene Ransome—had vanished from my side. The intense loneliness of the sea acted like poison on my brain. When I turned my eyes to the ship, I had a morbid vision of her as a floating grave. Who hasn't heard of ships found drifting, haphazard, with their crews all dead? I looked at the seaman at the helm, I had an impulse to speak to him, and, indeed, his face took on an expectant cast as if he had guessed my intention. But in the end I went below, thinking I would be alone with the greatness of my trouble for a little while. But through his open door Mr. Burns saw me come down, and addressed me grumpily: "Well, sir?"

I went in. "It isn't well at all," I said.

Mr. Burns, re-established in his bed-place, was concealing his hirsute cheek in the palm of his hand.

"That confounded fellow has taken away the scissors from me," were the next words he said.

The tension I was suffering from was so great that it was perhaps just as well that Mr. Burns had started on this grievance. He seemed very sore about it and grumbled, "Does he think I am mad, or what?"

"I don't think so, Mr. Burns," I said. I looked upon him at that moment as a model of self-possession. I even conceived on that account a sort of admiration for that man, who had (apart from the intense materiality of what was left of his beard) come as near to being a disembodied spirit as any man can do and live. I noticed the preternatural sharpness of the ridge of his nose, the deep cavities of his temples, and I envied him. He was so reduced that he would probably die very soon. Enviable man! So near extinction—while I had to bear within me a tumult of suffering vitality, doubt, confusion, self-reproach, and an indefinite reluctance to meet the horrid logic of the situation. I could not help muttering: "I feel as if I were going mad myself."

Mr. Burns glared spectrally, but otherwise wonderfully composed.

"I always thought he would play us some deadly trick," he said, with a peculiar emphasis on the *he*.

It gave me a mental shock, but I had neither the mind nor the heart nor the spirit to argue with him. My form of sickness was indifference. The creeping paralysis of a hopeless outlook. So I only gazed at him. Mr. Burns broke into further speech.

"Eh? What? No! You won't believe it? Well, how do you account for this? How do you think it could have happened?"

"Happened?" I repeated dully. "Why, yes, how in the name of the infernal powers did this thing happen?"

Indeed, on thinking it out, it seemed incomprehensible that it should just be like this: the bottles emptied, refilled, rewrapped, and replaced. A sort of plot, a sinister attempt to deceive, a thing resembling sly vengeance—but for what? —or else a fiendish joke. But Mr. Burns was in possession of a theory. It was simple, and he uttered it solemnly in a hollow voice.

"I suppose they have given him about fifteen pounds in Haiphong for that little lot."

"Mr. Burns!" I cried.

He nodded grotesquely over his raised legs, like two broomsticks in the pyjamas, with enormous bare feet at the end.

"Why not? The stuff is pretty expensive in this part of the world, and they were very short of it in Tonkin. And what did he care? You have not known him. I have, and I have defied him. He feared neither God, nor devil, nor man, nor wind, nor sea, nor his own conscience. And I believe he hated everybody and everything. But I think he was afraid to die. I believe I am the only man who ever stood up to him. I faced him in that cabin where you live now, when he was sick, and I cowed him then. He thought I was going to twist his neck for him. If he had had his way we would have been beating up against the North-East monsoon, as long as he lived and afterwards too, for ages and ages. Acting the Flying Dutchman in the China Sea! Ha! Ha!"

"But why should he replace the bottles like this?" . . . I began.

"Why shouldn't he? Why should he want to throw the bottles away? They fit the drawer. They belong to the medicine chest."

"And they were wrapped up," I cried.

"Well, the wrappers were there. Did it from habit, I suppose, and as to refilling, there is always a lot of stuff they send in paper parcels that burst after a time. And then, who can tell? I suppose you didn't taste it, sir? But, of course, you are sure . . ."

"No," I said. "I didn't taste it. It is all overboard now."

Behind me, a soft, cultivated voice said: "I have tasted it. It seemed a mixture of all sorts, sweetish, saltish, very horrible."

Ransome, stepping out of the pantry, had been listening for some time, as it was very excusable in him to do.

"A dirty trick," said Mr. Burns. "I always said he would."

The magnitude of my indignation was unbounded. And the kind, sympathetic doctor too. The only sympathetic man I ever knew . . . instead of writing that warning letter, the very refinement of sympathy, why didn't the man make a proper inspection? But, as a matter of fact, it was hardly fair to blame the doctor. The fittings were in order and the medicine chest is an officially arranged affair. There was nothing really to arouse the slightest suspicion. The person I could never forgive was myself. Nothing should ever be taken for granted. The seed of everlasting remorse was sown in my breast.

"I feel it's all my fault," I exclaimed, "mine, and nobody else's. That's how I feel. I shall never forgive myself."

"That's very foolish, sir," said Mr. Burns fiercely.

And after this effort he fell back exhausted on his bed. He closed his eyes, he panted; this affair, this abominable surprise had shaken him up too. As I turned away I perceived Ransome looking at me blankly. He appreciated what it meant, but he managed to produce his pleasant, wistful smile. Then he stepped back into his pantry, and I rushed up on deck again to see whether there was any wind, any breath under the sky, any stir of the air, any sign of hope. The deadly stillness met me again. Nothing was changed except that there was a different man at the wheel. He looked ill. His whole figure drooped, and he seemed rather to cling to the spokes than hold them with a controlling grip. I said to him:

"You are not fit to be here."

"I can manage, sir," he said feebly.

As a matter of fact, there was nothing for him to do. The ship had no steerage way. She lay with her head to the westward, the everlasting Koh-ring visible over the stern, with a few small islets, black spots in the great blaze, swimming before my troubled eyes. And but for those bits of land there was no speck on the sky, no speck on the water, no shape of vapour, no wisp of smoke, no sail, no boat, no stir of humanity, no sign of life, nothing!

The first question was, what to do? What could one do? The first thing to do obviously was to tell the men. I did it that very day. I wasn't going to let the knowledge simply get about. I would face them. They were assembled on the quarter-deck for the purpose. Just before I stepped out to speak to them I discovered that life could hold terrible moments. No confessed criminal had ever been so oppressed by his sense of guilt. This is why, perhaps, my face was set hard and my voice curt and unemotional while I made my declaration that I could do nothing more for the sick, in the way of drugs. As to such care as could be given them they knew they had had it.

I would have held them justified in tearing me limb from limb. The silence which followed upon my words was almost harder to bear than the angriest uproar. I was crushed by the infinite depth of its reproach. But, as a matter of fact, I was mistaken. In a voice which I had great difficulty in keeping firm, I went on: "I suppose, men, you have understood what I said, and you know what it means."

A voice or two were heard: "Yes, sir. . . . We understand."

They had kept silent simply because they thought that they were not called to say anything; and when I told them that I intended to run into Singapore and that the best chance for the ship and the men was in the efforts all of us, sick and well, must make to get her along out of this, I received the encouragement of a low assenting murmur and of a louder voice exclaiming: "Surely there is a way out of this blamed hole."

Here is an extract from the notes I wrote at the time:

We have lost Koh-ring at last. For many days now I don't think I have been two hours below altogether. I remain on deck, of course, night and day, and the nights and the days wheel over us in succession, whether long or short, who can say? All sense of time is lost in the monotony of expectation, of hope, and of desire—which is only one: Get the ship to the southward! Get the ship to the southward! The effect is curiously mechanical; the sun climbs and descends, the night swings over our heads as if somebody below the horizon were turning a crank. It is the pettiest, the most aimless! . . . and all through that miserable performance I go on, tramping, tramping the deck. How many miles have I walked on the poop of that ship! A stubborn pilgrimage of sheer restlessness, diversified by short excursions below to look upon Mr. Burns. I don't know whether it is an illusion, but he seems to become more substantial from day to day. He doesn't say much, for, indeed, the situation doesn't lend itself to idle remarks. I notice this even with the men as I watch them moving or sitting about the decks. They don't talk to each other. It strikes me that if there exist an invisible ear catching the whispers of the earth, it will find this ship the most silent spot on it. . . .

No, Mr. Burns has not much to say to me. He sits in his bunk with his beard gone, his moustaches flaming, and with an air of silent determination on his chalky physiognomy. Ransome tells me he devours all the food that is given him to the last scrap, but that, apparently, he sleeps very little. Even at night, when I go below to fill my pipe, I notice that, though dozing flat on his back, he still looks very determined. From the side glance he gives me when awake it seems as though he were annoyed at being interrupted in some arduous mental operation; and as I emerge on deck the ordered arrangement of the stars meets my eye, unclouded, infinitely wearisome. There they are: stars, sun, sea, light, darkness, space, great waters; the formidable Work of the Seven Days, into which mankind seems to have blundered unbidden. Or else decoyed. Even as I have been decoyed into this awful, this death-haunted command. . . .

The only spot of light in the ship at night was that of the compass-lamps, lighting up the faces of the succeeding helmsmen; for the rest we were lost in the darkness, I walking the poop and the men lying about the decks. They were all so reduced by sickness that no watches could be kept. Those who were able to walk remained all the time on duty, lying about in the shadows of the main deck, till my voice raised for an order would bring them to their enfeebled feet, a tottering little group, moving patiently about the ship, with hardly a murmur, a whisper amongst them all. And every time I had to raise my voice it was with a pang of remorse and pity.

Then about four o'clock in the morning a light would gleam forward in the galley. The unfailing Ransome with the uneasy heart, immune, serene, and active, was getting ready the early coffee for the men. Presently he would bring me a cup up on the poop, and it was then that I allowed myself to drop into my deck chair for a couple of hours of real sleep. No doubt I must have been snatching short dozes when leaning against the rail for a moment in sheer exhaustion; but, honestly, I was not aware of them, except in the painful form of convulsive starts that seemed to come on me even while I walked. From about five, however, until after seven I would sleep openly under the fading stars.

I would say to the helmsman: "Call me at need," and drop into that chair and close my eyes, feeling that there was no more sleep for me on earth. And then I would know nothing till, some time between seven and eight, I would feel a touch on my shoulder and look up at Ransome's face, with its faint, wistful smile and friendly, grey eyes, as though he were tenderly amused at my slumbers. Occasionally the second mate would come up and relieve me at early coffee time. But it didn't really matter. Generally it was a dead calm, or else faint airs so changing and fugitive that it really wasn't worth while to touch a brace for them. If the air steadied at all the seaman at the helm could be trusted for a warning shout: "Ship's all aback, sir!" which like a trumpet-call would make me spring a foot above the deck. Those were the words which it seemed to me would have made me spring up from eternal sleep. But this was not often. I have never met since such breathless sunrises. And if the second mate happened to be there (he had generally one day in three free of fever) I would find him sitting on the skylight half-senseless, as it were, and with an idiotic gaze fastened on some object near by —a rope, a cleat, a belaying pin, a ringbolt.

That young man was rather troublesome. He remained cubbish in his sufferings. He seemed to have become completely imbecile; and when the return of fever drove him to his cabin below the next thing would be that we would miss him from there. The first time it happened Ransome and I were very much alarmed. We started a quiet search and ultimately Ransome discovered him curled up in the sail-locker, which opened into the lobby by a sliding-door.

When remonstrated with, he muttered sulkily, "It's cool in there." That wasn't true. It was only dark there.

The fundamental defects of his face were not improved by its uniform livid hue. It was not so with many of the men. The wastage of ill-health seemed to idealize the general character of the features, bringing out the unsuspected nobility of some, the strength of others, and in one case revealing an essentially comic aspect. He was a short, gingery, active man with a nose and chin of the Punch type, and whom his shipmates called "Frenchy." I don't know why. He may have been a Frenchman, but I have never heard him utter a single word in French.

To see him coming aft to the wheel comforted one. The blue dungaree trousers turned up the calf, one leg a little higher than the other, the clean check shirt, the white canvas cap, evidently made by himself, made up a whole of peculiar smartness, and the persistent jauntiness of his gait, even, poor fellow, when he couldn't help tottering, told of his invincible spirit. There was also a man called Gambril. He was the only grizzled person in the ship. His face was of an austere type. But if I remember all their faces, wasting tragically before my eyes, most of their names have vanished from my memory.

The words that passed between us were few and puerile in regard of the situation. I had to force myself to look them in the face. I expected to meet reproachful glances. There were none. The expression of suffering in their eyes was indeed hard enough to bear. But that they couldn't help. For the rest, I ask myself whether it was the temper of their souls or the sympathy of their imagination that made them so wonderful, so worthy of my undying regard.

For myself, neither my soul was highly tempered, nor my imagination properly under control. There were moments when I felt, not only that I would go mad, but that I had gone mad already; so that I dared not open my lips for fear of betraying myself by some insane shriek. Luckily I had only orders to give, and an order has a steadying influence upon him who has to give it. Moreover, the seaman, the officer of the watch, in me was sufficiently sane. I was like a mad carpenter making a box. Were he ever so convinced that he was King of Jerusalem, the box he would make would be a sane box. What I feared was a shrill note escaping me involuntarily and upsetting my balance. Luckily, again, there was no necessity to raise one's voice. The brooding stillness of the world seemed sensitive to the slightest sound like a whispering gallery. The conversational tone would almost carry a word from one end of the ship to the other. The terrible thing was that the only voice that I ever heard was my own. At night especially it reverberated very lonely amongst the planes of the unstirring sails.

Mr. Burns, still keeping to his bed with that air of secret determination, was moved to grumble at many things. Our interviews were short five-minute affairs, but fairly frequent. I was everlastingly diving down below to get a light, though I did not consume much tobacco at that time. The pipe was always going out; for in truth my mind was not composed enough to enable me to get a decent smoke. Likewise, for most of the time during the twenty-four hours I could have struck matches on deck and held them aloft till the flame burnt my fingers. But I always used to run below. It was a change. It was the only break in the incessant strain; and, of course, Mr. Burns through the open door could see me come in and go out every time.

With his knees gathered up under his chin and staring with his greenish eyes over them, he was a weird figure, and with my knowledge of the crazy notion in his head, not a very attractive one for me. Still, I had to speak to him now and then, and one day he complained that the ship was very silent. For hours and hours, he said, he was lying there, not hearing a sound, till he did not know what to do with himself.

"When Ransome happens to be forward in his galley everything's so still that one might think everybody in the ship was dead," he grumbled. "The only voice I do hear sometimes is yours, sir, and that isn't enough to cheer me up. What's the matter with the men? Isn't there one left that can sing out at the ropes?"

"Not one, Mr. Burns," I said. "There is no breath to spare on board this ship for that. Are you aware that there are times when I can't muster more than three hands to do anything?"

He asked swiftly but fearfully:

"Nobody dead yet, sir?"

"No."

"It wouldn't do," Mr. Burns declared forcibly. "Mustn't let him. If he gets hold of one he will get them all."

I cried out angrily at this. I believe I even swore at the disturbing effect of these words. They attacked all the self-possession that was left to me. In my endless vigil in the face of the enemy I had been haunted by gruesome images enough. I had had visions of a ship drifting in calms and swinging in light airs, with all her crew dying slowly about her decks. Such things had been known to happen.

Mr. Burns met my outburst by a mysterious silence.

"Look here," I said. "You don't believe yourself what you say. You can't. It's impossible. It isn't the sort of thing I have a right to expect from you. My position's bad enough without being worried with your silly fancies."

He remained unmoved. On account of the way in which the light fell on his head I could not be sure whether he had smiled faintly or not. I changed my tone.

"Listen," I said. "It's getting so desperate that I had thought for a moment, since we can't make our way south, whether I wouldn't try to steer west and make an attempt to reach the mail-boat track. We could always get some quinine from her, at least. What do you think?"

He cried out: "No, no, no. Don't do that, sir. You mustn't for a moment give up facing that old ruffian. If you do he will get the upper hand of us."

I left him. He was impossible. It was like a case of possession. His protest, however, was essentially quite sound. As a matter of fact, my notion of heading out west on the chance of sighting a problematical steamer could not bear calm examination. On the side where we were we had enough wind, at least from time to time, to struggle on towards the south. Enough, at least, to keep hope alive. But suppose that I had used those capricious gusts of wind to sail away to the westward, into some region where there was not a breath of air for days on end, what then? Perhaps my appalling vision of a ship floating with a dead crew would become a reality for the discovery weeks afterwards by some horror-stricken mariners.

That afternoon Ransome brought me up a cup of tea, and while waiting there, tray in hand, he remarked in the exactly right tone of sympathy:

"You are holding out well, sir."

"Yes," I said. "You and I seem to have been forgotten."

"Forgotten, sir?"

"Yes, by the fever-devil who has got on board this ship," I said.

Ransome gave me one of his attractive, intelligent, quick glances and went away with the tray. It occurred to me that I had been talking somewhat in Mr. Burns' manner. It annoyed me. Yet often in darker moments I forgot myself into an attitude towards our troubles more fit for a contest against a living enemy.

Yes. The fever-devil had not laid his hand yet either on Ransome or on me. But he might at any time. It was one of those thoughts one had to fight down, keep at arm's length at any cost. It was unbearable to contemplate the possibility of Ransome, the housekeeper of the ship, being laid low. And what would happen to my command if I got knocked over, with Mr. Burns too weak to stand without holding on to his bed-place and the second mate reduced to a state of permanent imbecility? It was impossible to imagine, or, rather, it was only too easy to imagine.

I was alone on the poop. The ship having no steerage way, I had sent the helmsman away to sit down or lie down somewhere in the shade. The men's strength was so reduced that all unnecessary calls on it had to be avoided. It was the austere Gambril with the grizzly beard. He went away readily enough, but he was so weakened by repeated bouts of fever, poor fellow, that in order to get down the poop ladder he had to turn sideways and hang on with both hands to the brass rail. It was just simply heart-breaking to watch. Yet he was neither very much worse nor much better than most of the half-dozen miserable victims I could muster up on deck.

It was a terribly lifeless afternoon. For several days in

succession low clouds had appeared in the distance, white masses with dark convolutions resting on the water, motionless, almost solid, and yet all the time changing their aspects subtly. Towards evening they vanished as a rule. But this day they awaited the setting sun, which glowed and smouldered sulkily amongst them before it sank down. The punctual and wearisome stars reappeared over our mastheads, but the air remained stagnant and oppressive.

The unfailing Ransome lighted the binnacle lamps and glided, all shadowy, up to me.

"Will you go down and try to eat something, sir?" he suggested.

His low voice startled me. I had been standing looking out over the rail, saying nothing, feeling nothing, not even the weariness of my limbs, overcome by the evil spell.

"Ransome," I asked abruptly, "how long have I been on deck? I am losing the notion of time."

"Fourteen days, sir," he said. "It was a fortnight last Monday since we left the anchorage."

His equable voice sounded mournful somehow. He waited a bit, then added: "It's the first time that it looks as if we were to have some rain."

I noticed then the broad shadow on the horizon extinguishing the low stars completely, while those overhead, when I looked up, seemed to shine down on us through a veil of smoke.

How it got there, how it had crept up so high, I couldn't say. It had an ominous appearance. The air did not stir. At a renewed invitation from Ransome I did go down into the cabin to—in his words—"try and eat something." I don't know that the trial was very successful. I suppose at that period I did exist on food in the usual way; but the memory is now that in those days life was sustained on invincible anguish, as a sort of infernal stimulant exciting and consuming at the same time.

It's the only period of my life in which I attempted to keep a diary. No, not the only one. Years later, in conditions of moral isolation, I did put down on paper the thoughts and events of a score of days. But this was the first time. I don't remember how it came about or how the pocket-book and the pencil came into my hands. It's inconceivable that I should have looked for them on purpose. I suppose they saved me from the crazy trick of talking to myself.

Strangely enough, in both cases I took to that sort of thing in circumstances in which I did not expect, in colloquial phrase, "to come out of it." Neither could I expect the record to outlast me. This shows that it was purely a personal need for intimate relief and not a call of egotism.

Here I must give another sample of it, a few detached lines, now looking very ghostly to my own eyes, out of the part scribbled that very evening:

There is something going on in the sky like a decomposition, like a corruption of the air, which remains as still as ever. After all, mere clouds, which may or may not hold wind or rain. Strange that it should trouble me so. I feel as if all my sins had found me out. But I suppose the trouble is that the ship is still lying motionless, not under command; and that I have nothing to do to keep my imagination from running wild amongst the disastrous images of the worst that may befall us. What's going to happen? Probably nothing. Or anything. It may be a furious squall coming, butt-end foremost. And on deck there are five men with the vitality and the strength of, say, two. We may have all our sails blown away. Every stitch of canvas has been on her since we broke ground at the mouth of the Mei-nam, fifteen days ago . . . or fifteen centuries. It seems to me that all my life before that momentous day is infinitely remote, a fading memory of light-hearted youth, something on the other side of a shadow. Yes, sails may very well be blown away. And that would be like a death sentence on the men. We haven't strength enough on board to bend another suit; incredible thought, but it is true. Or we may even get dismasted. Ships have been dismasted in squalls simply because they weren't handled quick enough, and we have no power to whirl the yards around. It's like being bound hand and foot preparatory to having one's throat cut. And what appals me most of all is that I shrink from going on deck to face it. It's due to the ship, it's due to the men who are there on deck—some of them, ready to put out the last remnant of their strength at a word from me. And I am shrinking from it. From the mere vision. My first command. Now I understand that strange sense of insecurity in my past. I always suspected that I might be no good. And here is proof positive, I am shirking it, I am no good.

At that moment, or, perhaps, the moment after, I became aware of Ransome standing in the cabin. Something in his expression startled me. It had a meaning which I could not make out. I exclaimed:

"Somebody's dead."

It was his turn then to look startled.

"Dead? Not that I know of, sir. I have been in the forecastle only ten minutes ago and there was no dead man there then."

"You did give me a scare," I said.

His voice was extremely pleasant to listen to. He explained that he had come down below to close Mr. Burns' port in case it should come on to rain. He did not know that I was in the cabin, he added.

"How does it look outside?" I asked him.

"Very black indeed, sir. There is something in it for certain."

"In what quarter?"

"All round, sir."

I repeated idly: "All round. For certain," with my elbows on the table.

Ransome lingered in the cabin as if he had something to do there, but hesitated about doing it. I said suddenly:

"You think I ought to be on deck?"

He answered at once but without any particular emphasis or accent: "I do, sir."

I got to my feet briskly, and he made way for me to go out. As I passed through the lobby I heard Mr. Burns' voice saying:

"Shut the door of my room, will you, steward?" And Ransome's rather surprised: "Certainly, sir."

I thought that all my feelings had been dulled into complete indifference. But I found it as trying as ever to be on deck. The impenetrable blackness beset the ship so close that it seemed that by thrusting one's hand over the side one could touch some unearthly substance. There was in it an effect of inconceivable terror and of inexpressible mystery. The few stars overhead shed a dim light upon the ship alone, with no gleams of any kind upon the water, in detached shafts piercing an atmosphere which had turned to soot. It was something I had never seen before, giving no hint of the direction from which any change would come, the closing in of a menace from all sides.

There was still no man at the helm. The immobility of all things was perfect. If the air had turned black, the sea, for all I knew, might have turned solid. It was no good looking in any direction, watching for any sign, speculating upon the nearness of the moment. When the time came the blackness would overwhelm silently the bit of starlight falling upon the ship, and the end of all things would come without a sigh, stir, or murmur of any kind, and all our hearts would cease to beat like run-down clocks.

It was impossible to shake off that sense of finality. The quietness that came over me was like a foretaste of annihilation. It gave me a sort of comfort, as though my soul had become suddenly reconciled to an eternity of blind stillness.

The seaman's instinct alone survived whole in my moral dissolution. I descended the ladder to the quarter-deck. The starlight seemed to die out before reaching that spot, but when I asked quietly: "Are you there, men?" my eyes made out shadowy forms starting up around me, very few, very indistinct; and a voice spoke: "All here, sir." Another amended anxiously:

"All that are any good for anything, sir."

Both voices were very quiet and unringing; without any special character of readiness or discouragement. Very matter-of-fact voices.

"We must try to haul this mainsail close up," I said.

The shadows swayed away from me without a word. Those men were the ghosts of themselves, and their weight on a rope could be no more than the weight of a bunch of ghosts. Indeed, if ever a sail was hauled up by sheer spiritual strength it must have been that sail, for, properly speaking, there was not muscle enough for the task in the whole ship, let alone the miserable lot of us on deck. Of course, I took the lead in the work myself. They wandered feebly after me from rope to rope, stumbling and panting. They toiled like Titans. We were an hour at it at least, and all the time the black universe made no sound. When the last leech-line was made fast, my eyes, accustomed to the darkness, made out the shapes of exhausted men drooping over the rails, collapsed on hatches. One hung over the after-capstan, sobbing for breath; and I stood amongst them like a tower of strength, impervious to disease and feeling only the sickness of my soul. I waited for some time fighting against the weight of my sins, against my sense of unworthiness, and then I said:

"Now, men, we'll go aft and square the mainyard. That's about all we can do for the ship; and for the rest she must take her chance."

VI

As we all went up it occurred to me that there ought to be a man at the helm. I raised my voice not much above a whisper, and, noiselessly, an uncomplaining spirit in a fever-wasted body appeared in the light aft, the head with hollow eyes illuminated against the blackness which had swallowed up our world—and the universe. The bare forearm extended over the upper spokes seemed to shine with a light of its own. I murmured to that luminous appearance:

"Keep the helm right amidships."

It answered in a tone of patient suffering:

"Right amidships, sir."

Then I descended to the quarter-deck. It was impossible to tell whence the blow would come. To look round the ship was to look into a bottomless, black pit. The eye lost itself in inconceivable depths. I wanted to ascertain whether the ropes had been picked up off the deck. One could only do that by feeling with one's feet. In my cautious progress I came against a man in whom I recognized Ransome. He possessed an unimpaired physical solidity which was manifest to me at the contact. He was leaning against the quarter-deck capstan and kept silent. It was like a revelation. He was the collapsed figure sobbing for breath I had noticed before we went on the poop.

"You have been helping with the mainsail!" I exclaimed in a low tone.

"Yes, sir," sounded his quiet voice.

"Man! What were you thinking of? You mustn't do that sort of thing."

After a pause he assented. "I suppose I mustn't." Then after another short silence he added: "I am all right now," quickly, between the tell-tale gasps.

I could neither hear nor see anybody else; but when I spoke up, answering sad murmurs filled the quarter-deck, and its shadows seemed to shift here and there. I ordered all the halyards laid down on deck clear for running.

"I'll see to that, sir," volunteered Ransome in his natural, pleasant tone, which comforted one and aroused one's compassion too, somehow.

That man ought to have been in his bed, resting, and my plain duty was to send him there. But perhaps he would not have obeyed me. I had not the strength of mind to try. All I said was:

"Go about it quietly, Ransome."

Returning on the poop I approached Gambril. His face, set with hollow shadows in the light, looked awful, finally silenced. I asked him how he felt, but hardly expected an answer. Therefore I was astonished at his comparative loquacity.

"Them shakes leaves me as weak as a kitten, sir," he said, preserving finely that air of unconsciousness as to anything but his business a helmsman should never lose. "And before I can pick up my strength that there hot fit comes along and knocks me over again."

He sighed. There was no complaint in his tone, but the bare words were enough to give me a horrible pang of self-reproach. It held me dumb for a time. When the tormenting sensation had passed off I asked:

"Do you feel strong enough to prevent the rudder taking charge if she gets sternway on her? It wouldn't do to get something smashed about the steering-gear now. We've enough difficulties to cope with as it is."

He answered with just a shade of weariness that he was strong enough to hang on. He could promise me that she shouldn't take the wheel out of his hands. More he couldn't say.

At that moment Ransome appeared quite close to me, stepping out of the darkness into visibility suddenly, as if just created with his composed face and pleasant voice.

Every rope on deck, he said, was laid down clear for running, as far as one could make certain by feeling. It was impossible to see anything. Frenchy had stationed himself forward. He said he had a jump or two left in him yet.

Here a faint smile altered for an instant the clear, firm design of Ransome's lips. With his serious, clear, grey eyes, his serene temperament, he was a priceless man altogether. Soul as firm as the muscles of his body.

He was the only man on board (except me, but I had to preserve my liberty of movement) who had a sufficiency of muscular strength to trust to. For a moment I thought I had better ask him to take the wheel. But the dreadful knowledge of the enemy he had to carry about him made me hesitate. In my ignorance of physiology it occurred to me that he might die suddenly, from excitement, at a critical moment.

While this gruesome fear restrained the ready words on the tip of my tongue, Ransome stepped back two paces and vanished from my sight.

At once an uneasiness possessed me, as if some support had been withdrawn. I moved forward too, outside the circle of light, into the darkness that stood in front of me like a wall. In one stride I penetrated it. Such must have been the darkness before creation. It had closed behind me. I knew I was invisible to the man at the helm. Neither could I see anything. He was alone, I was alone, every man was alone where he stood. And every form was gone, too, spar, sail, fittings, rails; everything was blotted out in the dreadful smoothness of that absolute night.

A flash of lightning would have been a relief—I mean physically. I would have prayed for it if it hadn't been for my shrinking apprehension of the thunder. In the tension of silence I was suffering from it seemed to me that the first crash must turn me into dust.

And thunder was, most likely, what would happen next. Stiff all over and hardly breathing, I waited with a horribly strained expectation. Nothing happened. It was maddening. But a dull, growing ache in the lower part of my face made me aware that I had been grinding my teeth madly enough, for God knows how long.

It's extraordinary I should not have heard myself doing it; but I hadn't. By an effort which absorbed all my faculties I managed to keep my jaw still. It required much attention, and while thus engaged I became bothered by curious, irregular sounds of faint tapping on the deck. They could be heard single, in pairs, in groups. While I wondered at this mysterious devilry, I received a slight blow under the left eye and felt an enormous tear run down my cheek. Raindrops. Enormous. Forerunners of something. Tap. Tap. Tap. . . .

I turned about, and, addressing Gambril earnestly, entreated him to "hang on to the wheel." But I could hardly speak from emotion. The fatal moment had come. I held my breath. The tapping had stopped as unexpectedly as it had begun, and there was a renewed moment of intolerable suspense; something like an additional turn of the racking screw. I don't suppose I would have ever screamed, but I remember my conviction that there was nothing else for it but to scream.

Suddenly—how am I to convey it? Well, suddenly the darkness turned into water. This is the only suitable figure. A heavy shower, a downpour, comes along, making a noise. You hear its approach on the sea, in the air too, I verily believe. But this was different. With no preliminary whisper or rustle, without a splash, and even without the ghost of impact, I became instantaneously soaked to the skin. Not a very difficult matter, since I was wearing only my sleeping suit. My hair got full of water in an instant, water streamed on my skin, it filled my nose, my ears, my eyes. In a fraction of a second I swallowed quite a lot of it.

As to Gambril, he was fairly choked. He coughed pitifully, the broken cough of a sick man; and I beheld him as one sees a fish in an aquarium by the light of an electric bulb, an elusive, phosphorescent shape. Only he did not glide away. But something else happened. Both binnacle lamps went out. I suppose the water forced itself into them, though I wouldn't have thought that possible, for they fitted into the cowl perfectly.

The last gleam of light in the universe had gone, pursued by a low exclamation of dismay from Gambril. I groped for him and seized his arm. How startlingly wasted it was.

"Never mind," I said. "You don't want the light. All you need to do is to keep the wind, when it comes, at the back of your head. You understand?"

"Aye, aye, sir. . . . But I should like to have a light," he added nervously.

All that time the ship lay as steady as a rock. The noise of the water pouring off the sails and spars, flowing over the break of the poop, had stopped short. The poop scuppers gurgled and sobbed for a little while longer, and then perfect silence, joined to perfect immobility, proclaimed the yet unbroken spell of our helplessness, poised on the edge of some violent issue, lurking in the dark.

I started forward restlessly. I did not need my sight to pace the poop of my ill-starred first command with perfect assurance. Every square foot of her decks was impressed indelibly on my brain, to the very grain and knots of the planks. Yet, all of a sudden, I fell clean over something, landing full length on my hands and face.

It was something big and alive. Not a dog—more like a sheep, rather. But there were no animals in the ship. How could an animal. . . . It was an added and fantastic horror which I could not resist. The hair of my head stirred even as I picked myself up, awfully scared; not as a man is scared while his judgment, his reason still try to resist, but completely, boundlessly, and, as it were, innocently scared —like a little child.

I could see It—that Thing! The darkness, of which so

much had just turned into water, had thinned down a little. There It was! But I did not hit upon the notion of Mr. Burns issuing out of the companion on all fours till he attempted to stand up, and even then the idea of a bear crossed my mind first.

He growled like one when I seized him round the body. He had buttoned himself up into an enormous winter overcoat of some woolly material, the weight of which was too much for his reduced state. I could hardly feel the incredibly thin lath of his body, lost within the thick stuff, but his growl had depth and substance: Confounded dumb ship with a craven, tip-toeing crowd. Why couldn't they stamp and go with a brace? Wasn't there one God-forsaken lubber in the lot fit to raise a yell on a rope?

"Skulking's no good, sir," he attacked me directly. "You can't slink past the old murderous ruffian. It isn't the way. You must go for him boldly—as I did. Boldness is what you want. Show him that you don't care for any of his damned tricks. Kick up a jolly old row."

"Good God, Mr. Burns," I said angrily. "What on earth are you up to? What do you mean by coming up on deck in this state?"

"Just that! Boldness. The only way to scare the old bullying rascal."

I pushed him, still growling, against the rail. "Hold on to it," I said roughly. I did not know what to do with him. I left him in a hurry, to go to Gambril, who had called faintly that he believed there was some wind aloft. Indeed, my own ears had caught a feeble flutter of wet canvas, high up overhead, the jingle of a slack chain sheet. . . .

These were eerie, disturbing, alarming sounds in the dead stillness of the air around me. All the instances I had heard of topmasts being whipped out of a ship while there was not wind enough on her deck to blow out a match rushed into my memory.

"I can't see the upper sails, sir," declared Gambril shakily.

"Don't move the helm. You'll be all right," I said confidently.

The poor man's nerve was gone. I was not in much

better case. It was the moment of breaking strain and was relieved by the abrupt sensation of the ship moving forward as if of herself under my feet. I heard plainly the soughing of the wind aloft, the low cracks of the upper spars taking the strain, long before I could feel the least draught on my face turned aft, anxious and sightless like the face of a blind man.

Suddenly a louder sounding note filled our ears, the darkness started streaming against our bodies, chilling them exceedingly. Both of us, Gambril and I, shivered violently in our clinging, soaked garments of thin cotton. I said to him:

"You are all right now, my man. All you've got to do is to keep the wind at the back of your head. Surely you are up to that. A child could steer this ship in smooth water."

He muttered: "Aye! A healthy child." And I felt ashamed of having been passed over by the fever which had been preying on every man's strength but mine, in order that my remorse might be the more bitter, the feeling of unworthiness more poignant, and the sense of responsibility heavier to bear.

The ship had gathered great way on her almost at once on the calm water. I felt her slipping through it with no other noise but a mysterious rustle alongside. Otherwise she had no motion at all, neither lift nor roll. It was a disheartening steadiness which had lasted for eighteen days now; for never, never had we had wind enough in that time to raise the slightest run of the sea. The breeze freshened suddenly. I thought it was high time to get Mr. Burns off the deck. He worried me. I looked upon him as a lunatic who would be very likely to start roaming over the ship and break a limb or fall overboard.

I was truly glad to find he had remained holding on where I had left him, sensibly enough. He was, however, muttering to himself ominously.

This was discouraging. I remarked in a matter-of-fact tone:

"We have never had so much wind as this since we left the roads."

"There's some heart in it too," he growled judiciously.

It was a remark of a perfectly sane seaman. But he added immediately: "It was about time I should come on deck. I've been nursing my strength for this—just for this. Do you see it, sir?"

I said I did, and proceeded to hint that it would be advisable for him to go below now and take a rest.

His answer was an indignant: "Go below! Not if I know it, sir."

Very cheerful! He was a horrible nuisance. And all at once he started to argue. I could feel his crazy excitement in the dark.

"You don't know how to go about it, sir. How could you? All this whispering and tip-toeing is no good. You can't hope to slink past a cunning, wide-awake, evil brute like he was. You never heard him talk. Enough to make your hair stand on end. No! No! He wasn't mad. He was no more mad than I am. He was just downright wicked. Wicked so as to frighten most people. I will tell you what he was. He was nothing less than a thief and a murderer at heart. And do you think he's any different now because he's dead? Not he! His carcass lies a hundred fathom under, but he's just the same . . . in latitude 8° 20' North."

He snorted defiantly. I noted with weary resignation that the breeze had got lighter while he raved. He was at it again.

"I ought to have thrown the beggar out of the ship over the rail like a dog. It was only on account of the men. . . . Fancy having to read the Burial Service over a brute like that! . . . 'Our departed brother' . . . I could have laughed. That was what he couldn't bear. I suppose I am the only man that ever stood up to laugh at him. When he got sick it used to scare that . . . brother . . . Brother . . . Departed . . . Sooner call a shark brother."

The breeze had let go so suddenly that the way of the ship brought the wet sails heavily against the mast. The spell of deadly stillness had caught us up again. There seemed to be no escape.

"Hallo!" exclaimed Mr. Burns in a startled voice. "Calm again!"

I addressed him as though he had been sane.

"This is the sort of thing we've been having for seventeen days, Mr. Burns," I said with intense bitterness. "A puff, then a calm, and in a moment, you'll see, she'll be swinging on her heel with her head away from her course to the devil somewhere."

He caught at the word. "The old dodging Devil," he screamed piercingly, and burst into such a loud laugh as I had never heard before. It was a provoking, mocking peal, with a hair-raising, screeching over-note of defiance. I stepped back utterly confounded.

Instantly there was a stir on the quarter-deck, murmurs of dismay. A distressed voice cried out in the dark below us: "Who's that gone crazy, now?"

Perhaps they thought it was their captain! Rush is not the word that could be applied to the utmost speed the poor fellows were up to; but in an amazingly short time every man in the ship able to walk upright had found his way on to that poop.

I shouted to them: "It's the mate. Lay hold of him a couple of you. . . ."

I expected this performance to end in a ghastly sort of fight. But Mr. Burns cut his derisive screeching dead short and turned upon them fiercely, yelling:

"Aha! Dog-gone ye! You've found your tongues—have ye? I thought you were dumb. Well, then—laugh! Laugh—I tell you. Now then—all together. One, two, three—laugh!"

A moment of silence ensued, of silence so profound that you could have heard a pin drop on the deck. Then Ransome's unperturbed voice uttered pleasantly the words:

"I think he has fainted, sir——" The little motionless knot of men stirred, with low murmurs of relief. "I've got him under the arms. Get hold of his legs, someone."

Yes. It was a relief. He was silenced for a time—for a time. I could not have stood another peal of that insane screeching. I was sure of it; and just then Gambril, the austere Gambril, treated us to another vocal performance. He began to sing out for relief. His voice wailed pitifully in the darkness: "Come aft, somebody! I can't stand this. Here she'll be off again directly and I can't. . . ."

I dashed aft myself meeting on my way a hard gust of

wind whose approach Gambril's ear had detected from afar
and which filled the sails on the main in a series of muffled
reports mingled with the low plaint of the spars. I was just
in time to seize the wheel while Frenchy, who had followed me, caught up the collapsing Gambril. He hauled
him out of the way, admonished him to lie still where he
was, and then stepped up to relieve me, asking calmly:

"How am I to steer her, sir?"

"Dead before it, for the present. I'll get you a light in
a moment."

But going forward I met Ransome bringing up the spare
binnacle lamp. That man noticed everything, attended to
everything, shed comfort around him as he moved. As he
passed me he remarked in a soothing tone that the stars
were coming out. They were. The breeze was sweeping
clear the sooty sky, breaking through the indolent silence
of the sea.

The barrier of awful stillness which had encompassed
us for so many days as though we had been accursed was
broken. I felt that. I let myself fall on to the skylight seat.
A faint white ridge of foam, thin, very thin, broke alongside. The first for ages—for ages. I could have cheered, if
it hadn't been for the sense of guilt which clung to all my
thoughts secretly. Ransome stood before me.

"What about the mate," I asked anxiously. "Still unconscious?"

"Well, sir—it's funny." Ransome was evidently puzzled.
"He hasn't spoken a word, and his eyes are shut. But it
looks to me more like sound sleep than anything else."

I accepted this view as the least troublesome of any, or
at any rate, least disturbing. Dead faint or deep slumber,
Mr. Burns had to be left to himself for the present. Ransome remarked suddenly:

"I believe you want a coat, sir."

"I believe I do," I sighed out.

But I did not move. What I felt I wanted were new
limbs. My arms and legs seemed utterly useless, fairly worn
out. They didn't even ache. But I stood up all the same to
put on the coat when Ransome brought it up. And when

he suggested that he had better now "take Gambril forward," I said:

"All right. I'll help you to get him down on the main deck."

I found that I was quite able to help, too. We raised Gambril up between us. He tried to help himself along like a man, but all the time he was inquiring piteously:

"You won't let me go when we come to the ladder? You won't let me go when we come to the ladder?"

The breeze kept on freshening and blew true, true to a hair. At daylight by careful manipulation of the helm we got the foreyards to run square by themselves (the water keeping smooth) and then went about hauling the ropes tight. Of the four men I had with me at night, I could see now only two. I didn't inquire as to the others. They had given in. For a time only I hoped.

Our various tasks forward occupied us for hours, the two men with me moved so slowly and had to rest so often. One of them remarked that "every blamed thing in the ship felt about a hundred times heavier than its proper weight." This was the only complaint uttered. I don't know what we should have done without Ransome. He worked with us, silent too, with a little smile frozen on his lips. From time to time I murmured to him: "Go steady"—"Take it easy, Ransome"—and received a quick glance in reply.

When we had done all we could do to make things safe, he disappeared into his galley. Some time afterwards, going forward for a look round, I caught sight of him through the open door. He sat upright on the locker in front of the stove, with his head leaning back against the bulkhead. His eyes were closed; his capable hands held open the front of his thin cotton shirt baring tragically his powerful chest, which heaved in painful and laboured gasps. He didn't hear me.

I retreated quietly and went straight on to the poop to relieve Frenchy, who by that time was beginning to look very sick. He gave me the course with great formality and tried to go off with a jaunty step, but reeled widely twice before getting out of my sight.

And then I remained all alone aft, steering my ship, which ran before the wind with a buoyant lift now and then, and even rolling a little. Presently Ransome appeared before me with a tray. The sight of food made me ravenous all at once. He took the wheel while I sat down on the after-grating to eat my breakfast.

"This breeze seems to have done for our crowd," he murmured. "It just laid them low—all hands."

"Yes," I said. "I suppose you and I are the only two fit men in the ship."

"Frenchy says there's still a jump left in him. I don't know. It can't be much," continued Ransome with his wistful smile. "Good little man that. But suppose, sir, that this wind flies round when we are close to the land—what are we going to do with her?"

"If the wind shifts round heavily after we close in with the land she will either run ashore or get dismasted or both. We won't be able to do anything with her. She's running away with us now. All we can do is to steer her. She's a ship without a crew."

"Yes. All laid low," repeated Ransome quietly. "I do give them a look-in forward every now and then, but it's precious little I can do for them."

"I, and the ship, and everyone on board of her, are very much indebted to you, Ransome," I said warmly.

He made as though he had not heard me, and steered in silence till I was ready to relieve him. He surrendered the wheel, picked up the tray, and for a parting shot informed me that Mr. Burns was awake and seemed to have a mind to come up on deck.

"I don't know how to prevent him, sir. I can't very well stop down below all the time."

It was clear that he couldn't. And sure enough Mr. Burns came on deck dragging himself painfully aft in his enormous overcoat. I beheld him with a natural dread. To have him around and raving about the wiles of a dead man while I had to steer a wildly rushing ship full of dying men was a rather dreadful prospect.

But his first remarks were quite sensible in meaning and tone. Apparently he had no recollection of the night scene.

And if he had he didn't betray himself once. Neither did he talk very much. He sat on the skylight looking desperately ill at first, but that strong breeze, before which the last remnant of my crew had wilted down, seemed to blow a fresh stock of vigour into his frame with every gust. One could almost see the process.

By way of sanity test I alluded on purpose to the late captain. I was delighted to find that Mr. Burns did not display undue interest in the subject. He ran over the old tale of that savage ruffian's iniquities with a certain vindictive gusto and then concluded unexpectedly:

"I do believe, sir, that his brain began to go a year or more before he died."

A wonderful recovery. I could hardly spare it as much admiration as it deserved, for I had to give all my mind to the steering.

In comparison with the hopeless languor of the preceding days this was dizzy speed. Two ridges of foam streamed from the ship's bows; the wind sang in a strenuous note which under other circumstances would have expressed to me all the joy of life. Whenever the hauled-up mainsail started trying to slat and bang itself to pieces in its gear, Mr. Burns would look at me apprehensively.

"What would you have me do, Mr. Burns? We can neither furl it nor set it. I only wish the old thing would thrash itself to pieces and be done with it. This beastly racket confuses me."

Mr. Burns wrung his hands, and cried out suddenly:

"How will you get the ship into harbour, sir, without men to handle her?"

And I couldn't tell him.

Well—it did get done about forty hours afterwards. By the exorcising virtue of Mr. Burns' awful laugh, the malicious spectre had been laid, the evil spell broken, the curse removed. We were now in the hands of a kind and energetic Providence. It was rushing us on. . . .

I shall never forget the last night, dark, windy, and starry. I steered. Mr. Burns, after having obtained from me a solemn promise to give him a kick if anything happened, went frankly to sleep on the deck close to the binnacle. Convalescents need sleep. Ransome, his back propped against the mizzenmast and a blanket over his legs, remained perfectly still, but I don't suppose he closed his eyes for a moment. That embodiment of jauntiness, Frenchy, still under the delusion that there was "a jump" left in him, had insisted on joining us; but mindful of discipline, had laid himself down as far on the forepart of the poop as he could get, alongside the bucket-rack.

And I steered, too tired for anxiety, too tired for connected thought. I had moments of grim exultation and then my heart would sink awfully at the thought of that forecastle at the other end of the dark deck, full of fever-stricken men—some of them dying. By my fault. But never mind. Remorse must wait. I had to steer.

In the small hours the breeze weakened, then failed altogether. About five it returned, gentle enough, enabling us to head for the roadstead. Daybreak found Mr. Burns sitting wedged up with coils of rope on the stern-grating, and from the depths of his overcoat steering the ship with very white bony hands; while Ransome and I rushed along the decks letting go all the sheets and halyards by the run. We dashed next up on to the forecastle head. The perspiration of labour and sheer nervousness simply poured off our heads as we toiled to get the anchors cock-billed. I dared not look at Ransome as we worked side by side. We exchanged curt words; I could hear him panting close to me and I avoided turning my eyes his way for fear of seeing him fall down and expire in the act of putting out his strength—for what? Indeed for some distinct ideal.

The consummate seaman in him was aroused. He needed no directions. He knew what to do. Every effort, every movement was an act of consistent heroism. It was not for me to look at a man thus inspired.

At last all was ready, and I heard him say, "Hadn't I better go down and open the compressors now, sir?"

"Yes. Do," I said. And even then I did not glance his way. After a time his voice came up from the main deck: "When you like, sir. All clear on the windlass here."

I made a sign to Mr. Burns to put the helm down and then I let both anchors go one after another, leaving the ship to take as much cable as she wanted. She took the best part of them both before she brought up. The loose sails coming aback ceased their maddening racket above my head. A perfect stillness reigned in the ship. And while I stood forward feeling a little giddy in that sudden peace, I caught faintly a moan or two and the incoherent mutterings of the sick in the forecastle.

As we had a signal for medical assistance flying on the mizzen it is a fact that before the ship was fairly at rest three steam-launches from various men-of-war arrived alongside; and at least five naval surgeons clambered on board. They stood in a knot gazing up and down the empty main deck, then looked aloft—where not a man could be seen either.

I went towards them—a solitary figure in a blue and grey striped sleeping suit and a pipe-clayed cork helmet on its head. Their disgust was extreme. They had expected surgical cases. Each one had brought his carving tools with him. But they soon got over their little disappointment. In less than five minutes one of the steam-launches was rushing shorewards to order a big boat and some hospital people for the removal of the crew. The big steam-pinnace went off to her ship to bring over a few bluejackets to furl my sails for me.

One of the surgeons had remained on board. He came out of the forecastle looking impenetrable, and noticed my inquiring gaze.

"There's nobody dead in there, if that's what you want to know," he said deliberately. Then added in a tone of wonder: "The whole crew!"

"And very bad?"

"And very bad," he repeated. His eyes were roaming all over the ship. "Heavens! What's that?"

"That," I said, glancing aft, "is Mr. Burns, my chief officer."

Mr. Burns with his moribund head nodding on the stalk of his lean neck was a sight for any one to exclaim at. The surgeon asked:

"Is he going to the hospital too?"

"Oh, no," I said jocosely. "Mr. Burns can't go on shore

till the mainmast goes. I am very proud of him. He's my
only convalescent."

"You look . . ." began the doctor staring at me. But I
interrupted him angrily:

"I am not ill."

"No. . . . You look queer."

"Well, you see, I have been seventeen days on deck."

"Seventeen! . . . But you must have slept."

"I suppose I must have. I don't know. But I'm certain
that I didn't sleep for the last forty hours."

"Phew! . . . You will be going ashore presently, I suppose?"

"As soon as ever I can. There's no end of business waiting
for me there."

The surgeon released my hand, which he had taken
while we talked, pulled out his pocket-book, wrote in it
rapidly, tore out the page, and offered it to me.

"I strongly advise you to get this prescription made up
for yourself ashore. Unless I am much mistaken you will
need it this evening."

"What is it then?" I asked with suspicion.

"Sleeping draught," answered the surgeon curtly; and
moving with an air of interest towards Mr. Burns he engaged him in conversation.

As I went below to dress to go ashore, Ransome followed
me. He begged my pardon; he wished, too, to be sent
ashore and paid off.

I looked at him in surprise. He was waiting for my answer with an air of anxiety.

"You don't mean to leave the ship!" I cried out.

"I do really, sir. I want to go and be quiet somewhere.
Anywhere. The hospital will do."

"But, Ransome," I said, "I hate the idea of parting with
you."

"I must go," he broke in. "I have a right!" He gasped
and a look of almost savage determination passed over his
face. For an instant he was another being. And I saw under
the worth and the comeliness of the man the humble reality
of things. Life was a boon to him—this precarious hard life
—and he was thoroughly alarmed about himself.

"Of course I shall pay you off if you wish it," I hastened to say. "Only I must ask you to remain on board till this afternoon. I can't leave Mr. Burns absolutely by himself in the ship for hours."

He softened at once and assured me with a smile and in his natural pleasant voice that he understood that very well.

When I returned on deck everything was ready for the removal of the men. It was the last ordeal of that episode which had been maturing and tempering my character—though I did not know it.

It was awful. They passed under my eyes one after another—each of them an embodied reproach of the bitterest kind, till I felt a sort of revolt wake up in me. Poor Frenchy had gone suddenly under. He was carried past me insensible, his comic face horribly flushed and as if swollen, breathing stertorously. He looked more like Mr. Punch than ever; a disgracefully intoxicated Mr. Punch.

The austere Gambril, on the contrary, had improved temporarily. He insisted on walking on his own feet to the rail—of course with assistance on each side of him. But he gave way to a sudden panic at the moment of being swung over the side and began to wail pitifully:

"Don't let them drop me, sir. Don't let them drop me, sir!" While I kept on shouting to him in most soothing accents: "All right, Gambril. They won't! They won't!"

It was no doubt very ridiculous. The bluejackets on our deck were grinning quietly, while even Ransome himself (much to the fore in lending a hand) had to enlarge his wistful smile for a fleeting moment.

I left for the shore in the steam-pinnace, and on looking back beheld Mr. Burns actually standing up by the taffrail, still in his enormous woolly overcoat. The bright sunlight brought out his weirdness amazingly. He looked like a frightful and elaborate scarecrow set up on the poop of a death-stricken ship, to keep the seabirds from the corpses.

Our story had got about already in town and everybody on shore was most kind. The marine office let me off the port dues, and as there happened to be a shipwrecked crew staying in the Home I had no difficulty in obtaining as many men as I wanted. But when I inquired if I could see

Captain Ellis for a moment I was told in accents of pity for my ignorance that our deputy-Neptune had retired and gone home on a pension about three weeks after I left the port. So I suppose that my appointment was the last act, outside the daily routine, of his official life.

It is strange how on coming ashore I was struck by the springy step, the lively eyes, the strong vitality of everyone I met. It impressed me enormously. And amongst those I met there was Captain Giles of course. It would have been very extraordinary if I had not met him. A prolonged stroll in the business part of the town was the regular employment of all his mornings when he was ashore.

I caught the glitter of the gold watch-chain across his chest ever so far away. He radiated benevolence.

"What is it I hear?" he queried with a "kind uncle" smile, after shaking hands. "Twenty-one days from Bankok?"

"Is this all you've heard?" I said. "You must come to tiffin with me. I want you to know exactly what you have let me in for."

He hesitated for almost a minute.

"Well—I will," he decided condescendingly at last.

We turned into the hotel. I found to my surprise that I could eat quite a lot. Then over the cleared table-cloth I unfolded to Captain Giles all the story since I took command in all its professional and emotional aspects, while he smoked patiently the big cigar I had given him.

Then he observed sagely:

"You must feel jolly well tired by this time."

"No," I said. "Not tired. But I'll tell you, Captain Giles, how I feel. I feel old. And I must be. All of you on shore look to me just a lot of skittish youngsters that have never known a care in the world."

He didn't smile. He looked insufferably exemplary. He declared:

"That will pass. But you do look older—it's a fact."

"Aha!" I said.

"No! No! The truth is that one must not make too much of anything in life, good or bad."

"Live at half-speed," I murmured perversely. "Not everybody can do that."

"You'll be glad enough presently if you can keep going even at that rate," he retorted with his air of conscious virtue. "And there's another thing: a man should stand up to his bad luck, to his mistakes, to his conscience, and all that sort of thing. Why—what else would you have to fight against?"

I kept silent. I don't know what he saw in my face, but he asked abruptly:

"Why—you aren't faint-hearted?"

"God only knows, Captain Giles," was my sincere answer.

"That's all right," he said calmly. "You will learn soon how not to be faint-hearted. A man has got to learn everything—and that's what so many of those youngsters don't understand."

"Well I am no longer a youngster."

"No," he conceded. "Are you leaving soon?"

"I am going on board directly," I said. "I shall pick up one of my anchors and heave in to half-cable on the other as soon as my new crew comes on board and I shall be off at daylight to-morrow."

"You will?" grunted Captain Giles approvingly. "That's the way. You'll do."

"What did you expect? That I would want to take a week ashore for a rest?" I said, irritated by his tone. "There's no rest for me till she's out in the Indian Ocean and not much of it even then."

He puffed at the cigar moodily, as if transformed.

"Yes, that's what it amounts to," he said in a musing tone. It was as if a ponderous curtain had rolled up disclosing an unexpected Captain Giles. But it was only for a moment, merely the time to let him add: "Precious little rest in life for anybody. Better not think of it."

We rose, left the hotel, and parted from each other in the street with a warm handshake, just as he began to interest me for the first time in our intercourse.

The first thing I saw when I got back to the ship was Ransome on the quarter-deck sitting quietly on his neatly lashed sea-chest.

I beckoned him to follow me into the saloon where I sat

down to write a letter of recommendation for him to a man I knew on shore.

When finished I pushed it across the table. "It may be of some good to you when you leave the hospital."

He took it, put it in his pocket. His eyes were looking away from me—nowhere. His face was anxiously set.

"How are you feeling now?" I asked.

"I don't feel bad now, sir," he answered stiffly. "But I am afraid of its coming on. . . ." The wistful smile came back on his lips for a moment. "I—I am in a blue funk about my heart, sir."

I approached him with extended hand. His eyes, not looking at me, had a strained expression. He was like a man listening for a warning call.

"Won't you shake hands, Ransome?" I said gently.

He exclaimed, flushed up dusky red, gave my hand a hard wrench—and next moment, left alone in the cabin, I listened to him going up the companion stairs cautiously, step by step, in mortal fear of starting into sudden anger our common enemy it was his hard fate to carry consciously within his faithful breast.